The Chalice

PHIL RICKMAN was born in Lancashire and lives on the Welsh border. He is the author of the Merrily Watkins series and the Tudor historical series starring Dr John Dee. He has won awards for his TV and radio journalism and writes and presents the book programme *Phil the Shelf* for BBC Radio Wales.

PHIL RICKMAN

The Chalice

CORVUS

First published in Great Britain in 1991
by Gerald Duckworth & Co. Ltd.

This edition first published in Great Britain in 2013
by Corvus, an imprint of Atlantic Books Ltd.

1 3 5 7 9 10 8 6 4 2

A CIP catalogue record for this book is available from the British Library.

E-book ISBN: 978 0 85789 691 9
Paperback ISBN: 978 0 85789 696 4
Printed and bound by
CPI Group (UK) Ltd, Croydon, CR0 4YY.

Corvus
An imprint of Atlantic Books Ltd
Ormond House
26-27 Boswell Street
London WC1N 3JZ
www.corvus-books.co.uk

The Chalice

PROLOGUE

I had received serious injury from someone who, at considerable cost to myself, I had disinterestedly helped, and I was sorely tempted to retaliate . . .

Dion Fortune
Psychic Self-Defence, 1930

PROLOGUE

SEPTEMBER, 1919

There she was, lying across the bed, stretched out corner to corner, as though this could relieve the cramp inside caused by the way she'd been used . . . trifled with and slighted, yes, and humiliated . . . as if, as a young woman, she was natural prey, just another little hopping bird in the hawk's garden.

Oh! She might have felt better beating her fists into the pillow, but she'd never have excused herself for that. *Not* the behaviour of a trained psychoanalyst.

All the same, she would remember telling herself that if she didn't do something about it she'd quite simply implode. So perhaps that was what started the process.

It must have been going on, somewhere, while she was persuading her body into the relaxation procedure – not easy when her stupid mind insisted on re-enacting the appalling business, over and over.

Beginning with his proposal of a small adventure for her. That boyish grin through the bristly little moustache, the kind which all the men she knew seemed to have brought back from the Great War. The bantering baritone, smooth and slick as freshly buffed mahogany.

'Didn't you know, Violet? My goodness, didn't you know that we still had it here?'

The question causes, as he knew it would, a veritable flutter in her breast.

But Violet, still suspecting some prank, says lightly that she trusts he's speaking metaphorically, as anybody with even a perfunctory knowledge of such matters is aware that the Holy Grail does not exist and never did.

At which he puts down his wine, spilling some. 'The hell it doesn't, you arrogant minx!'

'Except, of course, as a symbol. Doubtless a sexual one.'

It's a numbingly dull and sultry afternoon, summer seeping sluggishly into autumn, and she's tired of his games.

'And what would *you* know about symbols?' His lips twisting in amusement. 'Or sex, for that matter.'

The room is gloomy: tiny windows and those monstrous black beams. They have not discussed sex. Only violence and pain.

'As much,' she informs him casually (although she's stung by his manner and infuriated by his blatant smirk), 'as *any* advanced student of the methods of Dr Freud.'

'Freud? That ghastly charlatan?' He laughs, oh so confident, now that his own demons are quiet. She decides not to react.

'A passing fad, Violet, you'll see,' leaning back behind his desk, handsome as the devil. 'But please – I'm intrigued – define for me this symbolism.'

What's his game now? Oh, she must not give in to the welling hostility. Or, worse, to that other undignified stirring which has made the leather seat feel suddenly hot where she sits. *Most* humiliating and hardly the response of a trained psychoanalyst.

'So . . .' He trails a finger through the spilled wine. 'Let's look at this. Joseph of Arimathea . . . uncle of Christ, provider of his tomb . . . begs from Pontius Pilate the cup used at the Last Supper and perhaps to collect the blood from the Cross . . .'

'Yes, a pretty legend, I accept that.'

'And then carries it with him on his missionary voyage to a place in the west of Britain, where a strange, pointed hill can be seen from the sea.'

'Yes.' She's seen it herself – in dreams – as if from the sea: the mystical, conical Tor on the holy Isle of Avalon.

And although she would never admit this to him, she's still secretly thrilled by the legend and has been many times to the place where Joseph was said to have buried the Grail, causing a spring to bubble up, the Chalice Well, which to this day runs red. Chalybeate, of course. Iron in the water.

'Obviously,' she says, 'I would not dispute that Joseph and his followers came to Avalon as missionaries. Or, indeed, that he was responsible for building the first Christian church in England. This is historically feasible.'

'How very accommodating of you, Violet.'

'Although I rather suspect the story that Joseph had once brought the child Jesus here is no more than a romantic West Country myth illuminated by the poet Blake.'

He says nothing.

'And surely, what Joseph introduced to these islands was a faith, not a . . . a trinket.'

That came out badly, sounding, even to her own ears, more than a little churlish. He smiles at her again, looking replete with superior wisdom.

She rallies. 'The symbolism is clear. The *idea* of a chalice is well known in Celtic mythology – the Cauldron of Ceridwen, a crucible of wisdom, a symbol of transformation. Upon which, the legend of the Holy Grail, seen from a twentieth-century perspective, is obviously no more than a transparent Christian veneer.'

'In which case,' he says, musingly, after a pause, 'the Grail would be even more significant, carrying the combined power of two great traditions, Christian and pagan. Would it not?'

'If there was such a thing, no doubt it would.'

'*If there was such a thing . . .*' He considers this for a while, hands splayed on the desk, eyes upraised to the blackened beams. 'If there was such a thing, and it had been secretly held by the monks of Glastonbury until the Reformation . . .' He stops.

His eyes are suddenly alight with zealot's fire.

'Oh, really.' Violet almost sniffs. 'Monks were always forging relics to improve the status of their abbeys. Anyway . . .' Pushing back her chair and standing up. 'I'm a psychologist. Not an historian.'

He also stands, but remains behind the desk. He seems to be considering something. 'Very well. What if I were to show it you? What if I were to show you the Grail itself?'

He's still wearing his uniform. Some of the men wear theirs because they have nothing else. But *his* wardrobe could hardly be bare or gone to moth. No, he continues to sport his captain's uniform because he knows its power. Over women, of course.

'Ha,' Violet says. Uncertainly.

In spite of herself, in spite of the teachings of Dr Freud and what he has to say about the all-consuming power of sex, she is beginning, as she follows this man out of the study and down a dark, low passage, to feel quite ridiculously excited.

In those days, Violet hadn't been terrifically good at containing emotion. Well, she was still a young woman, somewhat less experienced than her confidence might suggest.

She knew she was not what most people would call beautiful and that some men were intimidated by her direct manner. But, others – and quite often the better-looking ones, the ones whose arms might have been around slimmer waists – would seek her out. Faintly puzzled about why they found her attractive.

There had always been two sides to her, which she equated with the Celtic and the Saxon: the airy feyness and the no-nonsense earthiness. Although she'd been born in north Wales, she considered herself (because of her Yorkshire steel-working family) to be chiefly Saxon, as suggested by her flaxen hair and her solid, big-boned body. But she'd always needed the phantasmal fire of the Celts, their inbred cosmic perspective.

These two aspects had fallen unexpectedly into harmony over the past few years, during the Great War; all Europe might have been in roiling, smoking turmoil, but Violet had been curiously at peace.

Not that she was any great pacifist. She'd have quite liked to have been at the Front. To be tested. But the only women's work there was nursing, and she was the first to admit she didn't have the patience for it. Not then.

But staying at home had been a revelation. Elements of what she was had come together in an unexpected way. Serving in the women's land army, raising the crops, feeding the troops: fulfilment in a healthy, practical way, but also wonderfully symbolic. With all the young, strong men away in the forces, England – the essential England, of holy hills and fertile meadows – was at last in the care of women. The girls of the land army had taken on the traditional role of Mother Goddess.

It had changed her. She still found Freud stimulating and exciting and the logic of his methodology unassailable, as far as it went.

But there were areas of experience which psychoanalysis could not unveil. And she had lifted up the hem of the curtain and seen wonders.

However, to become truly initiated into the Mysteries, one needed the guidance of human beings who had been there before. And some of them could be . . . well, pretty unsavoury types in other respects. The sacred quest for enlightenment, it appeared, would often bring out the very worst in people.

One had to go jolly carefully, keeping one's eyes open and, quite frankly, one's legs together.

'Go on then . . . hold it.'

Vapour is rising from a small candle on the block of stone between them.

'No . . . please . . . this is not right!'

'You're wrong. It's absolutely right. Now. For me. For us. Violet. . .'

It lies in a black cloth between his hands.

'Grasp it.'

'No!'

'Clasp it to your breast.' He extends his arms, the cloth and what lies in it.

'Please . . . It's black, it's evil . . . I don't . . .' She's starting to sob.

'But it's what you want, my dear. It's what you've always wanted. This is 1919 and you're a free and enlightened woman . . . a trained psychoanalyst. Primitive superstition can't touch you now.' Standing between her and the way out, he adds lazily, 'And take off your clothes, why don't you?'

And so Violet was in a fairly hellish state when she flung her soiled body on the bed, making its springs howl. In retrospect she might have been better off rampaging through the grounds, taking it out on the last of the weeds.

The bed had a light green eiderdown, and the wallpaper was salmon pink. Colours of summer. A pleasant room on a sullen autumn afternoon. But it didn't calm her down today. The effects of such abuse did not just quietly fade.

There was an essential conflict here. One could adopt the Christian attitude, turn the other cheek and walk away: *very well, I tried to help you . . . I counselled you, taught you how to control your nightmares from the War . . . and you took advantage of me. Nevertheless, not my place to be judgemental. As a psychologist.*

Ha. Hardly good enough was it? Violet sighed, lay back and let her eyelids fall. The pillows were soft and cool. The back of her head felt heavy, like a bag of potatoes. She let her arms flop by her sides. The anger, still burning somewhere below her abdomen, was at odds, though not uncomfortably so, with the supine state of her body. She was, surprisingly, reaching a state of relaxation. But then, she was getting rather good at that.

Of course . . .

Violet smiled.

. . . one could simply allow oneself to go absolutely and utterly berserk.

She began a simple visualisation, letting loose her thoughts, to roam the wildest of terrain, those places of high cliffs and crashing waves, black and writhing trees against a thundery sky. As her body lay on its bed, on a sallow, sunless afternoon in the mellow, autumnal Vale of Avalon, her thoughts stalked the wintry wasteland of cruel Northern myths. In search of a suitably savage instrument of revenge. Oh *yes*.

She was starting to enjoy her anger and felt no guilt about this. Daylight dripped on to her eyelids like syrup. And in the cushiony hinterland of sleep, in those moments when the senses mingle and then dissolve, when fragments of whispered words are sometimes heard and strange responses sought, Violet's rage fermented pleasurably into the darkest of wines.

'Good dog.'

Its fur was harsh as a new hairbrush. It brushed her left arm, raising goosebumps.

It lay there quite still, as relaxed as Violet had been, but with a kind of coiled and eager tension about it. She could feel its back alongside her, its spine against her cotton shift. It was lean, but it was heavy. And it was beginning to breathe.

She didn't really question its presence at first. It was simply there. She raised her left hand to pat it. Then the hand suddenly seized up.

So cold.

And Violet was aware that the room had gone dark.

Not dark as if she'd simply fallen asleep and the afternoon had slid away into evening. Dark as in a draining of the light, of the life-force vibrating behind colours. The most horribly negative kind of darkness.

She opened her eyes fully. It made no difference. The wallpaper was a deepening grey and the fogged light inside the window frame thick and stodgy, like a rubber mat. The eiderdown beneath her was as hard and ungiving as a cobbled street.

The fear had come upon her slowly and was all the worse for that. It chilled her insides like a cold-water enema. A rank odour soured the room. The air seemed noxious with evil, almost-visible specks of it above her like a cloud of black midges.

Drawing a breath made her body lurch against the creature lying motionless beside her in the gloom.

And motionless it stayed, for a moment.

Violet knew what she had to do. She lay as still as she could, gathering breath and her nerve.

Then she put out her left hand. Out and down. Until her fingers found the eiderdown, hard as worn stone. There was an almost liquid frigidity around her hand, over the wrist, almost to the elbow, like frogspawn in a half-frozen pond.

It was very hard to turn her head, as though her neck was in a vice, everything she held holy crying out to her not to look.

But look she did. She managed to turn her head just an inch, enough to focus on her left shoulder and follow her arm down and down to where the wrist . . . vanished.

Somewhere through the greyness she could detect a dim image of her fingers on the eiderdown, while the beast's gaseous body swirled around the flesh of her arm.

As Violet began to pant with fear, it turned its grey head, and the only white light in the room was in its long, predator's teeth and the only colour in the room was the still, cold yellow of its eyes.

I am yours.

PART ONE

There is such magic in the first glimpse of that strange hill that none who have the eye of vision can look upon it unmoved.

Dion Fortune
Avalon of the Heart, 1934

ONE

FOR MYSTICISM . . . PSYCHIC STUDIES . . . EARTH MYSTERIES . . . ESOTERICA

CAREY AND FRAYNE
Booksellers
High Street
Glastonbury

Prop. Juanita Carey

14 November

Danny, love,

Enclosed, as promised, one copy of Colonel Pixhill's Glastonbury Diary. More about that later. After this month's marathon moan.

Sorry. I'm getting hopelessly garrulous, running off at the mouth, running off at the Amstrad. Put it down to Time of Life. Put this straight in the bin, if you like, I'm just getting it all off my increasingly vertical chest.

What's put me all on edge is that Diane's back. Diane Ffitch.

Funny how so many of my problems over the years have involved that kid. Hell, grown woman now – by the time I was her age, I'd been married, divorced, had three good years with you (and one bad), moved to Glastonbury, started a business. . .

I know. A lot more than I've done since. There. Depressed myself now. It doesn't take much these days. Colonel Pixhill was right: Glastonbury buggers you up. But then, you knew that, didn't you?

I've been trying to think if you ever met Diane. I suspect not. She was in her teens by the time our paths finally crossed (although I'd heard the stories, of course) and you were long gone by then. Although you might remember the royal visit, was it 1972, late spring? Princess Margaret, anyway – always kind of

11

liked her, nearest thing to a rebel that family could produce. As I remember you wouldn't go to watch. Uncool, you said. But the next day the papers had this story about the small daughter of local nob Lord Pennard, who was to have presented the princess with a bouquet.

Diane would have been about four then and already distinctly chubby. Waddles up to Margaret – I think it was at the town hall – with this sheaf of monster flowers which is more than half her size. Maggie stoops graciously to scoop up the blooms, the photographers and TV cameramen all lined up. Whereupon, Diane unceremoniously dumps the bouquet, hurls herself, in floods of tears, at the royal bosom and sobs – this was widely used in headlines next day – 'Are you my mummy?'

Poignant stuff, you see, because her mother died when she was born. But obviously, a moment of ultimate embarrassment for the House of Pennard, the first public indication that the child was – how can I put this? – prone to imaginative excursions. Anyway, that was Diane's fifteen minutes of national fame. The later stuff – the disappearances, the police searches, they managed to keep out of the papers. Pity, some even better pictures there, like Diane curled up with her teddy bear under a seat in Chalice Well gardens at four in the morning.

Years later she turns up at the shop looking for a holiday job. Why my shop? Because she wanted access to the sort of books her father wouldn't have in the house – although, obviously I didn't know that when I took her on.

But she was a good kid, no side to her.

She's twenty-seven now. Until very recently, Lord Pennard thought he'd finally unloaded her, having sent her to develop her writing skills by training as a journalist in Yorkshire. What does that bastard care about her writing skills? It was Yorkshire that counted, being way up in the top right-hand corner of the country. An old family friend of the Ffitches owns a local newspaper chain up there, and of course, the eldest son, heir to the publishing empire, was not exactly discouraged from associating with the Hon. Diane. Yes, an old-fashioned, upper-crust arranged marriage: titled daughter-in-law for solid, Northern press baron and the penurious House of Pennard safely plugged into a source of unlimited wealth.

But it's all off. Apparently. I don't know exactly why, and I'm afraid to ask. And Diane's back.

When I say 'back', I don't mean here at the shop. Or at Bowermead Hall. Nothing as simple as a stand-up row with Daddy, and brother Archer smarming about in the background. Oh no. Diane being Diane, she's come down from the North in a convoy of New Age travellers.

Well, I've nothing against them in principle. How could I, with my background? Except that when we were hippies we didn't make a political gesture out of clogging up the roads, or steal our food from shops, despoil the countryside, light fires made from people's fences or claim social security for undertaking the above. Hey, am I becoming a latent Conservative or what?

Anyway, she rang. She's with these travellers – oh sorry, 'pagan pilgrims' – and do I know anywhere near their holy of holies (the Tor, of course) where they could all camp legally for a few days? Otherwise they could be arrested as an unlawful assembly under the terms of the Criminal Justice Act.

Well, I don't basically give a shit about the rest of them being nicked. But I'm thinking, Christ, Diane winds up behind bars, along comes Archer to discreetly (and smugly) bail her out with Daddy's money . . . I couldn't bear that.

So I thought of Don Moulder, who farms reasonably close to the Tor. He's got this field he's been trying to flog as building land in some corrupt deal with Griff Daniel. Only, Mendip Council – now that Griff isn't on it, thank God – insists, quite rightly, that it's a green-belt site and won't allow it. So now the aggrieved Moulder will rent out that field to anybody likely to piss the council off.

I call him up. We haggle for a while and then agree on three hundred quid. Which Diane is quite happy to pay. She says they're 'really nice people' and it's been a breath of fresh air for her, travelling the country, sleeping in the back of the van, real freedom, no pressure, no cruel father, no smug brother. And at the end of the road . . . Glastonbury. The Holyest Erthe in All England, where, according to the late Dion Fortune, the saints continue to live their quaintly beautiful lives amid the meadows of Avalon and – Oh God – the poetry of the soul writes itself.

(The reason I mention DF is that, for a long time, Diane was convinced that the famed High Priestess was her previous incarnation – gets complicated, doesn't it?)

God knows what the great lady would have written had she been around today. Bloody hell, this is the New Age Blackpool! Shops that even in your time here used to sell groceries and hardware are now full of plastic goddesses and aromatherapy starter-kits. Everybody who ever turned over a tarot card or flipped the I-Ching sooner or later gets beached on the Isle of Avalon.

And the endless tourists. Not just Brits, but dozens of Americans, Japanese and Germans, all trooping around the Abbey ruins with their camcorders, in search of Enlightenment followed by a good dinner and a four-poster bed at The George and Pilgrims.

OK, I should moan. The shop's never been more profitable. I've had to take on assistance at weekends (Jim Battle, nice man). But I'm not enjoying it any more, there's the rub. I'm feeling tense all the time (mention menopause and you're dead!!!). I see the latest freaks on the streets and I can see why the local people hated us twenty years ago. I too hate the New Age travellers blocking up Wellhouse Lane with their buses, marching up the Tor to tune into the Mystical Forces, camping up there and shitting on the grass and leaving it unburied.

And I can see why the natives still don't trust us, because they think we're trying to take over the town. And maybe we are, some of us. We say we're all for unity and the kindly pagans are getting into bed with the Christians and everything, but basically we have very different values and when some local issue arises it all erupts. Like the proposed new road linking central Somerset into the Euro motorway network. Most of the natives are in favour because it will relieve traffic congestion in the small towns and villages, but the incomers see it as an invasion of their rural haven, the destruction of miles of wonderful countryside. So whichever way it goes, half of us are going to be furious.

It's not as if even the Alternative Community is united. We pretend to be, of course – old hippies, part of that great universal movement. But we're divided, factionalised: gay pagan groups, radical feminist pagans like The Cauldron. Everything in Glastonbury inevitably becomes EXTREME.

I lie awake, mulling over the old hippy thing – why CAN'T we all live in peace together on what's supposed to be the Holyest Erthe in all Britain?

And then I go back and read Pixhill's Diaries, making myself doubly miserable because we're the sole outlet for a book nobody wants to buy on account of his Nostradamus-like warnings of impending doom, souls raging in torment, the rising of the Dark Chalice, etc., etc. Well, you just don't say things like that about Glastonbury. Because this is a HOLY town and must therefore be immune from evil. The people who settle here want to bathe in the sacredness like some sort of spiritual Radox. They want to be soothed. They don't want anything to dent the idyll.

Anyway, you should see a copy, as Carey and Frayne are the publishers. Let me know what you think. I'll go now. I think I can see Jim Battle, my best male friend these days, wobbling down the High Street on what appears to be a new secondhand bike and looking, as usual, in need of a drink.

Look after yourself, wish me luck with Diane and be glad your posh London outfit doesn't have to publish anything like the enclosed!

Love,

J

TWO

A SOUND THINKER

Not knowing Archer Ffitch all *that* well, Griff Daniel decided on restraint.

'Dirty, drug-sodden, heathen bastards.' Griff scratched an itchy palm on his spiky grey beard. 'Filthy, dole-scrounging scum.'

Attached to the wooden bars of the gate at the foot of Glastonbury Tor was a framed colour photograph of a lamb with its throat torn out. Over the photo was typed,

KILLED BY A DOG NOT ON A LEAD.
DOGS WHICH CHASE SHEEP CAN BE SHOT BY LAW.

'What they wanner do, look,' said Griff Daniel, 'is extend that bloody ole law. 'Tisn't as if any of the bastards'd be missed by anybody. Double barrel up the arse from fifty yards. Bam.'

'Appealing notion.' Archer Ffitch was in a dark suit and tie and a pair of green wellies, even though it was pretty dry underfoot for November. Not natural, this weather, was Griff's view. Too much that was not natural hereabouts.

'Destroying this town, Mr Archer. Every time they come there's always a few stays behind. Squatting in abandoned flats, shagging each other behind the church, nicking everything that's not nailed down, and you say a word to 'em, you gets all this freedom-of-the-individual baloney. Scum.'

'Quite, quite.' Archer with that bored, heard-it-all-before tone. But Griff knew he'd have all Archer's attention in a minute, by God he would.

'And the permanent ones. Alternative society? Green-culture? What's alternative 'bout pretending the twentieth century never bloody happened? Mustn't have a new road 'cause it means chopping a few crummy trees down. Can't have decent new housing 'cause it leaves us with one less bloody useless field.'

16

'I hear what you're saying.' Archer nodding gravely, like he was being interviewed on the box. 'I'm appalled we lost a man like you from the council, and I agree. A few changes in this town are long overdue.'

Griff sniffed. 'What they all say, with respect. Your gaffer, he's been spouting 'bout that for years.'

'My father?'

'No, lad, the MP. Sir Larry.'

Archer went silent. He'd changed a lot. Gone into his thirties still lanky, overgrown schoolboyish; suddenly he'd thickened up like His Lordship, jaw darker, eyes steadier: watch out, here comes another Pennard power-pack. Griff wished his own son was like this; it pained him to think of the difference.

'What have you heard?' Archer's heavy eyebrows all but meeting in the middle, like a mantelshelf, with the eyes smouldering away underneath.

Griff smiled slyly. 'Not a well man, our Sir Larry. Might be stepping down sooner than we thinks? Make way for someone more . . . vigorous? That be a suitable word?'

'Radical might be a better one,' Archer said cautiously. 'In the Thatcher sense, of course.'

'Ah.' Griff gave his beard a thoughtful massage. '*Could* be what the place needs. Depending, mind, on what this . . . *radical* newcomer is offering to us in the, er, business community.'

'I understand.' Archer was gazing past Griff, up the Tor to where the tower was. Erected by the old monks back in the Middle Ages, that tower, to claim the hill for Christ. Dedicated to St Michael, the dragon-slayer, to keep the bloody heathens out. Pity it hadn't worked.

'Can't see a soul up there,' Archer said. 'You *are* sure about this, Griff?'

'Ah.' Griff decided it was time to dump his manure and watch the steam. 'Got it a bit wrong when I phoned you, look. They're not here. Yet. All camped down in Moulder's bottom field. Clapped-out ole buses and vans, no tax, no insurance. Usual unwashed rabble, green hair, rings through every orifice.'

'Sounds enough like mass-trespass for me.' Archer pulled his mobile phone out of his inside pocket, flipping it open. 'OK, right.

Why don't I get this dealt with immediately, yah? Invoke the Act, have the whole damn lot charged.'

'Aye.' Griff nodded slowly. 'But charged what with?'

The phone had played what sounded like the opening beeps of Three Blind Mice before Archer's finger froze, quivering with irritation.

Griff leaned back against the gate and took his time re-reading the National Trust sign: *Please avoid leaving litter, lighting fires, damaging trees.*

'Bastards are legal, Mr Archer. In Moulder's field with Moulder's permission. In short, Moulder's been paid.'

'These vagrants have money?'

'One of 'em does. Young woman it was stumped up the readies, so I hear. One as even Moulder figured he could trust.'

Griff leaned back against the gate, gave his beard a good rub.

'Quite a distinctive-looking young lady, they d'say.'

'Spit it out, man.' Archer was going to have to deal with this tendency to impatience with the lower orders. MPs should be good listeners.

'Of . . . should we say *generous* proportions? And she don't talk like your usual hippy rabble.'

Archer was hard against the light, solid and cold as the St Michael tower.

'What are you saying, Mr Daniel?'

Looking a bit dangerous. Like he could handle himself, same as his old man. Don't push it, Griff decided.

'Well, all right. It's Miss Diane. Come rolling into town with the hippies. In a white van. Big pink spots on it.'

Archer said nothing, just loomed over him, best part of a foot taller. Moisture on his thick lips now.

'Your little sister, Mr Archer.' Little. Jesus, she must be pushing thirteen stone. 'She come in with 'em and she rented 'em a campsite so they wouldn't get arrested. Don't ask me why.'

'If this is a joke, Mr Daniel . . . Because my sister's . . .'

'Up North. Aye. About to get herself hitched. Except she's in Moulder's bottom field. In a van with big pink spots. No joke. No mistake, Mr Archer.'

Archer was as still as the old tower. 'How many other people know about this?'

'Only Moulder, far's I know. Who, if any, like, action happens to be taken, requests that he be kept out of it, if you understand me.'

No change of expression, no inflexion in his voice, Archer said, 'I'm grateful for this. I won't forget.'

'Well,' Griff said. 'Long as we understands each other. I think we want the same things for this town. Like getting it cleaned up. Proper shops 'stead of this New Age rubbish. Cranks and long-hairs out. Folk in decent clothes. Decent houses on decent estates. Built by, like, decent firms. And, of course, the new road to get us on to the Euro superhighway, bring in some proper industry. Big firms. Executive housing.'

Archer nodding. 'You're a sound thinker, Griff. We all need a stake in the twenty-first century.'

'Oh, and one other thing I want. . .'

Archer folded his arms and smiled.

'I want my council seat back off that stringy little hippy git Woolaston,' said Griff.

Archer patted the leather patch at the shoulder of Griff's heavy, tweed jacket. 'Let's discuss this further. Meanwhile, I have a meeting tonight. With a certain selection committee. After which I may be in a better position to, ah, effect certain changes.'

'Ah. Best o' luck then, Mr Archer.'

'Thank you. Er . . .' Archer looked away again. 'Diane's . . . ill-ness . . . has caused us considerable distress. It's good to know she has chaps like you on her side.'

'And on yours, Archer,' Griff Daniel said. 'Naturally.'

As Archer drove off in his grey BMW, Griff looked to the top of the unnaturally steep hill, glad to see there was still nobody up there, no sightseers, no joggers, no kids. And no alternative bastards with dowsing rods and similar crank tackle.

He hated the bloody Tor.

Not much over five hundred feet high when you worked it out. Only resembled some bloody green Matterhorn, look, on account of most of the surrounding countryside was so flat, having been under the sea, way back.

So nothing to it, not really.

But look at the trouble it caused. Bloody great millstone round this town's neck. Thousands of tourists fascinated by all that cobblers about pagan gods and intersecting lines of power.

If it wasn't for all that old balls, there'd be no New Age travellers, no hippy refugees running tatty shops, no mid-summer festivals and women dancing around naked, no religious nuts, no UFO-spotters. Glastonbury Tor, in fact, was a symbol of what was wrong with Britain.

Also the National Trust bastards hadn't even given him the contract for installing the new pathway and steps.

Griff Daniel went back to his truck. *G Daniel & Co. Builders.* It would maybe have said . . . *& Son.* If the so-called son hadn't disgraced the family name.

When it came down to it, the only way you were going to get rid of the riff-raff was by getting rid of the damn Tor. He imagined a whole convoy of JCBs gobbling into the Tor like it was a Walnut Whip, the hill giving way, the tower collapsing into dusty, medieval rubble.

All the way back to his yard on the edge of the industrial estate, Griff Daniel kept thinking about this. It wasn't possible, of course, not under any conceivable circumstances. You couldn't, say, put the new road through it, not with a scheduled ancient monument on top, and also it was far too big a national tourist attraction.

But it did make you think.

THREE

QUEEN OF THE HIPPIES

It was rather an antiquated bicycle, a lady's model with no crossbar, a leatherette saddle bag and a metal cover over the chain. Terribly sedate, an elderly spinster's sort of machine, fifteen quid from On Your Bike, over at Street. But Jim could get his feet to the pedals without adjusting the seat, and, more to the point, it was the kind of bicycle no youngster would want to be seen dead on.

So at least he could park it in town with an odds-on chance of it not being nicked.

Jim unloaded himself from the bike outside Burns the Bread, in the part of Glastonbury High Street where the Alternative Sector was rapidly chasing the few remaining locally owned shops up the hill.

He was puffing a bit and there was sweat on his forehead. It was rather close and humid. And November, amazingly. He pushed the bike across the pavement and into a narrow alleyway next to the bookshop called Carey and Frayne. Got out his handkerchief to wipe his face, the alleyway framing a neat little streetscene from a viewpoint he'd never noticed before – quite a nice one, because . . .

. . . *by God* . . .

. . . above the weathered red-tiled roofs and brick chimney stacks of the shops across the street reared the spiked and buttressed Norman tower of the town centre church, St John's, and it had suddenly struck Jim that the tower's top tier, jagged in the florid, late-afternoon sun, resembled a crown of thorns.

While, in the churchyard below, out of sight from here, there was one of the *holy* thorns, grafted from the original on Wearyall Hill. It was as if the Thorn had worked its way into the very fabric of the church, finally thrusting itself in savage symbolism from the battlements.

Yes, yes, yes. Jim started to paint rapidly in his head, reforming sculpted stone into pronged and twisted wildwood. But keeping the same colours, the pink and the ochre and the grey, amid the elegiac embers of the dying sun.

By God, this buggering town . . . just when you thought you had it worked out, it would throw a new image at you like a well-aimed brick. Jim was so knocked-sideways he almost forgot to chain his bike to the drainpipe. Almost.

Twenty feet away, a youth sat in a dusty doorway fumbling a guitar. Jim gave him a hard look, but he seemed harmless enough. The ones with guitars *usually* were, couldn't get up to much trouble with an instrument that size to lug around. Penny-whistlers, now, they were the ones you had to watch; they could shove the things down their belts in a second, leaving two hands free for thieving.

Over the past eighteen months, Jim had had three bikes stolen, two gone from the town centre, one with the padlocked chain snipped and left in the gutter. Metal cutters, by God! Thieves with metal cutters on the streets of Glastonbury.

'Jim, you're painting!'

'No, I'm not.' Reacting instinctively. For half his adult life, painting had been something to deny – bloody Pat shrieking, *How many bills is that going to pay?*

'New bike, I see.' The most beautiful woman in Glastonbury bent over the bike, stroking the handlebars. 'Really rather suits you.'

'You calling me an old woman?' Jim pulled off his hat. 'I'll have you know, my girl, I've just ridden the buggering thing all the way back from Street in the slipstream of a string of transcontinental juggernauts half the size of the QE2. Bloody Europe comes to Somerset.'

'Just be thankful that bikes are still allowed on that road. Come the new motorway you'll be banned for ever.'

'Won't happen. Too much opposition.'

'Oh sure. Like the Government cares about the Greens and the old ladies in straw hats.' She straightened up, hands on her hips, and a bloody fine pair of hips they were. 'Tea?'

'Well . . . or something.' Jim followed her into the sorcerer's library she called a bookshop. He helped out here two or three days a week, trying not to look too closely at what he was selling.

He glared suspiciously at one of those cardboard dumpbin things displaying a new paperback edition of the silly novels of Glastonbury's own Dion Fortune. Awful, crass covers – sinister hooded figures standing over stone altars and crucibles.

'Over the top. The artwork. Tawdry. Way over the top.'

'Isn't everything in Glastonbury these days?'

Well, you aren't, for a start, Jim thought. He wondered whether something specific had happened to make Juanita distance herself from the sometimes-overpowering spirituality of the town and from the books she sold. You didn't open a shop like this unless you were of a strongly mystical persuasion, but these days she answered customers' questions lightly and without commitment, as if she knew it was all nonsense really.

Jim let her steer him into the little parlour behind the shop, past the antiquarian section, where the books were kept behind glass, most of them heavy magical manuals from the nineteenth century. Jim had flicked one open the other week and found disturbingly detailed instructions 'for the creation of elemental spirits'. He suspected it didn't mean distilling your own whisky.

Which reminded him. 'Erm . . . that Laphroaig you had. Don't suppose there's a minuscule drop left?'

'That rather depends how many minuscule drops you've had already,' Juanita said cautiously. Damn woman knew him rather too well.

'One. Swear to God. Called at a pub called the Oak Tree or something. Nerves shot to hell after a run-in with a container lorry from Bordeaux. One small Bells, I swear it.'

She looked dubious, puckering her lovely nose. In the lingering warmth of this year's strange, post-Indian summer, she was wearing a lemon yellow off-the-shoulder thing, showing all her freckles. Well, as many of them as *he'd* ever seen.

'Just that you're looking . . . not exactly un-flushed, Jim.'

'Hmmph,' said Jim. He let Juanita sit him down in an armchair, planting a chunky tumbler in his drinking and painting hand. She had quite a deep tan from sunning herself reading books on the balcony at the back. While most women her age were going frantic about melanoma, Juanita snatched all the sun she could get. Must be the Latin ancestry.

Watching her uncork the Laphroaig bottle with a rather suggestive *thopp*, Jim thought, Ten years . . . ten years younger would do it. Ten years, maybe fifteen, and she'd be at least within reach.

He coughed, hoping nothing showed. 'Erm . . . Happened to cycle past Don Moulder's bottom field on the way back. Guess bloody what.'

'New Age travellers?'

'Nothing gets past you, does it?' Jim held out his glass. 'Arrogant devils. Bloody thieving layabouts.'

'Not quite all of them.'

As she leaned over to pour his drink, Jim breathed in a delightful blend of Ambre Solaire and frank feminine sweat, the mixture sensuously overlaid with the smoky peatmusk of the whisky. Aaaaah . . . the dubious pleasure of being sixty-two years old, unattached again, and with all one's senses functioning, more or less.

'I'm sorry . . .' Shaking himself out of it and feeling the old jowls wobble. 'What did you just say?'

'I said at least one of them isn't a thief. Besides, oddballs have always drifted towards Glastonbury. Look at me. Look at you.'

'Yes, but, Juanita, the essential difference here is that *we* saved up our hard-earned pennies until we could do it in a *respectable* way. We didn't just get an old bus from a scrapyard and enough fuel to trundle it halfway across the country before it breaks down and falls to pieces in some previously unsullied beauty spot. You see, what gets me is how these characters have the bare-faced cheek . . .'

'Because Diane's with them.'

'. . . to call themselves friends of the buggering planet, when they . . . What did you say . . .?' Jim had to steady the Laphroaig with his other hand.

Juanita poured herself a glass of probably overpriced white wine from Lord Pennard's vineyard and lowered herself into a chintzy old rocking chair by the Victorian fireplace. There was a small woodstove tucked into the fireplace now, unlit as yet, but with a few autumn logs piled up ready for the first cold day.

Jim said, 'I'm sorry, I don't quite understand. You say Diane's back? Diane's with *them*? But I thought . . .'

'We all did. Which is . . .' Juanita sighed. '. . . I suppose, why I got them the field.'

Jim was bewildered. '*You* got them the buggering field?'

He'd thought she was over all that. Might have been Queen of the Hippies 1972, but she was fully recovered now, surely to God.

Juanita said, 'Comes down to the old question: if I don't try and help her, who else is going to?'

'But I thought she was working in Yorkshire.' The idea of Diane training to be a journalist *had* struck Jim as pretty unlikely at the time, considering the girl's renowned inability to separate fact from fantasy. 'I thought she was getting married. Peter somebody.'

'Patrick. It's off. Abandoned her job, everything.'

'To become a New Age buggering traveller?'

'Not exactly. As she put it, she kind of hitched a lift. They were making their way here, and she . . .'

Juanita reached for her cigarettes.

'. . . Oh dear. She said it was calling her back.'

Jim groaned. 'Not again. Dare I ask what, *specifically*, was calling her back?'

'The Tor.' Juanita lit a cigarette. 'What else?'

Jim was remembering that time the girl had gone missing and they'd found her just before dawn under the Thorn on Wearyall Hill, in her nightie and bare feet. What was she then, fifteen? He sank the last of the Laphroaig. He was too old for this sort of caper.

'Lady Loony,' he said. 'Do people still call her that?'

FOUR

A FINE SHIVER

The ancient odour had drifted in as soon as Diane wound down the van window, and it was just so . . . Well, she could have wept. How could she have forgotten the scent?

The van had jolted between the rotting gateposts into Don Moulder's bottom field. It had bounced over grass still ever so parched from a long, dry summer and spiky from the harvest. Diane had turned off the engine, sat back in the lumpy seat, closed her eyes and let it reach her through the open window: the faraway fragrance of Holy Avalon.

Actually, she hadn't *wound* down the window, as such. Just pulled out the folded Rizla packet which held the glass in place and let it judder to its favourite halfway position. It *was* rather an *old* van, a Ford something or other – used to be white all over but she'd painted big, silly pink spots on it so it wouldn't stand out from the rest of the convoy.

The smell made her happy and sad. It was heavy with memories and was actually a blend of several scents, the first of them autumn, a brisk, mustardy tang. And then wood-smoke – there always seemed to be woodsmoke in rural Somerset, much of it applewood which was rich and mellow and sweetened the air until you could almost taste it.

And over that came the most elusive ingredient: the musk of mystery, a scent which summoned visions. Of the Abbey in the evening, when the saddened stones grew in grace and sang to the sunset. Of wind-whipped Wearyall Hill with the night gathering in the startled tangle of the Holy Thorn. Of the balmy serenity of the Chalice Well garden. And of the great enigma of the West: Glastonbury Tor.

Diane opened her eyes and looked up at the huge green breast with its stone nipple.

She wasn't the only one. All around, people had been dropping out of vans and buses, an ambulance, a stock wagon. Gazing up at the holy hill, no more than half a mile away. Journey's end for the pagan pilgrims. And for Diane Ffitch, who called herself Molly Fortune because she was embarrassed by her background, confused about her reason for returning and rather afraid, actually.

Dusk was nibbling the fringes of Don Moulder's bottom field when the last few vehicles crawled in. They travelled in smaller groups nowadays, because of the law. An old Post Office van with a white pentacle on the bonnet was followed by Mort's famous souped-up hearse, where he liked to make love, on the long coffin-shelf. *Love is the law*, Mort said. *Love over death*.

Headlice and Rozzie arrived next in the former Bolton Corporation single-decker bus repainted in black and yellow stripes, like a giant bee.

'Listen, I've definitely been here before!' Headlice jumped down, grinning eerily through teeth like a broken picket fence. He was about nineteen or twenty; they were so awfully *young*, most of these people. At that age, Diane thought, you could go around saying you were a confirmed pagan, never giving a thought to what it really meant.

'I mean, you know, not in this life, obviously,' Headlice said. 'In a *past* life, yeah?' Looking up expectantly, as though he thought mystic rays might sweep him away and carry him blissfully to the top of the holy hill. 'Hey, you reckon I was a *monk*?'

He felt at the back of his head. Where a monk's tonsure would be, Headlice had a swastika tattoo, re-exposed because of the affliction which had led to his extremely severe haircut and his unfortunate nickname.

Rozzie made a scoffing noise. 'More like one of the friggin' peasants what carted the stones up the hill.'

She'd told Diane that the swastika was a relic of Headlice's days as some sort of a teenage neo-fascist, neo-skinhead. Headlice, however, pointed out that the original swastika was an ancient pagan solar symbol. Which was why he'd had one tattooed on the part of him nearest the sun, see?

He turned away and kicked at the grass. His face had darkened; he looked as if he'd rather be kicking Rozzie. She was a Londoner;

he was from the North. She was about twenty-six. Although they shared a bus and a bed, she seemed to despise him awfully.

'I *could*'ve been a fuckin' monk,' Headlice said petulantly. Despite the democratic, tribal code of the pilgrims, he was obviously very conscious of his background, which made Diane feel jolly uncomfortable about hers. She'd been trying to come over sort of West Country milkmaidish, but she wasn't very good at it, probably just sounded frightfully patronising.

'Or a bird,' she said. 'Perhaps you were a little bird nesting in the tower.' She felt sorry for Headlice.

'Cute. All I'm sayin' is, I feel . . . I can feel it here.' Punching his chest through the rip in his dirty denim jacket. 'This is not bullshit, Mol.'

Diane smiled. On her own first actual visit to the Tor – or it might have been a dream, she couldn't have been more than about three or four – there'd been sort of candyfloss sunbeams rolling soft and golden down the steep slopes, warm on her sandals. She wished she could still hold that soft, undemanding image for more than a second or two, but she supposed it was only for children. Too grown-up to feel it now.

Also she felt too . . . well, mature, at twenty-seven, to be entirely comfortable among the pilgrims although a few were ten or even twenty years older than she was and showed every line of it. But even the older women tended to be fey and child-like and stick-thin, even the ones carelessly suckling babies.

Stick-thin. How wonderful to be stick-thin.

'What it is . . .' Headlice said. 'I feel like I'm home.'

'What?' Diane looked across to the Tor, with the church tower without a church on its summit. *Oh no. It's not your home at all, you're just passing through. I'm the one who's . . .*

Home? The implications made her feel faint. She wobbled about, wanting to climb back into the van, submerge like a fat hippo in a swamp. Several times on the journey, she'd thought very seriously about dropping out of the convoy, turning the van around and dashing back to Patrick, telling him it had all been a terrible, terrible mistake.

And then she'd seen the vinegar shaker on the high chipshop counter at lunchtime and a spear of light had struck it and turned it into a glistening Glastonbury Tor. *Yes!* she'd almost shrieked. *Yes, I'm coming back!*

With company. There must be over thirty pilgrims here now, in a collection of vehicles as cheerful as an old-fashioned circus. At least it *had* been cheerful when she'd joined the convoy on the North Yorkshire moors – that old army truck sprayed purple with big orange flowers, the former ambulance with an enormous eye painted on each side panel, shut on one side, wide open on the other. But several of the jollier vehicles seemed to have dropped out. Broken down, probably. Well, they *were* all frightfully old. And fairly drab now, except for Diane's van and Headlice's bee-striped bus.

Mort's hearse had slunk in next to the bus. There was a mattress in the back. Mort had offered to demonstrate Love over Death to Diane once; she'd gone all flustered but didn't want to seem uncool and said it was her period.

Mort climbed out. He wore a black leather jacket. He punched the air.

'Yo, Headlice!'

'OK, man?'

'Tonight, yeah?'

'Yeah,' said Headlice. 'Right.'

Mort wandered off down the field and began to urinate casually into a gorse bush to show off the size of his willy.

Diane turned away. Despite the unseasonal warmth, it had been a blustery day and the darkening sky bore obvious marks of violence, the red sun like a blood-bubble in an open wound and the clouds either runny like pus or fluffy in a nasty way, like the white stuff that grew on mould.

Diane said, 'Tonight?'

'Up there.' Headlice nodded reverently at the Tor where a low, knife-edge cloud had taken the top off St Michael's tower, making it look, Diane thought – trying to be prosaic, trying not to succumb – like nothing so much as a well-used lipstick sampler in Boots.

But this was the terminus. They'd travelled down from Yorkshire, collecting pilgrims en route, until they hit the St Michael Line, which focused and concentrated energy across the widest part of England. They might have carried on to St Michael's Mount at the tip of Cornwall; but, for pagans, the Tor was the holy of holies.

'What are you – we – going to do?' Diane pulled awkwardly at her flouncy skirt from the Oxfam shop, washed-out midnight blue with silver half-moons on it.

'Shit, Mol, we're pagans, right? We do what pagans do.'

'Which means he don't know.' Rozzie cackled. Her face was round but prematurely lined, like a monkey's. Ropes of black beads hung down to her waist.

'And you do, yeah?' Headlice said.

Rozzie shrugged. Diane waited; she didn't really know what pagans did either, apart from revering the Old Gods and supporting the Green Party. They would claim that Christianity was an imported religion which was irrelevant to Britain.

But what would they actually *do*?

'I wouldn't wanna frighten you.' Rozzie smirked and swung herself on to the bus.

From across the field came the hollow sound of Bran, the drummer, doing what he did at every new campsite, what he'd done at every St Michael Church and prehistoric shrine along the Line: awakening the earth.

Diane looked away from the Tor, feeling a trickle of trepidation. She supposed there'd be lights up there tonight. Whether it was just the bijou flickerings of torches and lanterns, the oily glow of bonfires and campfires . . .

. . . or the other kind. The kind some people called UFOs and some said were earth-lights, caused by geological conditions.

But Diane thought these particular lights were too sort of *personal* to be either alien spacecraft or natural phenomena allied to seismic disturbance. It was all a matter of afterglow. Not in the sky; in your head. In the very top of your head at first, and then it would break up into airy fragments and some would lodge for a breathtaking moment in your throat before sprinkling through your body like a fine shiver.

Bowermead Hall, you see, was only three and a half miles from the town and, when she was little, the pointed hill crowned by the St Michael tower – the whole thing like a wine-funnel or a witch's hat – seemed to be part of every horizon, always there beyond the vineyards. Diane's very earliest sequential memory was looking out of her bedroom window from the arms of Nanny One and seeing a small, globular light popping out of the distant tower, like a coloured ball from a Roman candle. Ever so pretty, but Nanny One, of course, had pretended she couldn't see a thing. She'd felt Diane's forehead and grumbled about a temperature. What had happened next wasn't too clear now, but it probably involved a spoonful of something tasting absolutely frightful. *You're a very silly little girl. Too much imagination is not good for you.*

For a long time, Diane had thought imagination must be a sort of ice-cream; the lights too – some as white as the creamy blobs they put in cornets.

Years later, when she was in her teens, one of the psychologists had said to her, *You were having rather a rough time at home, weren't you, Diane? I mean, with your father and your brother. You were feeling very lonely and . . . perhaps . . . unwanted, unloved? Do you think that perhaps you were turning to the Tor as a form of . . .*

'No!' Diane had stamped her foot. 'I saw those lights. I *did*.'

And now the Tor had signalled to her across Britain. Called her back. But it wasn't – Diane thought of her father and her brother and that house, stiff and unforgiving as the worst of her schools – about pretty lights and candyfloss sunbeams. Not any more.

FIVE

A SIMPLE PERSON

Unwrapping a creamy new beeswax candle, Verity laid it down, with some trepidation, on a stone window ledge the size of a gravestone.

Still not sure, not *at all* sure, that she could go through with this.

It was late afternoon, but, even with all its hanging lights on, the room was as deep and shadowed as the nave of an old parish church.

The best-known old buildings in Glastonbury, apart from the Abbey, which was ruined – *so* tragic – were the one-time court-house, known as the Tribunal, and the George and Pilgrims inn, both in the High Street, both mellow and famously beautiful.

And then there was Meadwell.

Which was hunched among umbrella trees about a mile out of town, to the east of the Tor. And was terribly, *terribly* old. But not famous, not mellow and not what one would call beautiful.

Rather like me, thought Verity, who looked after Meadwell for the Pixhill Trust and ran it as a sort of guesthouse. Most of the time she was decidedly *not* a sad or introspective or *timid* person. But tonight was the night of the Abbot's Dinner – and, as the sourly humid November day dwindled into evening, she realised that her little cat, Stella, had still not come home.

Of course this was not the first time. Nor was Stella the first cat to decide that, despite the veritable *army* of mice, it simply did not wish to live at Meadwell.

But tonight being the night of the Abbot's Dinner, Verity could not bear to be entirely alone.

Because Meadwell was so venerable, Grade Two listed and starred, little could be done to relieve the dispiriting gloom result-ing from tiny, mullioned windows which must never be enlarged, oak panelling too delicate to disturb and enormous beams so oppressively low that even little Verity was obliged to stoop.

A touch of whitewash between the beams might have lightened the atmosphere a little, but there were sixteenth-century builders' marks to be protected. Also, in two of the upstairs rooms without panelling, repainting of the walls was forbidden because of what was described as Elizabethan graffiti – words, names perhaps, carved and burned into the sallow surface.

Of Verity's own presence here there was little evidence beyond, on a shelf inside the inglenook, a collection of novels by the great John Cowper Powys, whose sensually extravagant prose was her secret vice and her refuge. She considered it part of her role not to disturb the house's historic ambience, to flit mouselike about the place.

Most of the holiday guests – elderly, educated people, retired doctors, retired teachers, friends of the Trust – said how much they *absolutely loved* the house, with its *tremendous character*. In summer.

But even high summer entered Meadwell with uncharacteristic caution, pale sunbeams edging nervously around the oaken doors like the servants of a despot.

And it was getting darker. It *was*. Not simply because of the time of year; the house itself was gathering shadows, its beams blackening, its walls going grey like old, sick skin, its deeper corners becoming well-like and impenetrable.

It was as if only the Colonel had been able to keep the shadows at bay, and now the fabric of Meadwell was darkening around her, as if hung with mourning drapes. And in spite of her faith she was beginning to be . . .

. . . afraid?

But I do not see.

Verity Does Not See. It had become like a mantra – and after all these years in Glastonbury and attendance at hundreds of esoteric lectures at the Assembly Rooms, there was very little one could tell Verity about mantras.

'*I do not see.*'

Whispering it as she opened the door of the oak cupboard in the corner to the left of the great inglenook and took down the silver candlestick. It should have been cleaned and polished this morning, but she'd been putting it off ever since the upsetting telephone call from Major Shepherd.

'Awfully sorry, my dear. Most awfully sorry.' His wheeze had been like an old-fashioned vacuum-cleaner starting up, the bag inflating.

Verity had told him, in her bright, singing way, not to worry *in the slightest*. Just look after himself, drink plenty of water, keep warm, leave *everything* to her.

Not expecting, for one moment, that the Abbot's Dinner would be able to proceed without the chairman of the Trust. Without, in fact, any guests at all, only Verity, who would prepare the meal, and . . .

. . . and the Abbot.

Whom She Did Not See.

This day was almost invariably a dull day. Subdued. When the late Colonel Pixhill was here, it was the one day of the year on which he was never seen to smile. He would mope about the garden, gathering the first dismal crop of dead leaves, pausing occasionally to sniff thoughtfully at the air like an old English setter.

On this day nearly twenty years ago, the Colonel had come into her kitchen, put a sad hand on her shoulder and solemnly thanked her for all her years of service. Saying sincerely that he didn't know how he would have managed here without her.

It had occurred to Verity later, with a shiver of sorrow and unease, that he must have sniffed his own death that morning on the bitter wind coming down from the Tor.

Don't think of it.

Verity pursed her lips, straightened up and glared defiantly into the gathering dark of the dining hall.

'At least . . . at least I . . .'

Although, apparently, it had been the most essential qualification for a mistress of Meadwell. At her initial interview, some thirty years ago, the Colonel had approached the issue delicately but with persistence.

Quite an old place, this, Miss Endicott. Damned old. Damned cold. Bit grim, really. Lot of ladies would find that off-putting.

I suppose they would.

Might be . . . how shall I put it? . . . a trifle timid about sleeping here. If they were left alone.

Yes.

But not you? Think about it before you answer. Wind howling, timbers creaking sort of stuff.

You mean they might be afraid of . . . spirit-manifestation, Colonel.

Well. Hmm. That sort of thing.

I . . . I am not privileged to see the dead.

I see. Consider it a privilege, would you? If you could see the damn things?

No, I . . . I suppose I'm rather a superficial person. That is, I believe in God and have an interest in the spiritual, as . . . as a force for healing. And therefore I should dearly love to live in Glastonbury. But I don't think it necessary or desirable for us all to have . . . communion. If we believe, then that is enough, and if we do not wish to see, God will respect that. I am not afraid of old places. I try to be a simple person. I get on with what I have to do, and I . . . I do not See.

Each year she'd polished the candlestick and laid the table for the Abbot's Dinner, as if it was just another evening meal. After the Colonel's death, she'd imagined – and rather hoped – that the Dinner would be discontinued.

However, under the direction of the Pixhill Trust, it had become even more of an Occasion – now also as a memorial for Colonel Pixhill. It was, said Major Shepherd, one of the *most* important of the Colonel's conditions.

For ten years or so, the Dinner had been well attended by members of the Trust, two or three of them even staying on for a few days afterwards. This had pleased Verity, who found life in general rather dreary when the holiday season was over and Mrs Green, the cook, and Tracy, the maid, had disappeared for the winter.

But, as age and infirmity eroded the Trust, fewer and fewer chairs had been required around the dining table. Most of the original trustees had been, after all, the Colonel's contemporaries, fellow officers and associates. The new, younger ones – including the Colonel's son, Oliver – were apparently less concerned with the more eccentric traditions and, indeed, were keen to modernise the administration of the Trust.

Major Shepherd had been adamant that the Abbot's Dinner must not be allowed to lapse . . . even when, last year, he and Verity had found themselves alone at the huge table, the silver candlestick between them, the Major mouthing the words he claimed not to understand. And now it had come to this.

'My dear, none of us is getting any younger,' the Major had admitted on the telephone this morning. 'Except, perhaps, for you, Verity.' She could imagine the tired twinkle in his faded grey eyes. 'You never seem to change.'

Which she decided to take as a compliment to her vegan life-style and her beloved Bach Flower Remedies.

'I shall be *seventy* next year, Major. But . . .' She'd thought it a timely moment to remind him. '. . . I have absolutely no notion of *retirement*, you understand. I wouldn't know *where* to put myself.'

'Perish the thought.' And he'd gone on, somewhat hesitantly, to raise the question of the Abbot's Dinner, which she was convinced would have to be abandoned.

'I do realise, my dear, you must have been finding it increasingly something of a trial. And perhaps a little . . . well, sinister?'

'Oh, *no*, Major . . .'

Oh, *yes*, Major. Sadly.

'So obviously, I wouldn't dream of asking you to go through the whole ceremony on your own tonight.'

Verity had been so relieved that she had had to cover the mouthpiece to muffle her sigh. She would go *out* tonight. In the absence of a scheduled Cauldron meeting, she could perhaps invite herself to Dame Wanda's charming town-house for the evening. Or see if there was an interesting talk at the Assembly Rooms. Or even a potentially *tedious* talk – there would at least be people there and tea to share.

'But perhaps,' Major Shepherd had said at the end of a particularly painful wheeze, 'I could prevail upon you . . .'

'Oh. That is, you don't have to *prevail*, Major.' Verity's brightness had begun to dissipate.

'. . . to light the Abbot's candle?'

'Oh.'

'And perhaps . . .'

Verity had closed her eyes.

'. . . a short prayer?'

'I . . .'

'I'm so sorry, Verity. We'll be there with you in spirit. George Pixhill, too, I'm sure.'

'In spirit. Yes.'

I do not . . .

Now she brought out the silver polish, laid an oilcloth over the long, oak dining table and began to work on the candlestick. Her throat was parched, her chest tight.

But she had her duty. She polished and polished, until the candlestick shone in the dark air like the moon.

The Abbot was used to fine things.

It would be four hundred and fifty-six years since he was hanged on the Tor.

SIX

THE WEIRDEST PERSON HERE

'It knows we're coming.' Headlice was aglow with the excitement of being a pagan at what he said was the greatest pagan temple in Britain. 'Look at it . . . it *knows*, man.'

The Tor was temporarily free of cloud but losing definition in the darkening sky. You could no longer make out the ridges which ringed the hill and were supposed to be the remains of a prehistoric ritual maze.

It did look ever so mysterious now, with not a house in sight and no other visible hills. Diane, too, felt herself wanting to go up. But on her own. She didn't care to be part of a so-called pagan ritual. They'd come a long way for this; things could get rather, well, orgiastic.

Once, she'd said to Headlice, Why did you want to be a pagan? What does it *mean* to you? Headlice had mumbled something about his childhood near Manchester, being made to go to church and all the hypocritical bastards in their Sunday suits and the women in their stupid hats. How he'd grown up despising Christianity as a meaningless social ritual. Headlice said the difference with the old gods was that they had balls.

'But what will we actually do, when we get there?'

Headlice shrugged. 'All down to Gwyn.'

Everything seemed to be down to Gwyn. Gwyn the Shaman. She hadn't seen him since their arrival. He had his own van, very dirty on the outside, but newer than the rest. He kept himself apart from the others. Even the travellers, it seemed, had their aristocracy, and Gwyn was the adept, the man with the Knowledge. Since he'd joined the convoy in East Anglia the mood had been somehow less frivolous. Some people had even left.

'Aw,' Headlice said at last, 'most likely we'll just light a fire. Take our clothes off, you know? Under the shining goddess of the moon. Let the energy flow through us and, like, see what develops.'

Oh gosh. Don't like the sound of that!

'Er . . .' She hesitated. '. . . you know you're not allowed to do that? I mean, light fires. It's National Trust property.'

Not a very Molly thing to say.

Headlice stared at her and started to laugh. 'That means it belongs to the people, you daft bat.'

A naked toddler sprang up giggling from the grass, bottom smeared with her own faeces. Diane tried not to notice. She looked away, across Moulder's field with its new covering of beaten-up vehicles painted with wild spray-colours. It was supposed to have all the spontaneity of a medieval country fayre, but it looked sad and dingy, like a derelict urban scrapyard.

Headlice said, 'Be fuckin' great.'

The tower poked the streaky sky, a stubby cigar waiting to be lit.

'Won't be no bother about fires, Mol. Who's gonna try and stop us?'

Another kind of unease was forming around her like a thermal glow. To Headlice, paganism, with its loose talk of 'old gods' and 'old ways', was just a sort of *alternative* social ritual. But Glastonbury Tor was not the place for play-acting.

She saw Don Moulder leaning over his gate, watching them. He was waiting for his money.

'And keep it to yourself, Mr Moulder. About me, I mean.'

'I won't say another word, Miss Diane.'

Don Moulder's currant eyes were pressed into a face like a slab of red Cheddar.

Don was a sort of born-again Christian with Jesus stickers in the back window of his tractor. It meant he never *quite* lied. So he'd probably told someone already.

Three hundred and fifty pounds changed hands. This left less than two hundred in the pocket sewn inside Diane's Oxfam moonskirt.

The travellers didn't know she was paying for the land; that would have been against their code. They thought Don Moulder was Molly's uncle. He raised an eyebrow at that.

And then said, 'Hippies.' Dumping the word like a trailer-load of slurry. 'Gonner be pretty bloody popular, aren't I, lettin' the hippies on my land. What I'm sayin' is, I'm not sure three hundred covers it, all the goodwill I'm losin', look.'

Don Moulder held all the cards; it cost her an extra fifty.

When she'd first encountered them, the travellers had been camping up on the moor – illegally, but there weren't enough of them to qualify for instant arrest under the Act.

The news editor, an awful inverted snob who thought overfed, upper-crust Diane needed exposure to the lower strata of society, had sent her to do a story on them. Hoping, no doubt, that they would refuse to talk to her and she'd come back with her tail between her legs and he could smirk.

Determined that this would not happen, Diane had toned down her accent, adding a little Somerset burr which she thought at the time was rather good, actually. She'd even passed their very obvious test: accepting a mug of tea made from brown water scooped from a ditch.

This certainly broke the ice with Headlice; he'd begun to tell her things, despite Rozzie's attempts to shut him up.

You print what you like, luv, we're not stoppin' here, anyroad.

Where are you going next then?

Leave it, Headlice, she's only trying to . . .

Home, luv. Our spiritual home. It's a pilgrimage. Along the pagan way.

Shut it, shithead.

To the sacred Isle of Avalon. Know where that is?

Diane had gone weak. It was another sign. Like a magic carpet unrolling at her feet, and the carpet went diagonally through the spine of England all the way back to Glastonbury. She'd felt almost sick with a combination of longing and dread.

Still holding the tin mug between her hands to stop them shaking she'd heard herself say,

May I come with you?

She didn't even remember deciding to say it; the question just popped out, as strange and spontaneous as a lightball over the Tor.

I could, you know, write about it for the paper – what it's really like, what you're trying to do, all the hassle you get and the abuse. Would that be possible?

And she'd told them her name was Molly Fortune and she came from Somerset, and her accent went even fuzzier.

In a complete daze over the following two days, she'd drawn all she had out of the bank, paid £825 for the van and spent half an hour spraying pink blobs on the side. Absolute madness. Her father would have paled into one of his thin rages. In her father's Somerset, New Age travellers were the worst kind of vermin, the kind you weren't allowed to shoot.

For wealthy, handsome Patrick (fortuitously away at the time on an editors' conference) embarrassment would be the worst of it. Embarrassment tinged, perhaps, with a certain relief. He was very good-looking, slim, two years younger than she. But he had *affection* for her; he would have been faithful. Perhaps.

Diane had sealed up her beautiful antique diamond ring in a registered envelope and posted it to Patrick, with a letter full of babbling incoherence. *Sorry. I just can't. I'm so sorry, Patrick. It's out of my hands. I'll write properly soon. Please don't hate me.*

It had been just a week before the widely publicised engagement party at the biggest hotel in Harrogate.

The worst of it for Diane was that, in spite of everything – in spite of Patrick's being virtually the Chosen Suitor – she *could* have loved him. Probably. But something so far inside that she couldn't reach it loved Glastonbury more.

'So we start going up now, and we wait quietly.'

Mort had with him his new floozie, a slinky little redhead with a muted Germanic accent who seemed to be called Viper. She was wearing a loose, white shift and Mort's hand was up one of the sleeves, carelessly cupping a breast.

Mort had dark, swarthy skin, high cheekbones; his hair was pulled back into a tight braid. He looked like he ought to be wearing a broadsword at his belt.

'Ain't a piece of street theatre.' It was as if he'd picked up Diane's thoughts about play-acting. 'This is the real thing. The real place. *The* place.'

'What's with this quietness shit?' Headlice demanded. 'We're goin' to our church. We don't have to hide it.'

Mort sighed. 'This is your first time, init, Headlice? There's people don't like us being here. We don't want no Stonehenge situation.'

Even to Diane this seemed a little over-cautious. Stonehenge was a restricted area and the Tor was not. And this was the middle of November, not Midsummer's Eve.

'Also, we don't want local kids tagging along. So we go up in small groups.'

Headlice was right: this wasn't how it had been. Paganism was not against the law, and the whole ethos of the New Age travellers was a kind of defiant exhibitionism; why else have purple hair, lip-rings, nipple-rings and luminous pentacles on the sides of your bus?

The vehicles in Don Moulder's bottom field were now in rough, concentric circles, the night beginning to join them together, like walls. It was strangely silent; no ghetto-blasters blasting, no children squealing.

'Idea being that we're up there by nightfall,' Mort said. 'And no lights. You and Roz first, OK? I'll show you the path.'

'No problem,' Headlice said. 'Mol's been up loads of times.'

'Mol ain't coming.' Mort's voice had tightened like his hair. He'd taken his hand out of Viper's sleeve.

Headlice stared at him. 'Huh?'

Mort turned to Diane. 'Don't take this wrong. We got nothing against you, Molly Fortune, but we ain't forgotten you're a reporter, and Gwyn don't conduct rituals for the Press. Sorry.'

'You got to be fuckin' kiddin', man!' Headlice was furious. 'That goes against everything we're up for! Like we're a fuckin' secret society now? I mean, come on, what is paganism *about*, man? If you, like, worship the sun and the moon and natural stuff, you do it in the open.'

Diane wanted to tell him to calm down, it didn't matter, it wasn't right for her to be part of a pagan ceremony, certainly not the kind Headlice envisaged. But he straightened up, absurdly like a little war veteran.

'Listen, I'm *proud* of what I am, me.' He prodded Mort in the chest. 'I worship the earth, yeah? And that hill's not private land, so if nobody can stop us goin' up, what right you got to tell Mol she can't come?'

Mort's face had darkened. He snatched Headlice's prodding forefinger, bent it slowly back. Headlice went white. Mort forced him to his knees, towered over him.

'This is religion, Headlice,' Mort said. 'It's between us . . .'

There was a slight crack from Headlice's finger.

'And the gods,' Mort said.

'You fuckin' . . .' Headlice shoved his hand between his thighs. 'You've broken it.'

'I don't think so.'

'Oh look . . .' Diane thought she must be as pale as Headlice. 'You go. To be quite honest . . .' Inspiration came. She produced a hopeless sigh. 'It's a pretty stiff climb, OK? I'm not built . . . Sometimes I get sort of out of breath, you know?'

Rozzie twirled her black beads and dropped a tilted grin that was sort of, Stupid fat cow, why didn't you say in the first place?

'I'll mind the camp,' Diane said. 'See the kids are OK.'

'Thank you,' Mort said quietly. He turned and walked off down the field, his woman clinging to his arm. When he'd gone, Diane felt distinctly uncomfortable. A real journalist would have protested, been absolutely determined to go up the Tor with them.

'Who's that twat think he is?' Headlice struggled to his feet. 'We got a fuckin' hierarchy now?'

'It's, you know, it's all right. Really. I didn't want to cause any . . . I mean, it's not the same at night, anyway. You can't see the view, and it gets very cold.'

'What you sayin' here, Mol?'

Diane rubbed her goose-pimpled arms. 'I don't know.'

'Don't you?' She saw that Headlice was confused almost to the point of tears. 'I'm fed up wi' this. Everybody treats me like a fuckin' dickhead. And you . . .' Staring at her resentfully. 'Wi' your fancy accent slippin' through. You're a bit deep, Mol. You come on like fat and harmless. I reckon you're weirder than all of us. I reckon you're the weirdest person here.'

Diane was silent, biting her lip.

SEVEN

SLIVER OF LIGHT

Increasingly, the dusk obsessed Jim Battle. He supposed it was due to his time of life: slipping away, as everyone must, into the mauve and the sepia.

But still it was endlessly challenging. Midges, for instance. How were you supposed to paint midges? In clouds, perhaps? A thickening of the air? Or just a dry stipple.

'Dry stipple,' Jim said aloud. One of those phrases that sounded like what it meant. There was a word for that; buggered if he could remember what it was.

With a thumb he smudged the sun. In the finished painting, it would be merely a hazy memory, a ghost on the canvas. Same with the Tor; you should be able to *feel* it in the picture, but not necessarily see it.

Jim stepped away from the canvas. The tangled garden, by now, was all blues and greys and dark browns. As there were no lights on in the cottage, Jim could barely see the canvas. Time to stop. Time to wind up the Great Quest for another day.

Still, for once, time was playing on his side, staying the dead hand of winter, letting him go on painting outdoors into the early evening, using the very last of the light. For this was when things happened. Often, when he looked at the picture next morning, he'd find that the absence of direct light had wrought some marvellous effects, textures he'd never have found if he'd been able to see properly. All a matter of surrendering to the dusk.

And beyond the dusk . . . lay the Grail.

Of course, everyone came to Avalon in search of the Grail. And it was different for all of them. There was always the *possibility* of an actual holy relic somewhere. But for most people the Grail was simply the golden core of whatever you dreamed you might achieve. The vanishing point on life's horizon. Glastonbury being one of those spots on the Earth's surface where the phantasmal became almost tangible, where you might actually reach the vanishing point before you, er, vanished.

Jim's personal Grail – the mystical formula which would (he hoped) come to define a Battle painting – was to be found at the very end of dusk, the cusp of the day, the moment between evening and night when the world stopped.

It should happen at dawn too, but it didn't for Jim. He'd walked out in the drizzle and the dew, to wait. In vain. The moment never came, or he could not feel it. Time of life again: at his age perhaps you were just not meant to feel the stopping of the world at dawn.

Not that he greatly wished for youth – only to have come to Avalon as a younger man. Wasn't as if he hadn't known, then, what he wanted to do. *Plenty of time for painting*, bloody Pat had bleated, *when you've got your pension*.

God. Why do we listen to them? If he'd left his wife and met Juanita twenty years ago, when she was a very young woman and he didn't seem *so* much of an older man . . .

Well, he hadn't. It was enough of a privilege that she was his friend, that he could bathe in her aura. Jim left the canvas wedged into the easel and manhandled the whole thing to the house. He propped it against the open door and turned to accept the night.

The cottage was tiny but satisfyingly isolated, reached by a track too narrow for a car. Ten years ago, although his worldly goods were few, the removal men had been less than euphoric.

But Jim still was, much of the time. Especially when the sun had gone, leaving its ghost to haunt the lush, sloping grass in the foothills of Glastonbury Tor.

Behind the cottage was a wooded hillside which was always immediately activated by the dying sun. He could almost feel it starting to tremble with the stirring and scufflings and rustlings of badgers and rabbits and foxes and owls.

Before him, the dark brown fields rolled away into the tide of mist on the slopes of the Tor and the cottage snuggled into the huge ash tree which overhung it, as if its only protection against the night was to become part of this great organism.

The way that Jim himself wanted to go into the final night. To be absorbed, become part of the greater organism, even if it was only as fertiliser.

He grunted, startled. Two extra shadows were creeping along the hedgerow.

Headlice saw the little tubby guy in his garden, with his red face and his tweed hat. What a waste, eh? People like that should go and live in nice suburban cul-de-sacs and leave the power places for them that could still feel the electricity.

He dragged Rozzie into the shadow of the hedge. 'Ow!' she screeched. 'Friggin' thorns.'

'Thorns round here are sacred,' Headlice told her. 'That Joseph of whatsit, when he landed and planted his stick, it turned into a thorn tree, right?'

'That's Christian.'

'It's still earth magic.' Headlice gazed up towards the Tor, very big now, almost scary in the flatlands. One side of the tower sucking the very last red bit out of the sky, the other side, the one closest to them, sooty-black.

He was glad they'd been sent first, to find their own way through the tangled undergrowth to the Tor. This was how a pilgrimage ought to end. Except he wished it wasn't Rozzie.

A fragile half moon had risen in a thin mist above the holy hill's eastern flank.

'Fuckin' magic. In't it?'

'You ain't seen nuffin yet.' Rozzie smiled secretively. 'Stop a minute, willya? I've done me friggin' ankle.'

Headlice gritted his teeth. 'Been better off bringing Molly. Least she knows the country.'

'Yeah,' Rozzie said. 'And you could shag her afterwards, right?'

Headlice said nothing.

'What you had in mind, ain't it?' Rozzie said. 'You're a transparent little sod.'

OK, so maybe he did wish it was Mol he was with. Sure she was fat. Fat*ish*. But she was nice-looking. Open, where Rozzie was closed-up. Despite – and he'd always known this – her not being what she made out. Plus she smelled nice.

When they crossed the lane, only a hedge between them and where the ground started to rise, Headlice wanted to climb over and scramble up, but Rozzie said they'd better find the gate Mort had told them to use. When they reached it they could see a glowing path of concrete: chippings and stuff had been put in, with steps. All the way to the top, it looked like. For the tourists. Sacrilege.

There was a collecting box inviting visitors to contribute towards Tor maintenance. Oh yeah, like patching up the concrete path? Balls to that.

And then there was a National Trust notice board for the thicko tourists. Headlice started to read it anyway, striking a match and holding it close to the print.

Tor is a West Country word of Celtic origin meaning a hill. Glastonbury Tor is a natural formation composed of layers of clay and blue limestone, capped by a mass of hard, erosion-resistant sandstone.

'How do they know that, anyway?' It was almost too dark to make out the print. 'How do they know it's a natural formation?'

'What's it matter?' Rozzie said.

'Because it could've been *built* here, you daft bat. By the ancient shamans. Like the pyramids. According to the lines of force and the position of the heavens.'

The Tor is and has been to many people a place of magic, the focus of legend and superstition. One local story is that there is a hollow space inside; another, perhaps very ancient, that the hill has a secret entrance to the Underworld.

Headlice felt sick to his gut to see it spelled out like this, in baby talk, for every ice-lolly-sucking day-tripper. He wanted to rip down the board, smash the collecting box, hack up the concrete path. Then the Tor would be a secret place again. A place for pilgrims.

He turned away, needing to put this tourist shit behind him.

'Come on.' Pulling at Rozzie.

'Get your mits off. Wanna read this last bit.'

The Tor was the scene of the hanging, drawing and quartering of Richard Whiting, the last Abbot of Glastonbury, when Henry VIII dissolved the Abbey in 1539.

'Heavy,' Rozzie said.

'Yeah. Shit.' Headlice dropped the match as it burned down to his fingers. 'I didn't know about that.'

He looked up to where night had fused the hill and the tower into a single dark lump.

'Still.' He walked off along the shining path. 'Maybe the old git had it coming.'

Alone for the first time since she'd joined the convoy, Diane sat in Headlice's bus, a woollen shawl around her shoulders, and unwrapped a peppermint-flavoured carob bar.

She was sitting on one of the original vinyl-covered bus seats still bolted to the floor. The bus windows were purpled by a November night as soft and luminous as June.

So this was it. Breathing space over. She was back.

What happens now?

Part of her wanted to take her van and leave quietly. Drive to Juanita's. She'd really missed Juanita, the older sister she'd never had. She really ought to explain. But what on *earth* could she say? Juanita might run a New Age bookshop, but she could be rather disparaging about people's visions.

I was dreaming every night about the Tor. Vivid colours.

Common homesickness. You'll get over it.

Kept seeing things sort of metamorphose into the Tor. Salt pots and vinegar shakers in cafés. Plastic bottles of toilet cleaner. And flashing images of it when I closed my eyes.

Hyper-active imagination. Next.

Stopping at traffic lights behind lorries owned by Glastonbury firms. Or houses called Avalon.

Oh, really . . .

And sometimes I'd wake up in the middle of the night sensing her near me, in the room.

Oh God, not . . .

The Third Nanny.

You're nuts, Diane.

She began to rock backwards and forwards, holding herself tight in the shawl. *Oh God, Oh God, what am I doing here?*

Two weeks ago, Patrick had shown her pictures of his family's villa in Chianti country. Wonderful place for a honeymoon. Lovely place, decent man. Oh *God*.

A shadow passed the window. Then another. She sat very still for a moment. They'd all gone, she'd watched them. Mort and Viper the last to go. She heard a giggle and a hiss.

Kids. There were three or four children in a converted ambulance at the other end of the field, in the care of a sullen teenager called Hecate, a large girl who claimed to be sixteen but was probably younger.

There'd been quite a few babies in the convoy when it first set off, but by the time they reached the beginning of the St Michael Line at Bury St Edmunds, they all seemed to have gone, along with their parents. And the dogs. None of the remaining travellers seemed to have dogs with them. She was sure there'd been a few before, when they were on their way down from Yorkshire.

And musicians. Two guitarists and a flute player. Now there was only Bran, the dour shamanic drummer.

And there used to be lots of ghetto-blasters. Endless rock music. Old Rolling Stones albums and Oasis and The Lemonheads. Deep into the night, and the children were used to it and slept through it all.

The hiss came again. Diane got up and went out to the platform. 'What's going on?'

It didn't stop. She stepped off the platform and found herself looking into the shadowed face of the girl called Hecate.

'What's your problem?' Hecate said.

'What are you doing?'

There were four small shadows moving about. Children who were surely old enough to be at school. They were hovering around the bus, making hissing sounds.

'Hey!' Diane realised what was happening. They all had big aerosol sprays. It was almost dark, but she could see that several of the yellow stripes on the bus's bee-patterned panels had already vanished. 'Stop that, you little horrors. Headlice'll go mad!'

The children carried on spraying the bus black, didn't even look round. In the near-dark there was something unearthly about them. They were like silent gnomes.

Diane turned back to the older girl. 'Can't you stop them?'

'Why don't you mind your own bleeding business?' Hecate said. 'You nosy fat slag.'

'How dare . . .?' Diane calmed down, remembered to put on the Somerset. '*That's* jolly nice, I must say.'

'Look,' Hecate said. 'Headlice told us to do it, right? Good enough?'

'I don't believe you.'

'I don't give a fart what you believe.' Hecate put her face very close to Diane's. Her teeth were thick and yellow and her breath smelled putrid. 'Now get back on the bus, crawl into a corner and mind your own. Else when they've finished I'm gonna hold you down while they spray your fanny black. *That* good enough?'

No getting round it; Jim was shaken.

'I don't think so. I'm pretty sure I didn't see her, although . . .'

Juanita said, 'Jim, is there something wrong with this line?'

Jim coughed, realising he'd been almost whispering down the phone. Whispering. In his own buggering house! And with the lights out, so no one could see him standing by the window.

'Thing is . . .' He drank some whisky and then put the glass on the windowsill, pushing it behind the curtain as though she could see how full it was. '. . . it was very nearly dark when the last ones went past, but I'd gone down to the end of the garden by then to get as close as possible to the path.'

Standing behind a sycamore tree with plenty of leaves still on it. Holding his breath as they went past. Hiding in his own buggering garden!

'I mean, they tend to be pretty skeletal, don't they, these travelling types? So unless she's lost a few stone . . .'

Bloody angry with himself for feeling threatened. But it was the first time in seventeen years of living here that his sacred space had been penetrated so blatantly by so many people. And such bloody *purposeful* people.

'You could have asked one of them where she was,' Juanita said.

'I suppose I *could*. But I . . . it's strange, but I didn't like to speak to them. You know what these characters are normally like, either drugged up to the eyeballs or laughing and swigging cider and what have you, like day trippers.'

'Yes, I know.'

'Not these buggers. Could've been the SAS on night manoeuvres or something. Quite . . . well, unearthly I suppose. In fact if it hadn't been for the way they were dressed and the glint of the rings in the ears, I'd've . . . I don't know. They were just so *quiet*. Not a buggering word between them. And you're looking at – what? – over a hundred of them. Yes, I suppose I could quite easily have missed Diane.'

There was a moment's silence.

'I don't like the sound of this, Jim.'

'That's why I called you. Do you think I should phone the police in Street?'

'What, and have the camp raided and Diane herded into a Black Maria? No, let's play it by ear. I'll get the car. Pick you up at the bottom of your track in about ten minutes?'

'Right ho,' Jim said, relieved. 'Just . . . just be careful. Don't stop for anybody.'

'Jim.'

'Yes?'

'You sound scared.'

'Oh. No, no. Just out of breath.'

Diane stood on the deck of the bus, nervously nibbling another carob bar. It was quiet again now. The strange children had finished spraying the bus and gone. Was it supposed to be a joke? She was ashamed at having let the girl menace her like that.

The air was cooling. She drew her woollen shawl across her lower arms, dragged it tight around her, arms folded in the wool. She sat down in one of the slimy vinyl seats. She'd wait about an hour and then creep quietly away to the van, drive up to Don Moulder's farm and then down Wellhouse Lane into the town.

All the buses and vans were still as wooden huts and drained of their colours. It could have been a scene from centuries ago. The circle of vehicles, which might just as well be carts, looked almost romantically tribal when their squalid aspects were submerged in shadows.

When she'd joined the convoy it was all so noisy and jolly, with a real sense of community. It was a kind of fun paganism more concerned with stone circles and earth-forces and ley-lines and spreading good vibes. They were like a travelling circus. And yes, you really could imagine a new spirit of freedom being born and nurtured in an encampment of latterday gypsies dismissed by just about everybody as a bunch of dirty scavengers. There really had been a glimmer of ancient light here.

The smell on the bus was of sweat, grease and oil with an underlying cannabis sweetness. A misty wafer of moon rose in the grimy glass. This was the only ancient light now.

And yet, as the thought passed through her mind, there was another glimmer, some yards away. Diane froze and then, very quietly, stood up and peered through the window into Don Moulder's field.

The Tor, half a mile away, was still visible, the tower entwined in strands of moon-touched cloud. A tall figure was gazing over the fields towards the sacred hill. Gwyn the Shaman. He was still here. He must be waiting until they were all in position on the Tor before making his ceremonial entrance.

The shaman was the tribal witch doctor. The man who interceded with the spirits. Bearded Gwyn, with his aloofness and his whispered prophecies, seemed disturbingly like the real thing. It was when Gwyn had joined that the atmosphere had begun to change. The gradual shedding of the happier, noisier, more casual pilgrims, leaving the quieter, more committed ones.

And Diane. And Headlice.

She held her breath, moved back a little from the window. She could see that Gwyn wore . . . a robe or a long overcoat. His arm, the one nearest to her, was reaching up into the mist, his hand . . .

His hand was curled around one end of the spectral sickle moon.

Diane gasped. Gwyn stood tall and still, a god with the moon in his hand. Or so it seemed.

Until, with a feeling of deep dread, she became aware that the wan glimmer was from the blade of a real sickle.

Gwyn lowered the blade, in a slow and ceremonial fashion. She watched the curved sliver of light swinging by his side as he strode across the field towards the Tor.

EIGHT

ONLY IN GLASTONBURY

Towers. Everywhere in Glastonbury you were overlooked by towers.

Juanita hurried across High Street. As an established tradesperson, she was permitted a reserved space on the central car park below the fortified Norman tower of St John's.

Like St Michael's on the Tor, over half a mile away, the town's principal church had its own colour-chart of moods. In the sunshine of late afternoon, it could be mellow, sometimes almost golden with its four-cornered Gothic crown. But on a dull day it faded to grey and was outshone by the rusty-red tiles on the roofs of the shops and houses packed around it.

And at night it brooded behind its walls and railings. When you looked up, you could no longer make out the four crosses supporting the weather vanes on the highest pinnacles and there was not that sense of the sacred which Glastonbury Abbey always seemed to retain in its ruins, day or night.

There was also a sort of concrete, walled apron where groups of young pilgrims gathered to smoke or chant to bongos and tablas. Which seemed fairly innocent during the day but could be rather menacing after dark.

It was also a good place to get yourself mugged, so Juanita very nearly screamed when a shadow moved.

'Oh, my dear, I'm so sorry. Did I scare you?'

'Not at all.' Juanita put a hand to her chest and swallowed. 'Jesus, Verity.'

The little woman wore a quilted body warmer and an elflike velvet hat. She carried a shopping bag, even though almost nothing was open.

'Nothing will happen to you here, Juanita. It's a very warm and spiritual spot. And so *egalitarian*. And the young people know that, and they neither threaten us nor feel threatened.'

53

'Right,' Juanita said uncertainly. Sometimes you wandered into the church itself and it would be full of young New Age types of indeterminate religion, hugging each other and smiling at everyone. And OK, nobody had actually been mugged in the area recently.

Except, of course, by Verity, who prowled the streets like a small cat because she was lonely when the tourist season was over and there was nobody to stay with her.

'Well, I'm just going to pick up Jim Battle,' Juanita explained, because Verity would keep you talking here for bloody ever. It was rather sad, really, this middle-class, New Age bag lady. 'Going to the pub.'

'I must go too, Juanita,' Verity said surprisingly and actually hefted her shopping bag and half turned. But then she dropped the bait neatly behind her. I can't put it off for ever.'

Oh God. 'Put what off, Verity?' Juanita was trying not to sound over-patient.

'Silly of me, I know. But it's the Abbot's night, you see.'

'Ab . . .? Oh. Whiting.' Juanita didn't want to hear this at all. Some thoughts were just too damned creepy to carry around with you through darkened streets.

'Poor man,' Verity said. 'He comes for comfort, and there's nothing we can do. They'll still hang him tomorrow.'

Juanita shuddered, couldn't help it. When you knew the circumstances, it wasn't very funny. Verity managed Meadwell, Glastonbury's gloomiest guest house. Abbot Whiting was said to have spent his last night there before he was executed in the king's name. And then they took the Abbey apart and Avalon's dark age began. Every year the Pixhill Trust held a formal dinner in the Abbot's honour.

'I wonder', Verity said wistfully, 'if he will ever be at peace.'

'Well, who knows, Verity. But there's not a lot you can do about it, is there? Look, I have to . . .'

'People say that when there is spiritual unity in the town again, when the Christians and the pagans come together in harmony . . .'

'Verity,' Juanita said gently, 'old Whiting was a Benedictine monk with no documented pagan leanings.'

'But he was a *Catholic*, my dear. Therefore a follower of the *Goddess* Mary. In destroying the Abbeys, Henry VIII was . . .'

'Yeah, I know. It was a sexist, male-domination trip.'

Propaganda from The Cauldron, the town's fastest-growing goddess group. It was almost a New-Age women's institute these days with even people like Verity going to the Outer Circle meetings and lectures. And fashionable since the arrival of the actress, Dame Wanda Carlisle, who was apparently discovering the goddess in herself. They kept urging Juanita to join, but it seemed to have an underlying political agenda. Anyway, the idea of an outfit led by someone calling herself Ceridwen after the Celtic harridan goddess . . .

'You want to be careful there, Verity. That woman's on a power-trip.'

Verity smiled nervously; although Juanita saw only the gleam of her tiny teeth, she could imagine all the cracks in the walnut face of someone who seemed to have been born to be sixty and sprightly. Verity, surely, was no latent pagan; she could be observed every Sunday toddling along to both morning and evening services at St John's.

'Power,' Verity said. 'Yes. The power to heal and to help people find their way. The Church is embracing spiritual healing again. The Bishop is talking to the alternative worshippers. Glastonbury is becoming *whole* again. So they say.'

'Do they?' Juanita was slightly incredulous. 'Jesus.'

'If we could help the Abbot find eternal peace after nearly five centuries, wouldn't that be wonderful?'

'Terrific. But if I were you I think I'd just go to sleep and try not to think about it.'

'Oh no! It's my *duty* to receive the Abbot. Who, thank God, I do not . . . See . . .'

'Yes. Well.' Juanita eased herself away. 'Just you look after yourself, Verity.'

She was glad when she'd crossed the shadowed car park and was safely behind the wheel of the Volvo. If Verity was a little unravelled, she was at least in the right place for it.

Dear God, Juanita thought, *I used to revel in all this. The excitement of it. A spiritual Las Vegas. The thrill of high metaphysical stakes.*

A lot had changed. Or maybe it was just her. Her agitation threshold had lowered for a start. She worried.

About growing old alone. About the business and whether selling mystical books was a good and worthy profession any more in a town where mysticism had become a tourist commodity. About Jim Battle, who ate and drank unwisely and what would happen if he ever collapsed with a heart attack over his easel in a little cottage even Hansel and Gretel wouldn't have discovered.

About whether this fourteen-year-old car would start.

'Come . . . *on!*'

The Volvo did, though without much enthusiasm, and Juanita was able to get into some *serious* worrying. About Diane.

Dotty. Confused. Mixed-up. That's all.

That's *all*?

She edged past the rear entrance of The George and Pilgrims and round into High Street. Followed all the way by Lord Pennard's voice down a telephone nearly ten years ago. A cold voice, a voice honed by Gillette.

You, Mrs Carey. I hold you entirely responsible.

No. She wasn't having that. This town was a positive bazaar of the mystical. If it hadn't been Carey and Frayne it would have been some other bookshop.

Diane had looked so utterly forlorn, shuffling in that first time, another teenage waif appealing for a holiday job. If you could *have* fat waifs. What was she supposed to say? Be off with you, you over-privileged hussy?

You didn't know she was maladjusted? Don't tell me you close your ears to the local gossip, Mrs Carey.

Juanita drove past the venerable façade of The George and Pilgrims, where modern pilgrims with Gucci luggage slept in rooms with four-postered beds and sloping walls. Sometimes she drank at the Pilgrims with Jim and the others, amusing themselves by embellishing the Glastonbury legends for earnest German tourists, telling them a clear UFO sighting over the Tor was virtually guaranteed at just before four a.m. on every second Sunday, especially in winter.

As it happened, Juanita had never actually seen a UFO, which was a pretty shameful admission in Glastonbury.

Diane, of course, claimed she'd always seen balls of light in the sky over the Tor. Didn't everybody see them?

And the gossips said, *It's in the genes, isn't it? Always a danger with the upper classes. Interbreeding. You'll always get one like that, every couple of generations.* And they watched her padding down the street, Lord Pennard's strange daughter, and they called her Lady Loony.

It was, admittedly, at the Carey and Frayne bookshop that Diane had discovered the works of Dion Fortune, the Greatest Woman Magician of All Time. *Oh, Juanita, I'm so excited. Dion Fortune – Diane Ffitch. Same initials!* Diane, nose in a book, munching healthy snacks. Nobody should get fat, for God's sake, on quorn and tofu and carob-covered cereal bars.

She'd have found those books anyway, sooner or later. In Glastonbury, the nutter's Mecca, where gateways to altered states seemed as close as the nearest bus stop. Where, on nights like this, you could almost see the subtle merging of the layers, the way you could in Jim's paintings.

Further up the street, only one shop was fully lit: Holy Thorn Ceramics, owned by thirtyish newcomers Anthony and Domini Dorrell-Adams. The lights were on because the Dorrell-Adamses were reorganising their window, and . . .

'Jesus,' Juanita said.

Tony and Domini were together in the window. In fact it was hard to imagine how they could be *more* together while fully clothed and standing up – Domini arching backwards and you could almost hear the moans.

Only in Glastonbury.

Juanita tried to smile, accelerated away to the top of High Street. It could be a hell of an aphrodisiac, this town. Well, at first, anyway. Turning into Lambrook Street, she was ambushed by misty moments from twenty-odd years ago, when she'd left Nigel Carey (sad junkie; dead now) and she and Danny Frayne had opened the shop with about two hundred books, mostly secondhand, and a lot of posters. Danny was in publishing now, back in London. And while it still said Carey and Frayne over the shop, and they still occasionally exchanged daringly intimate letters on business notepaper, and now and then had dinner and whatnot in London, Danny – once bitten – never came back to Glastonbury.

Headlights on full-beam, Juanita drove the Volvo off left into secretive, tree-hung Wellhouse Lane, official gateway to the Tor.

Impressionable. That was Diane. Curiously innocent. Perhaps deluded. That's *all*. But if he found she was with the New Age travellers, her father would . . . what? Have her committed? Juanita was convinced he'd tried something like that once. Jim was right. Lord Pennard was not a terribly nice man.

It was very dark. Juanita drove carefully up the narrowing hill road, scene of many a near-collision, and took a narrow right, scraping the hedge.

Where the Tor should be visible, there was a night mist like a wall. The lane swooped steeply into a tunnel of trees, and at the end of it Juanita swung sharp left into a mud-packed track until the car could go no farther.

The great ash tree leapt up indignantly, as if rudely awoken by the Volvo's headlights.

She got out. 'Jim?'

A little chillier than of late, and it'd be quite cold on the Tor. Pulling on her coat, Juanita very nearly screamed when a hand patted her shoulder.

'My, my.' Jim grinned like a Hallowe'en pumpkin behind his lamp. 'We *are* being traditional tonight.'

'Say what you like about the Afghan.' Juanita pushed her hair inside the sheepskin. 'But it's damned warm. Help me reverse?'

Jim, also, was dressed for action. In his hat and scarf and overcoat he looked like something from *The Wind in the Willows*, Mole or Ratty. With Toad's physique, however, and probably just as hopeless. But without Jim Battle there'd be nobody quite sane enough to turn to in this kind of crisis.

'Leave the car here, Juanita. Better off walking. Take us about twenty minutes. The old feet can virtually find their own way after all this time.'

'You sound a good deal more cheerful than you did on the phone.'

'That's because I haven't been out with you at night for a good while.' She felt his smile.

'Yes. Well. Unfortunately, we won't have time for a candlelit dinner.'

'I've got a bar of chocolate.'

'We'll have it to celebrate, afterwards. How are we going to handle this, Jim?'

'Bloody hell, I thought you were supposed to be in charge. Suppose there's some sort of orgy going on up there? Wouldn't be the first time.'

'In which case, Diane'll be somewhere on the edge of it looking terribly embarrassed and a bit lost.'

'People do change, Juanita. Erm . . . before we go any further . . .'

'That's a myth. People don't really change at all. Sorry, Jim.'

'I was going to say, on the question of heroics . . .'

Juanita squeezed a bulky, overcoated arm. 'I'm not suggesting you barge into the middle of a bunch of naked, squirming travellers and sling her over your shoulder.'

'No, I . . .'

'I mean, I know you'd *do* it. If I asked you.'

'Actually, I was thinking more about you. What I'm getting at is, the Tor's a funny place.'

'Tell me about it.'

'Sometimes you can get carried away. You know what I mean?'

'No.' Juanita rammed her fists into the pockets of the Afghan. 'Not any more. Carried away is what I don't get.'

NINE

NO BOOZE, NO DOPE

It was like being on a strange planet.

Like they'd climbed up the night itself and emerged on to some other sphere, and the moon and the stars were so much nearer and so bright it was like they were swimming in and out of your head.

All this without drugs.

'*Magic*,' Headlice breathed, understanding at last why Mort had been handing out this strict no booze, no dope stuff.

The pilgrims, all standing up now, had gathered around the tower, which rose out of this small space on the summit of the Tor, over an ocean of lights far, far below.

The tower. So close. Like a silent rocket ship in the centre, and they were like joined to it and it was part of them. Literally. If he stretched out his legs his bare feet would touch the stone.

His feet should have been dead cold up here, in November, but this was a very special year, the summer heat clinging to Avalon, and the Tor was where the *real* heat was stored, all the sacred earth-energy. This was like the spiritual power station of Britain and tonight Headlice was gonna get charged up like a battery.

All the pilgrims were in a circle, holding hands. Headlice's left hand had found the clammy fingers of this raggy-haired older woman called Steve. His right hand had been grabbed, unfortunately, by Mort. Mort was holding the finger he'd bent, which still hurt, the bastard.

But – hey! – it was suddenly *immaculately* weird.

The mist had come up behind them, surrounding them like this chilly, fuzzy hedge, forming yet another circle. So they were kind of locked into the pattern of the old maze which had been around the Tor in prehistoric times.

And there was one more inner space: the tower was roofless, like a chimney; you could stand inside – the flags underfoot dead

60

slippery on account of all the zillions of pilgrims over the centuries – and you could gaze up the stone shaft into the night. *And the night could come down it.*

Gwyn was in there now, in the centre of everything, catching the night.

He hadn't seen Gwyn arrive. The man was just suddenly among them, in a long coat, no telling what he was wearing underneath.

Gwyn the Shaman, who walked with the spirits. Headlice didn't know who Gwyn was or where he came from. There were stories about how Gwyn had been in Tibet with the Masters, or been initiated into the Wiccan coven at the age of ten then studied for the priesthood just to get both sides. All this might be total bullshit, but if you knew for a fact that Gwyn was, say, an ex-garage mechanic from Wolverhampton or just some toerag who'd found a copy of *King of the Witches* in the prison library, it'd like seriously detract, wouldn't it?

Gwyn had lit a candle, in a glass lantern because of the breeze, and he stood behind it in the arched doorway which led into the tower's bare interior and then out through an identical arch on the other side. His beard was gilded by the candlelight. Bran had set up this slow heartbeat on his hand-drum. Then more lanterns were lit until there was a semi-circle of them around the archway, sending Gwyn's priestly shadow racing up the stone.

Shaman. Mort swore he'd once seen Gwyn conjure a fire out of dry grass from six feet away. 'Magic, eh?' Headlice said to Steve, and Steve glanced at him and smiled and said nothing.

The throb of Bran's drum made the air vibrate, like the night sky itself was one big stretched skin.

Then Headlice felt a tug, and they were moving. Round and round the tower. The only sounds the drumming and the slithering of their feet on the grass, and he felt like a cog in an ancient, sacred mechanism and was totally blissed out. At first.

'The problem is,' Juanita said, 'I don't know where I stand any more. Whose side I'm on.'

Watching the Tor by night.

From less than half a mile away, it looked mysteriously pretty, with the lights, above a band of mist, making a faint frill around the base of the St Michael tower. They'd stopped on the edge of a small wood, unsure about this now that they were so close.

Jim's lamp had found a tree stump, and Juanita sat on it and talked.

'When Danny and I arrived it was very exciting, in an innocent way. We used to come here and watch for flying saucers. There'd been that big flap over at Warminster. Close Encounters. And books by John Michell and then J. M. Powys, and this all-pervading sense of . . . optimism, I suppose. Simple and naive as that.'

'I do believe there was a special optimism then,' Jim said. 'Although, naturally, we were very po-faced about it at the building society. Love-ins and be-ins and squats – not many mortgages in all *that* nonsense. I suppose I was just annoyed because I was rather too old for it all.'

'Then the spontaneity seemed to dissipate.' Juanita lit a cigarette. 'It became institutionalised and politicised. And you ended up with what we have now – New Age cliques and elitism. Like The Cauldron.'

'Oh. That.'

'There you are, you're alienated.'

'I'm not alienated. I *like* women. The Cauldron's all right as far as I'm concerned.'

'But *you're* not as far as they're concerned, that's the problem, Jim.'

'Everybody's got the answer,' Jim said. 'They're all so certain about it. Nobody seems content with mystery any more. Except me. I love mystery for its own sake. I think a true appreciation of the quality of mystery is the most the majority of us can ever hope for.'

The glow on the Tor began to flicker in and out, as though people were moving through it.

'We never saw any saucers,' Juanita said sadly. 'I didn't, anyway. But we knew that when the star people landed they'd land here. Because this was the centre. And we knew they'd be good aliens who'd respond to our spiritual aspirations. I used to imagine them coming into the shop – you know, at night. I'd hear a noise and creep down, and there'd be a couple of benign beings in shiny suits leafing through the books. To work out how far we'd got up the spiritual ladder.'

Jim was silent for a while, looking up at the gauzy lights on the Tor. Then he said,

'That's why you've stayed, isn't it? In Glastonbury.'

'Sorry?'

'Unfinished business. The hippy dream. Peace and love. You still hope that out of all this chaos there might be the seed of harmony and this is the place to nurture it. You're still hoping the good aliens will land.'

'Don't be ridiculous.' Juanita felt herself blush. 'That would make me a *very* sad person, wouldn't it?'

She felt his smile. And his own hopeless longing.

> *waken stone and darkness gather*
> *waken stone and darkness gather*
> *nahmu nahmu nahmu nah*
> *in the bowl of darkness gather*
> *nahmu nahmu nahmu nah.*

The half-whispered chant was still hissing in Headlice's ears when the circle stopped turning.

When he was sure he was still, he looked up to find the whole of the sky was still revolving, going round and round and round the tower, moon and stars and wisps of cloud.

Moon and stars and wispy cloud, moon and stars and moon and stars and . . . and everything turning into a chant. Everything with its own rhythm. Magic.

Was it, though? Was it? He glanced at Mort, whose head was bowed into his chest, dead relaxed as usual. Headlice felt a pulse of anger.

Come on. Get real: you're just dizzy, man. Magic? Magic's the chemicals working on the brain. Magic's what you conjure up in yourself to get your head uncluttered of all that shit about finding a job and taking your place in, like, 'society'. This pilgrimage, this is a celebration of freedom. This is our country, man, ours, not yours to put fuckin' fences around. This is where we can come and breathe the free air and light fires and tell tales about the old gods and get

*well pissed and stoned and shag our brains out, and when we wake
up in the jingle-jangle Avalonian morning we'll sit around and talk
about what it was like up the Tor, all the presences we felt around us,
how, like, holy it was. But it'll all be in our heads, stoned memories.
On account of nothing happened, not really.*

Yet this was the real place. *The* place. Go with it. It may never
happen again like this. Like when they took you into all those St
Michael churches, made you go in backwards; you didn't question
that. How are you ever gonna change if you don't, like, submit,
roll with it?

He let himself go limp. Rolled with it.

Gwyn was on the stones outside the tower, the light from the
candles on his feet and all the objects around him, which included
a metal cup – like a chalice – and a whip with a leather handle and
kind of thongs, like a cat o'nine tails. And a curved, ritual knife,
like a little scythe with the moonlight in its blade.

A woman was handing a bowl to Gwyn. It was Rozzie, in a long,
dark, loose robe twitching in the night breeze. (So when, exactly,
had his woman been picked as Gwyn's handmaiden?)

Then the people either side of him, Mort and the woman called
Steve, tightening their grip on Headlice's sweating hands as the
cup was filled from the bowl – holy water from the Chalice Well,
someone whispered – and the hands parted to receive the cup as
it was passed around the circle. Holy water from the Chalice Well,
cold water, metal-tasting, passed round anti-clockwise and again
and again, and each time it got to him – *drink deep, drink deep* –
the cup always full, so maybe there were two of them or maybe the
sacred water was replenishing itself by . . . magic.

The hands joining again, like clasps in some kind of bracelet,
and the movement re-starting, the cog in the machine, round and
round and round and the drum drumming deep down in his gut
and the chant, *nahmu, nahmu*, and the sudden weight of the sky,
and when he looked up the sky was turning around the tower and
. . . and . . .

He couldn't feel his feet any more; he was starting to float. Aware
of Gwyn speaking, hearing the words but like making no sense of
it; like it was coming from way off, and some of it was in Latin,
which figured, if Gwyn had trained as a priest to get both sides.

Gwyn's mellowed-out voice was soaring.

'*Emitte tenebrae tua et medacia tua. Ipsa me deduxerunt et adduxerunt . . .*'

Headlice suddenly felt very emotional, felt like crying.

'. . . *in montem, sanctum tuum . . .*'

Hands. The skin on the hands gripping his seemed to be puffing up like foam rubber and then Headlice felt something streak through him, hand to hand to hand . . .

. . . like an electric current, and he . . .

. . . was well off the ground, the air sizzling coldly around him, all lit up, an ice cascade. Perspective somersaulting; St Michael's tower groaning at his feet; he was up there. In the darkness.

. . . *montem sanctum tuum . . .*

Gwyn's voice rising and sliding and the responses from the others, a drone, enfolding him like soft curtains. The drum so loud, like it was inside his head, like he was inside the drum. It was brilliant. He was truly alive, man.

And the priest said,

'. . . *oh, Gwyn up Nudd, lord of the hollow, guardian of the dark gates, we call upon thee and offer to thee this . . .*'

'Jim,' Juanita said. 'Jim, look, I think I'm changing my mind about this.'

She crouched, panting, in the grass which was slick with night dew.

They were almost halfway up the Tor. She looked over her shoulder; in the dark it was like being on a cliff-face; vertigo seized her and she grabbed at the hillside for support, her hand closing around something she realised was a hard lump of sheep shit. She ran her fingers convulsively through the damp grass.

'I mean, are we going to make fools of ourselves? When you think about it, what are we supposed to be preventing? After all, come on, nobody ever got murdered or anything on the Tor, did they?'

'Depends what you call murder,' Jim said. 'Don't imagine Abbot Whiting saw much justice in what they did to *him*. Anyway . . .' He suddenly expelled an angry sigh. 'I'm curious now. It's a free country. National Trust property. We've got as much right . . .'

'Jim, why don't we just get the police? I was stupid. They won't arrest Diane, and even if they did . . .'

'*They* won't want to know. What's in it for them? Couple of cannabis arrests? They haven't got the manpower any more.'

'It's just . . .'

Jim turned towards her. 'Too old to look after myself?'

'No, I . . . Oh God.'

What it came down to was, whatever these neo-hippies were doing she didn't want to see it. Because she'd been there and it was beautiful once and she didn't want to watch a sweaty parody of her youth, didn't want to feel old, didn't want to have to feel disgust.

'Why don't we get the car and drive down to Don Moulder's field and wait for them to come back to their camp? We'll see where Diane goes and we'll try and snatch her.'

'No.' Jim's voice was pitched almost at conversation-level. 'I'm tired of being timid. Too old to be a hippy. Missed the boat. Missed too many boats.'

'Jim . . .'

'Why don't you stay here with the lamp and I'll go up alone.'

Juanita looked down at the lights of Glastonbury, thinking, God, one minute I'm worrying about his heart and his liver and the next . . .

'Jim!'

He'd pushed the lamp into her hands and when she looked up he'd vanished into a wall of mist.

Bloody hell. He was going up there to make a scene. At some point tonight he'd got this image of himself as a bumbling, ineffectual little man considered too old to kick ass, and now he had something to prove.

No *way*.

Juanita went after him, stumbled, her Afghan falling open. She was aware of a fringe of lights, and a man's hollow voice lifted up into the night, rhythmic and ecclesiastical, and that didn't sound like what they used to do in the seventies, not at all.

It started to go wrong very quickly, all in a rush, and it was so strong Headlice was just dragged down, like he'd lost the use of his feet, like they'd rotted into mush.

Because he was no longer above the Tor, he was *inside* it.

In this giant cave, full of mist.

It didn't matter too much at first that he had no control . . . got to roll with it, man. *I'm a shaman now, me. This is where they go, inside the earth, inside themselves* . . . Until he realised that without feet you couldn't run away.

At some stage, he saw what seemed at first like only a darker part of the mist. It writhed. It became like a tree, with fuzzy outstretched branches and little knotty twigs, the kind of wintry tree you see through fog from a train.

And then it wasn't a tree because trees don't move like this: the branches were dark arms and the twigs were fingers, thin fingers, bony, wiggling like they were underwater and the currents were doing it, and he saw arms inside sleeves, torn sleeves, hanging like sodden leaves gone black.

He tried to clench his own fingers on Mort's hand and Steve's. Only nothing happened. He couldn't work the muscles. Clenched his fingers, but nothing clenched.

A ring. A ring on one of the wiggling fingers, a big one, size of a curtain ring. Headlice heard, . . . *let me go . . . let me go unto my Lord.*

A figure in black with stains down the chest, this rough cloth around it, ripped in places, and stains, stains everywhere and a hard, powerful smell of dirty sweat, fear-sweat, and wet, rusty iron, like when you pull an old pram out of a pond, all black, the fabric rotted and dripping and the frame poking through.

No, I'm not going for this. This is dope in the fuckin' water. You get me out of this, you bastards, hear me?

The body was coming towards him in this kind of lopsided crippled way; it couldn't stand up straight, couldn't lift up its head. He tried to scream, feeling his throat working at it, pushing, but nothing coming out.

And the reason this ragged thing couldn't lift its head was because it hadn't got one, only stains around the neck of its robe.

Help me. Help me to my Lord. Its hands groping out for Headlice, fingers waving like seaweed in shallow water, Headlice shrinking away. Fuck off . . . fuck off, old man. Leave me alone.

Dom, dom, dom. Heart banging away in his chest. Blood throbbing in his head. Drum going *dom, dom, dom*, and he could see the old man was offering him something. Something that had formed between his hands, a bowl, and Headlice reeled back; this was all he could do, throw his body back from the waist, because his legs had gone now, gone into soup.

And the old man pushed the bowl towards him, but it was still joined to his hands, this bowl, this chalice, his fingers throbbing like veins in the curved metal. The old man was giving off long sobs, ragged as his rotting clothes, because he was as helpless as Headlice, this old man, didn't know what he was at.

Holding out the bowl, the old man said, *Alan.*

Which was Headlice's real name.

The entity said, *Alan.* Real sick and sorrowful, and Headlice looked down and saw, briefly, a wavering shadow of himself in the mist, and he knew that he'd become part of it, another wiggling thing. Part of the darkness. He started to cry too, because there'd soon be nothing left of him but tears and snot evaporating in the dark.

Alan, however, *Alan* started to feel dispassionate about this, about his body floating away from his consciousness, or maybe the other way round, who gives a shit, roll with it.

And this was when the air thinned into a paler darkness, and he became aware that he was out of it, up in the night sky again, over the Tor and looking down, and he could see everything very clearly. He was up here in the sky – thank you, thank you, thank you, gods – and looking down on . . .

. . . some miserable little sod scrabbling on its knees in blind circles, right under the church tower, surrounded by candle lanterns, its stupid fingers dipping into the flames, but showing no pain. Just twitching and scuffling like a lost thing, helpless and pathetic.

They were lifting it up from behind, two people, an arm each and the drum was going *dom, dom, dom*, like one of them execution drums, *dom, dom, dom*, and he was looking straight down now, like looking down a chute, on to the very top of its head, where a swastika . . .

Oh shit! Oh shit, man, it's me. That's me!

Being propped up like a scarecrow.

68

Rozzie was there too, watching, white-faced, but the bitch was avoiding touching him, and there was ... it was Gwyn, but it wasn't. His face was long and black and pointed. His coat was off, his skin shone – he was naked – and so did his sickle raised, with the moon in it.

It was a hell of a shock at first, Mort and Steve holding the pathetic thing's head back, exposing its throat to the blade, but the next instant he'd realised this was only Headlice, a naive little tosser, so it didn't matter he was going to die. Anyway, it had begun ages ago, the death thing; the cut was like a formality.

Alan was above it all, directly above, exalted. Directly above the swastika, the sun symbol on Headlice's head, the head chakra, the opening he'd like projected out of – he could see the cord now, a thin strand of silver, like a wire.

All he could see of Headlice was a pair of hands waiting to receive the chalice, the Holy Grail, and then Alan dissolved into laughter because the Holy Grail was black and slimy and smelt of piss.

TEN

WITH YOU THIS NIGHT

Verity lit a candle for the Abbot.

Its light might have created the illusion of a warm area at the heart of ancient Meadwell. It didn't. The light was as wan and waxy as a lone snowdrop in cold earth.

The silver candlestick and a dusty wine bottle, two crystal wine glasses and two pewter plates rested at the top of the oak dining table, which was as crude as an upturned barge.

On one was a salmon steak. They ate mainly fish, the monks, Colonel Pixhill had told her.

From the other plate, at the bottom of the table, Verity (who had never before sat alone here, who habitually ate in the kitchen listening to *The Archers*) was picking at a green salad, which, in this sparse light, looked grey.

She was perched like a sparrow on the oak settle under the window recess. At the top end of the table, behind the candlestick, was a high-backed oak chair with arms. The chair sat before the platter of salmon. There was a knife, but no fork.

The Colonel had said they did not use forks.

Oh, let this soon be over.

Verity chewed on a lettuce leaf which felt like crêpe paper in the desert of her mouth. Among beams and pillars of oak, huge shadows shifted sluggishly, like black icebergs. The lump of fish islanded by juices on the Abbot's plate looked – although she squashed the thought at once – like some grisly organic remains on a surgeon's tray.

The curious thing was that Verity had searched through all the records, the Church histories, the local histories – and there had been many of them, as writer after writer sought to explain the holy glamour of Glastonbury – without ever finding documentary evidence that Abbot Richard Whiting had eaten such a meal, or indeed that his last, sombre night upon this earth had been spent at Meadwell.

Colonel Pixhill, you see, had always *said* it was so. After the Dinner, relaxing a little with a small Panatella, the Colonel would ruminate on the Abbot's fate.

Of course, quite apart from his differences with the church over, er, marital matters, Henry VIII was an extravagant blighter. Never had enough money: And here was Glastonbury, wealthiest religious house in Britain outside Westminster. Had to get his hands on that wealth somehow. Greed – that's the orthodox version. That devil Thomas Cromwell, Henry's hatchet man, as it were . . . only a matter of time before he was ordered to focus his scheming brain on Avalon . . .

The Colonel would pour red wine, brought up that evening from the cellar. Tonight Verity also had a bottle ready. Such a terrible waste, she drank hardly at all and hated the cellar. She'd taken the biggest flashlight in the house, but its beam down there had been but a flimsy ribbon. A cobweb was still laced around the bottle of vintage claret she'd snatched from the nearest rack, ramming it under her arm to grope for the iron handrail to the cellar steps.

But, of course, it was more than money. Henry was capturing Jerusalem, do y'see? Jerusalem Builded Here, as Blake was to put it, on England's green and pleasant land. How could the king break from Rome, establish himself as the head of the Church, if he didn't smash the power of the place where . . . where those Feet walked in ancient times. And old Whiting would've realised this, of course he would, and suspected his own days were numbered, poor chap. But he stayed, and he waited. For a miracle. How could God possibly permit the very Cradle of Christianity to fall?

For Verity, the Colonel had illuminated the history of Glastonbury as no book ever had. She pictured the great Abbey soaring, in all its golden splendour, into a flawless blue heaven. Who, indeed, could have imagined it then as broken and derelict? Certainly not the Abbot.

At last, laying down her knife and fork – she could not eat with only a knife, like the Abbot – Verity composed herself and said, in a tiny, tremulous voice like the *tink* of china, the words enunciated for so many years by Colonel Pixhill.

'Have courage, have fortitude, My Lord Abbot. We are . . .'

She paused to correct herself, nervously fiddling with the lace handkerchief in the sleeve of the woollen pinafore dress she wore against the cold in here. For November, it was quite a warm night. Outside.

'I mean, *I* am . . .'

No! She had to believe that Major Shepherd was here at the table and so was Colonel Pixhill himself. Had to believe she was not alone.

'*We* are with you this night.'

The candle flame swayed to the left, as if a fresh draught had spurted into the room. Verity sat very still and did not See.

. . . no possible escape, of course. Royal Commissioners searching the old boy's chamber and coming up with writings critical of the king's divorce – as if anyone would commit such things to parchment. Plus a book about – Ha! That other famous cleric with the temerity to criticise his kind, Thomas Becket. And then they find a gold chalice hidden away and accuse Whiting of robbing his own abbey!

The first time she heard this, Verity had asked hesitantly, Might this not have been . . .? I mean, a precious chalice that he was so anxious to hide . . .'

The Grail, Verity? I hardly think so. If the cup from the last supper was indeed preserved, it was surely not precious in that sense. Certainly not made of gold. Wood or earthenware, more likely.

The Colonel had raised his glass, peered into the clouded wine, repeating,

We are with you, Lord Abbot. With you this night.

Drawing an obvious parallel with the Abbot's own last supper.

In October 1539 – Verity remembered all the dates as clearly as if she had been there – Thomas Cromwell, the King's agent, had ordered that Richard Whiting, a kind old man who was always mindful of the poor and the sick and known for his generosity, should be 'tried and executed'.

The 'trial' took place at Wells, where the Abbot and two monks said to be his 'accomplices' were swiftly sentenced to death and brought immediately back to Glastonbury. This was November 14.

The following day, the Abbot was brutally stretched and bound to a wooden hurdle, dragged through the streets by horses past helpless, horrified townsfolk, past the forlorn Abbey.

And so to the Tor.

Verity now rose among the shadows, poured wine into the Abbot's crystal glass and a little drop to moisten her own parched lips. It tasted bitter and salty, like blood.

There was a hazy necklace of light around the St Michael tower, just where it sprang free of the watery mist that rose from the Levels and gathered on the sides of the Tor.

Clutching her shawl around her, Diane stepped off the bus platform. Somewhere, a sheep bleated, a rare sound at night outside the lambing season.

It was OK; this was ordinary light. Perhaps a circle of candles. It wouldn't be visible at all from the edges of the town. So they were all up there, doing whatever they'd come to do. Gwyn the Shaman presiding. With his ceremonial sickle.

That had been a pretty scary moment. All alone, and raising his sickle to the moon.

Another reason to get out of here. This was not the convoy she'd joined.

She moved silently across the grass, careful not to bump into any vehicles, always a risk when there was so much of you.

She'd moved her van closer to the field gate, knowing she'd probably be leaving before the others, knowing Juanita would let her stay at the flat for a couple of weeks while she sorted herself out.

Mort's hearse loomed in front of her. *Love is the law, love over death.* She'd seen another, unpleasant side of Mort tonight. Another side of all of them. She stopped. There was the glow of a cigarette.

The thin moonlight showed her the hateful Hecate, sitting on the bonnet of the hearse. Her van was on the other side of the hearse. She couldn't possibly reach it unseen.

Well, gosh, what did that matter? She could leave if she wanted to. Don't be pathetic!

But she *was* pathetic. She imagined getting into the van, trying to start the engine which always took absolutely ages to fire. And Hecate standing there watching her, this large, strong and horribly precocious child smoking a joint. Opening the van door, which she could do because its lock was broken, and dragging her out, the younger children hearing the noise and coming to join in, black gnomes swarming over her.

Shivering, Diane crept back to the bus. She'd wait until Hecate had gone – for a pee or something – and then creep past the vehicles to the gate and go on foot to Wellhouse Lane and the town. Knock on Juanita's door, beg for sanctuary.

She sat in the front of the bus, in the driver's seat. A night breeze awoke and made the bus rattle; more sheep began to bleat. Diane felt like a solitary spectator on the perimeter of an enormous stadium, the landscape primed as if for some great seasonal festival, Samhain, Beltane or whatever they called midsummer night.

November 14? A day, surely, of no particular import in the Celtic calendar. Not even a full moon. November 14 . . .

And then, in the sky over the Tor, she saw a light.

Not a torch, not a lamp, not a fire.

It hung there for a moment and then went out. Diane caught her breath.

When she was very young she used to go all trembly and run downstairs, and Father snorted impatiently and the nannies said, Nonsense, child, and felt for a temperature.

Nannies.

There was a certain sort of nanny – later known as a governess – which Father expressly sought out. Nannies one and two, both the same, the sort which was supposed to have yellowed and faded from the scene along with crinolines and parasols. The sort which, in the 1960s, still addressed their charges as 'child'. The sort which, as you grew older, you realised should never be consulted about occurrences such as lights around the Tor.

And then there was the Third Nanny.

Her memories of the Third Nanny remained vague and elusive. She remembered laughter; the Third Nanny was the only one of them that ever smiled. And one other thing: she would sit on the edge of the bed but never left a dent in the mattress when she arose.

She knew now what the Third Nanny was.

Diane tensed. Behind the Tor, the whole of the sky was now growing lighter. Like a dawn. But it couldn't be dawn; it was quite early in the night.

The light spread behind the Tor like a pale sheet. It was grey and quietly lustrous, had a sheen like mother-of-pearl. She wondered if Hecate could see it and suspected not.

Diane had certainly never seen a light like this before. The light-balls she'd watched as a child had fascinated her. They were benign, they filled your head with a fizzy glow like champagne. This light was ominous, like a stormcloud, and it stroked her with dread.

She wanted to turn away. She couldn't. She couldn't even blink.

Two dark columns had appeared either side of the silhouetted tower of St Michael. Rising above the tower into the lightened sky like arms of smoke culminating in shadow-hands, cupped.

And in the cup, a core of intense and hideous darkness.

We are with you this night.

But who was with him, Verity wondered, when they dragged him on his hurdle up the side of the Tor? The mud besmirching him, the bleak November wind in his face bringing water from his eyes so that it would appear he was weeping.

All the accounts said that Abbot Whiting went to his death with dignity and stoicism.

But the very act of hauling him up the steep cone of the hill, the *violence* of it! And at the summit, under the tower, the waiting nooses – three of them, an obscene parody of the execution, on another hill, of Christ.

The other two 'convicted' monks were Roger James and John Thorne, treasurer of the Abbey and a skilled carpenter and furniture-maker. All three went quietly to their God. But the humiliation of Abbot Whiting did not end with his hanging.

Took off his head. Soon as they cut his dead body down, they took off the Abbot's head . . . to be displayed upon the Abbey gate, a trophy, a warning. Final evidence that Roman Catholicism was terminated in Glastonbury. That the Church belonged to the Crown. Imagine the impact of that on a little town in the sixteenth century. It must have felt like Armageddon.

Colonel Pixhill could never go on beyond this point, but Verity knew the Abbot's body had been drawn and quartered, sections of his poor corpse sent for exhibition at Bath, Wells, Ilchester and Bridgwater.

Where did they carry out this butchery? Where did they take the axes or cleavers to the body? Not, surely, on the Tor. More likely indoors . . . somewhere.

Here? This was the inference, wasn't it. That the Abbot was drawn and jointed in this house.

And if not at this very table, which was insufficiently ancient, then perhaps on another table standing where this one now stood.

There *had* been a body here. It was here that the Colonel had lain in his coffin, for three days, as stipulated in his will. People had said how brave she was to stay in the house alone with the corpse, but it had been a comfort to her, a period of adjustment, of coming to terms with it.

Verity stared down into the well of shadows around her feet. Why was she doing this to herself, as if she was obliged to unravel every last strand of sadness and horror from the unhappy tapestry? She was unable to suppress the sickening image of the Abbot's body, chopped into crude joints of meat, and her eyes rose inevitably to the lump of red salmon on the plate and saw . . . that it had gone.

The Abbot's pewter plate was clean.

Verity felt her mouth tighten into a rictus; both hands grabbed at her face like claws, eyes closing as her nails pierced her forehead and cheeks in a sudden, raging fever of fear.

She stayed that way for over a minute, rocking backwards and forwards on the settle, feeling her chest swelling . . . but she must not scream, must *not* . . . moaning feebly through her fingers, not daring to open her eyes, because the membrane of darkness shut in by her eyelids, that at least was *her* darkness, not Meadwell's.

She should not have to go through this. Her fear was spiked with an anger now at Major Shepherd for being so ill, too ill to realise what it took out of her. *It's my duty to receive the Abbot*, she'd told Juanita Carey, almost gaily. In truth, it would be upsetting enough for anyone, woman or man, to prepare a meal for a person long dead and then sit down to dine. Alone. With that person's spirit.

Oh, but she was getting old. She'd be with them all soon, the Abbot and the Colonel and Captain Hope, her almost-lover who had died of peritonitis in 1959.

Telling herself again that the Abbot was such a *kind* man, known for his generosity towards the old and the sick, Verity rocked more slowly and became calmer, pulling her hands away from her face, making them relax on her knees under the table, retracting her claws like a cat. Of *course* the plate was not empty. With the worry and tension of the Abbot's dinner, anyone could be subject to minor hallucinations.

Why, the ancient stone and timbered dining hall was quite normal: silent and cold and still. *Quite* normal.

Until the very moment that Verity opened her eyes. When, as abruptly as if someone had plucked out the snowdrop or flattened it between two clapping hands, the candle went out.

And when the room was fully in darkness, not even the ghost of the flame still discernible, the Abbot's chair creaked. The way that a chair creaks when someone rises from it.

And Verity, alone in the reaching darkness – *where it no longer mattered that she Did Not See* – gave in at last to the pressure of that long-withheld scream.

ELEVEN

THE WRONG GOD

'What the buggering hell's going on here?'

It might have been the erratic candlelight making Jim Battle appear to quiver. Or it might – Juanita couldn't be sure – have been real, Jim trembling not, of course, with fear but with barely suppressed anger at these bloody pagan scroungers taking over his beloved Tor.

What the buggering hell's going on here? Juanita couldn't believe he'd said that. It was just so *Jim*, but so completely out of context. Standing there defiantly, shoulders back, on the concrete apron at the foot of the St Michael tower, candles all around him: Jim Battle, building society manager turned mystical artist, being a dumpy little hero.

Juanita just hoped the pagan Pilgrims had a sense of humour.

Actually, there weren't as many of them as she'd imagined. Maybe a dozen. People always exaggerated where travellers were concerned. Juanita stayed behind Jim on the fringe of the assembly, a foot on the last step of the path, her nostrils detecting a soiled sweetness in the air – *not* marihuana.

No music either. Not even the rattle of the wind which normally haunted the summit of the Tor. Jim's outburst had erupted into a yawning vacuum, as if he'd stormed into a church in that moment at the end of a prayer before the scuffling begins.

Juanita lightly squeezed his arm, a squeeze supposed to convey the message, *Back off, Jim. Make an excuse. Walk away. Pretend you didn't see anything. You don't have anything to prove. Say you're sorry for interrupting. Just back off.*

'Well?' Jim glared belligerently at the shadowy travellers. 'What have you buggers got to say for yourselves?'

Oh, Jim.

Nobody replied. The only sound was a choking gasp from up against the tower. Juanita felt Jim's hand groping for the lamp and before she could think about it she'd let it go and he'd flicked it on, stabbing the beam at the tower.

The gasping person wasn't much more than a boy. His eyes, speared by the lamplight, were glazed. A man and a woman were holding his arms. Juanita realised, with distaste, that the smell on the air was vomit. And it lingered; the air up here was dense, like wadding.

'What's the matter with this lad, eh?' Jim tried to spread the beam over the other travellers, but they moved away. 'Well? Too bloody stoned to explain ourselves, are we? I really don't know what to think about you buggering people, I don't indeed.'

Juanita peered over his shoulder as he sprayed the light about, looking for Diane and not finding her or any recognisable face.

Actually, it was all a touch unnatural. Only the candle flames were in motion, burning in a semi-circle of lanterns around the tower, the glowing buds magnified by glass. At Jim's feet, there was a chalked semi-circle around one of the entrance-arches; inside it, metal bowls and cups and implements of some kind. Probably some sort of altar. Juanita recalled fragrant summer nights here with Danny Frayne and bottles of Mateus Rosé. And laughter, lots of laughter. Why was nobody laughing? Why weren't they making fun of Jim, old guy in a silly hat. *Have a drink, dad,* Danny Frayne would have said. *Have a joint. Be cool.*

Jesus God. Juanita shivered under her Afghan. Something wrong here. She remembered Jim saying what *purposeful* people they were, not the usual semi-stoned rabble, and became aware of shapes on the edge of the candle-lit semi-circle, closing in around him. She wanted to shout a warning, but suddenly her mouth didn't seem to work any more.

Sensing movement behind him, Jim turned slowly and with dignity. He snorted.

'I don't know – you call yourselves bloody Green pagans, but you've really no idea what this place is all about, have you?'

For God's *sake*, how long was he going to keep up this Colonel Fogey routine? How utterly stupid men could be when forced into a confrontation.

'Well, I'll tell you. Tell you what it's *not* about, shall I? It's not about drugs and made-up bloody rituals involving lots of shagging.

It's not about littering the place with belching wrecks of buses. It's not about worrying sheep and ripping fences for fires and having a shit on the buggering grass and not even burying it. It's not about contaminating a sacred site, and ruining all the . . .' A fissure developed in Jim's voice as it became personal. '. . . all the mystery.'

Juanita flinched as something slid past her and moved, with a fleeting feral smell, through the circle of candles and into the lamp beam.

She flinched again when she saw what it was.

Saw Jim's mouth fall momentarily open. Saw a man (?) with long, tangled hair secured by a metal circlet. Saw, with a feeling like a kick under the heart, that the hair enclosed a face from old, old nightmares, from those books she never really liked to sell, from magical pornography.

An animal's face and a devil's face. Sculpted and textured, harsh-haired around black eyes. And its body gleamed, well-muscled arms and legs glistening with grease. She saw this because, apart from the animal mask, the man (man? Oh Lord, yes) was naked.

When he spoke it was not much above a whisper, but it carried like a fast train in the night.

'You've said too much.'

Juanita was shocked to see the lips move, then realised that the mask of hair and skin ended above the mouth but the beard below it was real.

Over the top of the tower, there was a curiously unhealthy glow in the sky. Juanita began to feel seriously scared. This was not your routine New Age extravaganza, and some part of Jim had known it from the start. *You know what these characters are like, drugged up to the eyeballs or swigging cider . . . day trippers. Not these buggers.*

Jim looked up bravely into the bearded face.

Please God, Juanita thought, don't let him say anything inflammatory.

Below, the lights of Glastonbury had been doused by mist; the Tor was an island again. It was no longer part of the world Juanita knew.

'And who the hell are you?' Jim demanded. 'Conan the buggering Barbarian?'

She shut her eyes in anguish. Her head seemed to fill up with cold mist. She felt the ominous nearness of other bodies, smelled the feral smell again, like tomcats. This was all so futile. Diane wasn't here. She'd have recognised Jim's voice by now, come dashing out to explain.

When Juanita opened her eyes it was to see the goat-face close to Jim's, as though it was going to kiss him. Jim didn't move his head away, but she saw his hands grip the flaps of his overcoat to stop them shaking.

That did it. Diane wasn't here and Juanita couldn't watch this any longer. She pulled her Afghan coat together and marched through the crowd.

The goat-man turned to her. Nothing moved behind the blackness of the eyeholes. She felt horribly exposed, as if *she* were naked, not him. She pushed her hands hard into her coat pockets.

'OK, look.' It came out as a croak. 'We made a mistake. Come on, Jim, she's not here.'

'Bloody hell, Juanita.' Jim stood there like a bulldog. 'Why couldn't you just leave this to me?'

He pushed irascibly past the goat-man-priest and advanced on the boy held against the tower.

'You all right, sonny? Look, bloody well let him go, will you?' Snatching at the wrist of one of the men holding the boy. 'He's been sick. What's wrong with him? Drugs?'

Jim was pretty strong. The man's grip broke; the boy stumbled away and then straightened up, swaying into the darkness. They heard him slipping and rolling down the side of the Tor, into mist.

'Jim, we're going.' Juanita took his lamp. 'Let them get on with their . . . religion.'

The goat-man moved under the archway, as if he needed to think. Well, Juanita didn't. Whatever they were doing they could get the hell on with it. She grabbed the end of Jim's scarf and tugged him towards the path. Still, nobody said a word, but the atmosphere was stiff now with menace. These were the new hippies? Christ.

'Listen, we're sorry. Sorry to mess up your ritual, whatever, OK? We were just looking for a friend.'

She heard Jim grunt, and his scarf came away in her hand.

'Jim!'

Her shoulder was gripped. She dropped the lamp in alarm. When she turned, she fell into someone's arms, was swung round and looked up into a stubbly, grinning male face. As she squirmed, she saw two men seize hold of Jim, slamming him against the wall of the tower, where the boy had been, his arms stretched above his head.

The naked man stooped to pick something up. When he stood before Jim it was glittering in his left hand.

He whispered, 'I did not say you could go.'

He was bent over the bonnet of Mort's hearse. His face was streaked with mud and blood from scratches on his cheek and jaw. His eyes were big in the lamplight and sort of glazed.

Diane raised the Tilley lamp. 'Head . . . Headlice?'

'Mol . . .'

He stared up at her. In the white light, the swastika on his head looked crude, like a knife-wound. He smelled of sick. Why was he alone? Where were the others?

He let her help him up and walk him over to the bus. He stood on the little platform, framed in the doorway. Somewhere behind him was the Tor, but there were no lights there now.

'We'll get those cuts bathed.' She found a plastic bottle of water. The little woodstove in the bus was still going, just about.

'No time.' Headlice shook himself as if remembering something then swung round, urgently scanning the dark. 'Gotta get the hell out, Mol.'

The plastic bottle went slippery in her fingers. 'What happened?'

They were alone. Hecate had disappeared, probably not wanting to be around when Headlice found out what they'd done to his bus.

Diane had lit the Tilley lamp when the Tor went dark again. She'd been afraid to leave the bus. She didn't know what she'd seen, but it had left an atmosphere tainted with a brooding evil she'd never felt before. Not here. Not anywhere. The blackness at its heart had seeped into the unnatural spread of light until it was a night sky again. But it was a different kind of night, as black and opaque as soot, with no moon any more.

'Shit.' Headlice glared down at his hands. 'Look at that. Shakin' like a fuckin' leaf. Bad shit, Mol.'

'Listen,' Diane said. 'All I know is that sometimes you can't trust your . . . what your mind's telling you. It does awfully odd things to you. Up there, I mean. On the Tor. Tell me what happened.'

'You're talkin' dead posh.'

'I *am* posh. Frightfully posh, actually. For what it's worth.'

'I wanted you to be there. I wanted . . .' He shrugged. 'Nobody got laid, anyroad. There was a . . . like . . . holy water and chanting and stuff in Latin. I don't remember. Don't fuckin' *remember* . . .'

The kettle began to whistle on the iron stove.

Headlice pushed it angrily away. 'I told you, we got no time! Gotta get this thing going, piss off.'

'Headlice, you have to tell me. What did they do?'

Headlice picked up the kettle and emptied the hot water into the stove's firebox, causing an explosion of hissing steam.

'Water. Holy water. Acid, mushrooms, some shit. Did me head in. I'm not down yet. Not . . . There was . . .' He stopped, as if he wasn't sure what he remembered. 'This old man. And like a black chalice.'

Diane went very cold inside. Arms. Huge smoky arms in the sky, hands cupped like a communicant's to receive . . .

Headlice sprang to his feet. 'Get the bus goin' before the bastards come back. You an' me, Mol. I'm trusting you, don't shaft me.' The Tilley lamp spread its gassy, wobbly light over his face, mud and blood on it like warpaint.

'*Tuum Montum* . . . Summat like that. That were part of it. He'd lift his arms – like that.'

'Lift his arms . . .?'

'*Monum Sanctum?*'

'*Montem sanctum tuum,*' Diane said. 'Your holy hill. It's from the Mass. *They have conducted me and brought me unto thy holy hill.*'

She sighed. 'They sent me to a convent. Once.'

'Gonna write about this, Mol? Gonna write it up for the papers?' He sneered and poured cold water from the plastic bottle into the stove.

'Headlice, oh my God, listen. Gwyn. Had you ever met Gwyn before?'

He shook his head, slammed the metal stove door.

'What about Mort?' Oh gosh, these people, she knew there was something wrong with them.

'Yeah. Mort was the guy got me into this. He was in a pub, back home. Salford. I told you before.'

Headlice was moving around the bus, throwing things on the luggage racks. She remembered him saying he'd been unemployed, living with his parents, devouring earth-mysteries books, dreaming of ley-lines. And Mort had introduced him to a man with an old bus for sale and Headlice had sold his motorbike to pay for it. How he'd met Rozzie was a mystery.

'Look,' she said. 'When Gwyn joined us at Bury St Edmunds – you remember? When Gwyn joined, the whole mood of the convoy seemed to change. Some people left.'

'Con and Daisy.'

'What?'

'At Bury. Con and Daisy, Irish travellers. Con says to me, he says, You wanna fuck off, man, this guy's heavy shit. I says, come on man, heavy shit's what I've *come* for. And he just shakes his head. That's it, Mol, we're off.'

He took out his ignition keys for the bus, threw them up in the air, caught them.

'Me an' you then, Mol. Back on the St Michael Line. And no more stopping at churches, goin' in backwards. No more shit.'

'What did you say . . .?'

But Headlice had leapt down from the platform to get into the cab. He was probably right; they had to get out of here. She'd go with him, as far as the town and then . . .

She heard Headlice yell, 'Who the f . . .?'

And then he screeched in pain and there was a bump.

'Headlice!'

Diane snatched up the Tilley lamp and stumbled down the deck to the platform. She leaned out from the top step, holding out the lamp by its wire handle.

'Headlice?'

She couldn't see anything at first, but she heard retching and moaning. A dark figure moved unhurriedly aside.

Headlice was writhing on the grass, clutching his stomach, his head flung back. She saw a heavy-booted foot crunch into his face, under his nose. Bright blood fountained up. Headlice started to snuffle.

The lamp was wrenched from her hand.

Juanita kicked backwards with the heel of her boot and someone went, *Aaah*. Then she was punched hard in the mouth, tasted salt-blood.

The naked man raised his hand and the blade of the sickle was white-gold in the candlelight.

Juanita screamed through swelling lips.

'Oh, come on.' Jim still trying to bluster through this. 'Don't be so damned stupid.'

Only about half a dozen so-called pilgrims remained, two of them gaunt, unsmiling women.

'Do you know me?' The voice, still a whisper but raised high like the blade, had a horrid triumphant ring.

'Thankfully no,' Jim snapped. 'Now tell your lackey to get his bloody hands off that woman.'

'I am Gwyn ap Nudd. Do you know me now?'

Juanita spat blood.

'Bring him here.'

Jim, spluttering, was pulled from the wall by the warrior-looking man with the tight plait, and the priest pointed with his sickle to a patch of grass beside the concrete path. One of the other male pilgrims – he had a black cap and two large earrings like a pirate – went down theatrically on one knee, and when they flung Jim down, his head was bent back across the shelf of the man's other thigh.

His hat fell off; they pulled his hair to hold his head back.

Most of the candles had been extinguished. Jim had to stare up at the moon. They had removed his scarf, exposing his neck. He'll catch cold, Juanita thought ludicrously.

'The date', said Gwyn ap Nudd, the goat-priest, 'is November the fourteenth.'

Not a goat-priest . . . a dog-priest. Hound. Gwyn ap Nudd, lord of the Celtic Hades which could be entered through the Tor, Gwyn's hall. Gwyn was the leader of the wild hunt. It was a dog-mask.

As if this mattered.

Jim retched. Someone balanced one of the remaining candle lanterns on his heaving, overcoated chest.

'On this day in the year 1539, the last Abbot of Glastonbury, Richard Whiting, was convicted of petty theft and treason, then brought up here, to the church above the hall of Gwyn ap Nudd, fairy lord of death. And then, side by side with two of his monastic underlings, he was . . . hanged.'

'Let him go,' Juanita pleaded. 'Can't you see he's choking? He's an old man, for Christ's sake.'

'Whiting was also an old man,' the priest whispered. 'A rich and powerful old man. His public execution, on the spot where we stand, signified the fall of one of the wealthiest monastic establishments in the land. His God couldn't save him.'

The lips smiled. 'He was worshipping the wrong god.'

The sickle was raised until the moon once more was in the blade.

'And so his death was a sacrifice. To me.'

Juanita expelled all her breath in a long scream, kicked out and kicked nothing, and then her head was wrenched back by the hair and some disgusting rag was shoved between her teeth and half-way down her throat until she gagged.

Out of the darkness, quite close, a drum started up.

Behind the man who presumptuously called himself Gwyn ap Nudd, the mist had cleared and Juanita could see the lights of Glastonbury, so bloody, bloody close. Where were the police? Where were the courting couples? Where were the night-joggers?

'Imagine it bump, bump, bumping down the Tor,' Gwyn said. 'Whiting's head. *Bump, bump, bump.*'

In time to the measured drumbeat.

Juanita's eyes streamed. This couldn't be happening, it couldn't. Not *here*, where she and Danny had lain and shared a joint, drunk cool wine, made love, watched for the good aliens . . . She felt her stomach heave and began to choke on her own rising vomit. She tried to close her eyes, and she filled her head with prayers to God and all the other stupid gods that lived up here.

'They hung his head on the town gate,' Gwyn said. 'Where should this one hang?'

In the end Juanita had to open her eyes, if only because she knew she couldn't close her ears to the whistle of air against blade.

Jim's mouth was slightly open. She couldn't see his eyes; they'd put his hat back on and tipped it raffishly over his brow.

There was no sound from him, but there was movement. It might have been the candlelight, or it might have been that his cheeks were quivering.

Gwyn, the goat-dog-priest, raised his sickle to the slender moon and Juanita saw his long, thin cock begin to rise to the thrill of hacking off the poor man's head.

TWELVE

A LITTLE CANARY

'*The number you have dialled has not been recognized,*' said the heartless computer-voice, and Verity cut the line again. Her finger dithered over the buttons on the receiver. It was easy to misdial because not only was her finger shaking but many of the numbers were obscured by blood.

She tried again. Telephones quite often malfunctioned in Glastonbury, especially cordless phones and mobiles. Because of the valley formation, according to the engineers. Because of the Shifting of the Veil, according to the mystics.

She'd brewed some camomile tea, sipping it with lips that still felt rigid with shock.

There was no comfort tonight in the kitchen, even though it was in the more modern part of the house. No matter how many jolly mugs and copper pans and tomato-red casseroles one placed around the room, the drabness would filter through. Nothing would glint. The electric lights hanging limply between the beams would glow as though on rationed power.

This time, thank God, the telephone rang at the other end. But Major Shepherd's wife was outraged at the disturbance. The Major was unwell; she did not wish him agitated.

'I'm so sorry, Mrs Shepherd, I just didn't know who else to . . .?' 'Is it the blasted guttering again, Miss Endicott?' Mrs Shepherd evidently thought Verity was a querulous old ditherer who should have been pensioned off years ago.

'No.' Verity almost sobbed. 'It isn't the guttering.'

'*Tim!*' she heard. 'What are you doing out of bed? Oh, very well, but don't blame me, when you . . .'

'Verity?' Major Shepherd was wheezing badly. 'Are you all right?'

'No,' Verity said after a pause. 'I really don't think I am.'

*

Funny how quickly you forgot how it was. The hard-pile office-type carpet. All those white or transparent lamp-shades, designed for illumination, never for mood. The dominant colour: dark brown; pervasive smell: wet leather.

The arrogant, rigid maleness of the place.

As if to emphasise it, her father took her into the gunroom, where she saw the old oak-panelled cabinets had been replaced by revolting metal ones, floor to ceiling. It was truly horrible, sort of semi-military.

'Basic security,' he said, noticing her dismay. 'Can't be too careful with guns any more.'

'You could always just get rid of them, of course,' Diane said. 'Then you wouldn't need security.'

He didn't even bother to react. Gerald Rankin hung around in the doorway, as if she might try to escape. She could still smell his glove over her mouth and nose; the whole house seemed to be impregnated with the oily essence of Rankin's glove and the sense of being closed in.

'Thanks, Rankin,' her father said. 'Good man. Close the door behind you.'

When his farm-manager had gone, Lord Pennard pointed to the worn leather sofa, scuffed as an old wallet. 'Sit down, please, Diane.'

Her legs felt weak, but she stayed stubbornly on her feet, her back to the bay window with its steely, industrial Venetian blinds. She folded her arms beneath the shawl, tightened her mouth.

'As you please. Drink?'

She shook her head minimally. Picked up and brought home, like a little girl again. So who'd informed on her this time? Don Moulder, doubling his three hundred and fifty? *Times is hard, my chicken, got to earn your crust where you can, look.*

Diane glared at her father, at the marbled coldness of him.

She knew how bitterly angry he must be at the way she had, as he would see it, let him down. But if she didn't go on the offensive, she'd be nowhere. It had taken her many years to learn this.

'Did . . . did you phone an ambulance?'

Her father raised an eyebrow. 'Did . . . *I*?'

Incredulity. He didn't waste words any more than cartridges in his twelve-bore. Rather like a double-barrelled shotgun himself: heavy, steely-grey, polished and greased and functional.

He went across to the dresser, the last remaining piece of old oak in the room. Coming through the house, she'd noticed how many pieces of fine furniture and pictures had gone. He poured himself a small whisky from a decanter. His movements so elegant for a big man. He was perfectly balanced, his stomach still tauntingly flat. He'd always made her feel like some sort of awful throwback: the fat one.

Diane thought of Headlice lying where Rankin and his son, Wayne, had left him, snuffling on his own blood.

'He could be really badly hurt, you know.'

'I'm sorry.' Lord Pennard sipped his whisky. 'Who are we talking about?'

'Damn it, you . . .'

Calm down!

'His name's Alan. He's actually a sort of human being who hasn't done you any harm.'

The foxes and the pheasants hadn't done him any harm either; unlikely to lose sleep over a hippy.

'Diane, I . . .' He raised his voice, grey eyes wide and unblinking. 'I rang Patrick to tell him you were safe. He offered to come and collect you. Told him there was no need. Pointed out there was a train tomorrow. Said you'd be on it.'

Frightfully precise. Absolute concrete certainty in every syllable. It should be her cue to run out of the room, hands over her face, mumbling *I hate you, I hate you*, in a pathetic, drowning voice. She felt familiar small prickly movements in whatever part of the brain was responsible for manufacturing tears. She thought, I can't. I'm nearly twenty-eight years old.

'Look . . .' Knowing her voice was all over the place. 'Are you going to call an ambulance? Or let me call one?'

He looked at her, his severely handsome face almost sorrowful. He looked her up and down, from the messed-up hair to the fraying shawl to the moon-patterned skirt of washed-out blue from the Oxfam shop.

'Yes I know,' she said. 'I know you won't have it done from here. I know that so far there's absolutely nothing to connect you or even Rankin with a . . . a hippy in a field. But why – *please* – why can't you let me at least go to a telephone box?'

His face darkened. 'Because . . .' His body flexed then straightened like a broken twelve-bore clacking into place. 'Because I won't have you wandering around the town like a streetwalker. Because Rankin tells me the injuries were superficial, nothing such an individual wouldn't get in a pub brawl. And because . . .'

He came close enough for her to smell the Scotch on his breath and see the small veins in his cheeks like the veins in marble or the palest Roquefort.

'Because, my dear, hippies and gypsies are like dogs. Give one a good kicking and it'll simply limp off into the undergrowth until it's recovered.'

Diane shook her head in disbelief.

'So let's be realistic, shall we?'

He turned away. Never had liked to look at her for long. Something she'd always remembered, the cursory inspection, as if she was livestock off to market. Well, naturally he'd had more time for his son, that was the way of things, that was the system.

'Good.' Making for the door. 'Good . . .'

Diane was sure he'd been about to say 'Good Man.'

He turned at the door, Lord Reasonable. 'Look, Diane, been a damn trial to us all your life, but you're not stupid. No money to speak of, no job. And I should imagine you've seen enough of life with these scavengers, haven't you?'

She gripped the edge of her shawl. He simply couldn't absorb the idea of people wanting more from life than money and property and power and influence. Especially when, in his case, one of these – money – was less plentiful than it might be.

A corner of his mouth made a brief excursion towards a cheek – the closest he ever came to smiling. He got rid of it quickly, as if it was a nervous twitch.

'Jennifer's prepared your old room. If you want to see me in the morning, I'll be here until eleven. Train you want leaves . . .'

'I'm *not going*!' Realising, to her horror, that she'd stamped her foot. 'How can you? My God, it's unbelievable! I'm a grown woman, you send your man to . . . to kidnap me. And you expect

me to meekly get out of town, get out of your hair ... it ...
Where's Archer?'

'This has nothing to do with Archer,' he snapped.

She knew that Rankin or Wayne would be loitering in the passage to make sure she went up the right stairs. She knew the hidden
alarms would be activated to make sure she didn't leave in the
night. She felt outraged, humiliated, but, as usual, defeated, and
said in a despicably small voice,

'You haven't even asked me why I left Patrick.'

Lord Pennard paused, hand on the doorknob. He looked
pained.

'Diane, had I wished to know that, I should have asked Patrick.
Goodnight to you.'

'You see, Verity, I . . .' Major Shepherd's voice was swamped in a
torrent of coughing from which it seemed he would not recover.
Finally, he said, 'This must sound awful, but for some years you
have been our little canary.'

Cuddling her cup of camomile tea, Verity recoiled when she
saw it was streaked with blood.

'Miners,' the Major said. 'Miners used to take a canary in a cage
into the shafts, as a test for poisonous gases. If the canary . . .'

'I know,' Verity said tightly.

'Of course, I don't mean it *quite* like that. We knew nothing
would happen to you. That little woman, George used to say, is the
strongest human being I've ever met. You know what he meant,
don't you?'

'He meant I was not sensitive. Not in that way.'

Verity wanted to protest. Just because she did not See, that
didn't mean she was without insight or intuition. The Spiritual had
become her life. And healing. All those years studying the Bach
Flower Remedies. And dispensing them here, in the ancient sanctity of Glastonbury.

Even if being here meant living at Meadwell.

'It's always been dark in this house, Major. And it's growing
darker. I mean quite literally. I don't know why that is.'

The Major sighed.

'But until tonight, I have never felt the nearness of . . .'

She could hardly bring herself to utter the word. It was not a Glastonbury word. In the town's mystical circles, people spoke of positives, negatives and mediators, never of . . .

'. . . evil. If this was the Abbot, then the Abbot was evil. Is evil. I'm so sorry, Major Shepherd.'

There was a long pause. His wheeze was like the bellows one used to use on a dying fire.

'Verity, listen to me. I know you're on your own. And that no mere wage is recompense. That George warned us to expect problems. As the Millennium approaches. Now listen . . .'

'If you're going to mention retirement, Major,' Verity said at once. 'I couldn't think of *deserting*.'

She held on bleakly while Major Shepherd went into another agony of coughing.

'. . . am trying to get you some help. Stronger than me. Younger. If you could just bear . . . bear to hold on. If you can't, I'll understand.'

'I shall not desert my post,' Verity said, and felt so *cold*. 'Even though . . .'

Even though the house hated her. It did. It threw darkness at her. It turned everyone against her.

And *everything*.

She'd heard the creak of the Abbot's chair and dared not move. Everywhere had been utterly, *utterly* dark. Verity had scrabbled about in the darkness, found her way to the wall where she knew the light switches were, moved her flattened palms from side to side and in circles and still could not find them. The wall had felt as rough and cold as it must have been in the sixteenth century. The electric switches simply *were not there*.

She'd panicked, naturally, pulling herself up just short of hysteria when her hand alighted on a box of matches, the ones she'd used to light the candle. But when she struck a match it was dead. All of them were. Little sticks which would not light, only snapped.

'This thing,' Major Shepherd said soberly. 'It must remain at Meadwell. Do you know what I'm saying?'

'I think so.' Did she?

When the lights had come on, slowly and blearily, revealing an empty chair, a sad salmon steak, a scattering of spent matches and all the switches on the walls, Verity had accused herself of being a weak, stupid old woman. She'd cleared the table, placed the Abbot's chair neatly against the wall. In the kitchen, she'd scraped the salmon steak into the wastebin; giving it to the cat, if the cat had still been here, would have seemed disrespectful.

Not that the creature would have deserved it. When Verity had opened the door of the cupboard by the yawning fireplace, to return the candlestick to its place for another year, she'd had a terrible shock. Out had come a whizzing, spinning, slashing Stella, leaving smears of blood over Verity's arms and hands before hurling herself out of the room and streaking out of the house with a violent snap of the kitchen catflap.

The greasy, tobacco-coloured oak pillars supporting the doorway had looked on, like the sour, sardonic, menacing old men who haunted the street corners of her youth.

Putting down the telephone, Verity wept for many minutes, tears mingling with the blood on her bony arms.

Everyone against her. Everything.

A little, old canary, and gases filling the house: who could really say how noxious they were?

THIRTEEN

NONE OF IT HAPPENED

He'd finished off all the whisky in the flask. What could she say to that, after all that had happened? He gave the flask a final glance – sorrowful or contemptuous, too dark for her to tell – before stowing it away in an inside pocket of his overcoat.

'Erm . . . before we over-react, are you *quite* sure about this?'

This was the first time he'd spoken since they got into the car. Juanita spun the wheel, letting out the clutch as gently as her mood allowed, feeling the ageing Volvo lurch and slide back, the rear wheels whirring uselessly in the mud.

Over-react? Jesus Christ, he was accusing *her* of over-reaction!

'Look, it was Diane. And it was a cream-coloured Range Rover. Who else do we know who has cream Range Rovers? There was a gloved hand over her mouth, did I tell you that? To stop her screaming.'

When she said that, Juanita tasted oil – someone trying to stop *her* screaming. Her throat was swollen and her bottom lip felt like a slashed tyre.

'Look, would you mind giving me a push?' She hauled on the handbrake, still not looking at him. 'Please?'

He got out without a word. By the time they were free of the rut, he was creaking like an old bulldozer.

'Rankin. He'd have sent Rankin. Jesus, he sent the staff to snatch his daughter, can you believe that?'

'This is not the night,' Jim Battle said, 'to ask me what I can or can't believe.'

It was still hard to categorise her emotions when they'd come down from the Tor. Anger? Shame? Embarrassment?

Appalled relief was close. The others came later, were still coming, in waves, like a *never-again* hangover.

Neither of them had spoken on the way down from the Tor. Not until they'd emerged from the gate into Wellhouse Lane and the Range Rover had surged through their lamp beam, and there'd been a muffled scream and a glimpse of struggling figures in the rear, wild eyes over a glove.

Back at Jim's, Juanita had opened up the Volvo and he'd gone quietly into the house and emerged with the hip flask. Offering it to her first.

She'd shaken her head. Felt unbearably tired. The walk to the cottage had almost finished her. But she'd said, 'I'm going to get her.'

Jim had climbed silently into the Volvo.

'Like a buggering black comedy, eh?'

'You're not laughing,' Juanita said.

In a way, she was grateful for this: something to set her mind racing in another direction, to put speed and distance between them and the humiliation. She hurled the car out of Wellhouse Lane.

'Please.' He put a tentative hand on her arm. 'Slow down. You know where they're going.' His voice was sounding dry and old and frail, a voice that couldn't laugh, not a voice she'd heard before.

'Yes.'

'You don't even know what you'll do when you get there.'

'I'll get out. You'll stay in the car. And this time *I'll* over-react.'

'Juanita. I'm sorry. I'm so sorry.'

She released the accelerator with a thud, threw both arms round the wheel and hugged the car into the kerb.

He didn't look at her, stared straight forward through the windscreen at distant lights.

'I really thought I was going to die, you know.'

'*I* thought you were going to die!' She was not going to burst into tears, she was bloody not.

'I'd accepted it. I mean, it does happen. In the States and places. Crazy sects. Mass-suicides. Inexplicable abominations. I can still hardly believe I'm alive, that's the worst of it. I still think it could have happened.'

'Yes.'

'He really might have done it. I'm not just saying this. I think he . . . I think he simply changed his mind. I think—'

'What *I* think,' Juanita said without emotion. 'And this is the last I'm going to say about it. I think he actually thought the hat would be a better joke.'

'The buggering . . . hat.' Jim crumpled up then in the passenger seat. She could sense his shoulders heaving, the shock finally coming down on him, like a landslide: the white moon in the sickle as it descended. The moment of singing silence. Before the gleeful chuckle.

I can chop it off. Or you can give it to me. As a sacrifice. As an offering to Gwyn ap Nudd.

And then, ultimate surrealism and humiliating degradation – the picture of Jim kneeling, getting his coughing over, wiping his face.

And then solemnly presenting the man who called himself Gwyn ap Nudd with his soft tweed hat – the last appalling image Juanita saw before they pulled the oily rag out of her mouth, put the lamp into her hand and prodded her on to the stony path.

Halfway down she was violently sick.

Then, moments before the blind rage, came that disgusting, craven sense of relief which almost amounted to being *grateful* to the bastards for sparing them their lives.

The only sound was the Volvo's engine ticking over; Juanita was always scared to switch off at such moments in case it wouldn't start again. Now she slipped into second gear as Jim said precisely what she'd been expecting him to say sooner or later.

'Swear to me, Juanita. Swear to me you'll never tell anybody about this.'

'They shouldn't get away with it, Jim.' She touched the lump in her cracked lower lip. 'They could be charged with assault. Robbery with menaces.'

'One tweed hat?'

Would he ever recover his self-respect, get over his humiliation? He hadn't backed down on the Tor, but God knows how it would look in the local papers if it ever came to court.

'OK,' Juanita said. 'If you don't mention it, I won't either.'

He didn't reply. She guessed he was thinking about what they'd done to her, convicting himself of cowardice, about to say, Bugger it, let's nail the bastards.

She got in first. 'It never happened, Jim. That's the finish.' She drove steadily out of town along Cinnamon Lane. To Bowermead.

Confrontation. It was all confrontation tonight. And menace.

Gerry Rankin was an ex-marines officer, hard, shrewd and clothed for action in a Barbour and a leather cap.

'Then get him,' Juanita snapped.

'You really are wasting your time, Mrs Carey.'

The Hall hulked behind Rankin: a fortress, very few lights on. But then, the place was better in the dark. The appeal of Bowermead Hall – sixteenth century but brutally Victorianised – began and ended with its misleadingly lovely name.

Juanita said, 'Oh come on, do you really want the police here?'

Rankin was smiling with closed lips, leaning casually against a stone gatepost under a security light, a hard light on Jim, who was slumped inside his overcoat like a refugee, keeping his promise to say nothing.

'The police?' Rankin shook his head in pained disbelief. 'To investigate an allegation that Lord Pennard kidnapped his own daughter? Diane? Mrs Carey, the police *know* about Diane.'

'What's that supposed to mean?' As if she couldn't guess.

'We all know what it means,' Rankin said affably. 'If that girl was a commoner like you and me she'd be in a foam-rubber boudoir in what's politely called a Residential Home. She had a real chance to make something of herself and reinforce this family.'

'You mean bring in some wealth and a couple of grandchildren to consolidate the future.'

'I'm not going to discuss family business with you, Mrs Carey.'

'You're not "family", Gerry. Anyway, you've confirmed she's here. Now go and get daddy. Tell him I'm offering his mentally ill daughter some care in the community.'

Rankin said, 'You really don't understand, do you? Lord Pennard doesn't *want* her in the community. Not this community. For her own good, Mrs Carey.'

'Hmmph.' Jim shuffled inside his overcoat. 'Soul of compassion.' Juanita glared at him.

Rankin stiffened. 'I don't know who *you* are, friend, but if you want to be abusive about Lord P, this is not the place.'

Jim grunted and moved back into the shadows of the gatepost. Juanita was quite glad Rankin didn't know him. He knew her, of course, because he'd once been into the shop, assuming it to be a general bookstore and requesting the lurid memoirs of some SAS hero.

There was silence. Then Jim whispered, 'Perhaps we should come back in the morning.'

Rankin had good ears. 'Yeah, I'd strongly advise that course of action.'

'I'm sure you would. God knows what you'd have done with her by then.' Juanita strode over to the gatepost, where he lounged in his well-worn Barbour, his leather cap shadowing his eyes. 'But I'll tell you one thing. If we do come back tomorrow, it'll be with a bunch of reporters and a couple of TV crews.'

He wasn't intimidated. 'Let me spell something out for you, Mrs Carey. You are not taking on the soft-bellied aristocracy here. This is a business fighting for survival in a hard world. Two hundred acres and shrinking fast. Lots of overheads. A real business, Mrs Carey, not spooky books and incense-burners and fucking tarot cards. We don't piss about. Am I making sense to you?'

'Perfectly.' Holding her Afghan coat together at the neck, Juanita stepped back into the full glare of the security light. 'But I do sound rather authoritative on the phone, when you can't see my beads and my crystals. They'll come, Mr Rankin. They'll all come, the papers, the radio, the television. They can't afford to take the chance. If there *is* a story, they won't want to have missed it. I just have to wave my wand and utter the magic word . . . Pennard.'

It went very, very quiet. Quiet enough to hear a barn owl in the distant woods. Rankin gave Juanita a look harder than a punch in the mouth, and she almost recoiled. Then he turned tightly and walked away along the drive. After about twenty yards he turned back to keep them in view, removing something from a pocket. Juanita wondered, not altogether fancifully, if they should take cover.

'Mobile phone,' Jim said. 'I think you've hit the right nerve.'

'Let's hope so.'

'But you haven't made a friend.'

'Who wants friends like that?'

'Equally,' Jim Battle said, 'who wants an enemy like that?'

It was almost midnight when the Volvo turned into Chilkwell Street.

'I'm sorry.' Diane was wiping her eyes. 'I'm really, really sorry. They're probably right. I mean, you never know it yourself, do you? Nobody *thinks* they're insane.'

'Shut up,' Juanita said.

Jim Battle sat behind them, hunched inside his muddied overcoat. Juanita thought she should take him home without delay to his cottage and his canvases. Turps and linseed oil acted on Jim like smelling salts. She probably wouldn't see him for several days. He had a lot to paint out of his system.

With Diane, it had been surprisingly easy. Rankin had come off the phone and they'd waited in silence until a familiar plump figure had appeared on the drive. Juanita and Rankin had not looked at each other as Diane had come slowly towards the gate. With the security light and everything, it was rather like one of those Cold War movies, Soviet and Western spies being exchanged at Checkpoint Charlie. And then the recognition and the tears, and a final glance between Juanita and Rankin confirming that none of this had happened.

Juanita thought, *The longest night of my entire life and none of it happened.*

Diane was saying, 'It's just that – I'm sorry – I've just got to know that Headlice is OK. If we could just perhaps go past the camp . . .'

She obviously meant the boy they'd had up against the tower, who Jim had sort of rescued.

'Forget it, Diane. They'll all be back by now. I'm not going into that field tonight, not after . . .'

She heard the breath go into Jim, who'd insisted that even Diane shouldn't be told they'd been on the Tor tonight.

'. . . I mean, after what happened to this guy, they're probably blaming you. Anyway, if he's been badly hurt, what can you do about it?'

She was in no mood, anyway, to trust Diane's assessment of the situation. This was the Diane who'd told her on the phone yesterday that the bloody travellers were *frightfully nice people, once you got to know them.* Jesus.

'We're taking Jim home, OK? Then we're going back to my place.'

Diane said, 'It's just that I'm sort of scared for him, anyway. There was some sort of frightful ritual on the Tor. I mean with hallucinatory drugs and things. I think they were using him in some way to . . . I don't know. He'd been sick. What I mean is, he was already in a bit of a state *before* the Rankins attacked him.'

'Shit,' Juanita said.

'Juanita . . .' Warning rumble from Jim.

'He might look like a hardcase,' Diane said, 'with the swastika on his head and everything. But he's really quite, you know, naïve and vulnerable.'

The lights of Glastonbury ahead. Also the turning to Wellhouse Lane. And to Don Moulder's bottom field.

'Fuck it,' Juanita said and spun the wheel.

At first she thought she really must be hallucinating when, at the entrance to the bottom field, the Volvo's headlights found Don Moulder himself with a big stick and a heavy-duty hand-lamp.

Moulder was wearing a bulky sheepskin jacket. Pyjamas showed in the gap between the jacket and his Wellingtons. He was shining the lamp across the field.

Juanita pulled into the side of the lane, just short of the ditch. 'Stay,' she said sternly to Diane.

When she got out, feeling quite unsteady, Moulder had his back to the hedge and his stick clutched under his arm, pointing down.

'Don't you be coming near me, I got a twelve-bore.'

'What's it fire, acorns? Calm down, Don, it's Juanita Carey.'

Don Moulder relaxed. 'Don't waste no bloody time, do you, Mrs Carey? Well, I'm telling you now, lady, 'twas their own decision. Can't say 's I'm sorry, mind, but a deal was struck and that's that, s'far as I'm concerned. That don't entitle you nor Miss Diane to no money back is all I'm sayin'. They coulder had the full time. Man of my word, always have been.'

He marched over to the five-bar gate and shone his lamp triumphantly into the bottom field.

'I don't understand,' Juanita said. 'Diane, no!'

Diane had tumbled from the car and pushed past them through the gate.

'What's to understand?' Don Moulder said.

As far as the beam would go, the field was conspicuously empty. No buses, no ambulances, not even debris. Just a single white van with pink spots.

Diane stood in front of the van, looking helplessly from side to side.

'They're off my land and good bloody riddance,' Don Moulder said. 'Just like they was never 'ere at all, look. Thought at least I'd 'ave some shit to clean up.'

'Headlice?' Diane cried out. 'It's me. It's Molly.'

Her voice faded into the empty night.

'I don't understand this,' Juanita said. 'Where have they gone?'

'Thin air, Mrs Carey.' Don Moulder cackled. 'Just like one o' them bloody UFOs, look.'

FOURTEEN

FOR MYSTICISM . . . PSYCHIC STUDIES . . . EARTH MYSTERIES . . . ESOTERICA

CAREY AND FRAYNE
Booksellers
High Street
Glastonbury

Prop. Juanita Carey

15 November

. . . I had to write about this, Danny, put it all down, tell someone, even though I'm never going to send this one. I can't. Promised Jim. Couldn't even tell Diane what happened on the Tor or even that we were there last night. Although there's a lot she's told me in the house between one a.m. and dawn, most of it stuff I really didn't want to hear.

It's seven-thirty a.m. I haven't been to bed. You don't even want to imagine what I look like. Diane's taken a cup of chocolate (couldn't supply hot carob) to the spare room, with instructions not to emerge until lunchtime.

And . . . oh, yes, the morning paper just came, Western Daily Press. With, at the bottom of page one, the item of news that explained everything.

Apparently, the Conservative Party last night chose the man it wants to replace our MP, Sir Laurence Bowkett, who has announced he won't be fighting another General Election due to his advancing arthritis.

The new prospective parliamentary candidate for Mendip South is one Archer Ffitch, son and heir of prominent Glastonbury landowner, the Viscount Pennard.

Get it?

There's Archer smarming his way through a selection meeting while his wayward sister is camped on the outskirts of town with a bunch of travelling vagrants living off the state and worshipping heathen gods. Well, imagine if the Press gets hold of this! So Lord P sends Rankin and son off to Don Moulder's field – Moulder having presumably tipped him off – to remove the troublesome child by night, as discreetly as possible.

OK, so one of the vagrants gets beaten up in the process. Big deal. Hardly going to report the assault to the police, are they? And even if they did, it's one of the accepted hazards of the travelling life, getting punched around by local vigilantes, etc.

Of course, I could report it myself, respectable High Street businessperson ... 'Well, no, officer, I didn't personally witness the assault on the poor traveller by Lord Pennard's man, but I have it on the very highest authority ... The Hon. Diane Ffitch, actually. You know, the one they call Lady Loony.'

Added to which, I could hardly reveal how I found out about Diane without telling the whole story. And obviously, after what happened – I may have nightmares about it for years to come – I'm not what you might call terribly well-disposed towards these particular New Age gypsies, anyway.

Keep shtumm, then. Say nothing to nobody. Try and forget it. That's the answer. Always benefit from talking things over with you, Danny.

Actually, that's the easiest problem to sort out. The big one is tucked up in the spare bedroom, dreaming of past lives.

When we got in I lit the woodstove. Didn't need one, especially at that time of night, but you can't talk meaningfully in front of an empty grate, and I really wanted to know why. What was the silly little cow DOING with people like that?

I'm no wiser. What I got was Diane at her most infuriatingly fey. I heard about dreams and visions and portents (including a vinegar shaker in a fish and chip shop which magically resolved itself into a little Glastonbury Tor). I heard (again) the story of the Third Nanny, who Diane believes to be the spirit of the High Priestess of Avalon, Dion Fortune, half a century dead.

The truth is, I can't take this stuff any more. Even rather read

Colonel Pixhill's Diary – at least the old boy was a confirmed pessimist. I used to think that, at the very worst, New Age was fun. I got a buzz out of being the mysterious woman who sold books full of arcane secrets and therefore I must know most of them. I don't really know precisely when I stopped getting a buzz out of it, or precisely why, but I suspect that seeing what it had done to Diane was at least a factor.

When your birth coincides with the death of your mother and your father blames you for that and you grow up in an all-male household of the worst kind, you become susceptible to the most absorbent kind of fantasy, and you start to live in your head most of the time. And when what's outside of your head happens to be Glastonbury, on the legendary isle of Avalon, and every time you look out of your bedroom window there's the magical Tor on the horizon . . . what hope is there for you?

Because she could always escape into her secret world, Diane let her family bounce her around, from relative to relative, boarding school to boarding school. Never known any other life, thought it was quite normal. Suddenly, at the age of twenty-seven she wakes up in Yorkshire in an arranged job, with an arranged marriage on the horizon, and she thinks, this is ridiculous, I'm a grown-up now, a person in my own right.

For the first time, she rebels. She finds a suitably outrageous way out, sends back her ring, joins the raggle-taggle gypsies. Been a long time coming; most of her contemporaries made their absurd gestures of independence at the age of about sixteen.

And because she really knows this is a fairly adolescent kind of stunt, Diane has to make it Significant by throwing the esoteric cloak over everything. Oh, it was meant . . . part of the great cosmic design . . . I was summoned back . . . I had magic signals from the Tor. It's my destiny!

Well, bullshit, obviously, but if she goes around telling people about it at this end of town, they'll just all screech, Wow, too much man, far out, and set her up as Avalon's Seer of the Week. Meanwhile, indigenous locals will shake their heads and mutter about what an awful cross old Pennard has to bear, with that Lady Loony.

And here's me in the middle again.

Pennard already hates me for exposing an unstable child to an unlimited supply of occult literature (I hate me for that as well, but it could've been worse, she might have gone to Ceridwen).

And now I've blackmailed the noble lord into letting the family madwoman loose in Glastonbury again, and he and Archer are going to be in a constant state of tension about what she might do to discredit the House of Pennard before the next Election. And when the Ffitches get tense – as amply demonstrated last night – they can do damage. The British aristocracy's full of genetic anomalies, and Archer – well, he's sort of Diane in negative, I suppose: hard and dark where she's nice and squashy and sort of pastel-coloured. But just as loopy, I reckon, in his way.

Everything in Glastonbury inevitably becomes EXTREME. Who said that? Me, I suppose. New Age mystic turned born-again agnostic. I'd decided that healthy scepticism was the key to survival in this town, but if you're a sceptic what's the point of being here anyway? Should I get out now, do you think, before something erupts? I don't know. Maybe I need a man again. Maybe I need a guru. Or God.

Talking of Whom, I'm told the Bishop of Bath and Wells has been making overtures to the New Age community. There's to be some sort of conference at which Liberal Christians are to 'interface' with well-intentioned Green pagans to try and build a framework for possible Spiritual Bonding in the run up to the Third Millennium.

Only in Glastonbury.

Are we ALL going mad, or what?

And can anybody out there help us?

Don't answer that. Can't anyway, if I'm not sending it.

Goodnight. What's left of it.

PART TWO

The pseudo-occultism of the present day, with its dubious psychism, wild theorising and evidence that cannot stand up to the most cursory examination is but the detritus which accumulates around the base of the Mount of Vision.

Dion Fortune
Sane Occultism

ONE

HARMLESS

THE WELSH BORDER

It was a moody frontier town squashed between dark English hills and even darker Mid-Wales hills. The stone cottage was at the end of a deep-sunk dirt track, two, three miles beyond the huddled town of Kington.

Locating the place by car had been a problem for publisher Ben Corby, who hadn't travelled much outside London for a couple of years now, except on planes. And who had always – despite his enthusiasm for *The Old Golden Land* – found the countryside basically hostile.

So this place immediately gave him the creeps.

It was a low cottage, barrack-block long, the last of the light making its windows opaque and sinister, like Mafia sunglasses. No sooner had he switched off the ignition than something came rushing out at his car: a black and white dog or maybe a big cat. Something disturbing about it, the way it moved. Ben nervously wound his window down as a shadow edged around a door at one end of the long cottage.

'OK, Arnold.' Was the voice familiar? Was it him?

Ben's headlights showed that the animal was, in fact, a dog.

And that it had only three legs.

Uncanny. The disabled dog was just sitting there in the headlights, not barking, not even blinking. Ben didn't get out; a three-legged dog was probably a dog with a grudge.

'It's a friend,' the dog was told by the shadow. 'Possibly.'

Possibly. He'd come to the right place then. And the author of *The Old Golden Land* was evidently prepared for the worst.

*

Half an hour later, relieved to be out of the wild country and by a warmish wood-fire with a can of lager on the arm of his chair, Ben came, in his blunt Yorkshire fashion, to the point.

'Be suicide, mate. For all of us.'

The dog lay on his intact side, eyes open and a furry stump pointing at Ben as if it was his fault, the dog having only three legs.

'If we go with this, we might as well pulp our entire back-catalogue. Britain's premier New Age publisher does not put out a book advising people to hang up their dowsing rods and trade in their tarot cards for a pack of Happy Families.'

The dog lay on a sheepskin rug under a table with a converted paraffin lamp on it. Next to this Ben had dumped Joe's manuscript: *Mythscapes: The Old Golden Land Revalued*.

Joe Powys stared into the fire. Ben thought, Where's his woman? Why just him and a three-legged dog?

He'd been on at Joe to write a book about what really happened at Crybbe and Joe had said nobody would believe it. He'd agreed finally to produce a follow-up to his New Age classic, *The Old Golden Land*, and here it was . . . and the bloody thing was anti-New Age.

Not to say anti-meditation. Anti-fortune-telling. Anti-ghost-hunting.

But only as much as Hitler had been anti-Semitic.

'So, Joe. How do you propose to live?'

Powys raised his eyebrows. Hair fully grey now (prematurely, just about). But the face on the back of the book could still help unload a few thousand copies on wispy, wistful ladies.

'You're still a young . . . youngish guy. And almost – you can't deny it – a cult figure, once, an icon. So, OK, you've had a change of heart, unfortunately a seriously uncommercial one. You want to talk about it?'

This was a phrase Ben Corby had learned never to use to an author whose book he'd turned down. The bastards *always* wanted to talk about it. At length. But this one he did want to know about. What turns a wispy mystic into a hardened sceptic?

'Don't make me feel bad,' Powys said. 'You drive all this way to bring me a customised rejection slip—'

'Because we're old mates.'

'Right. Well, I'm sorry, old mate. But how can you write a book you wouldn't have the nerve to go out and promote and say you believe in it?'

'You have got to be kidding,' Ben said. 'I can name you at least. . .'

Powys held up both hands to stop him. He was sitting on the arm of the overstuffed sofa, his white T-shirt merging with the white wall so it looked as if he was only semi-materialised, only half there. The wood-fire was tucked away in an inglenook, books to the ceiling either side of it. Above the fireplace, there was a framed photograph of an old man with a clerical collar and a big, white beard and another one, full length, of a slender woman with pale hair.

Something told Ben both of these people were dead.

He stared hard at Powys. 'So what is it you don't believe in? Apart from ghosts, ley-lines, mysterious forces in the landscape . . .'

On another wall was a framed print of an intoxicating Samuel Palmer moonlit cornfield. The kind of scene you associated with *The Old Golden Land*. Ben remembered when they were students and Joe Powys had discovered the enchanted world of standing stones and mysterious mounds and beacon hills. Lighting up boring old Britain for a whole bunch of them, even Ben for a while. The guy just had that gift. *Poet of the Unexplained*.

'. . . Fairies, witchcraft, UFOs . . .'

Powys didn't reply. He went into his cupboard-size kitchen and returned with a six-pack of Heineken Export. He detached a can from the pack and passed it across to Ben, his face blank.

Ben remembered how this cottage had been left to Joe Powys by Henry Kettle, the old water-diviner, whose own motto had been *Nothing psychic, nothing psychic.*

'This is not something you can talk about sober,' said Ben. 'Am I right?'

'Now I'm not trying to advise you, don't think that. I don't wan' you to do anything goes against your religion.'

Joe Powys saw that Ben was fairly pissed. Arnold watching him with some disapproval; his late master, Henry Kettle had drunk only sparingly, on the basis that you couldn't dowse under the influence. As far as Arnold was concerned, this was still Henry's house.

Powys leaned down and patted him. 'It's OK, this man is a publisher.'

Powys remembered sitting in a pub with Ben Corby, just after the Max Goff organisation, Epidemic, had bought Dolmen Books, and Ben had said, *It's time for the New Age to grab the world by the balls.* Business talk. Ben Corby had made a lot of money selling books about healing rays and ancient wisdom. Had actually made a lot of money out of Joe Powys.

'It's just you're a hero to these people,' Ben said. 'The tens of thousands of decent, well-meaning if totally humourless punters who buy Dolmen books by the handful to stick on the shelf under sprigs of aromatic herbs. And if their long-time guru starts telling them about seers who need glasses, and not to trust their little bodies to spiritual healers, they're . . . Hang on, gotta have a slash.'

The stairs rose from the living room. When Ben had gone up, Powys kneeled down and took Arnold's black and white head between his hands and stared into the dog's eyes.

'What do we do, Arnold? He's going to dump me. No more Choice Cuts. Back to the Tex chunks, economy size.'

But you kind of knew he would, Powys, didn't you? You knew he was never going to publish a book which proves crystals rarely work and the St Michael Line is a con.

'Yes, I did, Arnold.'

He wished Fay was here. Fay had this direct, broadcaster's way of putting things. Fay would convey to Ben Corby precisely why this book was not, as expected, another dollop of New Age blancmange. Because Fay had been at Crybbe.

She was programme-controller at Offa's Dyke Radio now. She hated local radio but she needed people. Ordinary people who were concerned about town planning, car-theft, more hospital beds and rail-cutbacks. Fay had a flat in Hereford. She came back most weekends. But she didn't like it out here any more, he could tell. She'd gone right off the countryside.

Ben had said, 'Why the hell do you stay here? It's so bloody primitive. If Henry left it to you, why don't you just sell it?'

'I can't sell it,' Powys said. 'It's Arnold's house, too. He's a dowser's dog. He has a feel for this place.'

'Now that,' said Ben delightedly, 'is a wonderfully New Age thing to say.'

'I'm embarrassed.'

'But you don't believe any of it any more.'

Powys sighed. This was it with publishers. They never read anything properly, not after they'd made the entirely arbitrary decision that it was going in the wrong direction.

Henry's old pendulum clock struck eight. The night was young. He was going to have to go into this.

Look, he didn't not *believe*. He accepted totally that there were . . . things . . . *out there*. But who was really equipped to mess with them? The trance-mediums who'd call up your grandad so he could tell you about the missing socks? The Kirlian photographers who'd do your etheric body for the family album?

Or what about the dowsers? *Not* Henry Kettle. Henry had been over-cautious, if anything. For years he'd dowse only for water, wouldn't get into anything he was unsure of.

'But now you've got all these bastards, been at it for about six months and they're claiming to feel the earth's pulse. Energy dowsing. Everybody's a bloody energy dowser suddenly. Everybody can tune into the Earth Force, Sunday ramblers, New Age travellers . . .'

'Yeah, yeah.' Ben snapped his way into another can of lager. 'But it's all harmless. I mean, it can't hurt anybody . . .'

He stopped. Sensing the change in Powys's mood, Arnold got to his three feet and began a low growl.

'It's OK, Arnold,' Powys said. 'I can't kill a man when he's pissed.'

Ben Corby looked warily at Arnold and then back at Powys. 'What did I say?'

'You said "harmless".'

Powys tossed a log on to the fire, crushing the embers of the last one and sending up a splash of red sparks.

'They go to Totnes. And they go to Glastonbury. And they're like kids in Toys R Us. It's like they've been given a New Age credit card. Think I'll have a go at that hypnoregressive therapy next week. Damn, really *must* have the old aura resprayed. And it's all *natural*. No drugs, no artificial sweeteners. Totally harmless.'

He held up the poker, its tip glowing with heat-energy.

'They'll stand in a stone circle on Midsummer Night and call down the supreme atavistic power of the Horned God, right? But you offer them a bag of crisps containing monosodium glutamate, and it's like you pulled a gun on them. What's that tell us?'

'Jesus,' said Ben, 'it's a pitiful sight, an old New Ager who's lost his life-force.'

'Yeah. Pass me another lager.'

'None left, old son. Got another pack in the fridge?'

'How many packs did we drink?'

'Three. And half a bottle of some filthy liqueur.'

'In that case, no.'

'Listen,' Ben said. 'If you insist on doing this, I'll show it to the guy upstairs.'

'God?'

'No, you pillock. We belong to Harvey-Calder now, as you know, since Goff's untimely demise. And being the smallest, least-credible part of this big, faceless, mindless publishing conglomerate, we're naturally in the basement and the literary guys treat us like shit.'

Powys smiled.

'Some joker hung wind-chimes outside our door,' Ben said gloomily. 'Bastards. But there's this not-bad guy upstairs in charge of Harvey's general non-fiction called Dan Frayne. If he publishes it, it's no skin off Dolmen's nose. I'll show it to him.'

'Oh.' Joe Powys stood up, feeling confused, and a little cool air through the peeling patch in the left knee of his jeans. 'Well, thanks. Thanks, Ben.'

'Don't thank me,' said Ben Corby, who didn't believe in anything you couldn't get into a wallet. 'Just because I don't want you to starve doesn't mean I don't think you're a complete arsehole.'

Ben slept – or tried to – in a spare room about the size of a double coffin. No soothing traffic noise, that was the problem, no police and ambulance sirens en route to somebody else's crisis.

It was very still and very dark. The panes in the little square window were opaque, like slates. There was no noise at all from outside, nothing, no owls, no wind through trees, no branches tapping on the glass. Only the creak from the bed when he turned over.

It would have made no difference.

It would have made no difference if there'd been a force-ten gale blowing or a fox got into somebody's chicken shed. It would have made no difference if a plane had crashed in the woods.

He'd still have heard it; he'd still have awoken around three in the morning with a chill running up his back, from his arse to his fuzzed-up brain.

No question: there was no sound quite like this for putting the shits up you.

Ben didn't move again until he heard another door open across the passage and Joe Powys's loud whisper. 'Arnold, no. Leave it.'

Ben rolled then from under his duvet, snatched up his bathrobe, staggered to the door, crouching because of the thought of beams, the way you did in the car going under a low bridge even though you knew there was plenty of room.

As he felt his way out to the landing, the ceiling light blinked on in its little pot shade, low-powered, but dazzling at first. The vibrating dots resolved into Joe Powys in his T-shirt and briefs standing very still, a hand on the switch on the wall at the top of the stairs.

Ben, his voice thick, said, 'What's up with him?'

But before Joe Powys could reply, another long, rolling howl began welling from the foot of the stairs, went on and on, spooky as hell.

'I didn't think dogs did that in real life,' Ben said stupidly.

Powys started to go downstairs into the living room, half-lit from the landing, and Ben followed him because, shit, what if Powys went out of the house and left him here on his own?

They were halfway down when the crash came.

A classic splintering crash of exploding glass. Ben was clutching at Powys's arm, hissing, 'Fucking burglars.' Swivelling his head, looking for a weapon, like he was going to find a poker in a stand at the top of the stairs or a baseball bat hanging from the wall.

The crash seemed to go on and on, with a coda of rolling splinters.

The dog was silent.

'It's over,' Powys said.

Ben stared at him. Couldn't move. Powys padded barefoot down the rest of the stairs. 'Mind the glass,' Ben said weakly.

Half-light from the landing was the best they could hope for. The paraffin lamp converted to electricity had been converted to glass shards and dented tin. It was in the middle of the floor, still rolling.

Ben looked fearfully around the room. Nothing seemed amiss, apart from the lamp. In the grate, the fire was almost burned out, one ashy log glinting like a redfoil sweet paper. On the chimney breast over the inglenook, the two pictures, of the old vicar-guy and the woman with ash-blonde hair, were perfectly in place.

So quiet now, Ben could hear his own nervy, staccato breaths.

Trying to convince himself this was another of Powys's scams. That he'd crept down in the night, maybe balanced the lamp on the very edge of the table.

Joe Powys hadn't said a word. He was standing by the fireplace looking at the two photos. Ben looked too and . . .

'Oh, fucking hell . . .' His leg muscles turned to porridge. 'You just did that. Didn't you?'

Powys just looked sad.

Ben went up close. Peered, horrified, at the pictures. And then backed off with his hands out, like he'd opened a door and a blast of winter had hit him full in the chest.

He fell back on the sofa, hands on his knees as if glued there. 'Tell me they aren't,' he said.

Joe went over to the pictures and carefully turned each one the right way up.

'It's OK. It's happened before.'

Ben said, 'You have to get out of here, Joe.'

'No.' Powys smiled. 'I know where I am with this.'

'Who are they? Those people.'

'The old bloke with the beard is Fay's dad, Canon Peters.'

'Dead?'

'And the woman was called Rachel.'

'Girlfriend? She's dead too?'

'I didn't know her long enough to put a label on it. We keep the pictures up there to remind us. In case we get blasé about certain things.'

Ben put his hands over his face, rubbed his eyes. 'Where's the dog?'

'Under the table, on his rug.'

'Maybe he upset the table, knocked the lamp off.'

'Could be,' said Powys.

'No it fucking couldn't.' Ben found himself breathing hard again, closest he could remember ever being to hysteria. 'And, anyway, why was he howling? He often howl like that?'

'Sometimes.'

'Why d'you say, It's over? Just now, on the stairs.'

He still felt too weak to get up from the sofa.

'Hang on,' Powys said. 'What's Arnold got?' He got down on all fours, scrabbled about under the table, and came up with something.

A book. A big, fat, heavy book.

'Now this is new,' he said (nervously? Was that a quiver of nerves under the voice?).

'This never happened before.'

He looked up and Ben followed his gaze to the very top book-shelf under a big, black beam-end to the left of the fireplace. There was just enough light to show up a gap in the middle of the shelf, the other books apparently stiff and firm to either side.

'It fell off,' Ben said. 'It fell on to the lamp.'

'Yeh. Looks like it.' Powys's voice was dry and flaky like the ash in the grate. He held out the book for Ben. It was a real doorstop, about three inches thick, probably over a thousand pages.

Ben couldn't prise his hands from his knees to take it.

But he could see the title, in faded gold down the spine, the author's name across it, the surname in big capitals.

POWYS.

And because he knew Joe had never written anything half that long, he figured this must be John Cowper Powys, novelist, mystic, nutter.

The title, in smaller lettering, confirmed it.

A Glastonbury Romance.

Ben was bewildered, spooked almost out of his head. A book, just one big heavy book, flies off the top shelf, a good nine feet across the fucking room, smashes a lamp. Smashes the only source of light.

'What's it mean?'

'I don't know,' Joe Powys said. He put a hand on the mantel-piece (to stop the hand shaking?).

'But it's all harmless, isn't it?' he said.

TWO

STRANGE PLACE, BUT GOOD FUN

As Ben ate his breakfast in Joe's living room, he kept glancing up at the bookshelves, searching out the middle of the top row.

You could read the lettering on the spine easily, at least the part that said

POWYS.

He buttered his toast, edging his chair a few inches to the left.

'Let's talk about John Cowper Powys.'

'Oh,' said Powys. 'Uncle Jack.'

'Uncle Jack? Uncle fucking Jack? You're telling me after all these years that JCP . . .'

'Well, I don't know, that's the truth. He had a complicated personal life.'

'You can say that again.'

Ben had lain wide awake and cold for what seemed like hours thinking, on and off, about John Cowper Powys. He'd never actually read *A Glastonbury Romance*, but he'd read one of the shorter ones (not much credibility for a New Age publisher who'd never read much JCP) and found it actually not that bad for something published half a century ago. Joe being a descendant of the great man was just a possibility they'd hinted at in publicity for *Golden Land* and never taken that seriously.

'He died in – what – sixty-five?'

'Sixty-three,' Powys said.

'Lived in North Wales, his later years, with this woman who'd been his secretary or something, right? And you were born . . .?'

'Wrexham. In theory, he could have been my father, but I don't think he was up to it by then. My mother used to talk about an Uncle Jack who was a famous author, but in those days close friends of your parents were always aunties and uncles. And Jack was a common name then.'

'You remember ever seeing the old guy when you were a kid?'

Powys shook his head.

'You never ask about him, when you grew up?'

'Once. Not long before my mother died. I asked her about this Uncle Jack, the famous author. I said – because I'd heard of Cowper Powys by then – was he, by any chance, possessed of a middle name beginning with C?'

Ben put down the marmalade. 'And she said?'

'She said, Uncle Jack? What Uncle Jack?'

'Shit. But you could find out.'

'Maybe. Who would it help?'

'Listen.' Ben glanced at the bookshelf, lowered his voice. 'Suppose he wants you to.'

'What?'

'Establish the link.'

'Get lost,' said Powys. 'You're leaping to conclusions. A book falls off the shelf . . .'

'Halfway across the room. And the dog howling.'

'These things happen. Best thing is not to react.'

'Stone me,' Ben hissed at his toast in frustration.

'It was only a book. Nobody got hurt.'

'Not just a book, Powys. Not just a book. OK, what else we got? Glastonbury. When were you last in Glastonbury?'

'Never been.'

Ben put down his knife in astonishment.

'You've never been to Glastonbury? The world centre for earth mysteries? Glastonbury Tor and all the UFOs? Healing rays? The Abbey ruins? The St Michael Line?'

'The St Michael Line's spurious.'

'You've never been to Glastonbury?'

'Well, you know . . .' Powys stood up and started gathering plates together. He seemed uncomfortable about this. 'I read the *Romance* the first time when I was quite young. Much of it I didn't understand.'

'Isn't it all about sex?'

'Yeh, it is really. Mysticism and sex, and how they can both screw you up. It didn't make me want to go to Glastonbury, made me want to avoid it. It's a powerful book, though. Tells you a lot about JCP, things you might not want to know if there's a possibility you were related.'

'He had some funny ideas.'

'But where did he get them?' Powys said. 'Did he force his ideas on Glastonbury or did it force them on him?'

'Strange place. But good fun. We sell a lot of books there.'

'As you would.'

'Don't knock it, it's all har . . .'

Ben stopped himself and looked up at the shelf. Had it moved, just a fraction of a centimetre?

'Keep on saying it,' Powys said. 'Maybe that's best.'

No more than an hour after Ben had gone back to London, the phone rang, and it was Fay.

She'd said she was coming over this weekend, from Hereford. She was supposed to have come last weekend, but the bloke who owned Offa's Dyke Radio had apparently arrived in town and she had to stick around for meetings. Powys had thought this was an excuse and that there was something else in the air she wasn't telling him about.

Fay said now, 'Joe . . .'

And when she said Joe, he knew it was going to be heavy. Most of the time she called him Powys; people did, it was a better name than Joe, had more resonance: whisper it and it sounded as if you were calling the cat.

'Joe,' Fay said, 'it's . . . I've been offered a job.'

At the BBC World Service. London wanted Fay back. There was what they called a six-month attachment for a features producer. Six-month attachments at the BBC were hard to come by these days, now it was run like ICI.

She said, what did he think?

He said – what was he supposed to say? – that he thought she ought to take it. He was about to say he was likely to be down in London himself soon, seeing this publisher, and maybe they could . . .

Or maybe they shouldn't.

Joe Powys was feeling very alone. Fay was the only person who understood. Their relationship had involved a lot of comforting each other, of saying, *Listen, you're not out of your mind.* And, in the end, the reassurances had themselves served as reminders of how bad it had been and reminders were useful, except for those involving books thrown from shelves.

Fay said they'd see each other properly, and Arnold and everything, before she went.

'Well good God, you're only going to London . . .'

'Ah,' said Fay.

It wasn't just London. The World Service was planning some kind of trans-Global Christmas link-up under the working title Peace on Earth. Fay would be involved in producing the European end. From Brussels and places.

'Ah,' Powys said.

'And then there's a few other things. Paris. Amsterdam. Back in March,' Fay said. 'Probably.'

'Sounds brilliant,' he said, hoping she'd think the hoarseness was on the line. 'Do it. Don't look back.'

But, she said, what about him?

Fine, he said. Really. And he told her about the book.

The book that Ben Corby was passing on to this guy Frayne at Harvey-Calder.

Not the book which came off the shelf, sailed halfway across the room and smashed the lamp.

'That's wonderful, Powys,' Fay said. 'So you could be back in business, then.' And there was a silence, and then the conversation became rather weepy.

Later that morning, Powys went for a walk with Arnold. They climbed to the top of the hill behind the longhouse, Arnold indignant at being carried part of the way. From here, you could see along Offa's Dyke, the earthwork which used to mark the boundary between England and Wales but was only an approximation these days. The dyke itself was not exactly the Great Wall of China and probably never had been. It was just a symbol of an old division.

In *The Old Golden Land*, Powys had argued that borders were very sensitive places, where the veil – yes *that* veil – was especially thin. It was a place where you might expect to have extraordinary experiences.

So what was he still doing here?

'Hiding,' he said aloud. 'Hiding out.'

But had something found him?

He had Arnold's ball in his jacket pocket, and Arnold knew it. Usually, Arnold would race about after it, proving he'd never really needed four legs anyway. Today he stuck close to Powys.

It was Fay who'd rescued Arnold from the dog pound after Henry Kettle, the dowser, died in the car crash. Fay was small, like a terrier. She'd held on as long as she could. Now, in taking the London job, she had, in theory, cut Powys loose as well. He'd told Ben he was still here because it was Arnold's home, and Ben had said that was a wonderfully New Age thing to say.

But it wasn't really true.

He looked back down at the cottage. Mrs Whitney next door was hanging out towels on her washing line. Mrs Whitney had known Fay wasn't coming back; he could tell by her expression.

'Let's go, Arnie. Home.'

Home?

When they got back to the cottage, Arnold stood in the doorway and growled. Powys made his senses go dead and uncaring, or, at least, that was the message he sent to himself. It's nothing, it doesn't matter, it's irrelevant.

The big black book lay in the centre of the hearth this time, its spine split.

PART THREE

On Wearyall Hill, the long, low spur jutting out into the marshes, the first firm ground between Avalon and the sea in those days, Joseph set foot on English land, and he drove his staff into the warm, red, Westland soil as he took possession of our islands for the spiritual kingdom of his Lord, a realm not made with hands, eternal in the heavens.

Dion Fortune
Avalon of the Heart

ONE

MYSTERY

AVALON OUT, SAYS CANDIDATE

A bitter attack on the 'New Age subculture' of Glastonbury has been made by the man chosen by South Mendip Tories as their next Parliamentary candidate.

The Hon. Archer Ffitch, son of local landowner Viscount Pennard, says the town will become a national joke unless it 'stops encouraging cranks'.

Mr Ffitch won a standing ovation from constituency party members when he told them, 'We must seize the future and stop mooning about our mythical past.'

He said the town had become saturated with pseudo-mystics, many of whom were blatantly pagan, and had become a Mecca for New Age travellers.

As a result, local house prices had dropped and businesses were reluctant to invest in the town.

Even the boundary signs identified Glastonbury as The Ancient Isle of Avalon in acknowledgement of 'a probably bogus legend'.

Mr Ffitch said, 'If the local authority wants a new slogan, I'll give them one: Glastonbury FIRST, Avalon OUT.'

Mr Ffitch's remarks followed his formal acceptance of . . .

'You bastard,' Jim Battle muttered, as dusk settled like mud around die red roofs.

His first thought was to screw the *Evening Post* into a ball and ram it into the nearest litter bin. Instead, he folded it into his saddle bag. He would show it to Juanita. If he could face her.

He'd waited until the end of the day before cycling into town. Nothing to do with not wanting to show his face in daylight for fear of people pointing at him: *That's him. That's the bloke who was executed last night, ho ho. Where's your hat, Jim?*

Nobody would, of course. Nobody knew and nobody would find out. Even the buggering travellers had spirited themselves away. He wouldn't have to face anyone. Except for Juanita and his own hatless head reflected in shop windows.

Perhaps his humiliation on the Tor had been a small payback for his self-indulgence in fleeing the city to reside amid ancient mystery. How bloody Pat would have enjoyed it: the invasion of Jim's little idyll, a barbarian's blade over his throat.

As it turned out, nobody commented even on the premature departure of the travellers. The report of Archer Ffitch's speech had greater implications.

'This is the kind of chap we need,' said Colin Border in the off-licence, pointing to the *Post*'s picture of Archer looking severe but dynamic. 'What I've been saying for years. How can you hope to attract new industry to a town where half the potential workforce appear to be pot-smoking sun-worshippers? Fourteen pounds 49p, please, Jim,' wrapping Jim's bottle of Scotch in brown paper.

'Won't be terribly popular down the street, though.' Jim put his money on the counter. 'Lot of New Age types running quite profitable businesses now.'

'What, vegetarian sandwich bars and poky shops specialising in bloody overpriced gimcrack jewellery that's supposed to have healing powers? Give me a Marks and Spencer any day. Not that Archer'll be losing any support in that direction. Most of these halfwits throw away their votes on the Green Party and the rest are bound to be Labour, the odd one or two Lib-Dems. What's he got to lose? Nailing his colours to the mast from the outset. I like that.'

'Hmm,' Jim said. Because of the way he dressed and his disapproval of thieving travellers, people like Colin assumed he must be as reactionary as they were.

'I like this bit, Jim. Listen to this, "Glastonbury enshrines the idea of a strong English and Christian tradition within an established, solidly prosperous country town. It stands for the Old Values. Whereas Avalon, said Mr Ffitch, is a place which exists only in legends and folklore. It has been adopted by those who choose to turn their backs on the real world, to inhabit a drug-sodden cloud-cuckoo land where no one has to work for a living and traditional family values are laughed at." '

'Yes,' said Jim. 'Quite.' He picked up his bottle and got out of there before he exploded.

Outside, he looked down the street to where the lights of the New Age shops began. He saw a twinkling display of assorted crystals. He saw tarot cards and dreamy relaxation tapes and a lone twilight candle burning in the window of The Wicked Wax Co.

Well, all right, one or two of the windows were rather lurid; some of the owners a little, erm, eccentric. But that candle, for instance, symbolised something important, something close to the essence of it all. Something Archer Ffitch wouldn't understand and many of his supporters wouldn't realise until it was too late.

Jim folded the evening paper, jammed it under his arm and mooched off towards The George and Pilgrims. He needed a couple of drinks.

'You bastard, Ffitch,' he murmured. 'Why must you murder the Mystery?'

The woman with hair the colour of old gold was drifting around the shop with her hands out – palms down, like a priest vaguely searching for children to bless.

'I don't quite know,' she said. 'I don't quite know what I'm looking for.'

Diane thought that went for an awful lot of people in this town.

The woman was frightfully beautiful, in an ethereal sort of way. Must be wonderful to be ethereal. Being slim and elegant would, of course, be a start.

'Juanita would know.' The woman had a long, slender nose; she looked down it at Diane. 'Juanita would know at once.'

'Well, she'll be back in a short while,' Diane said.

Juanita had tramped wearily off to see her reflexologist, leaving Diane in charge of the shop. Just like old times, really. Except that Juanita's weariness used to be feigned and after a glass of wine she'd be fine again, full of ideas and energy. Last night she and Jim had seemed bowed and burdened and today Jim hadn't been round. Juanita had glossed over how they just happened to be walking up Wellhouse Lane when the Range Rover went past. She said that awful split lip had been caused by a flying log chip when she was chopping wood for the stove.

Whatever really happened, Diane thought, it's all my fault.

She gestured hopelessly at the shelves of books; the arrangements had changed a lot since she was last here.

'Perhaps if you gave me an idea.'

The woman whirled on her. She was about thirty, with a lean, peremptory Home Counties accent that didn't go with her appearance at all.

'Celtic manuscripts.'

'What, sort of Book of Kells?'

The woman looked horrified. 'That's Christian, isn't it? No, no, no, no, no ... what I need, urgently, are the very earliest images I can find of the Goddess. You haven't been here long, have you?'

What a nerve, Diane thought. You live here all your life and someone who moved in maybe six months ago ...

'I'm helping out,' she said tightly.

Which goddess? she wanted to ask. A decision seemed to have been taken that all the goddesses, from Artemis to Kali to Isis, should be combined into a single symbol of womanpower. For this woman, perhaps, it wasn't so much about spirituality, as a kind of politics. Just like the Pilgrims, really, wherever they were now.

The woman pirouetted again, hands exploring the air, as if she could somehow divine the book she wanted. Her rich golden hair was a tangle of abandoned styles, rippling waves and ringlets. Did she always behave like this, Diane wondered, or was she *on* something?

As though she'd picked up Diane's thoughts from die ether, the golden woman leaned across the counter and smiled widely. Her eyes were somewhere else.

'I'm the artist,' she declared.

And then stepped back. As though this was some sort of epiphany, a moment of wondrous self-discovery.

'And *you* are?'

'I'm Diane.'

'Do you acknowledge the Goddess? You should, you know. She can help you.'

With what? With her weight problem? As though spiritual development was just another aspect of health and beauty.

'What are you doing tonight?' the woman demanded, homing in on promising raw material. 'Come with me. I'm in Holy Thorn Ceramics across the street. Domini Dorrell-Adams. Come with me and meet the Goddess.'

Gosh, was this an order? The woman leaned sinuously across the counter again. 'I'll call for you, shall I? At seven?'

'Oh, well,' Diane said. 'I've a sort of, you know, commitment tonight.'

'You should make a commitment to the Goddess. The very landscape of Avalon is shaped in her image, did you know that? There's just no place better in the world to learn how to be a woman.'

She drifted to the door. 'Remember The Cauldron,' she sang carelessly, as though she was dropping a pamphlet behind her.

'Right,' Diane whispered, as the door got into the mood and glided shut. She actually did remember The Cauldron. Formed, not long before she'd been dispatched to Yorkshire, by a rather dominant woman calling herself Ceridwen, who used to be a witch and had a Divination Consultancy (fortune-telling booth) somewhere at the rear of the Glastonbury Experience arcade.

Juanita, never the sisterly type, didn't like her at all.

Diane wished Juanita would come back. She felt exposed and nervous when anyone came into the shop, and yet she didn't want to leave it, imagining Gwyn and his sickle among the freaks outside St John's, imagining a cream Range Rover screeching into the High Street kerb, a gloved hand over her face.

She'd slept last night in Juanita's spare bedroom – it had been rather blissy, actually, being in a soft bed again after that sleeping bag in the van. Juanita had said she could stay as long as she liked. Awfully kind, but . . .

. . . There *were* questions to be asked, and pretty urgent ones. Like, what was she going to do, with no money, no job and the kind of family that was probably worse than having no family?

Why *had* she been called back? What were they trying to tell her, the lights and symbols in the sky, the pungent scent of old Avalon and, most disturbing of all, last night's dark and horrific exhibition in the night sky while the Pilgrims performed what sounded horribly like a Satanic ritual? Where had the Pilgrims gone? And, most worrying of all, what had happened to Headlice?

She'd half thought of going to the police. Which would immediately implicate Rankin and her father and cause the most awful fuss, possibly for nothing. *Hippies and gypsies are like dogs. Give one a good kicking and it'll simply limp off into the undergrowth until it's recovered.*

Worse than having no family at all.

Back home. And a stranger – the golden-haired woman had thought she was a stranger. The town seemed different: Juanita's weariness appeared to be general; there was that atmosphere of torpor you found during the Blight, the period towards the end of summer when stagnant heat seemed to stick like toffee to the Somerset Levels. Except this was November and it wasn't heat so much as a lack of cold. No breeze, no vigour. The people she recognised as they walked past the window seemed conspicuously older.

The shop door pinged open then, and Diane looked up in alarm, half expecting to see Gerry Rankin with a chloroform pad.

'Diane!' the customer yelled. 'Sheesh! Wow! It's true! You *are* back.'

He was wearing this awful, home-knitted, baggy scarlet sweater that stopped just above his knees – which you could see through the splits in his jeans. His beard was a little more grey, a little more wispy. His hair had all but vanished from the front, making his pony-tail look pretty silly. But his smile was still as wide as his face.

'Oh gosh, Woolly, it's so good . . .'

'Please . . .' Woolly drew himself up to his full five-foot-five, assumed a dignified expression. 'Councillor Woolaston, if you don't mind.'

Diane gasped. A hand went to her mouth. 'Oh no! Gosh! Really?'

'You didn't hear? Last May, my love. Old Hippy Shakes the Establishment. Electoral Shock Rocks Glastonbury As Longest-Serving Councillor Bites Dust. Pretty wild, huh? I'm on three committees: Planning, Environmental Health and . . . er, I forget the other, but it's really heavy and influential.'

Diane hugged him. She could quite easily get her arms all the way round. 'I can't believe it!'

'Yeah, well,' said Woolly. 'Neither can Griff Daniel. If one of his lorries is tipping out a load of bricks these days, I stand well clear.'

Diane was thrilled. Over the years, three candidates from the Alternative Sector had stood against their old enemy and been heavily beaten by the local votes. Whoever had thought of putting Woolly up, it had been truly inspired. He might be an old hippy, but he was a *local* hippy. The natives sometimes despaired of him, but they couldn't help liking him, and they knew he was ever so honest.

'It's just incredible,' said Diane.

'It's not that incredible.' Woolly tried to look hurt. 'But yeah, if Griff hadn't had this bit of hassle over jerry-building, over Somerton way. And if it hadn't, like, found its way into the *Gazette* . . . whoops! Aw shit, man, all's fair in love and politics. How long you been back?'

'Since yesterday. Didn't you hear about it?'

'Yeah,' Woolly admitted, with a crooked smile. 'Course I heard about it. Just us politicians got to be a bit guarded. Nothing wrong with the travellers, most of 'em. That your van, with the pink spots? Nice one. Pity they've all gone, mind. I'd like to've seen Archer's face. And your old man.'

'What?' Diane said. Had it got out about her being snatched from the camp?

'Aw, come on. You're saying you really don't know?'

'Don't know what?'

'Sheesh.' Woolly dragged a stool across to the counter. 'What a fucking family. He didn't tell you about Archer being put up as Tory candidate for Mendip South?'

'Oh gosh. I didn't know, Woolly, I really didn't. I didn't know he was even in the running.'

'Clever the way they're timing it,' Woolly said. 'Idea being, presumably, that he stands in for old Bowkett at *this* dinner and *that* garden fête and soon he's so well-integrated that, come election-time, half the voters'll think he's already the serving MP. Geddit?'

'Ah.' It was all falling into place. This was a crucial time for Archer. Her father would have been picturing the headlines: CAN-DIDATE'S SISTER IS NEW-AGE TRAVELLER. A picture of Archer shaking hands with the Prime Minister and another one of Diane in her moon skirt standing in front of a white van with big pink spots. No wonder they'd acted so ruthlessly. No wonder Rankin hadn't cared who got hurt.

It was also no wonder they'd handed her over when Juanita started threatening them with the Press and TV.

Handed over! Good God, what sort of hostage had she become?

'I'm not gonner ask what went wrong up in Yorkshire, look,' Woolly said. 'Not any of our business. But I'm glad you're back, Diane, man. Gonner need all the support we can get over this road business, if the public inquiry goes against us.'

'Is that likely?'

'A sham, that inquiry. They won't admit it, but this is the first stage in linking Somerset into the Euro superhighway. Biggest environmental threat in Britain today. Nightmare. Some of the finest countryside in the world sacrificed to the juggernaut. Once they've started, there'll be no end to it. Be nowhere to walk except from your house to your car, and no garden in between.'

Woolly laughed, embarrassed. 'Sorry. When you get on the council you stop talking to people normally, you just make speeches. What you got here?' He started turning over the pages of *Shadow of Angels*, a glossy, new book about the St Michael Line, mainly pictures, handsome but superficial.

'Hey, I heard this thing was out. Let's see if I'm in the index.'

Woolly was Glastonbury's biggest expert on leys and earth-forces. Which said quite a lot, as there was no town in Britain with more ley-lines or, indeed, ley-line experts per square yard.

'Yeah, *Woolaston E. T.*, pages 171–173. Three pages? Sheesh. I shoulda charged this lady. Specially as she's rubbished it, apparently. They dress it up in a lovely jacket with romantic photos and a little bit of text that ends up saying the Line probably don't exist anyway.'

'We followed it,' Diane said. 'The convoy. We went from church to church all the way from the abbey at Bury St Edmunds, stopping at the Avebury circle and all those places and . . .'

She stopped, suddenly remembering something Headlice had said last night in his manic, mud-splashed, lets-get-out-of-here state.

'Who? The Pilgrims?' Woolly spread his hands. 'Well, that's good, innit? Travelling the Line, near as you can, it helps keep the energy flowing. Here, listen to this . . . *A resident of Glastonbury, Edward "Woolly" Woolaston walks the full length of the Line from St Michael's Mount to Bury every five years in what has become a personal ritual. "When I'm too old to walk, I'll find somebody to push me," says Woolaston, who has been studying linear configurations in the West Country landscape for over twenty-five years.'*

Woolly closed the book and sighed. 'Picture of me, too. She made me wear the woolly hat and the long scarf. The full sixties throwback bit. I don't mind. I just wish these clever gits would try and understand that while the Line might not work out exactly on the map, it does . . . in here.'

Woolly patted his chest and Diane thought at once of Headlice looking up the Tor from Don Moulder's meadow and announcing, *I can feel it . . . here*, punching his chest through his pitifully torn clothing.

And later, minutes before he was attacked in Moulder's field, he'd said, *And no more stopping at churches, goin' in backwards . . .*

They'd made a point, on Gwyn's direction, of stopping at every church on the St Michael route as well as many of the old stones and burial mounds. They'd made Headlice go in backwards?

'Hey, don't worry.' Woolly was wearing one of his huge grins, patting her arm. 'We're not gonner let 'em deport you this time. You got Councillor Woolaston behind you now, kid. Not going back with the Pilgrims, are you?'

'I don't even know where they are. It was just a way of . . . getting here, I suppose.'

Woolly didn't question it. To Woolly, everything in life was about Getting Here. 'So you're OK, then? I mean, in the shop?'

'Oh, yes.' But Diane wasn't too certain. She couldn't help imagining another unsuitable headline: CANDIDATE'S SISTER WORKS IN OCCULT BOOKSHOP. Not quite so detrimental to Archer's prospects. But Archer didn't like anything at all in his way. Not if it could be removed.

'You know, I think I'm gonner buy this book, after all,' Woolly said. 'How much?' He turned the book over. 'Sheesh, that's a bit steep.'

'I'm sure Juanita would want me to knock a pound or so off,' said Diane, but Woolly looked stern.

'Councillor Woolaston never trades on friendship. I'll pay full whack.' Woolly pulled out a pink and blue canvas wallet, searched through it, looked up, did his grin. 'Er . . . slight cash-flow problem. I can give you a tenner, bring the rest tomorrow?'

Diane smiled and put the book in a paper bag for him.

''Tis good to have you back, my love,' said Woolly sincerely.

Verity loved Dame Wanda Carlisle's house. It was everything Meadwell was not – spacious and airy, with sumptuous sofas and deep Georgian windows letting in lots of glorious light.

It was also surprisingly close to the heart of the town, tucked into a discreet mews behind St John's Church, quiet but convenient for attending talks at the town hall and the Assembly Rooms.

'I'm totally convinced this will help you.' Wanda, large and strong and scented, placed a reassuringly regal hand on Verity's wrist. 'My dear, the man is said to be wonderfully charismatic.'

Verity raised a hesitant eyebrow. Most of Wanda's pronouncements were couched in similarly extravagant superlatives. All great actresses, Verity supposed, were long conditioned to project, project and project.

'I suppose, all the same, that I shall have to consult Major Shepherd.'

'Nonsense, darling.' Wanda reached for the gin bottle. 'This Major Shepherd, it's all very well for him, he doesn't have to live in the blessed house. So he has no right to pontificate. Now. I'll tell you what we shall do. Dr Grainger is appearing at the Assembly Rooms on . . . when? Wednesday. Oh . . . that's tonight!'

'What a coincidence,' Verity observed, covering her wineglass with a hand. 'No more for me, thank you. I shall be quite tiddly.'

'In Avalon . . .' Wanda mixed herself a large gin and tonic. '. . . I have found that coincidence does tend to be the norm.' She had come to Glastonbury last spring for *my soul's sake*. Retaining the Hampstead villa, naturally, because while London might be unbearable it did remind one of the need for the sanctity of Avalon.

Verity raised her eyes to the sculpted ceiling and the cut-glass chandelier which threw hundreds of beautiful light-splinters into the farthest corners. She thought of the soiled bulbs of Meadwell struggling against the shadows and supposed a similar comparison could be made between her and the incandescent Wanda.

'I don't know,' she said. 'I don't know at all.'

She was still flattered that such a distinguished person, well-known from the theatre and the television, should have so much time for her. Although, she suspected Wanda did prefer to be with people who were rather in awe. In the presence of someone manifestly powerful, like Ceridwen, the fêted actress tended to wilt into a sort of compliant vagueness.

Verity fingered the glossy pamphlet on the occasional table. The man in the photograph was shaven-headed, bearded and unsmiling. DR PEL GRAINGER: *Fear of the Dark – a misconception. An Introduction to Tenebral Therapy.*

Dr Grainger was an American author and academic who had recently moved into a barn conversion at Compton Dundon, just a few miles away. Apparently, his argument was that we only fear the dark because we do not fully understand its role, a natural balance of darkness and light being essential for our health, eyesight and spiritual development.

'They say', Wanda confided, 'that he's had all the sources of artificial light removed from his barn. He has no television, writes and reads only by daylight, while the nights are reserved for thinking, meditation, sex and sleep. Sleep of a sublime quality attainable only by those who are truly at peace with the dark.'

Wanda raised a theatrical eyebrow. 'About the quality of the sex one can only speculate.'

'It sounds . . . quite interesting,' said Verity dubiously.

'In Avalon – and this is part of the magic – there is always *someone*. Whatever your spiritual problem. Always someone near at hand.'

All *too* near, in Wanda's case. Her house had become the headquarters of The Cauldron, some of whose Outer Circle gatherings had been attended, a trifle timidly, by Verity. The Outer Circle concerned itself mainly with lectures about the role of the Goddess in the modern world.

Actually, Verity was becoming rather sceptical about The Cauldron. She'd first gone along having been told the group was researching the Marian tradition in Glastonbury. While not herself a Catholic, she had felt an urge to understand the power of the faith which had driven Abbot Whiting. Now, she rather suspected that references to the Goddess Mary were something of a sop. And while respecting pagan viewpoints, Verity had always avoided any practical involvement in that particular belief-system.

'Is Dr Grainger a pagan?' she asked.

She was very much regretting having raised the darkness problem with Wanda. This had been several weeks ago, when the nights were drawing in and she had hoped to be invited to a social evening the actress was hosting, the prime purpose of which was to introduce the recently inducted Bishop of Bath and Wells to leaders of the New Age community. The new bishop was said to be keen to talk, on the basis, apparently, that a pagan spirituality was better than no spirituality at all. Verity thought this was probably a positive move.

'Darling,' said Wanda, 'I have absolutely no idea of Dr Grainger's spiritual orientation. But if he can help you to survive in that hell-hole, does it really matter? Oh Verity!'

Wanda, who had taken to wearing white, priestess robes about the house suddenly surged towards Verity amid a billow of sleeves.

'I do feel – don't you? – that we are at the beginning of something quite, quite momentous.'

In Wanda's world, it seemed to Verity, nothing which was less than absolutely momentous was worth getting involved in at all. She smiled half-heartedly and gathered her bulky tapestry bag into her arms.

'Eight o'clock, then,' Wanda decreed. 'There's an Inner Circle meeting of The Cauldron downstairs tonight, and I *would* prefer to leave before they arrive, otherwise I shall just be striding about as usual; longing to know what they're doing down there.'

'It must be frustrating, I know,' Verity said. Ceridwen had insisted that it be at least three years before an initiate was exposed to a high degree of what she called 'live energy'.

'Very well,' she said. 'Eight p.m.'

'Darling, I truly believe it will change your life,' said Wanda.

TWO

LIKE A PUMA

'*The Avalonian*? What is that exactly?'

'God, Diane, you make me feel so old.'

Juanita came to sit in the rocking chair, a glass of white wine in hand, a battered boxfile on her knees.

'*The Avalonian* is the magazine Danny Frayne and I started in about 1973. I suppose your reading wouldn't have been much beyond Noddy and Big Ears in 1973.'

'I think Thomas the Tank Engine.'

Juanita raised her eyes to the parlour's cracked ceiling. Newly bathed, without make-up, Diane looked all of sixteen. She was perched on a stool, still wearing the faded skirt with the moons on it, washed again and even more faded. She was sipping hot chocolate from a mug, both hands around it.

The shop was closed. The shadows had consumed the High Street. Juanita was limp from the reflexologist, Sarah, who had detected from her feet that her diaphragm was tight and her life-force, in general, needed topping up. Juanita wasn't sure her life-force had been replenished, but she did feel more relaxed.

And she *had* come up with a diverting idea for the Hon. Diane Ffitch. Who couldn't, after all, be a humble shop assistant for the rest of her life, paid a pittance and living out of the shop owner's spare bedroom.

'Oh, this sort of floaty blonde woman came in.'

'Hmmm?' Juanita had opened the boxfile and was rummaging through its contents. 'I should have the very last issue in here.'

'Very self-possessed, but quite batty. Domini-something.'

'Oh, right. Dorrell-Adams. She and her husband run that pot shop across the street. Keep mauling each other in the shop window.' Juanita made a face. 'I tend to find that sort of thing quite embarrassing now.'

She scowled at herself. Miserable old hag. That it should come to this. She took out a magazine, A4-size, printed on thick paper browning with age. When she held it up, the paper felt dry and brittle.

The cover, dated August 1976, featured a pen-and-ink drawing of a mane-haired woman in see-through robes and a headdress of bound twigs. Both arms were uplifted, along with her nipples, towards a sunrise behind the Tor. It made Juanita, who'd posed for the drawing, instantly depressed. In retrospect, the list of contents didn't inspire her much either:

WELLS CATHEDRAL – *Its ancient secrets unveiled*
CRYSTAL MAGIC – *Getting started on a budget*
WICCA – *Which witch-way is your way?*

Diane put her mug on the hearth and looked at the magazine. 'Not a lot's really changed in two decades, has it?'

'You're kidding.' Juanita thought sadly of her own body. Everything now – autumn leaves, secondhand books with loose pages – seemed to make her think sadly of her body. And her lower lip still hurt.

'Consider,' she said. 'There was no animal-rights movement. Words like "shamanism" weren't in general usage. And if there were any gay and lesbian pagan groups locally they didn't do a lot of advertising. Not in *The Avalonian* anyway.'

'Juanita,' Diane said. 'Tell me about The Cauldron.'

'Not gay. Not even mildly happy. Avoid them.' Juanita wiped the air. 'Ceridwen. Awful woman. Oppressive.'

'I talked to her once, must be ten years ago. About Dion Fortune. I wanted to know, you see.'

'If you were the reincarnation, having the same initials and everything.' Juanita sighed. 'And what did she tell you?'

'She was very pleasant actually.'

'I bet she was.'

'But she said there were an awful lot of people who'd like to think they were the reincarnation of the most powerful magician of this century. I remember her standard charge was twenty pounds, which I'd saved up from my Saturday wages.'

'You gave the money I paid you to that . . .?'

'Actually, she gave me ten back. She said I wasn't ready.'

'For what?'

'To know one way or the other.'

'Really Diane, you were an awfully naive kid, weren't you?'

Diane said, 'It must have been frightfully exciting in Dion's time. In the twenties, I mean. They felt they were on the brink of something miraculous – finding the Holy Grail or something. A bit like you and all your friends in the sixties and seventies. Seems to go in cycles, doesn't it?'

'Diane,' Juanita said heavily. 'I doubt there's ever been a time when some people in Glastonbury didn't think they were on the brink of something miraculous. That's the trick of it.'

'Trick?'

'This town. It plugs itself into your adrenal glands. Over-the-rainbow stuff.'

'Isn't that good?'

'Not', said Juanita, 'if there's nothing at the end of the rainbow but a crock of shit. Listen. The fact that you didn't remember *The Avalonian* is actually quite encouraging. Means that lots of other people won't either. So if it was relaunched . . . as a different *sort* of magazine, not just aimed at the New Age community. See what I'm getting at?'

Juanita got up and opened the door to the darkened shop, whose blind was not yet down so that they could see the street through the shop window.

'It's not exactly a healthy, rounded community out there.'

A twenty-something couple drifted past the shop, hand-in-hand. Both partners were male, one had dreadlocks, the other wore short hair and a sports jacket.

'Gay pagans?' said Diane.

'Well, they're not locals are they? How many real locals do you see this end of town at night?'

'There's me.'

'I meant ordinary locals. Sorry, but you're not. Not in any respect.'

Juanita closed the door.

'I bet this town's never been as divided as it is now. The locals don't want the New Agers, and the New Agers think *they're* the people who're going to inherit the holyest erthe, so it doesn't matter a damn what the locals think. They've stopped even trying to understand each other.'

'Admittedly, there aren't many locals who wouldn't swap all these little shops for a branch of Marks and Spencer.' Diane put down her cup to unwrap a peppermint carob bar. She'd drink hot chocolate but eat only carob. Contrary was not the word.

'Let's face it, Diane, they'd swap us for a McDonald's.'

'Not me. I wouldn't. But then, they all think I'm bonkers. It's OK.' She bit into the carob bar. 'One gets used to it.'

Juanita wanted to snatch the carob out of her podgy hand and bang her head on the wall. How dare she get used to it?

'Listen, there has to be a glimmer of light in all this. Think about Woolly. He's an old hippy, but he's local and people trust him enough to put him on the council. That's got to be a small step towards integration.'

'It's probably just an indication', Diane said morosely, 'of how many people are living in leaky houses built by Griff Daniel.'

'Don't go cynical on me, Diane, it's not your style.'

'I'm sorry. What's your plan?'

Juanita went down on her knees by Diane's wooden stool.

'A revamped *Avalonian*. A totally Glastonbury paper that contains different viewpoints, input from different sides. Professional. Unbiased.'

Diane shook her head. 'The local people will think it's just another hippy rag and they'll ignore it.'

'Not if it tells them important things they didn't know.'

'Like what?'

'You're the editor,' Juanita said. 'You tell me.'

'Oh.' Diane looked apprehensive. 'I was wondering where all this was leading.'

It was dark by the time Jim wheeled his bike down to the bottom end of High Street, where The George and Pilgrims stood in all its late-medieval splendour. To convince himself he wasn't yet a total slave to the booze, he'd pedalled around the town a while, down Benedict Street, round the Northload roundabout, weighing up whether or not he should buy a new hat.

On the one hand, a new hat would remind him distressingly, every time he put it on, of what had happened to the old one. On the other hand, not having a hat reminded him all the time.

The George and Pilgrims looked more like an Oxford college than a boozer. Over the doorway were set the heraldic arms of Edward IV. On the hanging pub sign, a fully armoured knight with a red-cross shield brandished a broadsword while a bunch of standard medieval punters – monks and nuns and a kid – hung around in case he needed anybody to defend. In the top right-hand corner of the sign was the ubiquitous Tor.

Jim signalled to St George to keep an eye on his bike and went in, slotting himself into a corner of the bar with a double Chivas Regal and looking around.

He listened to two elderly ladies taking tea at a table in the passage outside: 'Oh, he's quite miraculous, Charlotte. Two weeks ago, I could only bend it this far. Now . . . see? Isn't that wonderful?'

There was only one other customer in the dark, woody bar. Young chap he thought he recognised, at a particularly shadowed table. On the table were a pint of bitter and a whisky chaser. But before Jim had had more than a couple of sips of Chivas, both glasses were dumped, empty, on the bar.

'Same again,' the young chap told the barman grimly. He had thick black hair and a pair of small, square, gold-rimmed glasses, baggy cord trousers and a practical Guernsey sweater.

Jim recognised him now. 'Tony, isn't it?' Tony something double-barrelled with the pottery a few doors up the street and the gorgeous if rather brittle wife.

'I'm sorry?'

Blinking. Voice a trifle slurred. Oh dear, and not yet seven in the evening. Jim knew this road all too well.

'Jim Battle. Came into your shop when you first opened to enquire whether you were interested in displaying examples of local, er, fine art.'

'Oh yes. Sure. The painter.' Tony peered at him without much interest. 'Another one?'

'Civil of you. Thanks.' Jim drained his glass and Tony jerked a thumb at it, for the barman.

'Married, are you, Jim?'

'Not at the moment.' Jim smiled. Not the most original way to open a conversation in a pub. 'Hope you're not going to tell me what a lucky devil I am, Tony. Not with a wife like yours.'

Dorrell-Adams, that was the name. Holy Thorn Ceramics.

Tony sank a staggering quantity of his new pint, still looking like a man who wasn't used to it.

'Bloody bitch,' he said eventually.

'Oh gosh, Juanita, it's ridiculous. I only did a year. And it's not as if I was any good.'

Diane was pacing the tiny parlour, nervously nibbling another carob bar.

'How are you on layout? Sub-editing.'

'Hopeless. I was just a slightly mature trainee reporter. Sort of. I know how to write stories. Sort of. I know how not to commit libel. Probably. And that's it.'

'Sounds OK,' Juanita said. 'Sam knows about layouts. Sam Daniel. Griff Daniel's son. Estranged, fortunately. Set himself up as a sort of printer, with an enterprise grant. Desktop stuff, computers. But there's also a local offset plant which could turn the thing out.'

'I remember Sam Daniel. Mostly by reputation. We didn't mix in the same circles. He's in business?'

'In a bolshy sort of way. We discussed *The Avalonian* about a year ago. I was thinking of doing it all by myself.'

'Why?' Diane sat down, looking flustered.

'Because it seemed like a really nice thing to do, Diane.' Juanita rolled her eyes. 'For the town? OK, it wound up on the back-burner, as these things do. But then you coming back like this, it just seemed . . .'

Jesus God, don't tell her it was a sign.

'It would be quite a costly venture,' Diane said.

'You mean, have I suddenly got money to throw away? Well, the old bank balance stands at about twelve grand. But I could write to Danny. I bought him out of the shop when he . . . when he needed to leave. Which put me in the red for quite a while, and fortunately he still feels bad about that. Also, I may approach the Pixhill Trust.'

Diane looked blank. '*Colonel* Pixhill?'

'You knew him?'

'I sort of remember him. My father claims he conned my grandmother over the sale of Meadwell after the War. Father was abroad with the Army at the time. He was furious. They kept trying to buy Meadwell back, but the Colonel wouldn't play.'

'Poor old Pixhill,' said Juanita. 'They say he lived his last few years on fresh air to keep that place together and then, when he died, his family couldn't even sell it because of the Pixhill Trust, this rickety charity seemingly run by the Colonel's old army pals, most of them miles away.'

Diane said, 'Archer was very friendly with Oliver Pixhill, the Colonel's son. Same school. Inseparable for a while.'

'Oliver was apparently seriously pissed off at not being able to flog Meadwell. His inheritance was zilch. But now they say he's a member of the Trust.'

'What's it do, this Trust?'

Juanita perched lightly on the arm of Diane's chair. 'Good works, my child. Worthy things, connected with – and I quote – the Spreading of the Light for the Furtherance of Peace and Harmony in a Troubled World. Does that sound like *The Avalonian* or doesn't it?'

'They'd give you money?'

'For services rendered. Hang on. Stay right there.'

Juanita went through to the shop and unlocked the cabinet where the antiquarian tomes were kept. She returned with a slim, pocket-sized, softbacked book. It had a rather drab, green, cloth cover.

'I may live to regret this, but you're bound to see it sometime.'

You had to hold the book up to the light to make out the wording, in black, on the cover:

GEORGE PIXHILL: THE GLASTONBURY DIARIES.

'Take it,' Juanita said. 'Won't take you long to read. Gets seriously depressing towards the end, but you might find you and the old guy have a certain amount, er, in common.'

145

Meaning an unhealthy obsession with certain aspects of Glastonbury. But at least it would show her where this sort of thing could lead.

Diane held the little book gingerly in both hands, like a child with a first prayer book. 'Why've I never heard of this?'

'Probably because it's only been published a couple of months. And because it's never exactly been advertised. You have to ask for it. Oh, and because this is the only shop that sells it.'

'What?'

Juanita lit a cigarette.

''Bout a year ago, an old buffer called Shepherd – "Major Shepherd, good day to you ma'am" – swans in with this dog-eared manuscript. Wants some advice on publishing it. An absolute innocent. Left the manuscript – the only copy, mind you – left it with me to read. I'm expecting some tedious old war-memoirs, Rommel and Me sort of thing.'

Diane put her knees together, her elbows on her knees and her chin between cupped hands. Juanita stiffened, her memory superimposing a plump schoolgirl with spots from too much comfort chocolate: Diane a dozen years ago when Juanita had given her Dion Fortune's *The Sea Priestess* to read.

Oh God.

'Not Rommel and Me,' Juanita said. 'Although he did serve in the Western Desert with Montgomery.'

Diane nodded eagerly. As if she knew what was coming. Jesus, Juanita thought, she'll see it as another of those portents.

'You probably think I'm pitiful,' Tony Dorrell-Adams said, not for the first time tonight.

'Not at all, my boy.' Jim thought it was best to sound fatherly, this was what he seemed to need. 'Women go through phases. Particularly, erm . . . particularly here, for some reason.'

Actually, he was bloody embarrassed. Chaps flung together in pubs, there were, after all, long-established ground rules about what might safely be discussed. Sport, work, the Government. Women as a species.

Certainly not – not even after four Chivas Regals – your, erm, intimate personal problems.

'She's a completely different person,' Tony Dorrell-Adams said miserably. 'We've been here nearly four months. It's getting worse. It's as if . . . well, as if it isn't me she wants. Not me as an individual. Just the male element. Like . . . like a plug for her socket.'

'Quite,' said Jim gruffly.

'Except she's the one that lights up. Last night . . .' Tony's eyes had a deceptive brightness, suggesting a man who hadn't slept in a long time. 'Last night, after dark, she made me do it in . . . in the window. I mean the shop window.'

Pause for effect. Jim just nodded. Strewth.

'And I . . . I nearly couldn't. You know? I mean, it's against the law, isn't it? In public? Not that anybody was about. Least, I don't *think* so.'

'Oh, you'd have heard.'

'Suppose so. You see, the very reason we came here . . . I'll tell you, shall I?'

'If you think it'll help.' Jim groaned silently.

'It wasn't all that good between us, you see. I'd had a bit of a thing going with another teacher, to be frank. Nothing important, but it left a gulf, as you can imagine. Well, coming here, that was supposed to be a new beginning. In a place that was, you know, blessed. I thought, if we were working together, in a compatible way, things would straighten themselves out. Especially somewhere like this. Somewhere steeped in magic and earth-energy. Somewhere that would *feed* our hearts. They say, you know, that Glastonbury is actually the heart chakra in the great spiritual body of the world.'

'You came here to put your marriage together?'

Jim shook his head in real sorrow. No wonder they were staring at each other across a gap the width of the Severn Estuary.

'Tony, this is the very last place. Yes, it is uniquely spiritual, but that doesn't make it an easy place to live. Quite the reverse. And as for marriages . . . same again, is it?'

He handed Tony a tenner and Tony went for more drinks. Jim leaned back, eyes half-closed. *I'm not like that, am I? I didn't come here expecting anything, surely? I'm just a painter. Came for the mystery.*

He was aware of the bar filling up. One or two locals, but mainly incomers – healers and psychics, artists and musicians – the ones who thought it was OK spiritually to drink alcohol. He saw Archer Ffitch come in, moving discreetly through the bar to sit at a table occupied by Griff Daniel.

'Have you seen our new range, Jim?'

Tony Dorrell-Adams, distinctly unsteady now, placed another Scotch in front of Jim, spilling some.

'I came to see you, old son,' Jim said patiently. 'You remember? I saw all your pottery.'

'*She's* actually the potter. Domini. Glazes are my thing. And design. On-glaze colours, you know? I thought we were becoming compatible at last. You saw my Arthurian range, didn't you?'

'Oh, yes. Very, er . . .'

He'd seen the plaques decorated with knights and ladies and heraldry, Morte D'Arthur manuscript stuff; nothing exciting, but that seemed to be Tony. Nothing too exciting.

'Going bloody well. Quite well. People liked it. And the ley-line stuff I did with Woolly Woolaston. Now we're doing this set of six plates on Joseph of Arimathea. Joseph and the boy Jesus on the Isle of Avalon. Joseph collecting the Blood in the Grail. Planting his staff on Wearyall Hill. Damned collectible. Expensive, but it's a limited edition. That's the way ahead, I think. Limited editions.'

'Indeed.' Jim was bored. He saw Archer Ffitch stand up to leave. Archer turned and smiled at someone who'd probably been congratulating him on his candidacy.

'It's this bloody goddess group,' Tony said, 'the bloody Cauldron. That's what changed everything. All female? You know? She goes twice a week now. It's supposed to be a consciousness-raising thing. Discussion and meditation. But who knows what goes on behind closed doors. Do *you* know?'

Jim shook his head. Never had liked single-sex outfits. Back at the building society he'd resisted all attempts to get him into the Masons, even the buggering Rotary Club.

'And so now she's been poring over pictures of fat, ugly Celtic fertility goddesses and producing these ghastly crude female figurines, sort of Earth-mothers with huge . . . you know . . .'

'Boobs?'

Tony glanced furtively around and then whispered it. 'Vaginas.' He swallowed.

'Who the hell's going to buy those things? I said. Finally, I said it. Tonight. That was all I said – who's going to buy them?'

'Reasonable enough question,' Jim said. Lord, not another range of pot goddesses with giant fannies.

'That's what I thought.' Tony slid close to the wall. 'We have a living to make. I thought it was a reasonable . . . reasonable question. So I asked it. Who's going to buy them? I said. That was it. All I said.'

Tony lifted the bottom of his Guernsey sweater, pulled it up over his stomach.

'Look at this.'

'Good God, man, what are you doing?' Jim inched away in discomfort. Was this a preliminary to what they called 'male bonding'?

'She . . .' Tears forming in the poor chap's eyes, Lord, oh Lord.

'Look, steady on, Tony old chap.'

'. . . She smiled, Jim, and came close . . . snuggling up, you know? Hands inside the jersey, and then . . .'

'Oh my God.' Jim recoiled.

'Like a puma.'

'Look, hadn't you better have those seen to?'

'Savaged me like a puma,' Tony said, displaying livid scratches, six or eight inches long, still half-bleeding.

He began to cry. 'Came here to find love and harmony. And she savages me. Like a puma.'

THREE

PIXHILL

Most people would have flicked through the pages, reading an entry here, an entry there, get the idea of what kind of book it was. Not Diane. Diane had to start on page one.

Juanita watched brown, wavy hair flop over the girl's face as her head bowed over the unappealing book.

Actually, it was quite gripping, the introduction, in its recounting of how Pixhill had first been turned towards Glastonbury, a place he'd hardly heard of.

And even in the introduction Diane would discover one or two parallels, as a young army officer lay in a wrecked tank in the Western Desert in May, 1942 . . .

A full moon, or very near.

I expect I was staring up at the damn thing when it happened, head and shoulders out of the hatch, like a ginger cat I once saw peering out of a dustbin.

Don't actually remember any of what happened immediately before and certainly nothing of the actual impact which, being a direct hit into the body of the Grant, must have been like having your legs shot from under you.

My driver and co-driver, down below there, wouldn't have heard the bang either. They must have died at once. Similarly Corporal Elliman, the gunner, took some chunk of metal, never knew precisely where it came from, into his brain via the left eye, I think it was.

It was Little, Charles Anthony Little, wireless operator, who caused me the most pain. He was the veteran among us at thirty-one, almost a father figure to me, his commander, Capt. Pixhill, twenty-two, and an immature twenty-two to boot, thinking back.

Libya, this was, May twenty-seventh, when Rommel pulled a fast one, the old werewolf rising to the moon and having us cleverly out-flanked. By dawn, the desert around Bir Hacheim was a veritable

150

ocean of metal, but I saw nothing of that. The battle, for me, was a battle with myself, to block out the pain of my smashed legs and the sounds of war and of Charlie Little dying. While, out of the morning sky, the arrogant moon still shone down through the open hatch like some freshly polished medal on a Nazi chest.

What happened, I quickly worked out, having nothing better to do, was that a mounting pin from Elliman's machine gun had flown off when the whole damn thing sprang back with him, and (someone had speculated about the danger of this only a week or so earlier, but Major Collier said it couldn't happen) took poor Little in the throat.

Not much conversation between us, as you can imagine. I remember the poor chap blubbing and gurgling. I remember the smell of cordite and blood and the smoke from a thousand Capstans, the last of them having fallen from Elliman's lips to his chest and burnt a hole through his shirt before expiring. I remember the extraordinary agony in my legs when I tried to reach Little, thinking that if I could pull the damn pin from his neck he'd be able to talk to me. Conversation. All I craved.

I could hardly move at all, so I lay there shivering and entertaining poor Charlie with what must have been a devastatingly tedious monologue about my life thus far and how I had hoped to become a clergyman but was more or less resigned to an obscure career as a history teacher at some minor public school. My uncle William it was, Archdeacon of Liverpool, who had talked me out of the clergy.

The Church, he said dryly, tended to frown on young chaps who 'claimed' to have had encounters with angels.

Well only the one angel, I assured Little. The figure of a kindly chap in cricket whites who first bent over my bed when I was seven and quieted my whooping cough and thereafter was sometimes vaguely discernible at the edges of my vision, when someone close to me had died or the situation looked generally black. Each time the Cricketer came out to bat for me, I would have new energy to pull myself through whatever crisis.

After Little died, with a dispiriting bubbling sound like a wet inner tube with a puncture, I looked around for that reliable old sportsman, wondering if there was room for him in the turret with me, but all I could see out of the corners of my eyes was death and dawn and moonlight, and I thought, this is it, George, not going to come out of this show, are we? Remember thinking, what IS the bloody point? And that even the whooping cough would have been a better death.

I wondered, quite distantly, how long it would take for the Door to close. Knew I had a head injury but had kept my hands away from the cranial region, not wishing to know how serious. I thought that someone would tell my family I had died a hero.

Was this what I had been preserved for? To die a 'hero's death'? To qualify for membership of the Valhalla Club, endless booze and loose women for all eternity?

Mine would be, in fact, an inglorious death: the inexperienced, not to say incompetent junior commander who managed to get all his crew killed first. After all, if I hadn't been halfway through the hatch, sniffing the desert air, I too would have been gone by now. I thought of the Cricketer and I saw him not so much in the image of an angel as some serene, pipe-smoking fool in a Brylcreem advert, and I thought, it's a joke, it's all a damned joke. There is no purpose to life, we can have no control over our individual destinies, there is no 'divine guidance' to be had. And I was, for a sick instant, almost in awe of Hitler, who believed he had been chosen to alter the destiny of the entire human race.

I think it was at that moment that I lost all desire to survive. The Allies, certainly, would be a sight better off without me.

Equally, though, I had no wish to go out gasping and weeping bitter tears on the blood-sticky floor of a Grant tank. And so I wondered how I might pull myself up to the hatch to show my head so that some sharp-eyed Panzer could shoot it off, quick and clean.

I lay for a long time, staring up the circle of smoky blue, at the fading moon like a chipped shilling, and feeling the numbness, a sort of permanent shiver, creeping up my lower body and –

Well, I suppose you will say I fell asleep. You will say I hallucinated or that it was due to the reaction of chemicals in my brain. For that is how we prefer to explain such phenomena in the nineteen-seventies, embarrassed as we are by the term . . . vision.

There was a strange sort of glow in Diane's eyes which Juanita had seen before and found disturbing. Not to say ominous.

'The Cricketer,' Diane said.

'Thought you'd spot that. Bit like your revered nanny, huh? Sits on the edge of the bed with a cool hand on the fevered young brow. Jung would've loved him.'

Diane looked disappointed. 'You're saying this is an archetypal thing. Sort of projected imagination. A child's comfort figure. My ghost, angel, whatever was a good nanny, because all my real nannies were nasty, and Colonel Pixhill's was a cricketer because he was a boy.'

'Something like that. Beats lying awake sucking your thumb, I suppose.'

Diane frowned. 'You've changed. You're ever so cynical now, aren't you?'

'Maybe I've come to my senses. I used to be a mystical snob like the rest, an elitist in a town full of them.'

'What you mean is, you used to be a seeker after some sort of truth,' Diane said primly. 'And now you've stopped searching.'

'If you want to put it like that. All the sects and societies and covens, they all think their particular Path is the True Way and everything else is crap. I've concluded it's safer to start off on the basis that it's all crap.'

'That's just as bigoted, Juanita.'

'Saves a lot of time though, doesn't it?' Juanita pulled her old blue mac from the back of the parlour door. 'Look, I'm off to the pub, see if I can find Jim. You coming?'

'I think I'd rather like to finish reading this.'

'Thought you would. Just remember he died a sad, rather isolated old man, deserted by his wife, stuck in a gloomy farmhouse he couldn't afford to heat and . . . Oh, remember not to open the door for anyone, cream Range Rover or otherwise.'

'I won't. Juanita . . .'

'Mmm?'

Diane held up the book, pointed to the tiny writing at the bottom of the spine, where it said Carey and Frayne.

'And yet you published this.'

Juanita shrugged. 'Well . . . at the Pixhill Trust's expense. A thousand copies, only a few of which have sold since word got round about what was in it. Left to me, there's no way it would have come out looking like that, but the Trust were calling the shots and they wanted dark green, no picture, no blurb, no publicity, no other outlets. It wasn't important if only a few people bought it. It just had to be . . . available.'

'Did they say why? I mean, he's been dead nearly twenty years.'

'"An obligation" was all Major Shepherd said. I imagine the Trust thought there ought to be some sort of memorial to Pixhill. Why they sat on the manuscript for so long I've no idea. I only agreed to get it printed because I felt so sorry for old Shepherd, who wasn't in the best of health. Obviously wanted to get the thing off his hands before he passed on.'

Diane held the little green book between her hands and looked thoughtfully at it. Almost as if she was looking into a mirror, Juanita thought. She hoped Diane would continue to find parallels between Pixhill's alleged visionary experiences and her own. And she hoped, as she let herself out of the shop, that by the end of the book the central message would be clear.

Glastonbury buggers you up.

It was a bright night, the crown of St John's tower icy-sharp. On a night like this, this time of year, there ought to be frost. Why wasn't there frost?

All was quiet, save for the clicking of Juanita's heels. Not even the usual semi-stoned assembly with guitars and hand-drums around the war-memorial. You could sense tonight the nearness of the Abbey ruins, hidden behind the High Street shops.

But surely, Juanita thought, the whole point of Pixhill's book was that he was saying, don't get taken in by this, don't surrender to the vibes.

He'd come here on the back of a vision. Delirious in his tank on May 27, 1942, he'd imagined himself to be lying out on the sand under that same moon, but when he looked up he saw no battle-smoke – indeed it was awesomely silent.

What he saw was a small bump in the sand, a swelling, something that was buried rising again. There was an eruption – quite silent – and then there it was, huge before him in all its mysterious majesty: a green hill in the desert.

A conical green hill with a church on top.

Next thing, Captain Pixhill awakes on a stretcher and within days is on his way back to England for months of operations on his legs. When he can walk again he's given some sort of admin job at the Ministry and ends the War as a full colonel.

By then, he's discovered Glastonbury, convinced it was the Tor he saw in his Libyan vision after coming so very close to losing his life and his Faith. Convinced this is where his future must lie and inspired to learn that this is where the Holy Grail itself is said to have been brought.

And so, after the War, he comes to Glastonbury, marries a local girl, buys an ugly old house and . . .

. . . and what?

As far as Juanita could tell, there was no record of Colonel Thomas George Hendry Pixhill having done anything significant with his life from the moment he arrived to the moment he collapsed with a coronary. He seemed to have moped around the place for thirty years, ingesting the vibes, contemplating the views, tipping his hat politely to every passing female and keeping an occasional diary of, in later years, unremitting pessimism.

For Pixhill, the Holy Grail of his youth had been replaced by the Dark Chalice, presumably a metaphor for an increasingly gloomy world-view. In his last few months he was seeing images of the Dark Chalice everywhere – over the Tor, among the Abbey ruins, above the tower of St John's. Well, he wasn't the only amateur visionary to have gone a bit paranoid towards the end.

'Juanita!' As soon as she entered the pub, Jim was up and beckoning, broad face like an overripe Cox's apple. It was Jim's kind of bar, all wood and stained-glass; he looked like a jolly squire from some eighteenth-century painting. 'Glass of something cold and white, barman, for my friend. Juanita, I was coming to see you. Least, I think I was. Time is it?'

'Time you thought about some black coffee and a sandwich', Juanita said, 'if you're planning to make it home without falling in the ditch.'

He was more than slightly pissed, but at least he was more like the old Battle, and if he waved goodbye to a few more brain cells it would wear away the memory of last night's ordeal all the sooner.

'Had something to tell you, didn't I? The paper. What'd I do with the buggering paper?'

'I think you were sitting on it.' She saw he was not alone. Tony Dorrell-Adams shared his table, looking just as flushed but less convivial.

'Was too. Bit creased, never mind.' Jim retrieved the *Evening Post* from his chair, placed it on the table, spread it out. 'It's Archer Ffitch. In the paper. Archer's been selected as Tory candidate for Mendip South.'

'I know, Jim. It explains a lot. Hello, Tony.'

Tony nodded, couldn't manage a smile, went back to his beer.

'Yes,' blustered Jim, 'but have you seen what the bastard's saying? Wants this town to be efficient, streamlined, hi-tech, have its own branch of Debenhams, no veggie-bars, no crystals, no mystical bookshops . . .'

'This is an exaggeration, right, Jim?'

'. . . no Avalon, no mystery. Wants us, in fact, to be another bland, buggering lay-by on the Euro super-highway.'

'Here, let me read it . . .'

She saw that people were glancing at him, amused. He was one of those official characters who, like Woolly Woolaston, were allowed, not to say expected, to go over the top. She tried to tug the paper from him.

'Never believe a word I say,' Jim grumbled as the *Evening Post* tore in two. Juanita collected the segments together and sat down.

'Now, which page?'

'Just look for a picture of a well-known smug bastard. Hey, that's another thing. He was in here tonight, was Archer, and guess who he left with . . . Juanita, are you listening?'

'Yes, just a minute, Jim.'

Juanita had found another story. Or at least a headline. Or, more precisely, the first word of a headline. It made the hubbub around her recede into mush. The word was 'swastika'.

'I think', Jim was saying from, it sounded like, a long way away, 'that this must be the time for you to think seriously about that scheme of yours for relaunching *The Avalonian*. I can sense dirty work afoot and somebody ought to be saying it. We have to preserve the buggering *mystery*.'

'I don't know.' Juanita, who had glanced through the swastika story, was sure she'd gone pale, just hoped it wouldn't show under the muted pub lights. 'I don't know about that any more.'

FOUR

THE HUNTRESS

'Essentially,' Dr Pel Grainger said, 'we are talking readjustment. Reprogramming the organism to self-regulate photo-sensory input. We're talking . . .'

Dr Grainger moved to the very front of the platform, a portly figure all in black. He breathed in through his nose, abdomen swelling. Then he exhaled languidly and noisily from his mouth, flung his arms wide . . . and all the lights died at once, as if he'd blown them out.

'Penumbratisation,' he said.

Although it was obviously staged, there was an intake of breath from the audience. Verity jumped in her seat before realising, after a fraught second, that this was not Meadwell, but the Assembly Rooms, the alternative Town Hall, centre for esoteric lectures, meeting place for all who sought, in Glastonbury, a new level of Being. At the Assembly Rooms one expected – even hoped for – the unexpected.

'Marvellous,' said Dame Wanda Carlisle. 'Bravo.' But her voice, normally warm and perfectly pitched, sounded strident and intrusive. Nobody else had spoken.

The now-invisible Dr Grainger waited for total silence before continuing.

'If you think that was a shock, my friends, it's nothing compared to the sense of dislocation I guarantee you will feel when we put on the lights again at the end of the session. For those who haven't figured it out yet, *penumbratisation* means permitting our consciousness to merge with the shadows. It is the preliminary to bonding with the dark. Lesson one: learn to *penumbratise.*'

So far, Verity had not been terribly impressed with Dr Pel Grainger (the Pel apparently short for Pelham) not least because of his somewhat theatrical appearance. In his long, black jacket, he resembled the magicians she remembered from children's parties before the War. He had a trim, black beard which contrasted so dramatically with his puffy, pale face that it must surely be dyed.

With the lights extinguished, however, Dr Grainger was in his element, his voice as rich as black coffee, the voice of a hypnotist or one of those evangelical American clergymen. It soothed. It was, Verity thought, a rather dangerous voice.

'You may think that you cannot see me. But the Tenebral Law says you can see me clearer than ever now, without the interference of light. Light itself is random, haphazard, volatile. Artificial light *is* an interference.'

He paused. The little hall was packed, but nobody shuffled or coughed the way they had when the lights were on.

'Only darkness,' intoned the voice of Dr Pel Grainger, 'can connect with our inner being. In tenebral therapy, we learn to locate what I will call the *inner* dark. The darkness inside ourselves . . . about which there are a number of ancient misconceptions.'

Verity tensed.

'People say to me, "but darkness . . . surely we fear the dark because darkness is the oldest metaphor for evil." '

Verity flinched.

'This,' softly now, 'brings us to the oldest misconception of them all. One so endemic in our society that the modern world seeks to cancel the dark. Throughout history, societies have run towards the light because the light is easy. It makes no demands upon us. See, what you have nowadays, people go for south-facing houses, right? They go for plate-glass walls, French-doors, conservatories – they got to open everything to as much light as they can get. Because light makes no demands.'

Verity felt people around her nodding agreement.

'OK, let's deal with evil. The word "evil" is a terse, blanket condemnation of anything it does not suit us to understand. We know that it is essential for the development of the soul to undergo periods of hardship and so-called negativity. We talk of the soul travelling *out of the darkness and into the light*. Therefore, the darkness must be "evil". To that I say . . . bullshit!'

Verity thought of what she'd said to Major Shepherd about the presence of Abbot Whiting exuding evil. Because the lights had gone out? Was that really all it was?

'Let us consider darkness,' said Dr Grainger, 'as a sentient being. As something sensitive and vulnerable. In the States, our cities are so damn bright at night now, you can no longer see the stars. Plus we have high-powered security lamps on our houses, we blast through the night with our headlamps. Instead of melding with the dark, we *brutalise* it.'

As he said this, he snapped his fingers and the house lights came on for a blazing instant before going out again, and Grainger shouted, 'What do you see? Tell me what you see now. Come on, tell me what you see!'

'Big yellow spots,' a man called out.

'Alarming purple circular things,' described Dame Wanda, 'with a sort of spongy core.'

'OK, OK,' Pel Grainger said. 'You've all seen them before, just you didn't know what you were seeing. Well now, I'm gonna tell you. What happened was we blasted the dark with brutal, arti-ficial light, and what you saw, maybe are still seeing . . . are the bruises. Now, you want me to do that again, you want me to hit the darkness one more time?'

'No way, man,' someone behind Verity said nervously, as if Dr Grainger had threatened to hit a child.

'Any of you? Anybody want the light back? Anybody feel happier with a little illumination around here?'

Silence.

'Good,' said Dr Pel Grainger. 'I congratulate you all. You have reached what I term First-stage Tenebral Symbiosis. Now we can begin.'

Verity sat with her fingers linked on her knees and felt some trepidation.

When I awoke in my room at The George and Pilgrims, sunlight had turned the stained glass in my window into a nest of gems and I felt at once a different person. It was the first time since before the War that I had slept the night through and awoken after sunrise. Or, if it was not the first time, then it certainly felt like it.

This was my rebirth. That morning I walked through the Abbey ruins, at first appalled at how little remained and then overcome with a sudden humility and a desire . . . to worship. This was something I had never before experienced; indeed I realised then that I had never really understood the meaning of 'worship'. Before I knew it, I had fallen to my knees, something I had not been able to do since leaving hospital, without the most excruciating pain. This time I felt no pain at all, only a growing sense of wonder.

I do not know how long I knelt there in the wet winter grass, gazing up through the noble arch of the Western Doorway. Even today it is still possible, in Glastonbury, to kneel alone and undisturbed in a wide open public place, although I should not care to predict how long this state of affairs will remain before the worshipper is derided or even attacked and robbed. But it seemed to me then, and sometimes still does, that these serene ruins enclose a level of holiness unexperienced in most of our great surviving cathedrals.

And something else: a sadness, which I perceived then as sweet melancholy but now, it pains me to record, seems closer to a bitter despair.

But I was full of an extraordinary optimism as, later that morning, I made my way to the Chalice Well, where the Blood Spring flows and the Arimathean was said to have laid down the Grail.

There to meet my Teacher and another person: the highly controversial writer and mystic Mr John Cowper Powys.

Mr Powys, it must be said, was not the most popular man in this town at this time, due to the publication before the War of his extremely lengthy novel A Glastonbury Romance. *It is a powerfully volatile tome which had left me with very much mixed feelings. Although its central inspiration is the Holy Grail, the Glastonbury it portrays is far from a sacred haven. Indeed it emerges as a divided community full of 'misfits'. One leading character is an extremely aggressive entrepreneur and there is a young man whose spiritual leanings are challenged by a pretty extreme case of sexual frustration. There is also an unpleasant Welsh pervert of the masochistic type whose peccadilloes are said to have been derived from aspects of Mr Powys's own psychology.*

And so the thought of an encounter with this depraved and opinionated windbag would normally have completely taken the shine off the day. However . . .

*

Diane looked up from Pixhill's diary in alarm. Someone was banging on the shop door.

Don't open the door for anyone, Juanita had warned, cream Range Rover or otherwise. Did she really mean that? Juanita had been a little strange, not only more cynical but seemingly less secure. Rather disturbing; she'd always been such . . . well, such a lovely free spirit, really.

Diane rose hesitantly. It was true that Glastonbury was not as safe as it used to be. Apparently, there'd been a couple of muggings in the past year, while she was away, and a sexual assault, and as for burglaries . . .

She opened the door to the shop just a crack. Through the shop window she could see . . . Oh gosh. A sort of floating thing in white.

'Oh, Diana!' she heard. 'Don't be tedious. I know you're there.'

Oh no. It was that woman, the artist. Domini-Something-Thing.

'Come on, do open the door. I need your help.'

Diane, sighing, went through into the darkened shop. Hadn't she told the woman she was busy tonight? Cautiously, she unlocked the door.

'Oh, Diana, really,' Domini said as though they were old friends. 'It's only me.'

She stepped lightly over the threshold. She was wearing a long, white dress, rather flimsy, a dress for a summer night but she didn't seem at all cold. Too animated. There was a gold-coloured girdle loosely around her waist, a torc of brass around her neck. She looked . . . like a goddess.

'It's Diane,' Diane said. 'Not Diana. Look, I'm terribly sorry . . .'

'Oh,' said Domini. 'You should call yourself Diana, it's more resonant. Diana the huntress.'

'I've never been much of a huntress,' said Diane.

'No. I suppose you haven't.' Domini looked at her with a tilted smile. 'You must be quite strong, though. Hold these, would you?' She reached down behind her to the pavement and came up with a cardboard wine box. 'Be careful, it's rather heavy.'

'Wine?' Diane was bemused, her head still full of the Pixhill diaries.

'Lord, no. Follow me.'

Domini glided diagonally across High Street, paying no heed to a motorcyclist who roared through her path. Behaving as though she was made of air and light and the bike would have passed straight through her.

Diane lumbered behind, clutching the cardboard box to her chest. People had always treated her like a servant. Even servants; her father's staff were always making her fetch mops and garden tools and things.

'Stay precisely there.' Domini had stopped outside her shop, Holy Thorn Ceramics. The window was in darkness. Domini went into the shop and returned with another cardboard wine box.

Diane stared around, blinking; this was like a silly dream. The buildings, the familiar mixture of old and older, glistened and glittered in a Christmas card sort of way, although the night was perhaps too mild for frost. The street was curiously deserted.

'OK, you can put it down now.' Domini dumped her own box on the flagstones and danced back from it as though it was dirty or radioactive or something. A wobbling clatter of crockery echoed in the silence.

Domini dipped delicately into the box and extracted a white disc, holding it up towards a street light like a conjuror demonstrating to the audience.

It was a plate, gold-rimmed with a stained-glass-style painting in the middle, of a bearded man below a towerless Tor with a barefoot boy.

'That's rather charming,' Diane said.

'Think so, do you?' A white sleeve dropped to the shoulder as Domini's arm came back, and she tossed the plate into the night like a frisbee.

'My God, what are you . . .?'

The plate spun in the air for about twenty yards, flashing in the streetlight, before smashing into coloured shards in the road. Domini let out a shrill whoop and shook her golden hair.

'Can you feel it, Diana? Can you feel the vibrations, the energy around us?'

She took out a second plate. The picture in the middle showed a table bearing a golden cup with a shimmering aureole around it. Domini's arm came back again.

'No!' Diane yelled. 'Please . . .'

Domini lowered her arm and looked at her. 'You're right. I'll wait for a car. Or, better still, a heavy lorry.'

'Why are you doing this? Didn't they turn out well or something?'

Domini laughed, a drunk's laugh, but there was no aura of alcohol about her.

'Old stock, Diana. As of tonight. Obsolete. The shop's changing. Holy Thorn Ceramics – that was his idea, too. I know why now, I know the truth about the Thorn. Holy Mother, can't you feel it yet?'

'Yes.' And she could. The night was as sharp as one of the shards of pottery. Everything was hard and clear. There was no wind. The air seemed to fizz.

Domini spread out her arms like a bird feeling the currents. Diane didn't like it. She didn't like the feel of Glastonbury since she'd returned – the unseasonal mildness, summer blight in November. It was as if the weather had been tampered with, the conditions altered for some purpose.

'Look. Don't do this . . . Domini. You'll regret it tomorrow, I know you will.'

'Tomorrow? Darling, I spit on tomorrow. OK, look, if you don't want me to smash them, help me display them. Will you do that, Diana?'

Domini began to take plates out of the box, like a child unpacking toys. She laid each one face-up on the pavement in a line, edging down the hill, dragging the cardboard box behind her.

'Well, what are you waiting for? Take the other box. Come *on*, Diana.'

'They'll get trodden on.'

'Maybe. But if you don't help me I'll tread on them all now.'

'This is mad.'

'Sanest thing I've ever done. Go on, the bending will do you good. You're too fat. What's the matter with you? Don't you walk anywhere? Don't you ever have sex?'

She's out of control. Oh gosh. Humour her. Then get away. Diane carefully took a plate out of the box. It showed the bearded man looking up at Christ on the cross.

'Can you believe it?' Domini said. 'I actually painted this shit.'

'I don't understand.'

'Christianity's a brash, male religion which insults women. If we accept, as I assume we all do, that the so-called Holy Grail is simply an unsubtle Christianisation of the Celtic chalice, the sacred cauldron of our ancient wisdom . . . We do assume that, don't we, Diana?'

'Well . . .'

'In which case, tell me this.' Domini faced her, hands on hips. 'Where does the Bible mention the Grail? Even the Christian propagandists can't seem to agree whether it was some cup from the mythical Last Supper or whether it was the vessel which caught the blood dripping from the cross.'

'Or both.'

'Or neither. It's a myth. It's smoke. The so-called Grail Quest is a clear-cut male-domination trip, an attempt by armed men to steal Woman's cauldron of wisdom and rape her in the process. Just like the raising of the Abbey, with its great phallic towers – no, listen! – by a male-oriented Roman religion on a spot which just happened to be the holy vagina of the supine Goddess.'

'Oh, *really*!' Diane had heard all this before.

'No, come on, think about this . . . The Holy Thorn story, OK? Central character: one Joseph of Arimathea, wealthy merchant, international wheeler-dealer.'

'I think it's a rather lovely story, actually,' Diane said staunchly. 'The old tin trader, who brought Jesus to Avalon as a boy, making that last journey back with the holy cup. It's really . . . resonant. When I'm on Wearyall Hill sometimes I can imagine it all as an island again and old Joseph being helped ashore, a bit unsteady, staggering up the hill with the help of his staff and then, when he can go no farther . . .'

'You really are a big schoolgirl aren't you?' Domini puffed out her cheeks as if she was going to throw up with contempt. 'Isn't it obvious? Sticking his staff into the ground . . . pulling out his . . . staff . . . and he pushes it into a sacred landscape formed into the contours of the body of the Goddess. This man Joseph symbolically *fucks* the Goddess . . .'

'No!' Diane was appalled. 'How can you . . .?'

'And his seed, Diana . . . his foul seed germinates into a misshapen, stunted tree full of vicious thorns. A tree which flowers in the dead of winter against . . .'

'Oh now, look . . .'

'Against all the laws of nature! That's the sick truth behind your pretty little legend. And that's why I could no longer bear to be fronting a business called Holy Thorn Ceramics alongside an idiot who thinks it's all sooooo romantic.'

Domini snatched the plate from Diane's hands, laid it carefully on a flagstone.

'If that's your idea of art you must be stupider than you look.'

Domini jumped on the plate with both feet. A middle-aged man and a woman holding hands, the first sign of normal life since this episode began, crossed the street to avoid them. 'Excuse me . . .' Diane shouted, but they ignored her and only walked faster.

'Don't be such a wimp.' Domini took two plates and clapped them together in the air like cymbals. Her brittle laughter exploded with the pottery.

FIVE

GODDESS

SWASTIKA CLUE . . . The evening paper was on the table next to Juanita's wineglass, folded through the headline.

Juanita had drunk three glasses of house white and hardly noticed them go down. Jim was chuntering on about preserving the mystery.

The paper had revealed another mystery. The police were investigating it. Juanita wished to God Tony Dorrell-Adams would drink up and go so she could discuss this development with Jim, decide what they were going to do. But Tony just slumped in his chair; whatever he'd been telling Jim earlier, he wasn't going to talk about it with Juanita around.

'It's like the Holy Grail,' Jim said. 'If somebody dug up an ancient cup under the Chalice Well and it was proved to be the actual Grail the whole thing would be diminished, reduced to another sterile antique in a glass case. There'd be no buggering *mystery*.'

'Bullshit, sir,' roared a voice from behind. 'The discovery of that Holy Grail would be the best thing as could happen to this town.'

Oh hell, Griff Daniel. Juanita looked up, throwing a defensive arm over the paper. Just what they could do without.

And a reborn Griff Daniel, it seemed. The last time she'd seen him he'd been grim-faced, his grey and white beard bedraggled, his eyes full of sour suspicion. Looking, in fact, exactly like a bent builder who'd lost his seat on the council to a hippy. Now, grinning savagely through a freshly trimmed beard, he'd virtually erupted at their table.

'Now you just imagine, Mr Battle, if we had that bloody Grail banged up in a glass case. No more weirdos with dowsing sticks claimin' they knew where it was buried. No more lunatics having visions of the thing and sayin' they'd been singled out by the Lord. No more bloody speculation. No more room for dreamers and nutcases. Think what that would do for this town.'

'Make it exceedingly bloody boring,' said Jim.

'Ah.' Griff accepted a pint of Guinness from the barman and paid. 'Now that's where we differ, Mr Battle. You look like a regular sort with a decent haircut, but behind it all you're still an immigrant. One o' them.'

'Listen, buster,' Jim said mildly, 'I'll have you know I'm not one of *them* or one of you either. There are a few buggering individuals left.'

'In this town, Mr Battle, there's only two sides: locals and hippies. Even if some of 'em does wear jackets and tweed hats and is old enough to know better.'

Juanita saw Jim tense at the mention of his hat.

'What gets me, look . . .' Griff burrowed into his pint and emerged with froth spiked in his beard like cotton buds, '. . . is they d' think they got somethin' to show us 'bout how to live our lives. By God, I wouldn't live like that if it . . .'

'They think', Jim said, 'that if they're living here, something will help them to become better people. That it's easier to be a better person here because of a spiritual atmosphere to which you appear to be oblivious.'

'Spiritual!' Griff's tankard connected decisively with a beer-mat. 'Bullshit, mister. You tellin' me we didn't have our abbey an' our bit of tourism 'fore they come flooding the town with their cranky fads?'

'That's not what I'm saying at all, and you . . .'

'And didn't we used to have a proper town centre back then, with real shops sellin' stuff ordinary folk wanted to buy? And wasn't our property prices on a par with Somerton and Castle Cary if not better? And did people laugh at us in them days? No, mister, they did not.'

'What days?' said Jim irritably. 'There's always been an alternative community in Glastonbury. If you go back to the twenties and thirties – Dion Fortune at Chalice Orchard. And then Cowper Powys wrote that enormous novel . . .'

'Gah,' said Griff. 'Filthy bastard. Bloody ole pervert. Never showed his face here after that come out, 'cordin' to my ole dad.' He finished his Guinness with a flourish. 'But I'll tell you what's behind all this, mister. That bloody hill. Brings out the hippies with their weird ceremonies and such. Pulls 'em in like a kiddies' playground. Take that thing away and what you got is an ordinary, decent country town with a ruined abbey.'

'But you *can't* take it away,' Jim said patiently. 'You're stuck with it.'

'No you can't, that's true.' A gleam arrived in Griff's foxy eyes and a little smile crawled out of his beard. 'But you can keep *them* away. You can make that nasty little hill into as near as dammit a no-go area. If you goes about it right.'

'Got a plan, have we, Mr Daniel?'

'Ah. Well. You could say that. You could indeed.' Griff Daniel stood up, looking smugly secretive. 'Glastonbury first, Mr Battle. *Glastonbury First!*'

'I'm sorry.' Tony Dorrell-Adams rose unsteadily to his feet. 'I didn't come here to listen to an argument.' He pushed past Griff towards the door. 'Not what this town should be about.'

'Who the hell's he to know what the bloody town should be about?' Griff dropped into Tony's seat.

'Just a dreamer,' Jim said sadly. 'Just a nutcase.'

'Aye, well,' said Griff, 'I got to say I'd hoped for better from you, Mr Battle. I knows you're a bit of an artist an' that, but . . . You're very quiet tonight, Mrs Carey.'

'And you', she said, 'are looking unusually buoyant, Mr Daniel.' He'd once made a pass at her when she and Danny had ventured down to the Rifleman's Arms and had a row and Danny had walked out. Griff evidently assuming, prior to getting his face slapped, that ex-hippies had few morals and no taste.

'I'll say this, lady.' Griff wagged a bloated forefinger. 'I'll say this an' no more. There's a change on its way. An' when it comes we're gonner have 'em out. Every phoney healer. Every fortune-telling charlatan. Every last cranky cult-follower. Run out of town, with their bloody jazz sticks up their arses. So them that's old enough to know better maybe oughter be thinkin' which side you're really on. 'Cause from now on, my friends, it's gonner be Glastonbury First.'

He beamed at them, smugly.

'It's, erm, joss sticks,' Jim said.

'What?'

'You said "jazz sticks".'

'Gah!' Griff Daniel pushed back his chair and slouched off in search of more malleable company. After a few moments he turned on his heel, raised a hand to the barman and went out.

'Oh my Gods! It's him. He's coming. Quick! Mustn't let him see us. Where can we go?'

'Into the bookshop.' Diane pulled out her keys, seizing the opportunity to get the crazy woman off the street. Inside, she steered Domini into the back parlour and flung a log into the stove.

'Energy.' Domini pulled at her hair. 'I had to use the energy. The spore's in the air. Now or never, Diana.'

She'd left a trail of coloured plates perhaps a hundred yards long from The George and Pilgrims to the door of Holy Thorn Ceramics. Except it wasn't Holy Thorn Ceramics any more. Domini had gone into the shop and switched on the lights in the window.

The lights were purple now. They spotlit a crudely repellent squatting earthenware woman with a hole between her legs the size of a chimney pot. Around her lumpen head with its jagged grin was a wreath of brambles.

'No more Holy Thorn!' Domini had screeched. 'The Goddess lives here now. The Goddess *lives*!'

'Tea, I think,' Diane said.

'No wine?'

'The last thing you need is wine.'

She'd half expected Domini would suddenly collapse into tears, shattered by the realisation of what she'd done while carried away on this dangerous overflow of energy.

But the golden woman had slipped gracefully into the rocking chair, crossing her legs, the diaphanous white dress gliding back along her thighs.

Diane put the kettle on. 'This is really ever so silly, you know. It's not incompatible at all.'

'That's what I thought at first,' Domini said. 'I became aware of the need for a religion, and this was the only really English one. I mean, all that stuff about Israel – the Holy Land. Well it never seemed very holy to me, all these Jews and Arabs killing each other. This was my holy land. England. I mean, why not?'

She stretched her neck, leaned her golden head into the spindly back of the rocking chair. At least some of the hyper-urgency had gone out of her. She was like a racehorse steaming in the winners' enclosure.

'That hymn, I suppose, turned me on to it, when I was at school. *And did those feet in ancient times* . . .? All those lovely lines, the *bow of burning gold* . . . Wonderful. Until you get to the last bit.'

'Till we have built Jerusalem . . .'

'Exactly. If you've got a green and pleasant land why deface it with a filthy warren full of Arab muggers? Anyway, our religion's so much older than theirs. They'd heard about this legendary holy island in the West with the power to transform people's lives, a place where you could walk with the spirits, and they wanted a piece of the action. Simple as that.'

A ragged voice came from the street.

'Where are you, you heartless, evil bitch?'

'Ah.' Domini didn't move. 'Tony seems to have found one of his plates.'

There was a ringing silence. Then a long wail of pure, cold anguish from the street. As if the man out there had suddenly taken a knife deep into his stomach.

And then a window shattered.

'Something afoot,' Jim said. 'Something involving Daniel and Archer Ffitch. You hear what he said? Glastonbury First. You see, that's Archer's new slogan. It's all in here . . .'

He fumbled at the paper. Totally ignoring the swastika story, Juanita noticed.

'Can Archer Ffitch afford to lose that much credibility?' she wondered.

'Don't underrate that man.'

'Which of them do you mean?' Juanita got up. 'Same again?'

'Either. Both. Stay there, sit down, I'll get them. I owe you more than a few drinks.'

'You don't owe me a thing.' But he'd already gathered up their glasses.

While he was at the bar, Juanita took the opportunity to open out the evening paper. The headline was no less shocking.

Swastika Clue in Bus Body Mystery

New-Age travellers all over the West were being questioned by detectives today following the discovery of a man's body in an abandoned 'hippy' bus.

The dead man, believed to have head injuries, was found inside the vehicle early this morning by a woman walking her dog in woodland at Stoke St Michael near Shepton Mallett.

Police say the battered black bus had false number plates and no road fund licence, and describe the death as suspicious.

Their only clue to the identity of the man, said to be aged 19 or 20, is a distinctive swastika symbol tattooed on the top of his head.

Avon and Somerset police are appealing for anyone who might have seen the man or the bus . . .

Juanita could still hear Diane in the back of the Volvo, trying to persuade them to go back to Moulder's field. *He might look like a hardcase, with the swastika on his head and everything* . . .

She and Jim hadn't been close enough to the boy to see that kind of detail, and presumably Jim hadn't heard or had forgotten what Diane had said in the car. Either way, he didn't know and, sooner or later, she was going to have to tell him.

Jim put down Juanita's fourth glass of wine. She thanked him and swallowed half of it. Jim looked at her with concern.

'Sorry,' Juanita said absently. She was still trying to get her head around the possibility that Rankin was a murderer and Lord Pennard an accessory.

'Sometimes delayed shock is even worse, you know,' Jim said. 'You were very strong last night. Me, I couldn't sleep, with or without the booze. But I've learned my lesson. I'm feeling better now. I think anger helps, don't you? Archer and his evil plans, Griff Daniel . . .'

Juanita looked at him and thought, quite calmly, We could stop him. If you swallowed your pride and we went to the police and implicated Rankin and Pennard in this boy's death; even if they got away with it, the scandal would touch Archer. Archer would have to resign the candidacy.

When she was younger the idea would have excited her. The adrenalin would have drowned all Jim's objections, carried the pair of them all the way to the police station at Street. Or to the Press.

When she was younger.

Juanita gripped the base of her glass to prevent her throwing back the rest of the wine. And to prevent her hand from shaking. The noise of the pub swelled and deflated around her, a dozen conversations boiled together, the way it was when you were very drunk. *Was* she drunk?

Just jittery ... OK, frightened. Frightened of jumping to the wrong conclusions. Frightened at the way everything was going out of control.

She was aware that Jim was looking steadily at her, his honest eyes unmoving in his honest, English-apple face.

It was a look she'd seen before, but never quite so obviously in the face of Jim Battle, sixty-three, a friend, a good friend in the best, the old-fashioned sense.

'Juanita ...' His voice coming towards her along a very circuitous route. 'I'm ... very fond of you, you must know that. *Very* fond.'

'Jim ...' He was drunk. He didn't know what he was saying. She had to stop him. Not here, not now, not ...

Not ever. How could she say that to him, her best friend? Her best friend.

'I mean ...' There was sweat on his forehead. 'That is, I don't have any illusions, of course, that ...'

Please God ...

It was, ironically, Griff Daniel who saved her. And saved Jim, probably. Griff back already, half-grinning, half-scowling. Making an explosive arrival at the bar.

'Bloody hippies. Bloody mad bastards!'

Everybody heard him, everybody turned. Griff ordered another pint of Guinness.

'Bloody drugs, it is. Sends 'em out their minds. One minute they're almost rational, the next ...'

'What they done, then, Griff?' somebody called out. 'Sprayed your ole truck luminous pink?'

There was laughter. Griff Daniel took delivery of his pint of Guinness, took his time about swallowing some. Knowing he had an audience, he composed himself.

'You wanner know what they done, you go out and see for yourselves.'

SIX

FLICKERING

It was like a street party, like New Year's Eve, the atmosphere weirdly electric, lights shining out of shop windows and from the windows of the flats over the shops. More people than there'd been in the bar, maybe a hundred among the wreckage on High Street, many of them wandering into the road because of the sparsity of traffic so late at night.

The colourful, otherworldly folk of Glastonbury's thriving New Age Quarter: mystics, psychics, healers and dealers in crystals and tarot cards. Under the utility streetlamps, didn't they all look so depressingly ordinary?

Juanita shook her head to clear it. Where the hell were the police? Always the same in a Glastonbury crisis: half a dozen trauma-counsellors, but nobody to redirect the traffic.

Tony Dorrell-Adams sat on the bench outside the darkened veggie-bar. He was sobbing quietly. One of his arms was being held up, as though he'd won a boxing bout, by a man with a white medical bag. Blood was oozing from a limp hand. A small circle of watchers kept a half-fascinated aloofness, like mourners around a distant relative's grave.

About five shop windows had been smashed. The veggiebar had come off worst, with a crack three feet long in its main window, a spiderwebbed hole at the end nearest the frame.

'What happened, Juanita?' Councillor Woolly came to stand next to her in the doorway of an antiques shop. Woolly's own shop (archaic string instruments) was safely tucked away in Benedict Street.

'All I know', Juanita said, 'is that when Tony left the pub he was not in an awfully good mood. And not entirely sober. What I gather is that he found a few dozen of his newly glazed picture-plates scattered in some sort of weird formation all over the pavement.'

'His plates?'

'Yep. The fair Domini disposing of them, apparently. In a fairly imaginative, if cruel, fashion. I wouldn't claim to understand. I think she's one trump short of a Major Arcana, as we mystics say.'

Making light of it, but she was shocked. Her voice was hoarse, as if there wasn't enough oxygen. There was something wrong with tonight.

'What sort of plates?' Woolly looked worried.

Juanita pulled a segment from her mac pocket. 'Here's one I rescued earlier. Sort of.'

Woolly stared at the picture of half a church on half a hill. ''Tis Burrowbridge Mump.' When he looked up he was almost in tears. 'These're *our* plates. I been working with this guy, working out earth-mysteries themes. We done this series on the St Michael Line, all the churches and Abbeys and stones and stuff. Set of ten, boxed. Jesus . . . I mean, why? Why the fuck she have to do that?'

'Possibly a statement about the aesthetic and spiritual validity of Tony's art,' Juanita said dryly. Her mouth was so parched she could hardly finish the sentence. She coughed. 'And she seems to have other ideas for the window.'

Nodding across the street to the crudely fashioned, unspeakably ugly female form, unsubtly spotlit in purple, with what looked like the entrance to a railway tunnel between its spread thighs. The window was cracked but intact.

'Sheesh, that's really gross,' said Woolly. 'No wonder the poor bastard lost his cool.'

'He didn't need to start hurling his works of art at everybody else's windows, though. Must be fifteen or twenty panes gone.'

Who would pay? The Alternative Community was already withdrawing into itself. Juanita supposed repair bills would be settled quietly. She supposed she'd have her corner pane quietly replaced without seeking recompense from either the Dorrell-Adamses or the insurance company. As would most of the other New Age shopkeepers. Covering up, because this sort of incident just did not happen in sacred Glastonbury.

No wonder Griff Daniel had looked so happy.

Woolly shook his head in sorrow. 'We had this whole range planned. My knowledge, Tony's artwork. Good team, eh? I work out the concept, he makes 'em, she dumps 'em in the street, he smashes 'em. Gotter be a philosophical message there somewhere.'

'The message', said Juanita, 'is Glastonbury buggers you up.'

'Pixhill,' Woolly said. 'Don't you go quoting Pixhill at me, Juanita. You'll have me all paranoid again.'

'How do you mean?' Juanita asked, but Woolly had spotted Tony.

'What's he done to himself?'

'Cut his hand on a shard of pot. That – what's-his-name, Matthew, the herbalist guy – is sedating him the Natural way and anointing his wound with cowslip syrup or something.'

'This is a real downer,' said Woolly, the only living local councillor to specialise in understatement. *A downer.* Christ, it showed how basically rickety the whole community-structure was.

If Tony Dorrell-Adams, a steady, middle-class, terribly boring ex-teacher from the Home Counties, could behave like this, what did it say about some of the others?

She wondered where Jim was, turned to look for him.

It was strange: just turning around, just moving made her want to go on moving. There was something . . . a tingle in the air, an underlying vibration that was horribly exhilarating. The shock-waves had broken the Blight. People's bodies were flexing as they moved about, the way they might emerging into a bright spring morning.

Something not at all right about this.

A single, undamaged plate with a glowing cup glazed upon it, rolled, as if from nowhere, on end down the pavement and fell flat at Juanita's feet. It seemed awesomely symbolic, like the most innocuous things did when you were on acid.

There was a moment of charged-up silence, the plate wobbling on the flagstones. Juanita had time to think, *This is Glastonbury, buggering us up . . .*

. . . before it all began again.

She heard someone shout, 'Hold him!' as Tony Dorrell-Adams struggled to his feet, scattering the herbalist's bottled preparations and screaming,

'Biiiiiiitch!'

The scream seemed to splatter the white walls above the shops opposite like a gob of spit, and Georgian windows rattled with its agony. The air was alive, fizzing like soda. The streetlamps were flickering, one crackling – as though Tony's scream had hit an electrical current and caused a short-circuit or something.

Tony sank to his knees, sobs coming out of him like ghastly, amplified hiccups. 'I want to die . . . Just want to kill that bitch and die.'

Poor old Tony. One night he's humping his wife in the shop window, like this was Hamburg or Amsterdam, and the next . . . well, this was how domestic murders happened, one of the classic scenarios: you mock a man's prowess, his skills, it's like trampling his balls.

Juanita's tongue found the swelling on her lower lip, where the pilgrim had punched her and it all muscled in on her, everything that had happened in the past twenty-four hours: small events in the great scheme of things – petty violence and humiliation and the unexplained death of a social reject Diane called Headlice.

Diane . . .

Where the hell was Diane? Who should have been padding around this bizarre street-scape, wide-eyed and worried and exuding that doe-like innocence.

'Oh my God . . .' On a night like this, she'd forgotten about Diane. Snatching out her key, Juanita ran for the door of Carey and Frayne.

'*Do it*,' Wanda Carlisle urged. 'You won't get another opportunity like this.'

'I can't,' said Verity, 'I really can't.'

'He can help you.'

'It isn't my *place* to seek help.'

'You really are a martyr.' Wanda swept her black and white chequered cape stiffly across her shoulder. 'And you know what happens to them.'

The hall had nearly emptied. Only half the usual lights were on but it seemed to Verity that most people would have been happy to grope their way out in complete darkness. They had discovered an exciting new environment. Within it, they had meditated, they had touched each other's features the way blind people did, reinventing themselves and their partners by discovering what Dr Pel Grainger had identified as their 'shadow selves'. There had been some very effective visualisation exercises and it seemed that everyone's world-view had, for tonight at least, been subtly altered.

Verity had been aware, at one stage, of someone coming in and muttering about some problem on the street, and one person – she thought it was Councillor Woolaston – had left quietly. But the interruption had been soon forgotten as Dr Grainger's audience moved towards First-stage Tenebral Symbiosis.

Now Dr Grainger was sitting on the edge of the platform talking to a couple who'd stayed behind. 'Why, sure,' he was saying nonchalantly. 'Just take out the bulbs first then you won't be tempted to rush for the switches.'

'Let's go,' said Verity. Who, precisely *because* it had all been so seductive, was wishing she hadn't come. Dr Grainger was a very persuasive person, especially in the dark, but there was darkness and darkness, and she couldn't help feeling that Meadwell's dark was not the kind one might 'bond' with.

'Fine,' said Dr Grainger. 'Good luck.' He raised a hand to the departing couple, slipped down from the platform, and then – to Verity's horror – Dame Wanda was upon him.

She didn't bother to introduce herself, assuming, as she assumed with everyone, that he would recognise her and be flattered by her attention.

'Dr Grainger, I should like you to meet a friend of mine who is, desperately, *desperately* in need of your help.'

The man in black smiled patiently.

Verity backed away. 'Oh no, really . . .'

'Verity, do not dare move.' Wanda turned again to Dr Pel Grainger and said apologetically, 'I am afraid my friend needs saving from herself.'

From where Jim stood, leaning on his bike, the lights of Glastonbury were too bright tonight, harsh with instability. At the tree-hung entrance to Wellhouse Lane, he paused, feeling cold without his overcoat. Without his hat.

Go on. It'll be all right after the first few hundred yards. There's nothing to be afraid of. They've gone. The travellers have all gone.

Never thought this would happen to him. Never thought he could feel fear in this place of ancient spirit.

But there was nothing to be brave for now. Not any more.

He kept thinking back to yesterday – only yesterday, it seemed like another life, another incarnation – when he was sitting in Juanita's parlour, looking through his Laphroaig (the colour of dusk) at the woman whose skin was like the warmest, softest dusk you could imagine.

There was so much hope then. Well, not really, but you could kid yourself. You could believe in miracles.

And now there was no hope, and he had only himself to blame, doing what he'd always sworn to himself he would never do (stick to the banter, keep it light, never, never let her know for sure).

His hands felt clammy on the rubber of the handlebars. He'd seen what had happened in High Street, briefly assessed the situation – wouldn't have raised an eyebrow in Bristol – and edged quietly out of the picture. Hated rubberneckers and voyeurs and all this counselling nonsense. You should never interfere in people's private tragedies.

Private tragedy.

His own had come in the very second that Griff Daniel had burst back into the bar to spread the good news about the man smashing the windows of the hippy shops.

He hadn't meant this to happen. Hadn't come out tonight with the least intention of making a suicide flight.

But something had got to him. Something – whatever had made Griff Daniel so manic – set Jim off.

He'd been watching Juanita's eyes so closely. He knew precisely what he was doing, feeling strangely detached – in reality, probably as unstable as young Tony. And he knew that she knew where it was leading: Jim Battle burning all his boats, with a ninety-nine to one chance of total annihilation.

But that one per cent. The intoxication of running a wild, death-or-glory bet, the odds almost too high, for she was so beautiful and he was nearly twenty years older, twenty buggering years, and never had been what you'd call much of a catch, as bloody Pat would point out every other week.

Juanita, Juanita.

If he'd been a knight he'd have swum the moat for her, scaled the buggering tower. If he'd been a young man he'd have simply swung her on to the back of his bike and pedalled for the border. If he'd been a dog, he'd have lain down at her feet, rolled over and wagged his tail.

Better to be a dog than poor, buggering Jim Battle. Better a dog and get the occasional tickle, have his fur brushed.

He pushed his bike past the last house in Wellhouse Lane. The Tor was on his right. Somewhere. He couldn't see the bastard thing. Maybe – God forgive him for even considering this – maybe Griff Daniel was right about the weird little hill, the hill of dreams, the hill of obsession. Maybe they'd all be better off without it.

And he would rather . . .

Jim swallowed this thought and went on pushing, feeling cold sweat in the small of his back, as though he was leaking like an old and rusting sump. Listening to the tick, tick of his bike chain, following the bleary beam of his battery-powered bike lamp.

Only the mystery. Only the mystery could save him now.

And yet mystery could betray you. He remembered the heat of bodies around him, the strength of the hands holding him down, exposing his throat. And he would rather . . .

Jim squeezed his eyes shut, trying so hard to summon the dusk, bring the old mellow warmth into his chilled, sagging body. No good. It wouldn't come.

He would rather . . .

. . . rather have had that moon-bright sickle slice slowly through the skin and the sinew and the bones of his neck than to have seen the quick flickering of relief in Juanita's eyes when Griff Daniel burst into the bar.

SEVEN

SYNCHRONICITY

Don Moulder had been up late doing his VAT return, last minute as usual, and it was while he was locking up for the night that he heard it.

Would've figured it was no more than his imagination – doing his VAT always made him a bit paranoid about people coming after him – if both sheepdogs hadn't heard it as well and started to whimper.

'Lord preserve us,' muttered Don Moulder.

It came again: the echoey groaning and grinding of a clapped-out old gearbox, some distance off. One of the dogs crept between Don's legs. 'Oh aye, that's right,' Don growled. 'You go'n hide yourself, bloody ole coward.'

When Shep joined Prince under the table, Don scowled at them and went to the boot cupboard where he kept the twelve-bore. 'Got to protect me own stock, then?' He glanced up at the plaster between the beams. 'Forgive me, Lord, but I knows not of a better way to deal with these devils.'

Don decided to say nothing to the missus, who'd been in bed an hour and was most likely well asleep by now. Shots'd wake her, mind, if it came to that.

Warning shots only, more's the pity. You blasted away at the beggars these days, professional rustlers or not, and they'd be straight down the police station, figuring to nobble a God-fearing farmer for damages, due to the trauma they'd suffered. Bloody ridiculous; got so's a man couldn't defend his own property no more. Well, Don Moulder played by the old rules: thou shalt not pinch thy neighbour's ox, nor his ass nor his best Suffolk ram, and if thou triest it thou gets what's coming to thee, mister, and no mistake.

Shrugging on his old Barbour, Don let himself out. He was half-way across the yard, gun under an arm, lamp in hand but switched off, when he had another thought.

Knackered ole gearbox noise. Lord, suppose it's . . . Them . . .?
They'd paid him for three, four nights – via the Hon. Diane, bless her – then cleared off halfway through the first. All right, their decision, no pressure from Don Moulder. But what if they'd come back to claim the rest of their time? How did he stand there? Hadn't given 'em no money back, not a penny; still he hadn't been asked, and there was nothing on paper.

So what you did was you brazened it out. Only Godless hippies, they got no rights. And Miss Diane, nice enough girl but a few bales short of a full barn, so no problems there.

Don Moulder shouldered his gun like Davy Crockett and followed the hedge towards the bottom field.

The lights were still out in the shop when the door opened before Juanita could even get her key in the lock and Diane hissed, 'Quick,' and pulled her inside. She was so glad to find Diane still on the premises that she didn't say a word until she arrived in the parlour and discovered the source of all the night's excitement sitting coolly in her rocking chair looking like Arthur Rackham's idea of a page-three girl.

'Oh,' Domini said. 'Hello, sister.'

'Bloody hell.' Juanita stood in the doorway. 'You've got a nerve.'

'I was in need of sanctuary and Diana took me in.'

'Diane,' said Diane.

Juanita said to Diane, 'Is she pissed or what?'

'I certainly am not. If you must try to explain everything, I think I'm probably in a state of heightened consciousness.'

'While your husband', said Juanita sweetly, 'is in a state of heightened stress, heightened bewilderment and heightened likelihood of being nicked for criminal damage. Plus he's cut his hand rather badly breaking somebody's window.'

Domini sniffed. 'Not a *terribly* inventive response, all told. But not bad for a boring little turd of a primary school teacher.' She uncrossed her legs and sat up. 'Hey, come on, this is what it's all about, Juanita. Change. No, don't look at me like that. This is what Avalon does for us. Challenges all our preconceptions. Forces us to change.'

'Get her out of here,' Juanita said wearily.

'Oh,' said Domini. 'It was different for you then, was it?'

'What?'

'When you threw *your* man out. When Carey and Frayne lost its Frayne.'

Diane said, 'That's not awfully fair . . .'

And then the phone rang.

'Excuse me,' Juanita said. Perhaps it was Jim. Perhaps he'd gone straight home. She hoped it was Jim. 'I'll take it upstairs.'

Juanita's sitting room was directly above the shop and overlooked High Street. It appeared much quieter down there now. Nobody seemed to have called the police. She could see a light on over the restyled Holy Thorn Ceramics. Tony must have gone home. Well, there was no room for bloody Domini to sleep here.

She picked up the phone from the windowsill. 'Hello, Carey and Frayne.'

All she could hear was some awful wheezing. Oh please, not a breather.

Through the window, she saw a large group of people drifting up the street from the Assembly Rooms where this utter dickhead Pel Grainger had been promoting his tenebral therapy. He'd been in the shop a couple of weeks back, suggesting she should place a major order for his forthcoming book, *Embracing the Dark*. Maybe she should, if he'd pulled a crowd that size.

'Mrs Carey?' A man. Not Jim. She was sorry. If Jim had been about to say tonight what she'd thought he was about to say, then they really needed to talk. Not in a pub.

Poor Jim. With his bikes and his brushes and all those paintings he was going to sell one day when he'd found his Grail. Poor buggering Jim, who she'd thought was just a Really Good Friend. Perhaps no man ever wanted to be just her friend; was that a compliment at her age?

'Sorry,' she said into the phone. 'Yes, it's me.'

'Mrs Carey, I'm so sorry, I'm afraid I'm not awfully well. Little short of breath. It's Timothy Shepherd. From the Pixhill Trust. Terribly sorry to telephone so late, I did try earlier but there was no reply.'

'I've been out. Sorry. No problem, Major.'

'You sound as if there is.'

'Do I?'

'You sound a little stressed.'

'Sorry. It's nothing. Nothing really. Look, Major, if you're ring-ing to see how the book's selling, I'm afraid not very well at all.'

Major Shepherd went into a prolonged coughing fit. God, what was the matter with him? Not just flu, that was for sure.

'Don't worry about the book,' he said eventually. 'Mrs Carey, I should like to see you, but I'm afraid I'm in no condition to travel to Glastonbury. Would it be possible for you to come up here?'

'To Cirencester?'

'I wouldn't presume upon your valuable time if I didn't think it was of some considerable importance. Could you come tomorrow?'

She thought about tomorrow's already-unnerving agenda. Jim to sort out, with extreme tact and delicacy. And the problem of the swastika boy. Should she urge Diane to tell the police what she knew?

'Major, quite honestly, tomorrow could be a problem.'

'Will you try?'

'I really don't think . . .'

'Friday, then. I beg you to try, Mrs Carey.'

'Is there a particular problem? About the book?'

'Forget the damn book.' She could hear his voice going into a wheeze, and a woman in the background, exasperated, *God's sake, Tim* . . .

'Major, do you think I could call you back tomorrow evening?'

'Look, Mrs Carey . . . All *right*, Rosemary . . . I'm sorry. Mrs Carey, how can I approach this with you? There are things you don't know. Parts of the diary we couldn't print for legal reasons. Elements of George Pixhill's past which have a bearing on what I . . . what I understand is beginning to happen in Glastonbury.'

Bloody Pixhill, Juanita thought. I wish I'd never heard of bloody Pixhill.

'All right,' she said. 'I'll come on Friday.'

'Thank you,' said Major Shepherd slowly. 'Bless you, Mrs Carey.' He said it in a peculiar way, as though it was an actual benediction.

'A pleasure,' Juanita said, strained. Through the window, she saw two women walking up the street; one was Dame Wanda Carlisle.

'And please,' the Major said, 'please don't let me down. Verity Endicott can no longer deal with this alone.'

She watched the two women pass under the window, Dame Wanda Carlisle flamboyant in a cape and – talk of the devil – Verity Endicott a pace behind, like a little chihuahua. Synchronicity.

Juanita hated synchronicity. She stood there holding the phone, pushing back the metal aerial. The button at its tip was missing and she kept pushing the point into her palm, to experience the reality of pain. More mystery. I don't *need* any more flaming mystery.

'Major, how does Verity Endicott come into this?'

She saw a man in a cap and a belted raincoat crossing the road towards the bookshop.

'Goodnight, Mrs Carey.' As though he hadn't heard.

'Major Shepherd . . .'

The man in the raincoat reached the kerb and pulled off his cap. Coils of thick grey hair tumbled out. It wasn't a man at all.

'Oh shit,' Juanita said.

Ceridwen.

Don Moulder could never approach that bottom field now without a feeling of resentment.

It was well out of sight of the farmhouse. Bloody perfect, it was: gently sloping, easy access from the road, magnificent views to the Tor.

Ideal for housing. Also, the only field he'd hardly notice if it had gone. When the snooty beggars at the council had turned the plan down, Don reckoned this was because Griff Daniel was involved and now he'd lost his seat the planners were putting the boot in. Seemed like the only way to get the scheme through now was to get Griff back on the council.

Don slowed up, gun pointing downwards now. No lights down there. Nothing.

Crafty devils.

Griff Daniel had been round earlier with a roll of posters for Don to stick on his fences, on telegraph and electric poles, trees. The posters said: GLASTONBURY FIRST.

All would be clear very soon, Griff had said.

What was in the bottom field was not clear at all. Even though there was a bit of a moon, so he didn't need his hand-lamp yet.

There was something – he could sense that, the way you could sense whether there was livestock in a meadow in the dark. Although, when Don put out a hand to the five-barred gate, he found the old length of electric wire still looped around the posts, and they *never* closed gates behind them, didn't hippies. Rustlers he'd ruled out soon as he figured the noise had to be coming from the bottom field.

Sneaky. Well, two could play that ole game.

Don undid the wire, gave the gate a prod, moved silently through and pushed it shut behind him. He crept out into the field, to the edge of where it sloped down towards the road, laid the unlit lamp at his feet and hefted his twelve-bore.

Stand by.

Don stood there a moment in the soggy grass, then he took a deep breath and stamped down with his right boot on the button of his lamp.

'Right then!' he roared. 'What's all this? Who give you per—'

His voice cut out like a wireless in a power failure. The bloody ole lamp hadn't come on. He snatched it up and shook it and still it didn't light up. He dropped the useless bloody thing in the grass and thought about firing a shot into the air.

Maybe not.

He looked up into the sky. A haze of light was wreathed around the moon and you could make out a bit of nightmist below the Tor.

You testin' me, Lord?

It wasn't cold, but it was damp, and Don shivered, wanting to be in his bed with his old woman. Whoever they were, they'd probably been scared off. He picked up his lamp, shoved his gun under his arm and turned away, tramping grumpily back towards the gate.

At least, he thought he was going back to the gate. But when he put out his hand to unloop the wire, he shouted in pain.

'Uuurgh!'

Bloody hedge. Fistful of damn thorns.

Angry with himself now. He must be in a wonky state if he'd got lost in his own bloody field. He kicked out with his left boot at where he figured the gate must be and it got snagged in the hedge and he was left limping about, in a right old mess, trying to drag his foot out and still keep the boot on.

While behind him, in the silence of the bottom field, came the hollow gasp-and-growl of an old engine starting up.

Don Moulder dropped his gun and lamp with the shock of it. He wrenched his foot out of the hedge, leaving the boot still ensnared there.

'All right, come outer there. Show yourselves. I . . . I can see you!'

And he could. Under the moon, in front of an old oak tree the Green beggars had got officially protected so he wasn't allowed to chop it down.

It sat there under the tree: a big, black hippy bus, engine throbbing.

'Come on then. I'm a-waitin' for you.'

Don standing on one leg, his bootless foot feeling cold. The Blight was over now all right, it was winter in that field. He could see the steam from his own breath rising, and he realised he was afeared. Lights were coming on in front of the bus: feeble, greasy, headlights that didn't light up anything, not the grass, nor the hedge, nor the gate. The lights hung either side of a radiator grille that was peeling off like a scab on a child's knee.

The bus lurched with a cackle of rusty-sounding gears and he thought, *Oh Christ, they're gonner run me over*, crouching and feeling for his twelve-bore but finding only the lamp.

This time, when he pressed the switch, it lit up at once. He shone it directly at the bus and it lit up the grass and the hedge and the old oak tree he wasn't allowed to chop down.

His mind spun. He blinked, lost his balance and fell to his hands. The bus was still making its rattling cough, but all he could see when, frantically, he shone his light at it, were the hedge and the oak tree.

The noise of the bus cranked up like catarrhal laughter and filled the night and his head, and all he could see in the lamplight was the grass and the hedge and the old oak tree he wasn't allowed to chop down.

Oh no. Oh Lord. Oh no.

His thumb found the lamp's switch. He had to do this. He had to. *Oh Lord, please let . . .*

Breath coming faster now, Don snapped off the light. The grass and the hedge and the oak tree vanished, and there was a moment of calm. Before the vibration began. The earth shaking under him. An acrid smell beginning to filter through, diesel and hot rubber.

Gears meshed in the air.

And there, in the roaring darkness, was the bus right in front of him, a halo of dirty smoke around it and wisps of grey steam dribbling out of its loose, grinning radiator and only smog and shadow where its wheels should have been.

EIGHT

CRONE

Ceridwen wasn't her real name. It was the name of the formidable Celtic Goddess of Rebirth and Transformation and thus was often brazenly assumed by seers and psychics with professional ambitions.

Her real name was Ruth Dunn and she used to be a nurse.

She also claimed to have been a witch since childhood, trained in 'the robed, Gardnerian tradition'. Now she worked part-time at a New-Age nursing home on the Pilton Road and had an apartment near the Glastonbury Experience arcade where she forecast the future by scrying with a mirror and a bowl of rusty spring water from the Chalice Well.

Ceridwen, the Goddess's representative in Glastonbury. Usually seen on the street dressed in a man's greatcoat or, as tonight, in a district nurse's gabardine mac, her dense grey hair clamped under a cloth cap.

'Thank you,' she said to Juanita. 'Thank you for looking after her. I've come to take her home.'

'Yessss,' Domini breathed. She looked radiant. 'I'm to be apprenticed to the Inner Circle. A neophyte.'

'Wow,' Juanita said. 'Somebody open a bottle of champagne.'

She was furious. Bloody Ceridwen. She'd come back to Glastonbury after her divorce – after losing custody of the children when her husband played the witchcraft card in front of a Methodist judge. Raging with malice and greedily gathering the wretched wives of Avalon to her embittered bosom.

Now, to Juanita's horror, Diane was presenting Ceridwen with a cup of tea.

'Thank you, my dear.' Ceridwen turned her large face on Juanita. 'You must be glad to have her back.'

'Yes,' Juanita said non-committally.

'She's grown up.'

'Yes. Big girl now, Ruth.'

'Ceridwen.'

'Oh, sorry.' Juanita smiled.

There was a silence. Ceridwen lowered herself into the armchair, sipped her tea. 'Diane, do you remember coming to see me some years ago?'

'Yes.' Diane glanced apologetically at Juanita.

'Used to like to call yourself Diane Fortune, do you remember?'

'When she was a little girl,' Juanita said. 'People tend to grow out of giving themselves silly names.'

Ceridwen didn't look at her, only at Diane. 'When she was in adolescence. When the psychic portals were opening to her.'

'When she was having problems at home,' Juanita said. 'When she was scrabbling for an identity in a family where women don't count for much, especially if they aren't slim and beautiful.'

Ceridwen smiled, still looking at Diane. 'I had heard you were going through a denial phase. Can't be good for business, Juanita, if you no longer believe in the books you're selling. Indeed, hard to see . . .'

She turned to face Juanita at last. Her industrial-strength Alice band had slipped and thick, grey hair obscured one glittering, ebony eye.

'. . . how can you go on living in Avalon. While contriving to block it all out.'

'Maybe I'm growing old and faded and bitter and cynical.'

'You're beautiful, woman.' A sharp rebuke. 'But you lack wisdom.'

'Thank you, Ruth.'

'And yet', Ceridwen shrugged. 'You may still have . . . untapped potential.'

Domini said, 'Ceridwen *could* help you to find it. If you showed some humility.'

'Right.' Juanita nodded seriously. 'You mean, I could learn how to scatter my books down the street and turn over my shop window to a plaster goddess with big tits and a cunt like a culvert.'

Diane gasped. Domini scowled. Ceridwen sipped her tea and smiled to herself. *Go on*, Juanita thought. *Turn me into a hamster.*

Ceridwen's eyes didn't move. She said, 'That's not what we do any more.'

Something cold and needle-thin penetrated Juanita's spine from within. Ceridwen sat in the stoveside chair like a big Whistler's Mother, face still and hard and varnished. She began to speak, slowly.

'The day will soon come, woman, when the only sanctuary to be found will be at the bosom of the Goddess. You know that we have to take full control of the spiritual life and welfare of this community. And soon. As for you . . .'

Ceridwen appraised Juanita, head to toe, like a fashion-shop manageress sizing up a customer. Or an undertaker estimating the amount of wood it would take for the coffin.

'. . . your time is close, woman. You have to come to terms with it. It'll happen sooner than you dread.'

'Are you threatening me?'

'Oh, Juanita.' Ceridwen laughed. 'I mean the hot flushes. Have you had the hot flushes yet? There are, as we say, three aspects of the Goddess. The virgin. The Mother. And . . .'

'Piss off,' said Juanita.

'And the crone.' Ceridwen placed her cup and saucer on the arm of the chair. 'The hag.' She stood up, stately and mature and wise.

'The last transition for a woman', she said gently, 'can be a wonderful and fulfilling time, full of enlightenment. If you are on the Path. A time of wisdom and reflection. And latent power.'

She paused. Her large bosom swelled under the tight gabardine.

'But it can also be a time of disillusion and decay, constantly chilled by the draught of death. If you reject the Goddess inside you.'

Juanita found she'd backed into the doorway. The bitch. The fucking bitch.

'That's what they said about HRT,' she said lightly and was gratified to see Ceridwen's face darken.

'Come, Domini,' Ceridwen said.

Juanita stayed in the doorway. 'Where are you taking her? Tony's in the shop.'

'Packing, I trust,' said Domini.

'We're going to a place of sanctuary,' Ceridwen said. 'Let us through, please.'

'Wanda's house?'

Ceridwen didn't reply. The actress's elegant town house had been virtually taken over by the bloody Cauldron. It had endless bedrooms; they would put Domini in one, surrounded by candles and ministering angels and the brainwash would be complete.

Bollocks to that.

'Why don't you stay here, Domini?' Juanita closed the parlour door, her back to it, both hands around its handle behind her. 'Take some time, think about it. You've a lot to lose. Tony's a decent guy.'

'I've been trying to tell her . . .' Diane said, as Ceridwen came forward, very much the nursing sister advancing down the ward. Briskly, she closed in on Juanita, rapidly detaching her hands from the doorhandle. Taking Juanita's hands in each of hers and bringing them tightly together.

Grey coils of hair settled around the broad, coarse face, looking down on Juanita's. It had all happened very quickly. Juanita flinched, half-expecting the woman to hit her, but when she spoke it was the voice of Ruth Dunn again, the firm but kindly nurse.

'You silly, silly woman. I think you're really quite unstable. I think you need counselling.' Ceridwen putting on a show of strength and sanity for Diane and Domini.

She was a much larger woman than Juanita, built for holding down distressed patients in the night. The grip was stronger than it looked.

'Oh, it's understandable,' Ceridwen said, the voice of experience. 'You're frustrated and depressed by your loss of belief. And by Diane's youth, because yours has gone. You're afraid that, before you know it, another twenty-five years will have passed and you'll look into the glass and your face will be the face of . . .'

She raised her heavy eyebrows.

'. . . Verity Endicott.'

Positioning both of Juanita's hands away from her body, moulded together, palm to palm, like an old-fashioned teacher showing a child how to pray.

'What lovely, slender hands you still have,' she said almost tenderly, and Juanita was suddenly and irrationally scared that her palms might be fused together for ever.

'But you're afraid, I think, that beneath the silky, brown skin which, sadly, now caresses only books . . .'

Juanita saw a splinter of spite in Ceridwen's eyes.

'. . . are an old woman's curling claws.'

'Let me go.' Juanita felt a coldness under her heart. 'How dare you? How fucking dare you?'

After a long moment, Ceridwen smiled, relaxed and let both Juanita's hands fall away like a discarded pair of silk gloves.

As the two women left, Domini smirking, Juanita felt sick and humiliated. Like Jim Battle after his Execution.

At first, she couldn't feel her hands at all. Self-consciously she rubbed her palms together to restore the circulation, experiencing a moment of relief followed by a palpitating insecurity. And a creeping, bitter shame.

Diane went to shut the shop door.

'No.' Juanita walked out on to the pavement. 'I need some air.'

It was gone midnight. The street was deserted, not even one of those stoned guitar-and-bongo duos under the church wall. The very air felt thin and exhausted, used up by lungs involved in excess panting and screaming and sighing. The town was full of madness tonight.

She walked across the street to the war-memorial, a good twenty feet high and carved like a Celtic cross. Iron railings separated it from St John's churchyard. Juanita leaned against the railings, pulled out her cigarettes.

'We've got problems here,' she said as Diane joined her.

'Look', Diane stared down at her trainers on the first step of the memorial, 'what she said. That was awful. Cruel. But . . .'

'But true,' Juanita said. 'It wouldn't have been cruel otherwise. I've looked at Verity Endicott more than once and thought, yeah, that'll be me one day. Toddling round the town with my shopping bag when all the shops have closed.'

'That's not what I meant. You're not remotely like Miss Endicott. I hope I look like you when I'm . . .'

'Forty-something.'

'I wish I looked like you now.'

'Oh, shut up, Diane.' Juanita lit a cigarette. 'Listen, we really have a problem. Nothing to do with that woman.'

'I wish you hadn't offended her.'

'Oh for God's sake . . . Diane, that boy, Headlice . . .'

Diane went still.

'He's dead,' Juanita said. 'I'm sorry to tell you like this. It was in tonight's paper. They found his body in an abandoned bus in a wood at Stoke St Michael.'

Diane stared across the street as if it were a distance of several miles.

'He had head injuries,' Juanita said. 'It has to be him because of . . . you mentioned a swastika.'

'On top of his head.'

'The police are suspicious. You know what that means, don't you?'

Diane put her arms around the stem of the Celtic cross. Her shoulders shook.

'They're appealing to anyone with pertinent information to come forward. Which probably includes anyone who might have seen the boy having his head kicked in by their father's farm manager.'

Diane laid her cheek against the stone.

'Diane?'

'Was it his own bus? That he was found in?'

'It was a black bus.'

Diane nodded.

'I really think you need to go to the police,' Juanita said. 'Tomorrow. I'll come with you.'

'They wouldn't believe me.' Diane's voice was tiny. 'My father would say I'd made it all up. He'd tell them I was unbalanced. Just like he always does.'

'They'd still have to check it out.'

But she was right. Juanita sighed. Lord Pennard and Rankin had had a whole day to make provisions for this incident getting out. They'd have something ready, some watertight story. Especially now the boy was dead. Also, Pennard would undoubtedly have connections at chief constable level and beyond. And with Archer's political career on the line and all it represented in terms of the future wealth and influence of the House of Pennard, there was nothing they wouldn't do.

'Listen, I'll get Jim to look after the shop. While we go to the police station.'

Of course, she'd have to promise Jim first that nothing would come out about the Execution. What a can of worms.

'They'll ask why I didn't report it before,' Diane said.

'Because you didn't know the boy was dead.' She put a hand on Diane's shoulder. 'Come on, Diane Fortune. I'll make us some hot chocolate.'

An amber streetlamp reddened and Juanita looked up warily.

Diane dabbed her eyes with a tissue. 'I was wrong about the Pilgrims. They weren't terribly nice people at all. They made Headlice go into church backwards and they gave him drugs.'

'Quite.' Juanita tried not to think about sickles and animal masks. If only she could tell Diane precisely what the nice pilgrims had done to Jim and her. But a promise, unfortunately, was a promise.

'He had a horrible life,' Diane said. 'He just wanted . . . something he could believe in.'

'Don't we all.'

As they walked back to the shop, Juanita found herself thinking of Colonel Pixhill and fancied she could feel wings of foreboding overhead, like some shadow hang-glider.

NINE

LIKE, SAY, 'GHOST'

Yesterday Joe Powys had been to Hereford Library and got out everything they had on Uncle Jack Powys. He'd brought back as many books as he'd been allowed to; they were all spread out now on his desk back at the cottage, eight of them.

It was six fifteen a.m. He'd awoken in the dark thinking about it, a little scared. Uncle Jack. Uncle bloody Jack?

Where did this come from? You grow up assuming a certain kinship with one of the greatest literary figures of the twentieth century, there has to be a reasonable basis for it.

But the more Joe Powys investigated, the more he found that there wasn't.

Last night he'd called up relatives he hadn't spoken to since he was a kid. *Joe. Joe Powys. P-O-W . . . your cousin. That's right, Mary's son . . .*

Feeling embarrassed as hell now. Arnold the dog sitting by his chair, laughing at him, the way he did, with his orb-like brown eyes.

None of the relatives had heard of any kind of link with John Cowper Powys. None of them remembered it being a family name. So he was the only one of them with the surname Powys? What did that say?

'I know what you're thinking, Arnold,' Powys said. 'I suggest you forget it.'

Arnold kind of shrugged, lay down and lowered his head to his paws.

One of the relatives had said, *All I remember, Joe, is for a long time we thought you must be Len's boy. Auntie Mary never discussed it.*

What his mum used to tell him was that his father had messed around with bad women and they'd got divorced when he was a baby, and Uncle Jack had looked after them until Len came along.

Later, Powys had figured that his mother and father had never been married at all, but he didn't push it, never searched out his birth certificate – pretty sure he'd find out he was registered under his mum's maiden name. Not Powys.

She used to talk about Uncle Jack until he was maybe ten. He had memories of books by JCP on the shelves when he was small, but not when he was old enough to read them with any understanding. His mum, in later years, read only magazines, and when he visited her two years before she died even the shelves had gone. Now Len was dead too.

That last time, when he'd asked his mother who was Uncle Jack and she'd looked blank, he'd smiled and not pushed it – what did it matter anyway? True, John Cowper Powys had lived not that far from Wrexham in the last part of his life. True, his mother had been a district nurse who'd moved around Merseyside and North Wales and might well have encountered the old bloke, maybe even nursed him.

'Old' being the key word here. JCP, born in the 1870s, had been very old when Joe was born. It really didn't seem at all likely that John Cowper Powys was his father.

Over the years Powys had tossed around a few more likely explanations. Say Mum arrives back in Wrexham with an illegitimate baby and she needs a name for him, and there on the shelf is some book by John Cowper Powys. Which is a nice name and doesn't sound phoney, and so maybe she becomes 'Mrs Powys' until she marries Len.

So the baby who should have been Joe Morris becomes Joe Powys. By the time she marries Len, he's nearly five years old and is used to the name, maybe can't get his mouth so easily around Devereaux, which is Len's name. And because it was JCP who saved her reputation when the chips were down, Mum retains a soft spot for the old guy, and the legend of Uncle Jack, the benefactor, is born.

It's a persistent kind of myth. Joe likes it. And when he comes to write a book about mystical aspects of the British countryside, which turns out to be a minor bestseller, and people ask him if by any chance he's descended from one or other of the famous literary siblings, Theodore, Llewellyn and John Cowper Powys, he . . .

well, he doesn't deny it. And Ben Corby never asked in case the answer was the wrong one.

None of which explained the incidents of the book in the night.

Powys was afraid of ghosts. He didn't use to think he was. He believed in them, believed they were just beyond the boundaries of human understanding, and *only* just. He used to believe in the tape-recording theory of ghosts: that they were emotional imprints on the atmosphere, events replaying themselves over and over.

Therefore ghosts were harmless.

Harmless, harmless, harmless.

Around nine a.m., Joe looked up from JCP's *Autobiography*, in which Uncle Jack confesses early on to being some kind of sado-masochist – hence the tortured figure of the self-crucifying Welshman Owen Evans in *A Glastonbury Romance*.

Powys thought, *Masochism*?

And went to the phone, scrabbling in the desk drawer for his contacts book. He had misgivings about this, what he might be opening up. And having to endure the scorn, of course. But he made the call anyway.

And was lucky, as it happened. Brendan Donovan had just arrived at the university. Nine a.m. Too early, surely, for really withering rhetoric.

'OK, Powys,' Brendan Donovan said. 'I may possibly be able to accommodate a five-minute argument. The full half-hour would require an appointment.'

Some years ago, Professor Brendan Donovan, of the Edinburgh University department of parapsychology, had reviewed the revised, mass-market paperback of *The Old Golden Land* for *The Scotsman*. Perhaps the most complimentary phrase in this review had been 'whimsical drivel'. Powys, unschooled in the etiquette traditionally observed between reviewer and reviewed, had telephoned Dr Donovan for a meaningful discussion. Others had followed over the years. Brendan Donovan had mellowed. Slightly.

'If you wish to discuss the spirit-path theory of ley-lines, with particular reference to linear anomalies in the Peruvian desert,' he said now, 'you'll find me a touch more amenable than I may have been regarding so-called earth-energies. Only a touch more, you understand, because ley-lines, of course, do not exist.'

'Poltergeists,' Powys said bluntly.

'Heavens,' Donovan said. 'My weak spot.'

'I know.'

'That is, Powys, so long as you do not attempt to try my patience by allowing any contentious words to intrude. Like, say, "ghost".'

'How about psycho-kinetic energy generated by a disturbed adolescent?'

'Well-trodden ground. Much safer.'

'In that case, how about psycho-kinetic energy generated by someone for whom adolescence is no more than a slightly feverish memory?'

'Like, who?' said Donovan.

'Like me.'

'Hmm,' Donovan said. 'Give me two minutes to summon a cup of fortifying coffee. I shall call you back.'

Well – let's be reasonable here – it wasn't Arnold, was it?

Nobody really knows what goes on down there. In the subconscious. Nobody knows what seeds planted in the psyche of a small child will start to germinate in the adult and with what effects.

OK, the trigger.

Joe Powys is alone, his woman has resumed her career, left him behind in a cottage in the sticks. Subconsciously, he knows she isn't coming back. His book has been rejected. And his home is not really *his* home; it's still Henry Kettle's, even though Henry is dead, because Henry had identity, which Joe doesn't have any more, maybe never did have.

The subconscious goes into mid-life crisis. Who is Joe Powys? Even the guy's name isn't real!

The subconscious gets extremely resentful. It reverts to the persona of a disturbed adolescent. It finds a focus for all that resentful energy.

Uncle Jack.

Bloody Uncle Jack.

*

'Well, it's interesting, Powys,' Brendan Donovan said. 'It possesses a certain flawed logic. However, I still have a problem with it.'

'Well, of course you do. What I'm doing here is groping for the psychological solution. I haven't said anything about the elements you don't like – power of place, earth-force, the thinness of the veil on the Welsh Border.'

'But it's there by implication, isn't it? Because the house was the home of this water-diviner, Kettle, it is more receptive, its atmosphere remains charged.'

'I didn't say that.'

'And therefore is capable of transforming the frustration of its unhappy occupant into psycho-kinetic energy, yes?'

'Well . . . could be.'

'Discounting all that, which I am, of course, predisposed to do, out of hand . . . the problem I have with all this is that the adolescent energy we suspect may cause poltergeist phenomena is essentially a sexual energy. I assume, Powys, you have not begun to find satisfaction in scourging yourself with barbed wire or something.'

'Occasionally I beat myself with Henry's old dowsing rods. Apart from that . . . Of course, *he* may have done.'

'Who?'

'John Cowper Powys always liked to think of himself as some kind of sado-masochist.'

'Ah. So you're obsessed with this man,' Donovan said.

'Curiously, I hardly ever thought of him. I'd forgotten that book was even on the shelf. *Consciously*, I'd forgotten.'

'Which book are we talking about?'

'*A Glastonbury Romance*. His masterpiece. About twelve hundred pages.'

'Haven't read it. Life's too short for fiction. What's it about?'

'It's basically a West Country soap-opera set in the 1920s. Far as I can remember, it's about people in pursuit of their ideas of the Holy Grail and the tensions between spiritual and commercial demands and people getting their rocks off, spiritually and sexually. I may be wrong, it's a long time since I breezed through it.'

'And this same book every time?' asked Donovan.

'Every time.'

'Too neat,' said Donovan. 'Too neat to be true.'

'Ah. You think I'm lying.'

'Indeed. I'm a scientist. What proof can you show me?'

'I've got a witness.'

'Your publisher. How very convenient.'

'Isn't it?' Powys admitted gloomily.

'Be a marvellous story for your own next publication.'

'No chance.'

'Before I could give a useful opinion, you would have to precipitate this book from its shelf under laboratory conditions. But then you knew that.'

'Brendan, if you bumped into your late granny at the tea machine, you'd make her take out her teeth under laboratory conditions.'

'And in the present circumstances, of course, my findings would have to include the probability of an author in decline attempting to kick-start his flagging career.'

'I knew you'd say that, too.'

'So why did you telephone me?'

'I'm a masochist. Runs in the family.'

Brendan Donovan laughed. 'Do you know what I might do in your place?'

'Resign,' Powys said.

'I might go to Glastonbury and open myself to all the wonderful earth-forces in the hope that my Grail awaited me there.'

'No, you wouldn't.'

'*I* wouldn't. I'm explaining what I might do if, perish the thought, I were you. Forget it, I probably had Glastonbury on my mind in a negative context, having received this very morning a review copy of a book even more foolish than your own revered opus. By an American, of course, one W. Pelham Grainger, PhD, who wants us all to enrich our lives by bonding with the living darkness. Absolute tosh. He lives near Glastonbury, as it happens. My, my, I must remember to record this coincidence in my Arthur Koestler Appreciation Society Diary.'

Powys shook his head.

'Away with you,' Donovan said. 'Away to your Avalon.'

'Thanks very much,' Powys said. 'I'll expect your bill in the mail.'

'My meter records . . . let me see . . . twenty-five minutes!'

'Prove it,' Powys said. 'Laboratory conditions.'

TEN

HIS STAIN

'Bastards.' Woolly threw the Daily Press on to Juanita's counter. 'Bastards, bastards, *bastards*!'

His roughened elbow poked through a hole in his shapeless orange sweater. The rubber band securing his stringy ponytail had snapped. He looked like an ageing Dickensian street urchin. There were tears in his eyes.

'I'm so sorry, Woolly,' Juanita said. 'But it's hardly a surprise, is it?'

She could see in his face that, no, it hadn't been a surprise. But there'd still been that final strand to be snipped before the rope broke and dropped him into the black pit.

She turned the paper around on the counter. The story was front-page lead.

Green Light for M-way

The controversial Bath-Taunton expressway is to go ahead – despite furious protests from environmentalists.

The report of the two-month public inquiry, published today, rejects claims that the proposed route would be a 'savage rape of Central Somerset'.

But a leading opponent of the plan said last night, 'We'll fight them to the last tree.'

The Government claims the road is the only way to end crippling congestion in several small towns and villages, especially during the holiday season.

It will also link the county firmly into the trans-European road network, opening up major industrial and commercial possibilities, according to local authority chiefs who have welcomed the decision.

'Got a call from the paper late last night asking for a quote,' Woolly said. 'Too choked to give a reasoned response, just wanted to get it over that we'd be re-forming the action committee, only it come out a bit stronger, like. Sheesh.'

Mendip Councillor Edward Woolaston, one of the original protesters, said, 'No way are they going to get away with this. This is going to be a nationwide issue, even a world issue, and we'll fight them to the last tree.'

Juanita didn't know what to say. The thought of an enormous public protest with the police and armies of security men guarding the site and people getting hurt made her feel faintly sick.

'The thing is, Woolly, it just never works. There've been so many full-scale road protests and it just leaves everyone beaten and bitter. Look at Newbury . . . Batheaston . . . Twyford Down . . . If the Government decides a road's going through, it goes through.'

She stared despondently through the window. All the shards of pottery had disappeared from the gutters, which streamed now with dark rain. Apart from Holy Thorn Ceramics being closed, you'd think nothing exceptional had occurred in High Street. Last night's spark in the air had fizzled out. There was no sign of either Tony or Domini.

'And the thing is, Woolly, if you organise a militant protest to stop the road, all it does is split the community even more because most of the locals think it's a good thing. They don't like the idea of the countryside being ripped up, but if it prevents traffic snarl-ups and children being run over and heavy lorries shaking their foundations . . . oh hell, you know all this better than I do, a lot of those people voted for you.'

'And won't vote for me again if I'm behind this protest,' said Woolly soberly. 'But I got to go with my conscience. We're fighting for the West Country's right to breathe. We're fighting for green hills, places to walk, places to be. We're fighting to stop them selling Britain for scrap. Sorry. There I go again, Councillor bloody Woolaston. It's all a sham, being a councillor. There is no democracy.'

Juanita pushed the newspaper away. 'So you want me to tell people . . . what?'

'Tell 'em there's an emergency meeting tonight. Put it round. Seven-thirty. Assembly Rooms. Now they've made a decision they won't hang around. It'll be bulldozers and chainsaw-gangs on every horizon before we know it. Still, you know how *you* could help.'

'Mmm?'

'Well don't sound so excited, my love.'

'I'm sorry. Lot on my mind.'

The idea of putting Rankin in the frame for murder seemed less straightforward than it had last night. You could never be sure what Diane was going to say, how much of her statement would include what *she* might consider normal but the police would see as the ravings of a certifiable psychiatric case.

'*The Avalonian*, I mean,' Woolly was saying. 'You get *The Avalonian* on the streets, we'd at least have a reliable mouthpiece to counter all the propaganda.'

'I have to tell you, Councillor,' Juanita said severely, 'that *The Avalonian* isn't going to be anybody's mouthpiece.'

'Well, yeah, I accept that, but. . .'

'But it will be fair and maybe consider certain viewpoints that the regular Press would be a touch queasy about.'

'Fair enough, fair enough. What's your schedule?'

'I don't know. February maybe. Things *are* moving. As it happens, I've just sent Diane to the print-shop to get acquainted with Sam Daniel. She's a little nervous, having heard that Sam thinks all upper class people should be placed against a wall and shot.'

'He's a good boy, is Sam. You only got to listen to his old man to know that.'

'I thought Griff Daniel hated the ground Sam walks on.'

'Exactly,' said Woolly. 'A good boy.'

In the square entrance hall, he stood on the flagstones, under one of the high, deep-sunk windows either side of the front door, and nodded approval.

'See, Verity, the old Tudor guys built this place, they had it right. They understood the importance of luminary-control. Hence the restrictive fenestration. Everybody says this was down to defence, but that was only part of the calculation.'

Dr Pel Grainger wore a formal black jacket over black jeans and black trainers. In daylight, he looked shorter and rather less imposing. As she supposed he would, given that the night was his chosen environment. Seeing him at the door so early had been quite a shock, rather like seeing an owl perching on one's bird table.

'Verity, you are just so lucky to have this place to yourself.' Dr Grainger smiled, showing small, rather stumpy teeth, their whiteness enhanced by the blackness of his close-mown beard. 'Which is how you got to look at the situation from now on in. Lucky.'

Cornered by Wanda last night, Dr Grainger had expressed – to Verity's dismay – immediate interest in Meadwell. It sounded the kind of place, he said, where just being there could virtually put you into Second-stage Tenebral Symbiosis.

When Verity had tried to explain to Dr Grainger that even in her time here Meadwell had not always been as dark as this, the American had nodded indulgently; he could explain this. Or maybe, he told her, when his therapy programme began to take effect, she wouldn't need to have it explained.

Well, perhaps it would work. Perhaps, after tenebral therapy, there would be more than the usual few precious moments of clarity when she first awoke, before her thoughts began to contract under the pressure of the house.

Dr Grainger moulded his body to one of the oak pillars, ran his hands up and down it. Verity had heard, at the Assembly Rooms, of people who liked to hug trees to share their life-force. But hugging centuries-old long-dead oak?

'And here's another thing . . .'

He stepped away, giving the oak a fraternal sort of pat, as if they had already established a rapport.

'I have been *horrified*, since I came here, to see how many owners of old houses kind of bleach their beams, to make them lighter. Can you believe that? See, oak is wonderful wood because it absorbs darkness so well. So . . . three, four centuries of storing the dark and these people want to take it all away. Can you believe that?'

'Perhaps they . . .' Verity swallowed. 'Perhaps they just want to make it more . . . cheerful.'

Dr Grainger almost choked on his own laughter. 'That's a joke, right?'

'Right,' said Verity weakly.

'You know, Verity, I could really use this house. It's hard to find one of these late medieval homes that hasn't been tampered with – windows enlarged, all this. Maybe I could hire it? Maybe a weekend seminar here in the summer, or around Christmas?'

He stood on tiptoe and slipped a hand into a dim space between the Jacobean corner cupboard and the ceiling.

'Yeah,' he said with satisfaction but no explanation. 'Tell me, why's it called Meadwell?'

Verity explained about the well in the grounds, as old as the Chalice Well and similarly credited with great curative powers. But unfortunately sealed up now because of a possible pollution problem.

'Uh huh.' A knowing smile. 'Uh huh. Now I begin to understand your problem here.'

How could he? This was utterly ludicrous.

'Seems to me that what may have happened is the house has become repressed because people have been afraid of it. Yeah? So what we got to do, Verity, is we got to alter the house's self-image. And yours. Remember, when you learn to embrace the dark, the darkness will embrace you back.'

'Yes,' said Verity. 'Thank you. You've made me feel better about it.'

But he hadn't. He'd made her feel worse. And when they went upstairs and Dr Grainger began to peer into the bedrooms in search of deeper and denser shadows, Verity could almost hear the voice of Major Shepherd, *Oh Verity, Verity, why didn't you tell me about this?*

Dr Grainger was crouching in a corner of the landing, both hands moving in empty air, trying to locate what he called 'the crepuscular core' of the house. 'This is commonly the place where most shadows meet. The repository of the oldest, the least disturbed darkness, you following me?'

I don't want to know. Verity almost panicked. *I don't want to know where this place is.*

And she was so grateful when there was a rapping from below. 'The front door. Excuse me, please, Dr Grainger.'

She almost ran downstairs to the hall, where a little light pooled on the flagstones. Probably the postman; it was his time. She unbolted the door.

'Oh.'

It was not the postman.

'Well, well. Miss Endicott.'

A deep, educated voice and there was something strikingly familiar about it that made her feel both afraid and strangely joyful.

She stared at him. A tall and slender man, in his late thirties or early forties. His face lean, his jawline deep. His eyes penetratingly familiar. When he smiled she noticed that he did not have a moustache.

Does not have a moustache. She caught herself thinking this and wondered why.

'You don't remember me, do you, Miss Endicott?'

'I'm so sorry.' Verity blushed. Something about him. Something so painfully known.

'But I was only a boy. When we last met.' He put out a hand. 'Oliver,' he said. 'Oliver Pixhill.'

One of the huntsmen – what appeared to be a savage snarl on his face – was beating a hound away from a dead stag. Too late; its head was awfully messed up and one of its antlers looked broken. It was very important to huntsmen that the head should be unspoiled.

Diane winced.

Across the bottom of the scene was pasted a page-heading from a holiday guide. It read:

THE QUANTOCKS: A REAL HAVEN FOR WILDLIFE.

The photo had been blown up, all grainy. The caption had a serrated edge, what Diane had learned on the paper in Yorkshire to call a rag-out. It made a pretty devastating poster and it hung uncompromisingly just inside the door.

'Sometimes we go out at night, a bunch of us,' Sam Daniel said. 'Paste 'em on a few tourist offices, show the visitors what it's really like in the pretty countryside. Plus, it shows bloodsports aren't what you'd call compatible with a tourist-based economy.'

He gave Diane a candid sort of look, as though defying her to report him to the police. Another test. People were always testing her, as though you couldn't expect automatically to trust anyone whose name was prefixed by The Honourable.

'Your old man done any of that? Stags?'

'Foxes,' Diane said. 'We haven't got many stags in our part of the county.'

Sam pulled on his earring. 'Ah, well, you know, I figured maybe he'd done a bit as a guest of one of the hunts over Exmoor way. They like to involve as many nobs as they can get, those bastards. Social cred.'

'I don't think so.'

'Or maybe you didn't like to ask him?'

'You don't,' Diane said. 'You don't ask my father anything like that. Or if you do, you don't expect to get a reply. Anyway, what about your father – doesn't he shoot?'

Like Griff, Sam Daniel was stocky, but not so heavy. He grinned through quarter-inch stubble. 'I don't ask him anything either. Mainly on account of we don't talk.'

The print-shop – the sign just said SAMPRINT – was on the corner of Grope Lane. Quite a central location. Diane didn't know much about computers and laser-printers, but it all looked jolly impressive. There was also a young boy called Paul, sixteen, his first job. Computer-whizz, Sam said.

Sam was about thirty and not so notorious nowadays. Not since he'd been dismissed from the County Planning department after his conviction for assault while sabotaging a hunt. The Beaufort Hunt, as it happened, the one Prince Charles sometimes rode with. Diane seemed to remember Sam had got off with a conditional discharge, but it still made all the papers, in the very week Griff Daniel had been installed as chairman of the district council.

Diane looked around the room at the equipment which must have cost, well, thousands. 'I thought you must have sort of made it up with your father.'

'What? Him invest in me?' Sam swept his buccaneer's hair back off his shoulders and rolled his head.

Juanita had said it was no secret in Glastonbury that Griff blamed his subsequent electoral defeat on the publicity over Sam's court case – despite his celebrated No Son of Mine statement to the *Gazette*.

'Business loan, this was,' Sam said. 'Achieved after a lot of grovelling and blatant lying. So if there's a chunk of the Ffitch fortune going spare, I can give you an immediate directorship, how's that sound?'

'Super,' Diane said. 'But, as my father likes to remind me every so often, my personal position is sort of, you know, what's the word? Destitute.'

Sam grinned and shook his head. He clearly didn't believe that; nobody ever could, quite.

'I've got a van,' Diane said. 'If that's any use. For deliveries and things.'

With pink spots and holes in the side. Just what he needed to boost his image within the business community.

'Can you write, is the main thing,' Sam said. 'Can you make this thing read like a proper paper, instead of the usual old hippy shit?'

She imagined huge stacks of *The Avalonian* piling up by the door, under the anti-bloodsports posters. The image was quite exciting and Sam did seem like the sort of person who could help make it happen. She knew Juanita had sent her along here in the hope that she would become inspired.

And also to take her mind off that trip to the police station. *And Headlice. I could have saved him.*

'Actually, I'm really not very good,' she said a little breathlessly. 'In Yorkshire I was always forgetting to ask people's ages and all that. My spelling isn't terrific either.'

Sam slowly shook his head. 'Ah 'tis the usual problem with you aristocrats. 'Always so arrogant and full of yourselves.'

A shadow fell across the window of the print-shop, accompanied by a thump on the glass, and Sam looked up sharply and then made a dive for the door. 'Hey! Piss off, pal!'

Something had been stuck to the outside of the window.

'Bloody Darryl Davey, that was.' Sam came back into the shop, holding a yellow printed sheet he'd torn from the glass. 'About all he's fit for, fly-posting. Thick bastard.'

He unrolled the yellow paper.

GLASTONBURY FIRST

A public meeting to launch a new initiative for the promotion of
Priorities in the town and its environs will be held

Tonight Nov. 16
at the TOWN HALL.
7.30 p.m.
GLASTONBURY FIRST.

Sam Daniel sniffed the paper suspiciously.

'The old man,' he said. 'I can smell the old man all over this.'

Verity was at once horribly anxious.

Oliver Pixhill. It must be thirty years since she'd seen him, and on that occasion she'd chased him angrily away.

'I hope it isn't inconvenient.'

'No.' She felt an awful blush coming on. 'Not at all. Besides . . .'

It had been not long after she'd taken over as housekeeper, Oliver and his mother having moved into the town. The boy had returned with his schoolfriend, Archer Ffitch, and an air pistol, both of them far too young to have such a thing in their possession.

'Old place doesn't change, does it?' Oliver Pixhill stooped to enter. 'Doesn't it frighten you, being here alone in the winter?'

Verity had found the dead bullfinch on the path, near the back door, the boys sitting on the wall, grinning at her, their legs swinging.

'I . . . I'm used to it,' she stammered, thinking of the American poking around upstairs looking for the heart of the darkness, wondering how he might alter the house's self-image. Oh lord, what was she going to do? How was she going to explain this? Oliver Pixhill was a member of the Trust; it would get back to Major Shepherd.

212

'I expect you're wondering why I'm here.' Oliver was soberly attired in a business suit. He was, Verity understood, some sort of corporate lawyer. In the City. Silly to judge him on that one incident from his childhood.

'You have every right to be here. That is, I'm very glad to see you, Mr Pixhill.'

There was the sound of footsteps overhead. Oliver glanced up briefly but didn't question it. Verity was struggling to put together an explanation in her head. About a man who was very interested in old, dark houses and . . .

'My father would never allow me to visit him here, you know.' Oliver walked languidly over to the stairs but didn't look up. He looked unnervingly like the Colonel as Verity first remembered him. Perhaps a little taller, sharper in the jaw.

'He'd come to my mother's flat two or three times a week and sometimes take me for walks. But he would never let me come here. Wasn't that odd. I used to think he was trying to protect me from something.'

'I suppose he simply thought it was a rather gloomy old place for a boy to grow up in,' Verity said lamely. 'Certainly your mother did.'

'That's what you were told, was it?' An eyebrow rose. 'I see.'

'I . . .' What could she say? How could she even start to explain? But she didn't have to. Black trainers appeared on the stairs.

'Verity, I found it.' Moving quickly and lightly for a man of his bulk, Dr Pel Grainger padded down the last few steps and arrived next to her, looking fulfilled, like a cat with a bird. 'The crepuscular core. A slight misnomer, but I like the phrase. Oh. Good morning.'

'Dr Grainger, this . . .' Verity held the oak pillar to steady herself. 'This is Mr Oliver Pixhill. The son of my late employer.' Her voice was small and dead. Like the bullfinch. 'Mr Pixhill, this is . . .'

'Hi.' Dr Grainger was already shaking hands with Oliver. 'Dr Pel Grainger.'

Oliver Pixhill shook hands, said nothing. He tilted his head enquiringly.

And did not have to wait long. Within a minute, to Verity's mounting distress, Dr Grainger had identified himself as a therapist specialising in Tenebral Psychosis, which, he explained, was not entirely dissimilar to Seasonal Affective Disorder, only all-year-round, more intense and usually connected to a particular dwelling.

He identified Verity as his 'patient'.

Verity burst into tears.

'Oh, have I been indiscreet?' Dr Grainger turned to Oliver Pixhill. 'I guess you knew nothing of this, right?'

'I certainly did not.' Oliver's deep voice was full of surprise and concern. He guided Verity through to the dining hall, hands on her quaking shoulders. 'I did not indeed.'

Oliver pulled out a chair for her at the long table. At which she hadn't sat since the Abbot's Dinner. He took the chair next to hers.

'Miss Endicott, this is utterly dreadful. None of us knew about this. I feel absolutely devastated. And guilty.'

'Please . . . it's my fault. I'm so . . .'

'I've been back in this house, Miss Endicott, for less than ten minutes and already I'm finding the atmosphere decidedly oppressive. We shall have to get you out.'

'No! You don't und—'

'Mr Pixhill,' Grainger said from the head of the table, where the Abbot sat. 'I can help this lady. I have got this . . .'

'I'm sure your therapeutic techniques are entirely creditable. What I'm saying is she should never have been left here alone and that is the responsibility of the Pixhill Trust. I'm going to make it my business to find Miss Endicott fully furnished accommodation in the short-term and then . . .'

'You don't understand!' Verity gripped the edge of the table. 'This is *my* responsibility. I made a promise to your father.'

He looked astonished. 'Good God, you really think my father was in a fit mental state to extract a promise from anyone?'

'Your father was a great man,' Verity whispered.

'My father?' Gently, Oliver took her hands in his. He hesitated. He took a breath. 'Miss Endicott, my father was a deeply unhappy man with a paranoid and obsessive nature. Who ruined his own and other people's lives through . . .'

'No!' Verity snatched her hands back. 'That's a . . . that's untrue.'

214

Oliver said, with compassion, 'I do know how you felt about him, you know.'

She stared at him through a blur of angry tears. Saw an unexpected pain in Oliver's eyes. His father's eyes.

'He was my father, and I'm frankly tired of having him venerated. It's time the truth was acknowledged.'

'What can you know of the truth?' Hard to get the words out, her throat was so tight.

'Verity, I've made it my business to find out the truth. You never wanted to. You loved him too much.'

Verity gasped.

Oliver held up a placatory hand. 'Oh, not in any physical sense, I don't suppose. I doubt he was interested in that side of things any more.'

'Stop it.' Verity drew a handkerchief from her sleeve, wiped her eyes. 'I don't want to hear any more of this.'

Oliver shrugged. 'All I know is, the oppressive darkness I felt when I entered here was nothing to do with the age of the building. Nothing to do with the legend of Abbot Whiting. You know that.'

Verity rose and backed away from him.

'It's him, Miss Endicott. You know that too. You've always known it. Him and his obsessions. His delusions. His self-importance. His invented visionary experiences. His crazy, rambling diaries. The darkness in here is *him.*'

'How can you say these things?' Verity wouldn't look at him.

'He destroyed my mother, he neglected his parental responsibilities. And he's left his stain on this place. Jesus, you can feel him. The self-inflicted misery of him.'

Verity covered her ears, but his voice was low and insistent.

'I asked you if you were afraid and you said you were used to it. Well, of course you are. Part of you wants to feel he's still here. That's what he left you. His stain.'

'No.' Verity began to beat her knuckles on the table. 'No!'

Oliver stood up. 'This is the source of your darkness, Dr Grainger. George Pixhill. Last and most pathetic of a long line of pseudo-mystics who've thrown away their lives in Glastonbury. You don't need to teach her how to wallow in it. She's been doing it for half her life.'

Verity said quietly, 'I think you should leave, Oliver.'

'I haven't told you why I came.'

'I do not wish to know.'

'I think you do,' Oliver said softly. 'I came to tell you that Major Shepherd was rushed to hospital late last night.'

Verity went very still.

'And died early this morning, I'm afraid,' Oliver said. 'I'm so sorry.'

ELEVEN

THE BELL

Mrs Whitney said, 'It's not my place to say it, Joe, but you are looking just terrible.'

She'd come round from next door with some of her homemade soup, leek and lentil. She'd done this once or twice a week since he'd been on his own.

'Sorry,' Joe Powys said shakily. 'Didn't get to bed until late. Bad habit to get into.'

He'd fallen asleep in the chair. Sat down to mull over his conversation with Brendan Donovan and just dropped off. Woken to Arnold whining softly beneath his chair and . . . thud.

It couldn't. Not in broad daylight.

'I don't know at all.' Mrs Whitney punched his arm in exasperation. 'Look at the size of them great black circles round your eyes. You look like one of them pandas. Didn't ought to be all alone out here, with just that dog. Isn't normal, young chap like you.'

She stood in the doorway, rising up in her bobbled slippers, trying to peer over his shoulder. Perhaps thinking she might be able to spot a syringe and bag of white powder. Unfair, Joyce was OK; Henry Kettle had thought so too.

'I'm fine,' Powys said. 'Honest to God.'

'Ho,' Mrs Whitney said scornfully and bustled past him. She didn't get far. He heard her gasp.

'All it is,' Powys said, 'I was looking for something. A book. Got carried away, Joyce. You know how it is when you start moving things, you can't stop.'

Well. Yes. On the whole, about as convincing as a mad axeman in a pool of blood claiming to have had a small mishap clipping his toenails.

Mrs Whitney left very quickly, her face as white as the tops of the hills after this week's short-lived snow.

It wasn't just the lamp this time. No indeed. Jesus.

Inside the house, the phone rang. He let it. It had rung several times, starting just as he'd opened his eyes to the sight of *A Glastonbury Romance* in the centre of the hearthrug. He'd picked up the phone and the line had been dead. Not the dialling tone, not the breathy echo of somebody with the wrong number or making a hoax call. Just dead: the sound you'd get if you were holding a banana to your ear.

About a minute later it happened again; he'd put it down and picked it up and there was a perfect, clear dialling tone, and this was when the whole shelf had collapsed and the books had come out horizontally, not falling, actually spraying into the room, taking the lamp and the radio with them, and Powys had thrown himself behind the sofa and screamed at the wall. At least, he'd intended to scream, but it came out like a whimper, and Arnold flew out from under the chair and began to snarl.

Which was when Mrs Whitney knocked on the front door. Mrs Whitney and the leek and lentil soup. 'Better come and have this in my kitchen, Joe. Be warmed up in ten minutes.'

Less than five minutes later, he came out, followed by Arnold. The air was chilly. The mist was a flimsy tent over the forestry, blotting out the hillfarms so that there was just the two cottages, one of them occupied by a bloke who only had to close his eyes now for something to happen. Maybe when he went to sleep, some kind of energy escaped from him and . . .

Oh, come on, you know better than to start theorising. These things happen. Leave it alone, don't be afraid, don't respond and it'll stop. Sooner or later it will stop.

Next door, Mrs Whitney sat him down by the Rayburn, warmed up the soup and stood over him while he spooned it up, Arnold lying across his trainers.

'Mr Kettle, now, he had this trouble more than once,' she said conversationally. 'I remember when he was dowsing for a new well at the old Bufton place, by Kinsham.'

'What trouble exactly?'

'Oh, don't you go taking me for a fool, Joe. I lived next door to Mr Kettle for too many years. Magnet for it, that man.'

'So, what do you think I should do?'

PHIL RICKMAN

'Well, it's not *just* the house, is it? Never is just a house, that's what Mr Kettle used to say. Just that house reacts quicker than most houses, on account of Mr Kettle, if anything comes in. I don't know where *you* could've picked something up though, Joe; you never goes anywhere much.'

'Maybe it was looking for me. God, I said I wouldn't do this again. If you respond to something, you just encourage it.'

'This is deep waters, Joe.' Mrs Whitney put the teapot on the Rayburn. 'I don't know what to say. Mr Kettle, now, he knew how to deal with this sorter business, but you, if you don't mind me saying so, you prob'ly don't.'

It could be deeply comforting having a neighbour like Mrs Whitney who had lived next door to Henry Kettle for many years and accepted dowsing (and everything it brought with it) as just another aspect of traditional country life, like blacksmithing and septic tanks.

'Get somebody in, you think I should do that?'

'Mr Kettle never liked to get nobody in. He was against all that. *Nothing psychic*, he used to say, *nothing psychic*.'

'Go away, then? Get myself sorted out?'

'I don't know what to say,' said Mrs Whitney. 'Your Fay – she's not coming back, is she?'

Through the wall they could hear the phone ringing in Powys's living room.

'Sooner or later you're going to have to answer that,' Mrs Whitney said.

'I think there's a fault on the line. No, I don't think she'll come back. Fay will probably go through life without anything happening to her again. If . . .'

He accepted a cup of strong tea.

'If she keeps away from you,' Mrs Whitney said. 'That what you mean?'

That probably was what he meant.

'That's no life, Joe.'

'She'll find somebody.'

Mrs Whitney sat down opposite him. 'I meant for you. No life at all, just you and that dog. Writing your books and walking the hills and trying to ignore stuff, and your hair going greyer

219

and them circles under your eyes getting bigger. No life, Joe, that isn't.'

It took him nearly an hour to put all the books back and assess the damage. For instance, the radio wouldn't work. It had fallen face-down and now it was dead. Possibly, something had drained the batteries; this had been known to happen.

He stood looking at the shelves, an unstable cliff-face. He put his hands flat to the books, leaned in. Like you stop an avalanche.

The phone wobbled as if it was about to ring, but it didn't.

I can't stand this. But if I leave it'll go with me. At least, if I stay here, there's Mrs Whitney and the leek and lentil soup.

The phone rang.

He stared at it. He could see his own fingermarks sweat-printed on the white plastic. He contemplated picking it up, hurling it at the wall. Wanted to do some violence back, didn't want it to think he was spooked.

When he picked up the phone it wasn't dead any more.

'Hello. Joe Powys?'

He hadn't got the breath to reply.

'I'm sorry, is that J. M. Powys?'

No detectable threat here. Nothing untoward. The voice sounded quite agreeable.

'Yes.' He coughed. 'Sorry.'

'Joe, my name's Dan Frayne. At Harvey-Calder. I've been looking at your manuscript.'

What? This was bloody quick. Unbelievably quick. Even if Ben Corby had dashed straight into the office with the manuscript as soon as he'd got back, told this bloke Frayne it was wonder-ful, unmissable, and Frayne had read it immediately, it still didn't figure. This was not how publishers worked.

'Do you ever get up to London?' Dan Frayne asked.

'Hang on . . .' Powys changed hands, put the phone to his other ear. 'I don't understand. I mean, you can't have had time to read it, Mr Frayne.'

'Well, that's true,' Dan Frayne said. 'But I've read *The Old Golden Land*, which I thought was wonderful – at the time. And, uh, Ben Corby told me all about the new book. About the way your attitude had changed.'

'He tell you anything else?'

Dan Frayne laughed. 'I have to say that when Ben got back he, er, he kind of wanted to talk to somebody. Old Ben was a little bit shaken. Not himself. Amazing.'

Powys looked up at the big, fat novel on the top shelf. He'd put it back on the shelf rather than keep it on a table or locked in a cupboard; you mustn't respond.

'There's an idea I've been tossing around for some time,' Dan Frayne said. 'Book I thought an old friend of mine should write, though I've never mentioned it to her. Then I thought she was too close to it, maybe someone should do it with her. But it would have to be someone of a like mind because this friend of mine . . . Anyway, I'd like to talk to you.'

Powys was confused. 'Let me get this right. We are not now talking about *Mythscapes*, we are talking about another book entirely.'

'We're talking about adapting and expanding the ideas in *Mythscapes* in a way that would make it rather more publishable.'

'I don't like the sound of it.'

'Come down and discuss it, huh? We'll meet all expenses.'

Had Ben Corby told this bloke Joe Powys was financially challenged? So broke, in fact, that he would write stuff to order?

'Say, this weekend?' Dan Frayne suggested. 'Or . . . Hey, can you get a train tonight?'

Powys was about to say no way, piss off, when he looked up at the book again. He thought he saw it move. He had an alarming vision of it emerging from the shelf, as if someone had slotted a forefinger into the top of its damaged spine, and hurled it with hurricane force at his head.

The voice in his ear said, 'Look, OK, I'll tell you when it clicked. It was when Ben told me – and he hated telling me, he made me swear not to mention it to anyone upstairs – it was when he told me about the book. *A Glastonbury Romance*. That was when the little bell did this ping.'

'The little bell?'

'The little bell that only pings for publishers. Maybe once or twice a year.'

'*That* bell, huh?'

Powys looked up at the book again. It sat comfortably in its space, between John Cowper Powys's *Weymouth Sands* and *Owen Glendower*, neither of which Powys had read.

He got the feeling the book, like Frayne, was waiting for his answer.

TWELVE

RESCUE REMEDY

Jim's living room was all studio now.

It had started as a gesture against bloody Pat, who he fervently hoped would never see it: the sofa pushed back to make space for the easels, the coffee table acting at first as a rest for the palette, then *becoming* a palette – colours mixed directly on to the varnish. Bloody Pat would have thrown a fit.

Gradually, the painting had crowded the rest of Jim's needs into corners: the cooker where he made his meals, the table where he ate, the TV he hardly ever watched, the armchair where he sometimes fell asleep pondering a composition problem, knowing that as soon as he awoke he could go for it, everything to hand.

Interior walls had been taken out, wherever possible, exposing the whole of the ground floor, where two pillars of ancient oak helped keep the ceiling up.

At the western end of the room, opposite the dingy little fireplace, half the wall had been taken out and replaced with glass, almost floor to ceiling. Most artists were supposed to prefer Northern light; not Jim. He called it his sunset window, and on good nights it had become a sheet of burning gold, as in

Bring me my bow of burning gold
Bring me my arrows of desire.

A bad joke now.

He'd fired off his pathetic arrows of desire. Shot his buggering bolt this time and no mistake.

Awakening to filthy grey light, he'd closed his eyes again in weariness, remembering he was supposed to be in the bookshop today. And at once had seen Juanita's lovely face with its gorgeously expansive smile, the tumble of heavy hair, the brown arms, those exquisitely exposed shoulders. Who might paint her nude? Degas? Renoir? Modigliani?

Certainly not Battle.

No more. Spell broken. Done it himself, like crunching a delicate glass bauble in his fist. No going back to that shop today. Nor ever. Couldn't face her again, would never be the same. No laughter. No banter. Surely she'd realise that.

Jim had rolled sluggishly out of bed, peered out at the mist, couldn't see farther than the buggering ash tree.

Thinking, at first, that he would paint. In the very centre of the studio, the three old-fashioned black, metal easels were set up in a pyramid formation. His Works in Progress. The glorious dusk. Over the past few weeks, he'd digested so much dusk he should be able to summon its colours and textures at any time of day. Even on a lousy, damp morning, the lousiest dampest morning of his buggering lousy life.

But when he'd stood in front of the canvases there'd been a congestion in his head. It felt soggy, spongy, and he'd found himself wondering, absurdly, if it had been his hat which had held his creativity together, helped to contain the glowing dusk, keep it burning in his head.

He'd inspected the paintings on the easels. Skies of clay, fields of carpet and lino. No mystery. No mystery there at all.

They were rubbish. He couldn't paint. What the hell had ever made him think he could paint?

Poor bloody Pat. Right all along, eh?

The sense of loss had settled around Jim like a grey gas. Like the first morning after the unexpected death of someone loved.

Which was one way of putting it. He'd gone back to bed, taking with him a bottle of Johnnie Walker.

Intermittently he'd awoken, feeling cold. Clouds obscuring the day, whisky obscuring his thoughts. What was left of life with his muse gone for ever? What could even Glastonbury ever mean to him again.

Sometimes he'd hear a distant ringing as the rain rolled like tears down the windows.

*

'He isn't answering.'

'Perhaps he's out painting,' Diane said.

'In the rain?'

'Well, perhaps he's painting inside then. You know how he hates to be disturbed while he's painting.'

'He shouldn't be painting at all. He knows he always comes in on a Friday. He . . .' Juanita broke off, looked hard at Diane. 'You don't want to do this, do you? You don't want to go to the police.'

Confusion was corrugating Diane's forehead. She'd been looking almost cheerful on her return from Sam Daniel's print-shop. Did Juanita know about this Glastonbury First meeting? No, Juanita didn't. Well, well, Griff and Archer obviously weren't letting the grass grow. A coincidence, too, that it should be held the same time as Woolly's road protest meeting. Or was it? They ought to keep tabs on this; perhaps she could go to one meeting and Diane to the other. Assuming they were back from the police station in time.

And then Juanita, looking at her watch, had said perhaps they really ought to be going soon, if only Jim would turn up. Diane hadn't answered, and that was when Juanita, not wanting to give her any more time to change her mind, had rung Jim.

And now Diane said, 'I've been thinking, Juanita. Perhaps I should talk to my father first. I can't just, you know, shop him.'

'You're shopping Rankin.'

'It's the same thing.'

'Listen, if you talk to your father, he'll stop you. Somehow he'll stop you. He'll convince you you didn't see what you know you did see . . .'

Juanita stopped, tried to hold Diane's eyes but Diane turned away.

'You really *did* see it, didn't you, Diane? You saw Gerry Rankin or his son or both of them kicking this boy's head. You saw the blood. Come on, I need to hear you say it.'

'Yes.' Diane stared hard at the counter. 'Yes, but . . .'

'Oh God, I knew it.'

'Why was he found miles away? The Rankins didn't take him to Stoke St Michael, they took me back to Bowermead. They left Headlice in Don Moulder's field.'

Juanita shrugged. 'So the Pilgrims found him, got scared . . .'

Scared? Those bastards?

'. . . and . . . and . . . listen to me, Diane . . . and they loaded him into his bus and somebody drove it off and dumped it in that wood. Then they got the hell out of Somerset. It makes perfect sense to me. These people will avoid the police even if they've done nothing wrong.'

She had to change the subject then because a couple of customers came in, elderly teacherish types, the kind who browsed for ever.

'Actually . . .' Lowering her voice. '. . . I can't help thinking I may have upset Jim. He was obviously leading up to saying what I didn't want him to say when Griff Daniel came into the bar and we all ran out into the street. I didn't see Jim after that.'

'He's a nice man,' Diane said.

'Yes,' Juanita carelessly dusted the counter. 'And only a few years older than Harrison Ford.'

This morning she'd contemplated what looked like a very sad and drooping face in the bedroom mirror and hadn't fallen into the usual routine of giving herself a what-the-hell consolatory grin before turning away.

Several of Jim's paintings hung in the flat. One showed a flank of the Tor below which the sun had set, the afterglow concentrated into a thin, vibrating red line, like a bright string pulled taut. It was clear that within a few seconds the line would have gone, and the earth was straining to hold and feel the moment.

Feel the moment. Jim had risen to feel the moment and she'd been horribly relieved when a force of nature called Griff Daniel had knocked him down. But that wouldn't have been obvious from her face, would it?

Verity put down her tea cloth and stepped into the middle of the kitchen, putting her hands together and closing her eyes as if about to pray. Then, very slowly, she opened them, like the arms of Tower Bridge.

Keeping her wrists joined together and raising her arms, bringing the cupped hands to face-level.

. . . like a priest presenting the chalice for High Mass, was how Dr Grainger had put it.

She opened her eyes and stared into the space between her hands. The light from the high window unfurled around her like a flag. She felt like a tiny Joan of Arc, the quilted body-warmer serving as a breastplate.

'Do this every hour,' Dr Grainger had instructed. 'And then when night falls and the window turns black – and this is the important part – *you continue to do it.*'

There was another exercise, which had to be done upstairs. It involved hugging an upright, perhaps the newel post at the top of the stairs, and at the same time feeling the walls closing around her, feeling the house hugging *her*.

She would assiduously practise both these exercises for a week, as instructed. She would embrace the dark.

She remembered the dramatic effects of the communal exercises led by Dr Grainger at the Assembly Rooms. It was not wrong. She would feel Colonel Pixhill beside her. And poor Major Shepherd. Abbot Whiting she was less sure about now, since the Dinner.

'That guy has a problem,' Dr Grainger had said when Oliver Pixhill had gone. 'He has a problem with his father. I don't buy what he was saying about the darkness in this house being down to the Colonel's essence. House this old, it shrugs people off. His problem is personal, I doubt it need concern you.'

'Oh, but it must, Dr Grainger. You see, he's a Trustee now. He has influence. The Old Guard, the people who knew the Colonel, they've all gone. All gone now. Major Shepherd was the last.'

'He can fire you, this Pixhill?'

'It's not quite as simple as that, if I refuse to leave. Which I shall, most certainly. But . . . Oh, I don't know what I'm going to do. I don't know what I'm *supposed* to do, except stay here and wait. There's no one to advise me. Poor Major Shepherd.'

She'd put a drop of Dr Bach's Rescue Remedy on her tongue, Dr Grainger nodding approval.

'This major, he was the Colonel's right-hand man?'

'They served together in the War. Dr Grainger, it's not true what Oliver said about the Colonel. He was a good, kind man. He wouldn't have harmed anyone. He loved people. He loved Glastonbury.'

'Sure. I'm sure you're right.'

'I'm probably speaking out of turn, but perhaps Oliver expected the house to be left to him until the Trust was set up. Oh dear, I don't even know how or when he became a Trustee. His name was just there.'

'These trusts, sometimes they like to have a relative. Usually to see that the wishes of the founder are adhered to.'

'He was just a boy,' Verity said. 'What could he know of the Colonel's wishes?'

Dr Grainger had nodded sagely as Verity put the kettle on the Aga for camomile tea.

'You see, only two days ago Major Shepherd said that someone would help me. He said things were coming to a head, but if I could hold on . . .'

'That's what he said? If you could hold on, someone would come along who could help you?'

Verity bit her lip. Dr Grainger smiled, brushing a cobweb from the sleeve of his black jacket. It was the kind of jacket that vicars used to wear.

'Maybe someone did, Verity.'

'Did?'

'Come along. To help you.'

'You mean . . .?'

'I told you, I can make it easier for you here. You just have to trust me.'

Thinking of Colonel Pixhill and his desire to experience the Holy Grail, Verity opened her hands, keeping them joined at the wrist.

As if to receive a chalice.

THIRTEEN

A SPIRITUAL HOTHOUSE

Harvey-Calder UK had a new building, near Canary Wharf with its Empire State obelisk. Some London New Age group claimed this was the crossing point of major metropolitan leys, a significant power centre. Ben Corby was probably in the process of publishing a book on it.

Powys stared at the tower. He'd only seen it in pictures before.

He couldn't believe he'd done this.

Leaving Arnold with Mrs Whitney, he'd driven into Hereford and jumped on the Intercity before he could change his mind. He didn't even know if there was a train, but he walked into the station five minutes before it got in.

He was getting this feeling of being on a conveyor belt, everything going as smoothly as if it was pre-programmed. As if it was fate.

He'd thought of ringing Fay at the BBC. In the sure knowledge that if she had an engagement tonight, she'd cancel it. She would be there. Whenever. He knew that; he'd be the same. So he didn't call, it wouldn't be fair. Also, if he looked to Fay as bad as he'd looked to Mrs Whitney, she probably wouldn't let him go back home. Which would help neither of them.

Dan Frayne's office was on the third floor. It was all open-plan, like the Stock Exchange, computer terminals everywhere. This maybe told you something you needed to know about publishing in the nineties.

'Joe Powys,' Dan Frayne said. 'Hey. Amazing. Jesus, man, you look all-in. Heavy journey? Bobby, coffee. Coffee OK for you?'

He was probably in his late forties. He had cropped grey hair and an earring with a small green stone in it. His shapeless clothes emphasised how thin he was and made Joe Powys, in clean jeans and a new sweater, feel overdressed. He stared at Powys for a long time over his glass-topped desk.

'No. You don't look like him. Not at all. Of course, I'm only going off the pictures.'

'Pictures? Oh. Him. Ah well,' Powys said, 'I never claimed to be related.'

Dan Frayne leaned forward, put on a mysterious whisper. 'Why, then? Doesn't he like you cashing in on his name, or what? Why's he doing this to you?'

They switched to a nearby wine bar, where everybody seemed to know Dan Frayne. 'I'm not trying to impress you,' he said. 'I need this. I need to be surrounded by dozens of people who know me superficially. Superficially. That's important.'

Joe Powys liked people who were full of nervous energy. They couldn't hide what was on their minds, came out with it, rarely lied.

'I used to have this shop in Glastonbury. Brrr.' Frayne shuddered. 'Bad news, Joe. I mean, for me. Too much closed-in, heavy stuff.' He spread his arms. 'I like to be surrounded by lightweights. I am not a heavy person.'

Powys looked around. Everybody else in the glass and leather bar looked, to him, to be pretty intense.

'No, no,' said Frayne. 'This is really superficial. Money is superficial. I love saying that. People think I'm crazy. Like, "Get outa here, you old hippy, what do *you* know about the real world?"'

Powys smiled.

'Well, it's true. I'm an old hippy. But – this is the point – I'd rather be an old hippy among the suits. I'd rather publish straight books than be down in the basement with Ben Corby, peddling esoterica. Ben, he copes with it because he's not a hippy and he really does value money and possessions. This make sense to you?'

'Possibly.'

'Now you're being cautious. You're like I was when I came out of Glastonbury.'

'You make it sound', Powys said, 'like coming out of Pentonville.'

Dan Frayne became quite sober. 'I never go back to Glastonbury. I can't function there. I can't stand to be an old hippy among old hippies. In Glastonbury you don't know anybody superficially. You know them intensely, deeply, intimately. You know their star signs and the colour of their auras. Amazing. They don't have superficial in Glastonbury. They either put their arms around you and hug you till you squeak or they ignore you. Listen, this book of yours, I've been reading it. I see Ben's point. I'd've binned it too. *Golden Land* was OK, this one I'd've binned.'

'Well, thanks,' Powys said.

'Except . . .' Dan held up both hands '. . . I noticed something. I noticed that in neither of those books do you ever refer to the celestial city. Not the merest mention in the index. The only earth-mysteries tomes in the history of the cosmos that don't go banging on about the legends of Glastonbury.'

'No mystery about that. I've just never been.'

Dan Frayne pretended to pass out with shock.

'Put it this way. If your name was Constable and you were a bit of a painter, would you buy a bungalow near Flatford Mill?'

'Ben Corby would,' said Dan Frayne.

'Ben Corby would buy the mill.'

'This is true,' Dan said.

'But anyway, it'd been done. To death. Everybody discussing earth-mysteries has to do Glastonbury. I'd got nothing new to contribute.'

'When did that ever put a writer off?'

'Anyway,' Powys said. 'Now you know, you can bin the book with a clear conscience.'

Gloom descended. You spend a long time isolated in the country, it's not easy psyching yourself up to come to London with what looks like a begging bowl.

'I'll tell you something,' Dan Frayne said. '*Mythscapes*. I would've dumped the book, but I still like the idea because it's an antidote to the New Age that isn't written by either a sceptic or a born-again Christian. It's that bit different. I just think it would be a better book, a more interesting book, a book with wider commercial appeal . . . if it was also about, uh . . .'

'Don't say it.' Powys felt a certain big book winging through the air, over fields and hills, through towns and industrial estates, on the great ley-line leading to . . .

'Glastonbury,' Dan said. 'As it really is. Today. The pressures it imposes on people living in Jerusalem Builded Here. The tensions between the Christians and the New Age pagans. Reflecting a friction that's been there in Glastonbury for centuries, millennia . . . aeons, I don't know.'

Silence. Or the nearest you could get to silence in a wine bar in Canary Wharf.

'Well.' Powys stood up. 'It's been nice meeting you.'

'Aw, come on, Powys, siddown. Hear me out, man.' Dan signalled to a waitress dressed like Powys's idea of a top-drawer callgirl. 'Same again, Estelle. The thing is . . .' He put his briefcase on the table between them. 'Can I talk to you? Do you mind? Personal stuff?'

'What happened to superficial?'

'I just want to tell you why. Explain the background to this. Hey you look pretty rough, did I tell you that?'

'I drop a lot of Valium,' Powys said. 'Go on.'

'OK,' Dan said, 'I didn't know much about Glastonbury except everybody said it was Camelot and Jerusalem rolled into one and you could get high there without drugs. So twenty-odd years ago I went out West with my lady. If I'm honest, Glastonbury wasn't the major pull. It was her. Gorgeous is not the word, but I'm only a publisher, never been good with words.'

He took a large, brown envelope from the briefcase, slid out a photograph and handed it to Powys. It was from the days when coloured photos tended to come out all blue and mauve. It showed a girl in a long white dress standing in a shop doorway. Over the door was a sign, hand-painted in vaguely psychedelic Celtic lettering. Carey and Frayne, it said.

Powys said, 'What about "lustrous"?' He peered at the picture again. '"Mesmerising"? "Iridescent"?'

'Half-Spanish,' Dan said. 'Well, Mexican, I suppose. Her father was a British doctor working out in middle America after the War, met this Latin beauty and brought her back to Blighty. Result: an English rose with a hint of something more exotic. She was a few years younger than me. I was, as you can imagine, a man-of-the-world figure, with a set of Grateful Dead albums and a regular supply of you-know-what. Golden days, Joe.'

'I was too young.'

'That's what they all say. Thank you, Estelle, that's super. Keep the change. Buy yourself some woolly socks.'

Dan Frayne watched Estelle's bottom all the way to the bar and explained how his lady had had a small legacy from granny, and he'd sold his Triumph Vitesse and they'd run away to the Isle of Avalon where they'd rented a little shop to specialise in second-hand books and underground magazines and privately published hippy stuff about UFOs and ley-lines.

'You think you've arrived in the Elysian Fields. You think you'll be there for ever. Then it starts to get to you. It's like a spiritual hothouse. What you think of as your spirit grows like rhubarb in shit. Amazing.'

Dan swallowed some golden beer.

'Suddenly you've got more bloody spirit than you can cope with, and you can't breathe for it. I'm on paradise island with the most beautiful girl in the world, and we . . . we'd fight. All the time. Over nothing. Over anything. You're pulled to extremes. No half measures. No compromises. Everything's a big issue in Avalon. Everybody you know is a healer and a seeker after wisdom. There are days in August when the air's like incense. I couldn't stand it. To cut a long, long, *long*, story short, I pissed off.'

His mood had changed.

'Broke me up, leaving her, but I wouldn't go back. I didn't trust myself. You know?'

'Because you might have stayed,' Powys said. 'Tried again.'

Dan Frayne nodded vigorously. 'I'd've stayed, and after a few months it would've been exactly the same. I've never been back. She stayed. She's stubborn. And, all credit to her, the shop's grown and it's a good business now. We've kept in touch. Not so much now. I'm married, three kids, you see the problem.'

Powys glanced at the photograph of the girl in the doorway.

Dan said, 'The only way I'd have gone back to Avalon was with the family as insulation, and how would she have felt then? Don't get me wrong, she wasn't always alone – you know, this and that, over the years.'

Dan began to unpack the brown envelope. It was full of letters, some hand-written, some printed.

'When you look like her, there's no shortage of suitors. But it was clear – you can read this stuff – that she'd built a wall around herself. Maybe that's how you do it. Survive. You know, mentally.'

'And this is the woman you wanted to do the book? The definitive Glastonbury exposé.'

Dan Frayne finished his beer.

'I'm worried about her,' he said. 'I get a feeling, I . . . nothing like that, I'm about as psychic as a microwave oven. I'm just worried. Maybe a little latent guilt. I'm sorry, this isn't what you expected to hear.'

'You want to commission a book because you're worried about a woman you left in Glastonbury?'

'Um . . .' Dan Frayne considered. 'Yeah.' He put his glass down. 'Yeah, I suppose that's the size of it. Amazing.'

234

FOURTEEN

SOMETHING HANGING
FROM IT

It was a Gothic-shaped doorway six steps up at the end of an alley framed by High Street shops. Over the door a sign said: ASSEMBLY ROOMS.

The alternative town hall, in fact. On occasion, Juanita could be induced to admit a certain affection for the place.

Diane said, 'I'll let you know what happens, then.' With her usual fashion flair, she was wearing an old and patched red woollen coat over a baggy turquoise sweatshirt and jeans.

'Er ... slight misunderstanding.' Juanita smiled innocently. Diane had got away with enough today; because of Jim not showing up they hadn't made it to the police station. 'I kind of thought you might go to the other one. Would you mind?'

'Glastonbury First? But I thought ...'

Diane was looking at Juanita's outfit, which comprised a plain charcoal-grey formal jacket with a skirt, a creamy silk top and a pink chiffon scarf. Not very Assembly Rooms.

'Would that be a terrible imposition, Diane? I thought you might recognise a few of the people I wouldn't.'

Diane looked resigned. 'Do you want me to take notes?'

'I don't think so. Let's not make your *Avalonian* role too obvious at this stage. Try and blend into the background.'

Some chance of that, Juanita thought, watching Diane drift down the street, as inconspicuous as a pheasant in a chicken run. But at least she wouldn't be in the same meeting as the predatory Ceridwen.

The church-type wooden doors of the Assembly Rooms had been thrown back to reveal yellow walls, more steps inside and a stand-up poster reading: RESIST ROAD-RAPE.

Woolly wandered up to stand with Juanita at the entrance to the alleyway, watching the punters going in, shaking his head in disappointment.

235

'Two real locals, maybe three.'

'And the rest we know,' Juanita said.

It was a shame; Woolly had also tried to give the meeting an element of conventional respectability. He was wearing a suit, had his hair pulled tightly back and bound with a fresh rubber band, looked almost like a regular person.

'That bastard Griff Daniel. You reckon he had advance warning about the road?'

'Well, the word is some posters went out yesterday. But they only went up this morning. Archer?'

'Bastard.' Woolly shook his head.

Still, he couldn't have been expecting a vast crowd. Apart from the easing of traffic congestion and rush-hour holdups, most people would be thinking about all the extra jobs the road would bring, how it would open up central Somerset to Euro-money.

'Trouble is, the Government's got the bloody moral high ground,' Woolly said. 'Take the juggernauts off the village roads, make the towns safer for the kids, you got the mums and dads on your side before you start. But it's all bullshit – you put this bloody road in and traffic expands to fill it, as traffic invariably does, and the lorries start hitting the village lanes again and kiddies still get mown down, and then you need another new road, and so it goes, until the whole of the West is a sea of metal.'

'That's what I love about you old hippies,' Juanita said. 'You never lose that dewy-eyed optimism.'

'Unless we stop it now.' Woolly pulled Juanita into the shadowy doorway of a picture-framing shop. 'I got this leaflet through the post the other day. Offering the support of the eco-guerrillas.'

'God,' said Juanita. 'I'm not sure I like the sound of that.'

'They got a point. Public inquiries and stuff, 'tis no more than a charade. But if contractors find their diggers getting vandalised, the bosses' fancy cars getting scratched . . .'

'Oh, Woolly, that's not you.'

'Yeah, I know. I hate that stuff. Man of peace. But what d'you do, Juanita?'

'Well, you don't do anything undemocratic. You're a councillor.'

'Sure,' said Woolly. 'But when you get on the council, you find out pretty soon how helpless local authorities are. Thing is, with this bunch in there and no *local* locals, you're gonner get demands for the extreme option anyway. Not counting the ones who'll recommend curses and laying out the runes and stuff.'

'Ceridwen's there, then,' Juanita said.

Woolly grinned. 'Least *you* done me proud, Juanita. You look . . . sheesh.'

'Well, thank you, Woolly. I decided to pass up on the pearls.'

'Anyway.' Woolly straightened his tie; it was actually a kipper tie, *circa* 1974, featuring Andy Warhol's Marilyn Monroe. 'I better get in there, strut my stuff.'

'Just don't go over the top, there'll almost certainly be Press there.'

'Yeah,' said Woolly dismally. 'They're the ones not smoking joints. Sheesh, I can't even see Jim Battle. He'll be coming, surely?'

'Yes,' Juanita said tightly. 'I'm sure he will.' She glanced over her shoulder and went into the meeting.

He poured another Scotch, pulled three bristle brushes from the sink, putting aside the linseed oil; time for neat turps. Got to work fast. Get this down while the energy's there.

The three paintings on their easels were all part of the same picture. He could see it now. The afterglow, usually close to the centre of the canvas, should in fact be on the perimeter, a *before* glow. The paint burning through from the edges, to the heart of the experience, the core of the pyramid.

Where lay the Grail.

Why had he never seen this before? To reach the inner light, you had to pass through darkness. Every experience, no matter how negative, was a force for progress. Even the worst humiliation – the sickle over your head, rejection by the woman you'd yearned for . . . all part of a rite of passage, through the deepest darkness, to the core of it all.

He was feeling so much better now he was painting. He'd been hoping for a good dusk to fire him, but the rain had kept on. Only when a bough of the ash tree tapped on his window, awakening him – and he saw something hanging from that bough, yes, yes – did he realise he could ignite his own:

Inside: he'd poured more whisky, finishing off the Johnnie Walker, starting on the Chivas Regal he'd been saving for Christmas. Arousing a glow in his gut and feeling it spread.

And *outside*: he'd pulled out the dog grate and lit a fire on the stone hearth, building a pyramid of oak logs, watching the sparks shoot out until the logs began to turn red, and then he'd wedged more logs around them, making a hard, hot funnel.

By the time it got dark, the whole room was glowing with a roaring, red energy.

Never lifting his gaze from the canvas, Jim Battle rummaged like a blind man among the tumble of tubes on his worktable to find a fat, full one he rarely used.

It would be labelled *Lamp Black*.

The association calling itself Glastonbury First was clearly not a sham after all. For a start, you had to be seriously confident to hold your inaugural public meeting at the Town Hall.

The building was next to the Abbey gatehouse and a little taller – nineteenth-century officialdom overseeing ancient sanctity. The town hall was lit up, the gatehouse an archaic silhouette.

The worrying part was that the main hall was nearly full. Must be close to four hundred people. Diane sat at the back, near the doors, as a sober-looking band filed on to the stage, among them Griff Daniel, discreetly followed by her brother Archer, and a wave of spirited applause from the floor.

She hadn't seen Archer in months. He'd put on a little weight, the chest-expanding, shoulder-widening kind she supposed heavyweight boxers like to acquire before a fight. Archer's hair was coiled and springy; he looked well.

Would Archer chair the meeting? Couldn't, surely, be Griff Daniel; he didn't have a terrific reputation for integrity.

It was neither of them. A bulky figure in a pinstriped double-breasted suit stood up at the table, perusing his notes through half-glasses. Oh gosh, Mr Cotton, Quentin Cotton MBE, noted charitable fund-raiser and the Ffitch family solicitor.

Credibility. *Mega* credibility.

Mr Cotton coughed for silence.

After thanking everyone for coming, he said, 'It saddens me that such a gathering as this should even be necessary. One might reasonably have thought that everyone in this town would put Glastonbury first. But this, regrettably, is not the case.'

Oh well; obvious what was coming.

'An increasing number of persons in our midst – although I doubt that any at all is here tonight – appear to give higher priority to bizarre beliefs of a quasi-religious nature, which for various far-fetched reasons, they appear to consider appropriate to our pleasant old country town . . . a town which, let me say at the outset, *has no use for this nonsense!*'

An awful cheer arose. Mr Cotton smiled grimly and nodded.

'Where once we attracted the more discerning visitor, we now draw, on one level, the lunatic fringe and, on another, what I can only describe as the dregs of the inner-cities. Those who exist on state benefits and prefer to steal from our shops rather than expend any of their hard-claimed money, which they prefer to go on drink and drugs.'

Clapping, general noises of affirmation, and a dusting of bitter laughter.

'But you're not here to listen to my opinions. You want facts. And behind me is a distinguished panel of experts ready and waiting to supply them. First, may I introduce a local businessman, well known to most of you – Mr Stanlow Pike, of Pike and Corner, estate agents and valuers, who will outline for you precisely how the value of the very fabric of this town has declined. By the fabric, I mean your homes. By decline, well, I think I am talking – and Mr Pike will confirm this – in the region of twenty per cent. Calamitous. Mr Pike . . .'

An anxiously overweight man in his fifties, Mr Pike began by saying that his business had been established in this town for three generations.

'I can see among you many of my clients, past and . . . and present. Among the, er, present clients are . . .' Stanlow Pike was pressing the tips of his fingers into the table, his body leaning back then forward like a large bird on a perch. '. . . Are several who have had properties for sale for more than a year and been unable to find a satisfactory purchaser. This is, to an extent, a national problem as you all must be aware. And a problem shared by every other agent in this town. However, it is worse here. Worse than Somerton, worse than Street, worse than Castle Cary. Because this most beautiful and historic town is no longer . . . no longer considered such a desirable place to live. And . . . and we all know why.'

One after another, they arose. The chemist, who had suffered two drug-related burglaries. The local official of the National Farmers' Union, whose members had been obliged to blockade their land against the thieving, trespassing travellers.

Griff Daniel's own speech was brief and, at first, restrained. He was a local man. He remembered a time when these mystical types were just a handful of harmless cranks. When they wore suits and ties like everyone else. When they did nothing more threatening than picnic on the Tor.

Which brought him to the point of this gathering.

''Tis a pretty place, the Tor, on a summer's morn,' Griff said lyrically. 'But after dark . . .'

He thumped the table once with his fist.

'. . . after dark, 'tis a threat and a menace to us all.'

Griff's face broke into a grim smile.

'But they also know the law, these scum. They know they're legal. Now don't that make you sick?'

'Disgraceful!' someone shouted.

'Indeed. But that's a public place, and if there aren't more'n six vehicles, they can do pretty much what they like there. And I know that most decent people in this town do not want these layabouts and are deeply, *deeply* frustrated that we cannot keep 'em out altogether. Now I'm not a lawyer and not a politician, except in the most amateur way, look . . .'

Diane was pretty glad at this moment that Juanita was not here.

'. . . so I took my problem to a man whose roots in this area go back farther than mine and probably farther than anybody else's in this room tonight. Now he's a new boy in the political game . . .'

'Oh really!' Diane exclaimed crossly. A woman in a hat turned and gave her a hard look.

'. . . but he's got his head screwed on and he knows how people in this town think and feel. Ladies and gentlemen, we are pleased and honoured to have with us tonight, the Hon. Archer Ffitch, MP-elect for Mendip South.'

In the midst of the applause a lone voice was raised.

'Just a bloody minute!' Five rows in front of Diane, a man had shot to his feet. 'I object! If you're gonner do your arse-licking in public, Dad, at least get it right.'

Oh gosh, Sam Daniel.

Griff's eyes bulged like a frog's. He strode angrily towards the edge of the platform, as though ready to jump down and attack his son.

Archer arose easily and put a large, firm hand on Griff's shoulder.

'Thank you, Mr Daniel. And thank you, also, to the gentleman who pointed out that understandable error. I am, of course, not quite MP-elect. The term, at this stage, is Prospective Parliamentary Candidate. Although, perhaps – who can tell, strange things happen in Glastonbury – perhaps exposure to the atmosphere at the bottom end of High Street has bestowed upon Mr Daniel the gift of prophecy . . .'

This caused an immediate eruption of mirth. Diane raised her eyes to the plaster mouldings.

Sam Daniel sat down. The young woman next to him looked furious. Diane recognised her at once. Charlotte Lovidge: dark-haired, undeniably chic, a trifle haughty. Diane saw Sam try to take Charlotte's hand, whereupon she turned pointedly away from him.

They were an item? Gosh. Charlotte, who couldn't be more than twenty-four, worked for Stanlow Pike, possibly training to become a valuer and auctioneer. It seemed an unlikely liaison for Sam. Diane supposed it came down very much to basics: Charlotte was extremely attractive.

Diane huddled into her coat, feeling fat and frumpish, as her brother Archer began to speak.

*

Against the greystone walls of the Assembly Rooms, they looked a fairly joyless bunch tonight, Juanita thought. They'd shelved the quest for the Grail for the present. They were here to plan a crusade to protect their holy land from the infidels.

'My information,' Woolly was saying from the makeshift black-box stage, 'is that they'll be making a start pretty soon after Christmas.'

There was a rumble from the more committedly Alternative types sitting cross-legged on the carpet below the stage.

'They've learned a few lessons from other road-protests – use the bad-weather months, don't make it easy, don't let the protest turn into a holiday camp with open-air music, stuff like that, don't attract tourists. Anyway, they'll start by clearing woodland. Chainsaw gangs.'

'Savages,' a woman yelled. Road-construction seemed to have taken over from nuclear power as the number one ecomenace.

'Do we know where?' another woman asked. A strong voice, Juanita noted. A voice with a sort of cello effect.

Dame Wanda. Just what the campaign needed. Ha.

Woolly shrugged. 'You tell me. That's what we got to organise. Intelligence. People on the ground who'll report anything suspicious. But this is a preliminary meeting, and there's things we can't very well discuss in a public place, so I suggest we form a Road-rape Action Committee. For which we need an office. Got to get it together under one roof. Somewhere we could have manned round the clock.'

'*Staffed!*' It was Jenna, the wire-thin Cauldron member. 'Staffed around the clock.'

'Staffed,' said Woolly wearily. Jenna sat down amid a cluster of women in the centre of the room. To her left, Juanita saw the free-floating blonde hair of Domini Dorrell-Adams. To her right the grey coils of Ceridwen.

Ceridwen whispered something to Jenna, who was back on her feet at once.

'I propose Wanda Carlisle as a kind of president or something, because . . . because she's a famous person and will attract publicity to the cause.'

And because you can control her, Juanita thought.

'All right,' Woolly said without enthusiasm, doubtless realising he wasn't going to be running the campaign much longer. 'You all wanner take a vote on that one?'

And when the hands rose, Juanita rose too and left. It was all so predictable. Anyway, she wanted to ring Jim again, maybe go up there and drag him out to the pub.

She wasn't prepared to lose a friend.

Funny, all those evenings outside on the hill, the stage all set, the sun primed like the canvas. All those evenings, summer and winter, vest and overcoat. Never realising that on the other side of the dusk was an intensity of energy he'd never dared dream of.

And when he was at last closing in on the mystical vanishing point, when he'd finally found – so to speak – the burial plot of the Grail, it was happening inside his cottage on a grey and sodden evening in no-hope November.

Jim had come through. He lurched from canvas to canvas, pushing the paint before him, as the bronze heat gasped from the fireplace, turning his studio into an alchemist's laboratory, a cave . . . a cave within the Tor itself.

He felt like a god. The god of the cave. The old god Gwyn ap Nudd, Celtic lord of the dead, in his chamber at the heart of the Tor.

The thought of the other Gwyn ap Nudd, the pagan goat-priest, no longer made Jim shrivel inside. What the priest had taken from him, he had summoned back. He'd seen it. In the ash tree. It was a sign; he was in control again.

Well into the bottle of Chivas Regal now, he thought about Juanita with her heavy, dark hair, her big Spanish mouth, her breasts, like brown, freckled eggs.

He lunged with his brush and was only half-aware of it tearing the canvas. He thought he saw faces in the sunset window, but he didn't care.

He was close to breaking through to the Grail. The ash tree stroked the wall, something hanging from it.

FIFTEEN

A BEAUTIFUL DUSK

The rain was easing as Juanita walked quickly along High Street. She'd made up her mind: she would ring Jim once more and then take a drive up there.

She caught sight of her reflection in the darkened window of the veggie-bar. From a distance of five feet, in an almost-sophisticated ensemble, under an umbrella, backlit by the golden streetlamp, she could almost be a refined version of the sylph with the headdress on the front of that long-ago *Avalonian*.

Maybe she ought to change before going to Jim's.

The door of the former Holy Thorn Ceramics – its sign had gone – opened suddenly, making her heart race, some primitive part of her quite ready to see the goddess standing there in all her dark glory.

But it was only Tony Dorrell-Adams and a suitcase.

'Tony?'

He scowled at first, then saw her, the way she was dressed.

'Oh. Hi, Juanita. You look . . . normal.'

'Thanks.'

'You know what I mean.' She could almost feel the accumulated sorrow and the bafflement vibrating around him.

'Yes. I do. I'm sorry, Tony, I really am.'

'I bet you are.'

His car was parked by the kerb, an old Cavalier hatch-back. He put his suitcase on the wet pavement, released the rear door.

'Look,' Juanita said. 'I'm not part of this, you know.'

'You're a woman. That makes you part of it.'

'Why don't you come over to the shop, have a cup of tea? Talk about it? You can't leave like this. Can't just give up.'

'Watch me,' Tony said. 'I've been given the car. Wasn't that kind? I get custody of the car so I've got the means to remove myself. It would be appreciated if I do this quietly, while every-body, including my wife, is in the protest meeting.'

Tony threw the suitcase into the boot and slammed the door, lamp-lit drops ricocheting into the night like angry sparks.

'This stinks, Tony.'

'Oh, no. This is Glastonbury. It's too holy to stink.' Tony wiped rain out of his eyes. Probably rain.

'Where will you go?'

'Back to teaching, I expect. I'll find something. Naturally, I'll fight the cow for everything I can get. She wants to keep this place open, she'll have to get some money from her precious Sisters of the fucking Cauldron. Not that anybody's going to want to buy pot goddesses with big . . . I'm sorry, I'm sorry. OK, maybe you weren't involved. In which case, I'd watch my back if I were you.'

'They can't touch me.'

'No?' He looked her in the eyes, half-pitying. 'They can touch anybody, destroy anything. Christ, I used to think we were ulti-mately inseparable, Domini and me. Meeting of minds, spiritually attuned. Good sex. Bit of a blip, stupid fling that meant nothing, but this was going to be where we got it all together again. That chap who works in your shop . . .'

'Jim.'

'Jim, yeah. He said last night that this was the last place you should come to repair your marriage. Wise man. There should be barbed wire around this town.'

'Come and have a drink.'

'No. I've got to get out of here.' He wiped his eyes again; it cer-tainly wasn't rain this time. 'I don't claim to understand any of this. I won't be able to explain it to anyone. I wish I could, but I can't.'

'Just hang on a minute, OK? One minute.'

Juanita gave him the umbrella to hold and ran across the road to the bookshop. She was back inside the minute to find Tony stand-ing at the kerb, arms by his side, the umbrella pointing at the pave-ment. Soaked through and he didn't seem even to have noticed it was raining. She shoved the book into his cold, damp hands.

'What's this?'

'You said you wished you understood. It might help.'

He peered at the book. 'I can't see.'

'It's Colonel Pixhill's Diary.'

'Oh. That.' He didn't seem impressed. 'Domini had one, threw it away.'

'People do,' Juanita said. '*Some* people do. He can make you feel very depressed. Until something like this happens and then maybe he's the guru you've been searching for. I'm not even supposed to sell it to people unless they specifically ask, so I'm giving it to you. Read it when you get to wherever you're going.'

'Harlow, Essex. Harlow New Town. My parents live there. No legends. No history to speak of. A real sanctuary. Thanks. Thanks for the book.' Tony raised a hand, unsmiling, climbed into his Cavalier and started the engine.

But it was a while before he could pull out into the road, and a while before Juanita could cross it. Because of the sudden traffic.

From a distance, it looked like a motorbike. When she saw what it was, Juanita went weak.

A bus with only one headlight and an engine like a death-rattle. Then a converted ambulance with NATIONAL ELF SERVICE across its windscreen. And then a hump-back delivery van, the kind the Post Office used to have, only with a window punched in the side. And then an old hearse. And more of the same, gasping and limping through the endless rain, a mobile scrapyard.

Oh no.

Juanita shrank into the Holy Thorn doorway, both hands around the umbrella stem. Holding the thing in front of her like a riot-shield, as they rumbled past and clattered past and groaned past, under the diffident, crane-necked gaze of the seen-it-all Glastonbury streetlamps.

The convoy from hell.

The umbrella shook rigidly in Juanita's hands. A sick ritual on the Tor, followed by a death. And they had the nerve, the arrogance, to come back.

Maybe they'd returned for the meeting – that was all poor old Woolly needed.

But no. She watched them proceed like a ramshackle funeral cortège, along High Street. For Chilkwell Street. For Wellhouse Lane. And the Tor.

*

The house lights dipped dramatically and Archer Ffitch became a powerful silhouette against a pure white rectangle.

He was suddenly so much like their father. Because all you could see was his shape, thicker but no hint of fat. Because you couldn't see their mother's moist lips and their mother's grey eyes. Because, like Father, he seemed at his most relaxed standing up, or erect on a hunter. And he was awfully relaxed at the moment.

'I want to show you some pictures,' he said. 'I want to show you a possible solution. But I want, first of all, to make it clear that I am acting here not as a politician but as a concerned resident of this area. What I am about to outline is a preliminary proposal, to be tossed around the democratic arena, adjusted, refined and perhaps, at the end of the day – who can tell? – rejected. I hope this will not be the case, because I believe it is the only way to correct an unhealthy imbalance in this fine old town.'

The hall was hushed.

'I believe,' said Archer, 'that the only solution to the problem must lie in restricting the activities of hippies, travellers and undesirables, without in any way diminishing the rights of local people.'

Archer lifted a hand and a picture appeared on the screen behind him: the top of Glastonbury Tor, the St Michael tower filling the screen from top to bottom.

'The Tor,' said Archer, 'is the property of the National Trust, a body responsible for making our nation's heritage accessible to the general public, and none of us would wish that to be otherwise.'

The next picture was an aerial photograph, looking down on the St Michael tower and the discoloured grass around it.

'I have been unable to establish,' said Archer, 'precisely how many tons of earth have been replaced here in recent years because of erosion caused by human feet. Or how many sheep have been killed by uncontrolled dogs. I would hate to estimate how many tons of human excreta have remained unburied by people flouting the fairly unenforceable laws about camping out on the Tor. And there are no records of how many innocent people – and children – have been disturbed or disgusted by the most shameless and perverse sexual shenanigans taking place in full public view. Is this – I ask you now – what we expect of a National Trust site?'

The response was immediate and deafening.

Diane didn't reply; she was struggling with a terrible sensation of foreboding. Oh, Archer would be canonised, all right. Archer was very good at sincerity.

The slide changed to a less dramatic picture: a close-up of an Ordnance Survey map intersected by hand-drawn black lines. Archer tapped the map on the screen with a pen.

'Let us first of all ask ourselves why these members of what they like to describe as an Alternative society flock like lemmings to this tiny hill. It is because of an unfortunate legacy.'

Archer paused.

A memory came to Diane of a Christmas when she was seven or eight, a Boxing Day afternoon spent hiding in her bedroom, trying to read her book and blank out the sound of the hunting horn. She'd fallen asleep in her mother's old rocking chair and awoken to find . . .

'. . . a legacy of nonsense from that most unstable of decades, the nineteen-sixties, when a so-called culture founded upon psychedelic drugs and led, I imagine, by bearded gurus from Tibet decided that the Tor was A Place of Power . . . where many so-called ley-lines intersect. The fact that no archaeologist or anyone with even basic common sense gives any credence whatever to this fatuous rubbish . . .'

He would know, of course, that the person in Glastonbury most obsessed with leys was Councillor Woolly Woolaston, whose reputation would be seriously eroded tonight. Diane briefly closed her eyes.

And remembered half-waking in her mother's chair that Boxing Day and stroking fur. She'd wanted a dog as a pet; her father had refused; he said dogs were for working and hunting, dogs were for outside.

Archer was laughing. '. . . gullible and rootless people who believe that they can get "high" on Glastonbury Tor. With or without the use of mind-altering drugs. Is this what that august body, the National Trust, exists to promote?'

This was just awful.

'Now the Tor,' Archer said, 'is, as my friend Mr Daniel pointed out a few minutes ago, a pretty place on a summer's day. A place where, doubtless, some of you would like to take your children or visiting relatives, were you not afraid of what they might see.'

'Or tread in,' Griff Daniel commented from a few yards along the stage.

'Quite. I'm also quite sure that none of you would wish to go there at night, or on some pagan solstice, or for the purpose of altering your perceptions . . . So let me outline to you a comprehensive plan.'

As a new slide appeared on the screen, Diane remembered sleepily stroking the fur in her lap, wondering vaguely why her skirt was wet and her hand sticky. Oh dear, perhaps the puppy had . . .

But it hadn't been a puppy at all. It was a fox. Or rather its head. A trophy from the Boxing Day hunt. One of its eyes was missing. Its jaws had been prised open. Its needly teeth gleamed with blood. Blood from its neck had soaked through Diane's Christmas kilt.

The old image brought tears of horror and pity to Diane's eyes. She blinked them away, tried to focus on the screen. The picture on the screen was not of Glastonbury, but it was instantly familiar.

Diane remembered Archer denying having anything to do with the fox's head, denying it with such appalled vigour and absolute sincerity that, by the end of the afternoon, Father was almost accusing Diane of having planted it to get her brother in trouble. *Blooded at last, eh?* Archer had whispered in her ear as they left the room.

On the screen, stormclouds glowered over the grey sentinels of the world's most famous prehistoric monument, Stonehenge.

'No . . .' She clapped a hand over her mouth.

He couldn't. He *couldn't* be suggesting . . .

But Archer didn't do anything he wasn't fairly sure of. Archer hated the thought of ever looking silly. Which, always the picture of sober sincerity, he never did. Diane stood up slowly, her back to the rear wall. She felt as cold as marble. Realising she'd always hated him; it just never seemed right to loathe your only brother.

Archer explained his proposal simply and concisely, connecting with the fears and prejudices of his audience. Diane felt an undercurrent of excitement in the hall, as if each person was linked to the people on either side, to the front and the rear, by a thin copper wire. With the ceiling lights out and Stonehenge still on the screen, she looked down and thought she saw a softly glowing net, a grid of pulsating energy.

She felt an utter despair. And something else that squirmed inside her, wanting to get out.

'So you see,' Archer was saying, 'there is a very clear and obvious precedent for these restrictions. All I need to know, at this stage, is . . . do you, the people of Glastonbury, want it to happen?'

'Too bloody true,' a man shouted out. 'Soon as possible.' And there were other cries of affirmation and support. A mindless response, the most alarming sound Diane could ever remember having heard.

She couldn't see Archer's eyes across the darkened hall, but she knew they were focused on her. As their gazes locked, triumph with dismay, an odd smell came to her: salty, earthy and fleshy. Not the fresh-blood, violent-death smell of the poor fox. More like the inside of an old-fashioned butcher's shop. There was a horrible warmth to it and a sour kind of voracious life; it pulled at her stomach; she felt disgusted, and somehow strengthened.

On her other side, in the dark canal of the aisle, she knew that a shadow-form crouched, could feel it rising with her own bruising fury.

She moved into the aisle. At once, something swirled around her denimed legs. There was a roaring in her head. The stage seemed miles away, the screen a distant window.

'Archer!' Diane called out in a voice so loud and precise that it scared her.

Silence made a hollow in the hall. Diane felt as if she was standing in mercury.

Oh my God, what am I doing?

Her jaw fell. She felt limp and soaked with sweat.

'I . . .'

Heads turned. People recognising her at once.

'I . . .'

No . . .

She could feel a cool but urgent pressure. A hand on her wrist. Resist, it said. Resist.

'Nanny?'

People began to laugh as Diane turned, stumbled and ran sobbing from the hall.

Juanita called Jim, for the eighth time that day, on the cordless from the upstairs sitting room. *Come on, come on, answer the damned phone, you stupid, proud, opinionated old bastard.*

The phone still ringing out, she went through into her bedroom, put on the lights, flung herself on the bed, kicked off her shoes. She was still wearing her grey jacket, all dressed up for Woolly's meeting. She started to laugh, halfway to tears.

No answer. He might be in bed. He might be lost in his painting. He might simply be drunk. But with the travellers camped in Wellhouse Lane, there was no way she was going up there to find out.

Juanita lay back, suddenly fatigued, and gazed moodily at the picture on the wall opposite. The table lamps either side of the double bed were perfectly placed to bring out the subtleties of Jim's twilight masterpiece, the tight red thread over the Somerset Levels.

She lay on the bed, half closing her eyes so that there was nothing but that rosy slit and she thought, *Sorry Jim. Sorry, sorry, sorry, sorry . . .*

He fumbled himself into his old khaki shirt, covering his bare chest. Stood there feeling very confused. And not too well. His throat was burning. The thick air was full of flitting shadows, so was his head, and it ached dully.

Where had he been?

His palette lay on the edge of the worktable. He saw that all the colours on it were dark. There was a smell of turps, more than a smell; he could taste it; he could taste the buggering turps.

The bottle of white spirit was on the floor at his feet, upright but empty. Jim fell to his knees beside the bottle.

He gagged, wiped the back of a hand across his lips, smelled it. Clutched at his throat. He'd finished the whisky . . . and drunk the buggering turps. He tried to spit; his throat was too dry. He had a sickening image of his tongue, like a flattened toad on the floor of his mouth. He covered his face with his paint-smeared hands and sank to his knees, sending the empty turps bottle skittering away.

What had he done?

As he tried to pick himself up, long-suppressed images of his old life burst like blisters. In the spouting pus of memories, he saw the wife he'd deserted: bloody Pat, poor bloody Pat, all she wanted was for him to be ordinary, pursue his pension, relegate his art to evening classes, Jim's hobby – how he'd hated that word; nobody in Glastonbury had a paltry hobby; coming to Glastonbury was a buggering quest.

For a Grail.

Jim staggered to his feet, self-disgust and revulsion fluttering frantically in his stomach, as if he'd swallowed a small bird. His insides felt raw, abraded, as if the wings of the bird were tipped with razor blades. He looked round for something to touch, either to prove he wasn't asleep or to wake him up. All he saw were the three metal easels in a Tor shape.

With a feeling of explicit foreboding, Jim advanced on the conical formation, the three canvases, which should be aglow with the holy fire of dusk.

All three were black. He'd painted every square buggering inch black.

Jim began to weep. Went to the fire for warmth, where he found all the logs reduced to black, smouldering husks.

Then where was the light coming from? How could he even see the black paintings? In a last, vague hope that this was all a sour, whisky dream, he stumbled to the sunset window.

And saw ... the rearing ash tree, something hanging from a branch ... two yellow moons, the source of the bleak light in the room.

He saw – it couldn't be, it just couldn't *be* – that the yellow moons were the weak and vapid headlights of an old black bus, parked where no bus could possibly park, in his small, square garden, surrounded on four sides by a hornbeam hedge.

Jim cowered, hands over his face. He'd gone mad.

Black. *Black, black, black* – sound of the rain slapping at the windows. He turned his back on the window, peered in dread through his fingers at a room which was cold and drab and full of failure, reeking of regret.

He began to moan aloud. He'd broken through the darkness expecting images of such intensity that they would fuel his paintings for ever, make them burn with Rembrandt's inner light and vibrate with the wild energy swirling in Van Gogh's cypresses. So that Juanita, his beautiful Juanita, would be drawn into the vortex. He'd thought she was already there with him, thought he'd seen her face in the sunset window.

But there was nothing, after all, on the other side of the darkness but a darker darkness, and he'd done something very bad. Killed it. He'd killed a beautiful dusk.

Jim began to scrabble in the hearth, among the ash and cinders and the exhausted, flaking logs grizzling on the stone. Had to get it back. The sacred energy. Had to relight the dusk.

Impulsively, he snatched a handful of greasy paint-rags from the worktable, thrust them into the fireplace. For kindling, he snapped his long brushes, the ones oozing black paint, the black he'd avoided for years, like Monet.

It was the right thing to do. A sacrifice.

He groped for the matches on the mantelpiece, struck three at once and watched the paint-rags flare and hiss until the broken brushes began to crackle.

Logs. He needed more logs. Apple logs from local orchards which burned sweet and heady. Avalonian sunset.

Behind his eyes he saw his lovely Juanita as she'd been the day he'd first arrived in Glastonbury, his middle-aged life a fresh canvas. He saw her leaning in the doorway of her shop: summer dress, brown arms, those gorgeous, ironic, frankly sensual brown eyes.

Woman of Avalon.

He was warmed. For him, she was always standing in the doorway of her shop.

But the flames were fading; he needed flames to feed her image.

Jim picked up the coffee table he used as a palette, swung it round by the legs and smashed it into one of the supporting pillars. Smashed it again and again into the iron-hard oak until the table was in fragments. Then fed the pieces to the fire, and watched the oil and varnish flash golden.

He pulled out a flaming table-leg, held it aloft like a sconce. He was the god of the Tor again.

Was there time? Oh yes.

Jim felt almost triumphant as he plunged the blazing log into the nearest canvas. No blackness now. He watched Juanita's warm, brown eyes glistening with compassion. She held out her arms and he reached for her.

The cottage began to fill with a red fog. Through it, he saw the generous mouth, darkly sparkling eyes under the tumble of hair.

Until, with a soft smile of regret, she turned away and walked back into her bookshop.

Sorry Jim. Sorry, sorry, sorry.

He watched the shop door slowly close.

SIXTEEN

THE SUNSET WINDOW

There was the sound of a key in the shop door below Juanita's bedroom window.

She called out, 'Come on up, Diane.'

Was the Glastonbury First meeting over already? Maybe it had been a total flop, about four people in the audience.

Sure. And maybe a UFO had come down on Wearyall Hill and Joseph of Arimathea had strolled out with his staff and the teenage Christ in tow.

'Juanita, I'm frightfully sorry.' Diane appeared, puffy-eyed and flustered, in the bedroom doorway. 'I sort of . . . I couldn't stand to hear any more.'

'That bad, huh?' Juanita sat up and swung her legs from the bed.

'Juanita . . .' Diane sank down, making the mattress howl. 'You can't imagine just how bad.'

'They couldn't do it.' Juanita walked to the window. High Street looked damp, detached and faintly hostile. 'There's no way they could get that through.'

'They got away with it at Stonehenge when all the hippies and travellers and people went to worship the sun at midsummer and started having festivals and things and causing chaos. They got a special Act of Parliament to make it into a restricted area.'

'Yes, but . . .'

'And now nobody can get in at all. You have to look at the stones from behind a fence or through binoculars from across the road or something.'

'But the Tor isn't an ancient monument, apart from the tower. I mean, it's an ordinary hill . . . Well, OK, an *extra*ordinary hill, but you can't fence off a hill.'

'Juanita, they've got it all worked out. It begins with a complete parking ban in Wellhouse Lane. The next step would presumably be some kind of tasteful wire-mesh fence, with metal gates, and no access to anyone after dark.'

'That's impossible. Anyone wants to get in, they'll do it.'

'It worked at Stonehenge. They say it's a completely sterile place now. The great temple of the sun where nobody can go in and watch the sun rise any more or feel the rays on the stone. And now if Archer gets his way, nobody'll be able to see it set, looking out from the top of the Tor to Brent Knoll and Bridgwater Bay. There'd be security patrols at the solstices, they'd have . . .'

Juanita blinked. 'People supported this in there?'

'They loved it. No more hippies. No more pagan rituals. The farmers were ever so excited. There were all these muddy Mendip growls of approval. "You're one of us, zurr," this sort of thing.'

'God,' Juanita said. 'Woolly will blow a fuse. I mean, the Tor would, you know, lose all its magic, all its mysticism, if you had to buy a ticket or something.'

'Oh yes, rather, and Archer was absolutely up-front about this. The undesirables don't come to Glastonbury to see the Abbey ruins or the Tribunal building, they come for the Tor, and if the Tor's no longer accessible, Glastonbury will lose its magnetism and we'll get "decent" tourists and "decent" shops and local people will be able to walk the streets without tripping over drug-addicts and if they want to go to the Tor they'll be able to go at a "civilised" time without having to tread in faeces and vomit and, oh Juanita, it's just awful, awful, *awful* . . .'

She saw that Diane's eyes were full of tears. Stains all down her cheeks. Which didn't seem as plump as they used to. Was she losing weight?

'It's terribly personal for me, you see,' Diane said. 'I've loved the Tor all my life.'

'It won't happen, Diane. There'll be an outcry.'

'There was an outcry over the new road, but that's going to happen. It all depends on who's crying out . . .'

She stopped, fingers at her mouth. Sitting on the edge of Juanita's bed, she began to sway.

'You OK, Diane?'

'Oh gosh.'

'Diane?'

'Crying out. That explains it. It was the Tor crying out.'

'What?'

'The visions. The vinegar bottle . . . the salt pot . . . the washing-up liquid. Don't you see?'

'I'm afraid not.' But Juanita was awfully afraid she actually did.

'It knew! The Tor knew! The Tor was crying out. Something bad was coming and the Tor knew, Juanita!'

Suddenly, Juanita was rather glad she hadn't taken Diane to the police station.

'It was calling out,' Diane whispered. 'To those who are close to it.'

'Diane, listen to me.' Juanita sat down next to her on the bed. 'I hate what Archer and Griff are planning as much as anyone. And I'll fight it on freedom-of-access grounds. We can't have them putting Britain behind bars. But if you start putting two and two together and getting sixteen . . .'

'Juanita, I know this in my heart. It called me back.'

Juanita said gently, 'Colonel Pixhill thought it had called him back too, and he wasted the rest of his life trying to work out why and never did, just went bonkers.'

But Diane wasn't even listening. She wouldn't even look at Juanita, just gazed at the walls, at Jim's picture, anything.

'I was thinking, Why me? I'd concluded that it wasn't me at all it wanted, it was Nanny Three. Violet. Dion Fortune. I thought Ceridwen could perhaps explain it, if . . . you know . . . if they could get through to her. But now I know it *is* me.'

'No, Diane . . .'

'Because Archer's the threat. To the Tor and all the magic of Glastonbury. Avalon out. Don't you see? It wants me because I'm Archer's sister. It wants me to stop him.'

'Sure. Fine. As long as . . .'

'And you were right, Juanita. With *The Avalonian*. It was meant. You have a purpose too.'

'Well thanks. Thank you very much, Diane.'

There was a long, fraught silence, Diane staring hard at the picture on the wall. Then she said,

'That's the same picture, isn't it? The one you've had for ages.'

Diane had gone pale. She looked close to fainting. It was ridiculous. She shouldn't go dashing about, working herself into a state. People carrying too much weight around, there was always a danger.

'I'll make some tea,' Juanita said.

'No.' Diane didn't move. 'Why's it gone dark? The sun-line in the picture. Why's it gone dark, Juanita?'

'I'll ring him again.' Trying to sound calm, but her too-thin, nervous fingers prodding at the wrong numbers. She held the phone up to the light, began again.

And the phone rang and rang and the old bastard didn't answer.

Juanita puffed feverishly at her cigarette. There was a time when she didn't actually need to smoke. Didn't need the wine. Never over-reacted.

The breeze tossed some rain at the window like a handful of pebbles.

'OK. How did you mean?' Her voice limp. 'How did you mean it had darkened?'

Diane swallowed. 'That red line. Like a red-hot wire. It had gone black. It was a black line. It was like a thin cut bleeding . . . black. All over the painting.'

'Why can't I see it?'

'I can't see it now. These things don't last.'

Juanita started to shake her head, wrapped her arms around herself, began to pace the room, staring down and rocking.

'Diane, you'd . . . OK, listen, you'd come in off the street, into a darkened shop, darkened hallway, and then you burst into a lighted room . . .'

'Juanita, sometimes you've got to trust me.'

Juanita blinked. 'Look, OK, I'll go over to Jim's. Check him out. You stay here. Stay by the phone, just in case.'

'You're not going on your own.'

'Well, you're not coming.'

'Juanita, I can be frightfully stubborn. You are not going on your own. If I have to get the van going and follow you.'

Juanita told her why it was impossible. She told her that her friends, the Pilgrims, were back. Not all of them. Maybe half a dozen. But back. They'd be spread all over the hill.

'Oh.' Diane became very still. 'In that case, there're a few things I need to ask them. About Headlice.'

Juanita's calves ached: varicose veins, was it, now?

Your time is close, woman. It'll happen sooner than you dread.

Diane said, 'I'll get the van.'

'No. OK. We'll take the Volvo.' Juanita was sweating. Her posh, grey jacket felt like rags.

Hot sweat, cold sweat, menopause, *hag.*

St John's church tower was watching them from above, unfeeling behind its lagging of rain and night.

Juanita pulled car keys from her shoulder bag, gripped them until the jagged edges bit into her palm.

'Listen. OK. Just listen.' Facing Diane over the bonnet of the Volvo. 'We go directly to Jim's. We don't stop for anybody. Is that understood?'

Diane nodded; Juanita didn't trust her. She pulled the old Afghan coat out of the boot, dragged it on. The rain was relentless as they drove into Chilkwell Street – a few cars parked, a little light traffic. Small town, rainy night.

Halfway up Wellhouse Lane, they came to the first vehicle. The old Post Office van. 'You agreed,' Juanita snapped. 'You agreed we don't stop. I don't care who you recognise, we keep going.'

Then the hearse.

'Mort,' Diane breathed.

'Shut up.'

Dim lamplight in some of the buses and vans. A few people plodded from one to another. Metallic music rattled the Volvo's windows.

'It's them, it's Mort's hearse.'

'I don't care if it's Storming Norman's bloody tank, we're not stopping.'

'I don't think I want to any more.' Diane actually seemed a little scared.

'Good.' Juanita trod on the gas, eased forward past the hearse. And then collapsed on the brake . . .

'What the hell?'

. . . as a grey cliff-face arose in their path.

259

The motor coach was in the middle of the road. Not moving. No lights. The Volvo stalled. Juanita wound down the window in rage, and screamed at anybody, 'What do you think this is, the municipal dump?'

Laughter came like breaking glass.

'Stay!' Juanita hissed at Diane. 'Just don't move an inch.' She slammed out into the road. There was a group of people, or it might have been people and bushes; it didn't move.

What if he's here? With his sickle. Gwyn ap Nudd. In his animal mask. Juanita tasted oil and wanted to run away, but she made herself speak to them.

'Excuse me. We need to get past.'

'Can't be done, lady.' A calm voice, unhurried. 'You're gonna have to turn back.'

All she could see was a tall grey figure and a cigarette end too small to fizz in the rain. Did whoever it was recognise her from the other night? Did they all recognise her?

'Mel's bus broke down, OK? We can't fix it tonight. You gotta go back. There's another way. Wherever you're headed, there's, like, always another way, lady.'

'Not to where we're going. I don't get this. What are you guys doing back here?'

'Lady, we are the army for Avalon. Public meeting, yeah? About the road? We're the public.'

'Can't you just reverse it down the hill?'

'It's fuckin' clapped. Don't you listen? We'll get it seen to when the morning comes.'

'I do like your coat.' A cruel, female cackle. 'My granny had one like that.'

Juanita was preparing an acid reply when she saw that Diane was at her side.

'Mort? Are you there?'

'For Christ's sake, what did we agree, Diane? The road's blocked, anyway. One of their buses broke down.'

'Mort!' Diane cried out shrilly. 'Where's Mort?'

'Shiiiit,' one of the female travellers drawled from the darkness. 'We got bleedin' Fergie?'

'Rozzie? Is that you? It's me. Di . . . Molly. It's Molly F-f-Fortune.'

'She on about?'

'Interbreeding, it is,' the man said. 'Been poking their cousins for centuries. All got brains the size of fuckin' walnuts.'

The mild rain between them was as dense and muffling as a velvet curtain. Diane shouted, 'Mort, we have to talk. I know you're there, I've seen the hearse.'

'It's my hearse, darlin'. Paul Pendragon at your service. There's nobody called Mort. And, listen, you shouldn't be here hassling us, you should be down at that meeting. Got to stop this fuckin' road, ladies. You come down with us, we'll look after you.'

'Diane, come on.'

'She yours, lady?'

'Diane, will you . . .?'

'Why did you leave?' Diane screamed. 'Why didn't you take poor Headlice to hospital? Why did you let him die? Why'd you leave him?'

Silence. Juanita had a horrible sense of *déjà vu*. She tensed, snatched at Diane's arm.

Somebody laughed and held up a hurricane lamp that passed from face to face, and there were beards and plaits and dread-locks and face-paint, and Juanita didn't recognise, thank God, anyone.

'Sweetheart,' Paul Pendragon said, 'if we took every case of headlice to hospital the Health Service'd grind to a bleeding standstill.'

Diane was all fuzzy and bewildered.

'They aren't the same. They're different.'

Well, they had to be. No way the last lot would return after the death, the possible murder, of one of their tribe.

Juanita was entirely relieved, if you wanted the truth. They got back into the car and she reversed about twenty yards, pulled into the side of the lane, half in the bushes, switched off the engine and the lights.

'I think what we do is we walk from here. But we let them go past first.'

Juanita leaned across Diane, pulled a torch from the glove compartment as a bunch of them came down the hill with the hurricane lamp. The army for Avalon marching to something mournful played on a tin whistle. She opened the driver's door and stood in the bushes until all she could hear was faint music and the echo of laughter.

She and Diane moved past the vehicles. Six, Juanita counted, including the bus blocking the road.

It was still raining, but they were less than half a mile from Jim's. A stupid exercise, really.

When, after nearly ten minutes' walking, a light appeared ahead of them and there was the sound of solid footsteps, Juanita was convinced it was Jim himself and started thinking of an excuse. It would have to be the Headlice issue: they wanted Jim's opinion before going to the cops. Tried to ring . . .

The footsteps stopped immediately in front of them, like a soldier coming to attention, and he turned the beam of his lamp on himself, lighting up a Barbour so old and worn it could have been Mr Barbour's prototype, and a face like a round of rough Cheddar.

'Is it the fire of hell, Mrs Carey? Or is it the wrath of God? Cursed, it is, this place. The devil in a black buzz and now the fire of hell.'

'Don.' Juanita wondered if she'd ever squeezed more disappointment into one syllable. 'I think we can do without the evangelism tonight.'

'She thought you were Jim Battle,' Diane said.

'Oh.' Don Moulder let his lamp arm fall to his side, the beam trailing in the road. 'Mr Battle. Aye. When I heared your voices, I did hope as he were comin' up with you. I called 'em already, look. Soon's I seen it, went back up the house, called 999. Told 'em to get their fingers out.'

Juanita felt herself go limp.

'Now don't you start worryin' nor nothin'. He couldn't be in there, no way, my love. When I seen it, I thought it were them hippies an' their paraffin again. I mighter smelt it and went down there earlier, look, but for this rain, and . . . and things.'

'Oh God,' Juanita howled. She pushed past Don and tore blindly down the little lane which led to Jim's track. She could smell it herself now, sour and acrid.

'I wouldn't go there,' Don Moulder shouted out, coming after her. 'Mrs Carey, you wait for me.'

She ran down through the trees. Her skirt snagged on some brambles and she ripped it free, feeling the material tearing under the Afghan coat.

Don Moulder stumbling behind. 'You won't get no nearer than I could, Mrs Carey.'

The air grew bright around her, rosy as dawn, but no dawn ever smelt like this.

'You wait for the fire brigade. They d'have machines as'll get down that track, no trouble. You'll get trapped down there, look.'

Juanita found the track at last, ran across the turning area where she'd parked the other night. On to a grassy hump, stumbling over a root and sinking to her knees.

'. . .'s far enough, I tell you! Don't be s' damn stupid, woman!'

When she stood up, it was like thrusting her head into an enormous blow-drier. She couldn't breathe, her mouth filled up with fumes and she fell back into the wet grass, Don Moulder screeching, '. . . Godzake, woman!'

She crawled on hands and knees around the grassy mound until she came to the little wooden gate leading into the tiny, square cottage garden where Jim would erect his easel on warm evenings, a high hedge protecting his privacy. She stood up by the remains of an old trellis, where roses had once hung. Her eyes were already sore and streaming and she had to blink four, five times before she could see the whole picture.

The whole terrible bloody picture.

Jim's cottage and the garden were in a little flat-bottomed bowl with a bank rising up behind it and the enormous ash tree, one and a half times as high as the cottage. The bowl looked like a frying pan, with a straight piece of track forming the handle, although she'd never seen it that way before.

But, then, she'd never seen it all lit up like this.

The lower windows of Jim's cottage were bright and warm, like the welcoming windows of a storybook cottage. Especially the floor-to-ceiling studio window, the sunset window. Looking now as if it had stored up all those thousands of liquid red sunsets and was starting one of its own.

The November night was as warm as a kitchen. The air carried the breathless rise and fall of distant sirens.

Diane and Don Moulder came to stand on either side of Juanita.

'That's far enough, Mrs Carey. Brigade's here now, look.'

The fire-sirens went on and on and got no louder.

'He's surely out here somewhere.' Don Moulder was wiping his eyes with a rag. 'He's not daft, isn't Mr Battle.'

The roof timbers of Jim's cottage produced a cheerful, crackling as fierce little impish flames began to poke through like gas-jets. And still the sirens went on and on and got no louder. In a gush of panic, Diane realised.

'Oh, gosh Mr Moulder, they can't . . . the fire brigade won't get through! The whole lane's clogged with buses and wagons, we couldn't even get the car past!'

'Whazzat, Miss?'

'Travellers. There's a bus broken down right in the middle of the road.'

'A buzz?'

'It's blocking the road.' Diane was aware of Juanita pulling open her Afghan coat and ripping at her skirt.

'Oh my God,' Juanita said. 'Oh my God. Look!' Pointing at the ash tree, something hanging from it.

'Aye,' Don Moulder was saying. 'A buzz. Maybe you seen it. But were it a real buzz? That's the big question, Miss Diane. Were it a real . . . Christ, are you mad, woman?'

Beside Diane, a muffled, ragged figure, cloth-faced like a scarecrow, began to run towards the inferno.

The sunset window cracked first, like a gunshot, and then it exploded, a thousand fragments of hot glass blown out at Juanita, muffled like a Muslim woman, a torn-off length of her skirt wound around her face as she threw herself at the cottage.

Diane rushed forward, squealing like a piglet, but Don Moulder grabbed her, both arms around her waist, and held her back.

A huge gush of fire lunged out of the cottage and hit the ash tree with a lurid splash of sparks, like a welding torch in a foundry.

Whatever was hanging limply from a branch was lit up very briefly before the flame pounced like a cat on a rat and consumed it.

Diane screamed wildly inside Don Moulder's arms.

Juanita had disappeared.

Brittle, burning dead leaves from the ash tree danced like frenzied fireflies to the futile warbling of the trapped fire-engines.

As out of the shattered sunset window toppled a frightful thing, a monstrous shape . . . a fossil tree with rigid projecting branches, a twisted, blackened pylon.

Coughing and retching, with Don Moulder's leathery farmer's hands clasped over her spasming stomach, Diane saw just about everything.

She saw that the tree was something entangled and kept upright by a metal artist's easel. Or maybe two easels, or even three, entwined, fused together into a single, horrific fire-sculpture, all black and flaking.

At the top of this twisted creation was spiked a charcoal ball, like a Hallowe'en pumpkin which had fallen into the bonfire. When the construction teetered, the ball twirled to display . . .

It was impolite to be sick on someone. Diane found the strength to pull away. Vomiting into the grass, she could still see it.

The grisly twinkle of teeth as the charred remains of Jim Battle toppled into Juanita's flung-open arms and the cottage roof collapsed into a gush of pumping blood-orange smoke.

Before she fainted on Don Moulder, Diane glimpsed something at the very centre of the billowing.

Obscenely like the hands of a conjuror letting loose a black dove, it was a smoking cup of shadows, a dark chalice.

SEVENTEEN

OF THE HEART

The cottage was fine, just as peaceful as it had ever been. Arnold limped contentedly around, Mrs Whitney brought homemade soup and all the books stayed on the shelves. Outside, there was snow on the hilltops and a stack of logs, nicely dried and split, in the old barn.

Winter was at the door, season of rough walks and hot fires, and whatever had been happening inside Joe Powys to cause that period of upset, that blip, it was obviously in remission.

So . . . fine.

Well, except for the no-Fay aspect, and even that was fine for Fay, who was a people-person and had been getting increasingly restless through the summer. It hadn't been love – Joe Powys kept telling himself this – so much as mutual need, the need for someone who had also experienced these things to be there when you awoke before dawn, in terror and self-doubt. Would Fay still awake in terror in Brussels or Munich or Amsterdam? Perhaps not.

So, fine. OK. Really.

Anyway, there was another woman now.

In hazy sepia, a cheerful, buxom lady in a hat and a long woollen skirt pushes a bicycle with a shopping basket over the handlebars. Colours slowly fading into the picture as she crackles through autumn leaves in a half-wooded lane to a steep and narrow path; at the end of this, a big shed with lace curtains at the windows, the shed built into the flank of a hill of cucumber green rising, almost sheerly it seems from here, to a church tower of grey-brown stone, a church tower without a church.

Her real name was Violet Firth, Evans when she married. She was born in 1890 in North Wales, although her family later moved to Somerset. As a young woman, during the years of World War I, she became quite a successful psychotherapist, initially attracted to the new ideas of Sigmund Freud.

Which she rapidly outgrew, realising there were phenomena of the mind and spirit which Freud could not approach. During this period she discovered she was telepathic, psychic and a natural medium.

She also discovered Glastonbury.

Somebody gave her a redundant army hut and she put it up directly under Glastonbury Tor and it was here that she founded the mystical order which became the Society of the Inner Light.

Powys already knew a little about her. During his research for *The Old Golden Land* he'd learned that she was the first writer to discuss the psychic aspect of leys, those mysterious alignments of ancient sites across the countryside.

What had put him off further reading was the name under which she produced her novels and magical studies: Dion Fortune. It was developed, apparently, from her family motto *Deo Non Fortuna*. Not her fault that, from this end of the century, it sounded like a fifties rock and roll singer.

Anyway, this was probably one of the reasons he'd never got around to reading *Avalon of the Heart*.

'All hokum, well over the top,' Dan Frayne had said, presenting him with the paperback to read on the train home. 'But it left me with a kind of warm glow, you know? Made me feel, yeah, this is The Place. Dangerous stuff, in retrospect.'

Powys read it twice. It was just over a hundred pages long, a personalised guide to Glastonbury and its mysteries in a style which was kind of Helen Steiner Rice meets Enid Blyton.

Dan Frayne was right. It was wonderful.

When he came off the train, he went directly to the Hereford Bookshop (beside a famous ley-line near the cathedral) and ordered everything of Dion Fortune's still in print. Then went to the library to find out who she was, really.

The book glowed. It was concise, vivid and haunting. It was a love story, about a torrid affair between a woman and a town. It told you exactly why people did what Dan Frayne and this Juanita had done – going to Glastonbury in search of something they couldn't define.

While Uncle Jack Powys, in a book more than ten times as long, explained why they all failed.

No wonder Fortune hadn't exactly taken to *A Glastonbury Romance*, published just two years earlier. *Do we behave like that at Glastonbury?* she wrote. *I must have missed a lot. We do not quite come up to Mr Powis's specifications.*

Mischievously misspelling Powys.

Joe Powys decided he really liked this woman. The night he got home he made a space on the shelf next to the *Romance* and inserted *Avalon of the Heart*.

The antidote.

Powys grinned and went to bed and slept the whole night through without interruption. And another six.

But last night he'd been appalled to find himself lying awake almost wishing it would happen again. Having awoken first of all feeling cold, feeling empty, missing Fay. And then wondering, Am I slightly mad?

This was an unnatural situation. Mrs Whitney had said as much. *No life, Joe, just you and that dog . . . walking the hills . . . hair going greyer . . . circles under your eyes getting bigger.*

And Dan Frayne, before he left London: *All I'm asking, Joe, is why not spend a couple of weeks in Glastonbury? Absorb the vibes. I guarantee a pivotal experience . . . alter your life, one way or the other. If you agree there's a book in this, I'll have the first instalment of the advance in the post inside a week. I'm empowered to go to twenty grand, half up-front. Can't go higher for non-fiction, these are hard times.*

Powys, down to his last two thousand in the bank and *Golden Land* royalties slipping fast, had said, 'Can I think about this?'

He could have had ten thousand pounds in his hand by now and he'd said coolly, 'Can I think about this?' Mad? Probably. And cold and lonely and his hair going greyer. Was ten grand going to change any of that? Plus, he'd have to write the book with Frayne's ex-girlfriend. Plus . . .

. . . what I'd also like from you, right up in the introduction . . . don't get up, don't hit me . . . is the Uncle Jack story. The stuff Corby

told me about. The Glastonbury Romance *bit. Gives us a hook for the marketing department.*

Well, sod that for a start. Be like hanging a sign around your neck that said CRANK. And somebody with expert knowledge of the Powys family tree would be sure to come out of the woodwork screaming, CHARLATAN . . . IMPOSTOR.

He was all mixed up. He needed to read some more Dion Fortune. A calming influence. She'd gone to Glastonbury, another seeker after spiritual truth, but she hadn't been screwed up by it like the amateurs, like Dan Frayne.

Read more Fortune, this was the answer. Slowly. By which time it would be nearly spring. And perhaps Fay would have come back and they could go down to Glastonbury together. Maybe Fay could get a radio programme out of it.

Joe Powys got up and made some tea for himself and Arnold. Who was he kidding?

Not long after nine a.m., the phone rang.

'You asked for time to think.'

'I'm still thinking,' Powys said. This was unusual. At this stage of the game publishers hardly ever chased you.

'What's the problem?' Dan Frayne didn't sound cool any more, didn't sound laid back, didn't sound superficial.

Powys tried to think of an answer. A strange, choked silence coming down the line.

'Listen, you have to get your act together, Joe. You read the stuff, yet?' Dan Frayne didn't sound right, lacked coherence. 'Her . . . you know . . . letters?'

'I've been a bit busy.'

'For fuck's sake, Joe. Listen, the thing is, I can't go down there, you know that. I have to be in New York next week anyway.'

Powys felt he was missing something. 'Why do either of us have to go? Where's the urgency?'

There was a ragged pause. Then Dan told him, his voice like there was a dry twig stuck in his throat.

'I nearly missed it. Wouldn't have known. It only made a couple of paragraphs in the national papers. I mean, there are lots of fatal fires all over the place. They didn't have any names at that stage, anyway. Relatives hadn't been told.'

'I'm really sorry, Dan.' Powys knew there were a lot of questions he should be asking, but this wasn't the time.

Giving him a big brown Jiffy bag containing the collected letters of Juanita Carey, Frayne had said, 'Written to me at least three times a year for twenty years. If I wasn't here, I think she'd still write, to unload the shit. Read and I guarantee you'll see the book mapped out before your eyes.'

Powys read for nearly two hours, Arnold lying gloomily across his feet, sleety rain coming like tin-tacks at the cottage window.

He read about the people of present-day Avalon, as seen by Juanita Carey.

June, 1989
   News just in: Alice Flood, the curate's wife, has left her husband for the guy who runs the Wearyall Wine Bar. The proposed Astral Festival has been attacked by one of those fundamentalist Christian sects claiming it'll attract satanic influences. One of the women at the tourist office in the Tribunal building has resigned because she says it's being haunted by a ghost in monk's robes and . . .
   Oh hell, just another week in bloody Avalon.

Powys smiled sadly, went back to the earliest letter, April 1975, and discerned a different tone, less cynical, more wide-eyed. Mrs Carey was writing it while listening to Alan Stivell's 'totally transcendent' Breton harp music. She was organising an earth-mysteries book fair in Glastonbury and was a little nervous about inviting the bigger names. Did Danny think Colin Wilson might be persuadable?

You never found out whether the book fair had been a success; Mrs Carey's next letter was about a relationship she was developing with an astrologer called Matt Rutherford who was 'a bit magnetic around the eyes'. The Matt thing lasted, on and off, nearly seven years, though Juanita didn't write much about it. Powys could imagine Dan Frayne seething with jealousy. But the general mood was changing.

In the eighties, the Thatcher subtext – greed is patriotic – was penetrating Glastonbury. Shops hadn't actually been selling chunks of holyest erthe in cans, but the possibility was in the air. There were now people in town who were seeing the New Age as New Money, and one of them was Matt Rutherford, who set up an agency offering astrological services to industry: star-screening employees and job-applicants to calculate their suitability for particular posts.

Juanita Carey had been furious to think that Rutherford was getting people fired because Pluto and Venus happened to be badly aligned when they were born.

Exit Matt.

Quite right too, Powys thought. Mercenary bastard.

He became aware that the letters were laying out for him a ground-plan of post-Fortune Glastonbury. He could see High Street, with all the New Age shops clustering at the bottom of the hill, near the ancient George and Pilgrims. He could see the lofty tower of St John's with the war-memorial outside, where the hippies gathered to play and sing with guitars and whistles. He had a sense of the Abbey ruins amid hidden green acres enclosed by streets full of shops and strange music. And, on the edge of the town, the tunnel lanes leading to the pagan enigma of the Tor.

I suppose this means you'll be going now, then, Powys? After what's happened.

'I suppose so, Arnold.'

Powys sighed. On the evidence of the Carey letters, the contrasts and tensions of Glastonbury hadn't actually altered much in the sixty-odd years since Uncle Jack had fluttered the dovecotes: commercial interests squeezing into bed with the spiritual, a lot of seriously screwed-up people and frustrated visionaries, endless petty disputes, and maybe a wriggling vein of kinky sex.

In the mid-eighties, after Matt Rutherford had left town to pursue his business interests in – where else? – Los Angeles, Juanita rarely referred to men.

The last letter – very recent – was a cool and cynical overview of New Age Glastonbury. It also discussed the problems of a scatty female of semi-noble birth called Diane Ffitch and the publication of the gloomy diaries of a certain Colonel Pixhill.

There was a copy enclosed. It was a dismal dark green with no picture on the front. Dan had said he really couldn't face reading it.

Joe Powys had another look at the photo of the girl in the white dress, Juanita Carey: iridescent, mesmeric . . . If you looked closely you could make out some kind of amulet around her neck. If you held the picture away from you, you were even more dazzled by the wide, white smile and the laughing brown eyes.

More than all this, Powys had liked her style.

He was deeply sad that she couldn't help him now.

PART FOUR

Mr Powis (sic) . . . has fluttered our local dovecotes to a painful
extent. Do we behave like that at Glastonbury? I must have missed
a lot. I am afraid that if people make the Glastonbury pilgrimage
expecting to find Glastonbury romance . . . they will be disappointed. We do not quite come up to Mr Powis's specifications.

Dion Fortune
Avalon of the Heart

ONE

AFTER THE FIRE

The caller said, 'This is Lord Pennard. I wish to speak to my daughter. Now.'

No question, it definitely was him, voice straight out of the freezer compartment. Sam Daniel, the printer, had seen him around, as you might say, heard him ordering his huntsmen about. Very big man in these parts, and oh yes, this was definitely Lord P on the phone, no doubt about that.

'Sure it is,' Sam said. 'And I'm the Pope. Now piss off and stop bothering us or I'll call the police.'

Diane looked up from the oldest and simplest of Sam's office word-processors.

'Your old man,' Sam said. 'And not a happy old man, if I'm any judge. What if he shows up at the door?'

'He's left a couple of messages on the answering machine at the shop,' Diane said. 'I just wipe them off. He won't come here. He's always employed people to show up at doors for him.'

'Fair enough.' Sam turned back to his computer screen. He was laying out this illustrated feature-piece by Matthew Banks, one of the five million local herbalists, about the Glastonbury Thorn. It listed all the Holy Thorn trees in and around the town, suggesting which was the oldest and examining the case for the various thorns being actual descendants of the staff of Joseph of Arimathea.

Complete load of old horseshit, in Sam's view, but Diane said the Thorn was a potent symbol which united the Alternative types and the locals. Local people were proud of the Thorn, Diane said. Well, Samuel Mervyn Daniel was about as local as you could get, and proud was putting it a bit strong.

Paul's digital clock said 8.20. Twenty past bleeding eight and they'd been at work for over an hour, marking up copy, transferring it to the computer, experimenting with layouts. It hadn't even been light when he'd unlocked the print-shop. He hadn't had a shave for two days, nor a proper meal, nor seen any telly, nor been in any fit state to do much with Charlotte.

The upper classes. Always been good at getting the peasants working the clock round for a pittance.

Except Diane was always here too, head down, a woman driven. A lot of grief, a lot of upset inside. But she wasn't letting any of it out, not in front of Sam Daniel. She had guts, and you didn't expect that. Or else it was another aspect of her reputed insanity.

Diane pushed her chair back. 'I've got to go. Got to open the shop.'

'Bet you've not had any breakfast, have you?'

She was losing weight, too. Not that she couldn't afford to lose a couple of stone, but not this way. And her face was always pale. It was like somewhere behind her eyes there was always an image of what she'd seen that night.

'Oh, well, you know, I've got some carob bars at the shop.' Diane pulled her red coat from the peg. The kind of coat you'd think twice about donating to Oxfam in case the Third World sent it back.

Sam raised his eyes to the ceiling. 'Bloody carob bars. I'm not saying the humble carob hasn't got its place, look, but a slice or two of toast, soya marg, a dab of Marmite, nothing would've died to bring that to the table, would it?'

'Thank you so much for your concern, Sam.' Diane gathered her stuff together in a plastic carrier bag. 'Listen, could you let me see a proof, printout, whatever of the piece on the town-centre enhancement scheme when you've finished it? No hurry, but if I could have it by three at the latest . . .'

Strewth.

'Anybody, excluding family, wants to see you, Diane, what shall I say?'

'Oh, send them round to the shop. They'll have to join the queue. Bye.'

He watched her through the window walking quickly, head held high, out of Grope Lane on to Magdalene Street. Gonna crack. Nothing surer.

After the fire, and no Juanita, Sam had figured the magazine idea would be straight down the tubes. But then, the day following the funeral, Diane had appeared, pale-faced, in the print-shop, a cardboard folder under her arm. Talking about getting started on *The Avalonian*. Like, pronto.

'I owe it to her, OK?' was all she'd say. Then they started work on the first dummy.

How do we know, Sam read on the screen, *that the thorn tree on Wearyall Hill is even in the same spot as what we like to think of as the Original?*

Matthew Banks's original draft had been a sight more cumbersome. Diane had ripped into it, subbing it down to neat sentences, short paragraphs. 'The Alternative Community,' Diane had said firmly, 'have to learn from the outset that this is our paper, not theirs.'

Sam grinned, remembering that bloody tight-arsed Jenna – a 'voice therapist' – coming in with a piece written by The Women of the Cauldron, with its own headline on top: WHY THE ANGLICAN CHURCH DENIES THE GODDESS MARY. Diane giving it back without even reading it, pointing out politely that *The Avalonian* would be doing its own headlines and any comment pieces would be specifically commissioned. Suggesting they cut the piece by half and submit it as a reader's letter with actual names at the bottom. Jenna'd gone out with a face like an old shoe.

Sam was starting to warm to Diane. One thing about the upper classes, they knew how to put people down with style.

And slave-driving, they knew about that. Three weeks after starting from nothing – no design, not even a paper-size – they now had almost enough for a respectable dummy, with real features, real news stories. Idea being they could take it around and show to people to stimulate advertising.

The plan was to start out as a monthly then come down to fortnightly. Anything beyond that, they'd need staff, which they couldn't afford. Diane insisted every contribution had to be paid for, even if it was just a token amount. Couldn't rely on volunteers like the guy with the three-legged dog.

You had to start out, Diane said, how you meant to go on: professional. Incredible. She'd seemed so soggy, that first time she came in.

Ah well. Sam stood up. Twenty to nine. Young Paul'd be in soon, then he could get some breakfast. No carob bars for Sammy, not after another dawn shift. Funny, everybody was up early this morning. Even Lord Pennard, who was obviously monitoring Diane's movements. Having her watched.

And with this family, it had to be more than just paternal interest.

Like she didn't have enough problems.

Mid-December already. The town-centre Christmas tree had just gone up in front of the Victorian Gothic market cross. There was a thin glaze of merriment on the streets – carol singers and also bands of pagan mummers with shamanic drums.

The former Holy Thorn Ceramics – now called the Goddess Shop – had a banner wishing customers a Happy Solstice.

Carey and Frayne had no specific wishes for anyone. Diane had found a box of Christmas ornaments for the bookshop window, including a chubby little electric Santa Claus with coloured lights around his hat which Woolly had made last year in his workshop. She hadn't the heart to display it; it reminded her too much of Jim Battle.

Jim's funeral had been awfully depressing. Woolly had rounded up a bunch of local mourners for the sake of appearances, but there was no family. His abandoned wife, unsurprisingly, had not attended; neither had his son, who also lived in Bristol.

An inquest had been opened and adjourned until the New Year. After taking her statement, the police had told Diane an open verdict was possible, although Accidental Death or Death by Misadventure were more likely. There'd certainly been nothing to suggest suicide. Unless she knew otherwise?

Diane had shaken her head. In truth, she didn't know what to think.

Through the shop window, she saw a lanky red-haired man in black jeans and one of those lumberjack shirts slapping something to the side of a yellow litter bin on a lamp-post.

Darryl Davey. The biggest boy at Sam Daniel's school, apparently. *Like a shark in a goldfish tank. Case of premature development. Shaving at about ten and a dad at sixteen, but now his son's sixteen and Darryl's pissed off that nobody looks up to him any more.* He seemed to be employed by the Glastonbury First people to display their material all over town. Probably illegally, but nobody stopped him. He was certainly quite open about what he was doing now, standing back to admire it.

It was a sticker, about four inches in diameter, like a NO ENTRY roadsign. Diane went to the window to examine it.

It was horribly effective. You just knew that it was going to be all over the old-established shops and pubs in Glastonbury. In the back windows of cars and delivery vans and farm vehicles. On the sides of buses.

The idea of restricting access to the Tor had caught on in a big way ... given immediate and urgent impetus by the fire. Before that inaugural Glastonbury First meeting had even finished, fire engines had been struggling to reach the top of a Wellhouse Lane effectively blockaded by travellers' vehicles.

One of those frightful coincidences for which Glastonbury was famous. The local and regional Press had seized the angle, giving a tremendous boost to Glastonbury First. And, of course, to Archer, who had been interviewed on the local TV news.

'Had this system been in operation,' Archer had said soberly and sorrowfully, 'I believe we should not now have a tragedy of this proportion on our hands. I hope these people, wherever they may be skulking, can sleep at night.'

Efforts by the Press to find these particular travellers had, of course, failed. Woolly said they'd never even arrived at the road-protest meeting. Eventually, the rescue services had managed to remove the old bus which had broken down in the road. It apparently had carried no licence disc, and all the other vehicles had gone.

The following day, an entirely innocent travelling couple, just passing through, had returned to their van on the central car park to find all four of its tyres slashed and the words MURDERING SCUM spray-painted along one side. The chairman of Glastonbury First, Mr Quentin Cotton, had appealed for calm and restraint although, as he told the *Evening Post*, it was understandable that emotions were running high.

Poor Jim Battle would have been sickened.

*

As the afternoon trailed dismally away, Verity Endicott sat in the deepest corner of the dining hall and welcomed the dark by inhaling it.

Dr Grainger had taught her how to do this. You breathed in, expanding the diaphragm, imagining the air inside your body to be of the same consistency and texture as the atmosphere in the room. And then you directed the smooth, dark air to the extremities of your body, to your hands and feet and along your spinal cord until the restful darkness filled your head. Finally, you exhaled through the mouth, sending some of your essence out into the room. A mingling.

Thus, Verity had taken her first tentative steps along the path to penumbratisation: fusion with the dark. Dr Grainger had spent hours with her over the past few weeks, refusing to take any payment because, he said, Meadwell was 'a real palace of shadows' in which it was a privilege to work.

He was an earnest, humourless man, and Verity seemed to be becoming rather dependent on him. On three occasions, they had meditated together in one of the upstairs rooms, sitting side by side on straight-backed chairs with their hands on their knees, a tincture of moonlight on the rim of a wardrobe. Here, Dr Grainger had instructed her in the techniques of tenebral chakra-breathing which, he said, would put her in tune with the dark physically, mentally and emotionally.

'There are five other stages after this,' he said, 'but it's gonna take you maybe a couple more weeks of nightly exercise before you're ready to move on up.'

Verity clung, with little confidence but certainly no misgivings any more, to the tenebral exercises. The house might be growing ever darker, but the real oppressor was Oliver Pixhill, whose undisguised intention was to dispense with her services, presumably seeing her as the final link with his despised father.

Dr Grainger was right. If she could not love the dark as he did, at least she might learn to live with it. It was her duty to stay, to resist all attempts to force her out. To hold out until . . .

Until when? Colonel Pixhill had always said she would know. Major Shepherd had said someone would help her, that she would not have to be a canary until she finally succumbed to the gases.

All she was sure of was that the person coming to help her was not Oliver Pixhill.

She just couldn't get him out of her head. He had never returned, but his sneers lingered. He obviously hated Meadwell too; had he inherited it, he would doubtless have sold it at once. Which was perhaps one of the reasons the Colonel had laid the foundations of the Pixhill Trust.

Verity felt very lonely. Day to day, she seemed to see only Dr Grainger. Wanda never telephoned; she was, it seemed, spending much of her time persuading influential people to support the campaign against the Bath–Taunton Relief Road. And was also, apparently, involved in setting up some sort of Christmas event uniting pagans and Christians in the person of Dr Liam Kelly, the liberal-minded new Bishop of Bath and Wells.

All fine and good in its way. This, surely, was what Glastonbury was about: a healing of ancient rifts. So was Christmas. It should be a time of rejoicing. But on the town streets there were few smiles to be seen. She missed very much the joviality of Mr Battle, with his sketchbook and his bicycle. And the careless elegance of Juanita Carey, even if she was always too busy to talk for long.

Such an unbelievable tragedy. In its wake and in the aftermath of the unpleasantness at Holy Thorn Ceramics, there seemed to be in the air of Glastonbury a cold hostility which Verity had never before experienced. Not what the holy town was about. It was as though Avalon itself – awful thought – was going the way of Meadwell.

At least Woolly looked cheerful, in orange trousers and a yellow jacket over a lurid Hawaiian shirt. But then he always looked cheerful; apart from that one suit, clothes like these were all he had.

His face was doleful though, today.

''Tis slipping away from me, Diane. I can feel it. They're taking over.'

He pulled a stool to the counter.

'Daft to complain. On one level, 'tis a wonderful job she's doing.'

'Dame Wanda?'

'Knows more famous folk than I even heard of, that woman. Actors, artists and such.'

'Yes, but Woolly, the sad fact is that when it comes to infra-structure, I'm afraid it's the kind of people Archer and my father know who really count.'

'Infrastructure. There's a clever word. You gonner use words like that in *The Avalonian*?'

'Certainly not,' Diane said. 'It's going to be simple and direct.'

'It's really gonner happen?'

'Of course it's jolly well going to happen.' Diane lowered her eyes. 'I think.'

She worked on *The Avalonian* every waking hour, even when she was in the shop, with the little laptop she'd borrowed from Sam. Studied the customers for people who might be recruited as correspondents. Preferably straight people. Well, as straight as you could find among customers at an Alternative bookshop.

'You know I'll help all I can,' Woolly said.

'I know. And don't think I'm not grateful, but there's a limit to how much you *can* help. Or at least be seen to help. You're a politician now.'

'Sheesh, do I look like a politician?'

'We have to be seen to be independent.'

In the window, a sign Sam had printed said, COMING SOON – *the avalonian*. She'd been a little worried about that: suppose people remembered the old hippy magazine and thought it was going to be the same sort of thing.

The phone rang. Diane never answered the phone in case it was her father. She waited for the answering machine to cut in, Juanita's voice still on it. There was silence, the caller not sure whether to leave a message.

'Er . . .'tis Miss Diane I wanted.'

'I know that voice,' Woolly said. 'It's—'

''Tis Don Moulder here. I, er, I needer talk to Miss Diane . . .'bout . . .'bout them hippies, look. I . . . right.'
The line was cut.

'Well, there's a man really at home with the new technology,' Woolly observed. 'You gonner call him back?'

'I might actually go and see him,' Diane said. 'I keep hearing rumours that he's gone sort of strange.'

'That's no rumour, my love.'

'Apparently he's put up a huge cross on his land. I thought it might make a piece for *The Avalonian*. For the dummy. I mean he's not an Alternative person, is he?'

'You mean he's like a straight religious maniac. Yeah, I suppose so. I do admire what you're doing, you know. The way you've thrown yourself into it. At a time like this.'

'It's *because* it's a time like this,' Diane said.

TWO

JACKET POTATOES

Standing under the swinging sign of The George and Pilgrims, Joe Powys watched Diane Ffitch walking down from Carey and Frayne, hands plunged into her coat pockets, a beret plopped on tangled brown curls, a stiff-backed folder under her arm.

She smiled shyly. 'This is awfully good of you. Although, I mean, it might actually be OK. It might just make the journey.'

'Then again, it might fall off.' He went to unlock the Mini.

'Well. Yes. I suppose so.'

Returning to the inn tonight, Powys had encountered her in the car park. Sitting in her pink-spotted van with the engine running; it was making a noise like a small aeroplane. Diane had said, *Does this mean it's sort of broken?*

It was only a hole in the silencer, but it looked like a very old exhaust system. Not safe to drive it to Bristol, especially at night.

Diane squeezed into the Mini, put her folder behind the seat. 'At least, there's a place at the hospital where you can go and get a cup of tea or something. While you're waiting.'

'Or,' Powys said, 'perhaps I could pop in and see her for a couple of minutes. Just so I can tell Dan something.'

'Oh gosh.' Diane fluttered, embarrassed. 'Bit of a prob, there, actually. She won't see anyone. Well, you know, except me. She's in quite a bad way. I mean emotionally, too.'

'Yeh, I can imagine.' Powys drove up High Street. The headlights of an oncoming car flash-lit a yellow poster in the window of an empty shop. It said, LET'S TAME THE TOR.

'She's feeling a lot of guilt about Jim's death. One way and another. I mean, she was sort of . . . sort of close to him. But I think not as close as he would've liked, if you see what I mean.'

'Oh. Right.'

'I mean, no one's saying he . . . you know . . .'

'Killed himself?'

'No one's saying that. He just seems to have got rather drunk and careless. People have been muttering about the Artistic Temperament. Meaning drink. But he actually wasn't like that. He was terribly balanced, really. Ever so stoical. Even after a few drinks.'

Diane went quiet for a while, a big girl squashed on to a tiny bucket seat in a car so small that she and Powys were almost touching.

'I do find it easy to talk to you,' she said at last. 'So I'm going to say it. I think . . .' She took a deep breath. 'I think this was, you know . . . meant.'

They were leaving town. Powys saw, in his rear-view mirror, the sign that said:

GLASTONBURY
Ancient Isle of Avalon

He felt a tingle of unreality at the very base of his spine. *This is a town ruled by legend, secretly governed by numinous rules.*

Bollocks.

He glanced at Diane. She was looking directly at him. He could see her face very clearly. Its openness seemed to belie everything he'd read about her in the letter from Juanita Carey to Dan Frayne.

Lady Loony. Arnold was sitting placidly on her knee, her arms around him.

Let it go, said his Wiser Self. *Don't react. Change the subject.*

Joe Powys sighed. His Wiser Self had quit years ago, disillusioned.

'Meant?' he said. 'How exactly do you mean, "meant"?'

Dan Frayne had said, 'I've rung the hospital and she won't speak to anyone. I've rung this Diane Ffitch, can't get a word of sense. Just goes on about this fucking Pixhill. Jesus, Joe, all I want is to know what's going on. Christ, forget the book if you like, go for a winter bloody break at Harvey-Calder's expense. Just help me.'

Powys had driven down a week ago under deep, grey skies, the famous Tor looking passive, disconnected. As though this crazy plan to have it fenced off had already diminished it.

He'd booked into The George and Pilgrims, into a dark room with an uncurtained four-poster bed and Gothic windows edged with richly coloured stained glass. From his window, if he leaned far enough out, he could see the bookshop, Carey and Frayne.

On the first day, Powys had walked Arnold round the streets, buying flimsy, small imprint books on the Grail, the Goddess, King Arthur and Joseph of Arimathea.

On the second day, he'd led the dog halfway up the Tor and then carried him to the top, where mist over the Levels obscured the views and a man with a red beard and two pigtails played a tuneless tin whistle into the wind battering the empty, hollowed-out church tower.

On the third day, he'd driven up through a housing estate to Wearyall Hill, where no signpost marked the path to the Holy Thorn. It proved to be a wind-thrashed little tree, absolutely alone on the hillside, protected only by a wire-netting tube. There were views to both the Tor, to the right, and the Abbey ruins behind the town centre. Of all the places he'd been in Glastonbury, this was somehow the most moving. He'd wished Fay had been here to share the moment and then, feeling as lonely and exposed as the Thorn, he had blinked away tears.

On the fourth day, he'd planned to visit the Abbey which was totally hidden from view until you went under a medieval gate-house in Magdalene Street and paid your admission fee. He'd left it until last, maybe worried he'd be disappointed. This would be an unfortunate reaction to the holyeste erthe in all England.

Finally he'd decided to save it, and gone into Carey and Frayne.

Waiting until there were no customers. Noting five paperback copies of *The Old Golden Land*. Watching Diane working on a laptop behind the counter. And then going over to request a copy of the little book he'd already read four times.

Diane had fumbled under the counter. The seaweed-green volume of Colonel Pixhill's diaries, as the letters had implied, was not exactly on display.

'I know your face.' Diane looking up to meet his eyes, as if the exchange of a Pixhill was a secret sign, like a masonic handshake. 'Don't I?'

'Shouldn't think so.'

But she'd surprised him, diving across the shop for a copy of *The Old Golden Land*. A bit unnerving because . . .

'Hang on, there's no author picture on the paperback.'

'No.' Diane had blushed. 'But there was on the hard-back. It lived in my locker, you see, for an entire term.'

It was lunchtime. She'd closed the shop, taken him into a little room behind, made some tea. Kneeling down with a saucerful for Arnold, as if a three-legged dog was yet another sign. As he was to learn, Diane Ffitch was always spotting signs and symbols.

It emerged that she'd been packed off at sixteen to this *absolutely frightful* private school near Oswestry, all outdoor pursuits and lukewarm showers, feeling like a fish out of water on the cold Welsh Border, so far from the mystery and allure of Avalon, feeling so utterly *miz* the whole time. Until Juanita had thoughtfully sent her *The Old Golden Land*.

Inspired by the book, she'd found a Bronze Age burial mound on the edge of the school grounds, seen how it aligned with the village church and then a hill fort on the horizon . . . and realised that the Welsh Border was actually quite mysterious, not such a ghastly place after all.

Powys had told her about Dan Frayne's proposal, Diane never taking her eyes off him. After a while he'd begun to feel a little uncomfortable. 'I'm messing up your lunch hour.'

'I've not been having one actually. Takes up too much time. I tend to just sort of nibble things.'

Telling him about the magazine she was trying to put together, determined to have it all organised for when Juanita came out of hospital because she'd need something to take her mind off everything.

Well, Powys said, if there was anything he could do to help . . . Thinking that working unobtrusively on a little local magazine would get him discreetly into the centre of things in Glastonbury, and if there *was* to be a book . . .

He felt her eyes somehow looking into him.

'We can use all the help we can get,' she said. 'In Avalon.'

The following day, again in her lunch hour, she'd taken him to see the guy at SAMPRINT, who'd struck Powys as being fairly cynical about *The Avalonian* venture but at least had never heard of

The Old Golden Land. He'd made a big fuss of Arnold, asked how he'd lost his leg.

'A farmer shot him. Accused him of worrying sheep. But it was a fit-up.'

Sam the printer said, 'What did you do?'

'His shotgun kind of wound up in the river,' Powys said. 'It was a family heirloom.'

Sam had shrugged approvingly. Then Diane had asked Powys if he'd interview the new Bishop of Bath and Wells about his attempts to reconcile Christian and pagan elements. Again, Powys had begun to feel detached from reality. It was like a half-waking morning dream where you watched yourself being drawn into unfolding situations, too lazy to pull yourself out.

Even after reading the Pixhill diaries.

'All I know is it's itching like hell,' she said.

This nurse was small and bossy but not unsympathetic. She was called Karen.

'That's a good sign. Let's have a look.' She leaned across the bed, the only one in the side-ward. 'Hey, don't back off. It won't hurt.'

'Sorry. Oh, I do need to get out of here.'

'Don't we all? Only some of us have to feed our kids. Just be glad we're not kicking you out before your time. You get the best bits now – relaxing and being looked after and not having to worry. That's the idea, anyway.'

'Sorry. I'm just a natural-born ungrateful bitch.'

The looking-after bit – that was the worst of all. You had to drink from a baby-cup with a spout, sometimes with a nurse holding the cup, although recently she'd learned how to grip it between her wrists, so long as it wasn't hot tea or coffee.

What she hadn't learned was how to turn on taps with her toes, and obviously she couldn't sink her boxing-glove bandages into hot water, so they had to give her a bath – sitting there with her arms in the air having her bits washed. The unutterable degradation of it.

Juanita sighed. 'I thought I'd be out in a week.'

'Well, we didn't order you to develop pneumonia.'

Because of the pneumonia – caused, they said, by shock – they'd had to delay the skin-grafts. You couldn't have a general anaesthetic with lungs seemingly committed to becoming a no-go area for oxygen. They'd pumped her full of antibiotics, but it was two weeks before they could get around to pulling the skin off her thighs and applying it to her hands.

For all that time, she actually hadn't wanted to smoke. Now the need was acute. This morning, she'd got Karen to take her down the corridor and put one in her mouth, unlit.

The fury was building too. But that was irrational, wasn't it?

'There you go.' Karen straightened up. 'Everything's fine. They'll probably take the dressing off again in the morning.'

'Do they have to? Can't I wear a permanent dressing?'

'It's only you who'll notice most of the time.'

'Exactly.'

The sight of the bandage balls at the end of her arms still inflicted horrendous, scorched images of Jim fragmenting in his jagged, molten cage, falling at last into her arms because . . . *because, Oh God, I couldn't turn away from him again.*

And then, like a wound slowly turning septic, the other insidious imaginings would begin to manifest.

'You were very lucky,' said Karen, who cleaned her teeth and – God help us – wiped her bum. 'You want to thank your lucky stars.'

'Sorry. Thanks, lucky stars. Actually, they tell me it was the lucky Afghan. But for the Afghan, my tits would've been jacket potatoes.'

'Don't think about it, all right?'

'Sure,' said Juanita. She looked down at her pure white cotton nightdress and the image of the jacket potatoes brought her to a decision. 'Listen, I need to ask you something.'

Diane asked him, 'Who was John Cowper Powys?'

It had been an easy run to the hospital, along the M5. Powys explored the parking area for a space.

'He was a famous author.'

'I know that. I mean, to you. What relation?'

'Forget it,' Powys said. 'Not your problem.'

'In the diaries,' Diane said, 'there's a bit where Pixhill comes into Glastonbury and meets his teacher, whom he doesn't identify, and John Cowper Powys, who he thinks he isn't going to like much. But he seems to get on with him in the end.'

'I'm glad somebody could.'

'The suggestion is that Colonel Pixhill and Mr Powys were involved in something together. It . . .' Diane hesitated. 'It's become very important to me to find out what this was.'

He said nothing. He was finding that if you asked Diane direct questions you were apt to scare her off. Better to wait.

'Because, you see, the other person, the teacher, the person Colonel Pixhill doesn't name . . . I think that was someone close to me. He writes several times about visiting his spiritual teacher. Twice he mentions going up Wellhouse Lane. Which was where . . . where she lived.'

Diane went quiet.

'You think his teacher was a she,' Powys said carefully. 'Why do you think that?'

'Because she's my teacher too,' Diane said, not looking at him. 'That is, she was . . . my nanny.'

Powys did some quick calculations. They were clearly not edging around the same person.

'Sorry,' he said. 'I thought we might have been talking about a woman who lived in a converted army hut at the foot of the Tor.'

She turned to him. They were in a shadowed area of the car park but he didn't need much in the way of lights to know her eyes were aglow.

'Diane,' Powys said. Very carefully, treading eggshells. The sound of a distant ambulance echoed the warning sirens going off in his head. 'Dion Fortune died more than twenty years before you were born.'

Diane considered this.

'I don't think she would consider that a problem,' Diane said eventually.

'Sorry.' The nurse rearranged the bedclothes over the cage thing that prevented them touching Juanita's upper thighs, where the skin had been removed. 'Ruth who?'

'Dunn. Nursing sister.'

'What, here?'

'Don't know where she was. It might not even have been anywhere in the West Country, but it probably was.'

'Don't recall. Friend of yours?'

Juanita laughed shortly.

'Like that, is it? I can ask the girls tomorrow. Anything in particular you want to know about her?'

'Just . . . whatever. Look, Diane's here, don't say anything to her about this, OK?'

'Offended you in some way, has she, this Dunn woman?'

'No,' Juanita said. 'She paid me a compliment.'

What lovely slender hands

Ceridwen had said.

Juanita stared grimly at the white boxing gloves. They covered scar tissue and transplanted skin. But not the unspeakable memory of gripping a melting, metal easel and staring into Jim Battle's fried eyes.

THREE

DOESN'T MATTER

With her hair around her shoulders, no make-up and the pristine white shift, she looked very young, Diane thought. Like a recumbent version of the sylph on the front of the old *Avalonian*.

But awfully vulnerable, with her hands inside those enormous bandages.

'They're taking them off tomorrow,' Juanita said.

'That's super.'

'Least it means I can get out of here.'

'When?'

'I'm thinking about it.'

'You mean you'll discharge yourself,' Diane said disapprovingly. She really didn't think Juanita was ready to face Glastonbury. She never spoke of the fire or Jim.

Juanita said, 'You know, you're looking distinctly washed-out. You've lost weight. Are you eating?'

'Sure. It's just been a bit sort of frenzied, what with people placing orders for Christmas, and ... look, I wanted to get your opinion on this.'

She pulled her folder on to her knees.

The artwork had *The Avalonian* across the top in lettering which was only modestly Celtic. The rest of the front cover was a black-and-white photograph of the Tor, surrounded by a high barbed-wire fence with two searchlight towers.

'We got the fence from one of those postwar pictures of Belsen or somewhere. Paul put it all together on his computer.'

With a practised elbow, Juanita prodded a pillow into the small of her back and studied the mock-up.

'I'm impressed. But it doesn't make any secret of where we stand on the issue, does it? I mean, Belsen?'

'I've also written to Quentin Cotton, asking if he'd like to write a piece expressing his views.'

'Not Archer? Not Griff?'

'This way neither Sam nor I have to deal with estranged relatives.'

'You and Archer are officially estranged?'

'I don't know, I haven't spoken to him. Oh. Gosh. I meant to say. You know who his new constituency agent is?'

'Domini Dorrell-Adams?'

'Oliver Pixhill.'

Juanita's eyes widened.

'It's true. Woolly rang to tell me just before I came out. Apparently, the constituency party isn't awfully well off at the moment so Archer offered to bring his own agent. Free of charge, as it were.'

Juanita's eyes narrowed. 'What's the scam?'

'He just wants somebody he can trust, I suppose.'

'Oliver's a shit,' said Juanita. 'Even as a kid he was a shit, so I'm told.'

Diane shrugged. 'Archer's a shit. Do you think we should run the contents along the bottom or down one side?'

'You could start off a column aligned with the *The* in the masthead. If you see what I mean. Actually, as an example of a first issue I suspect there ought to be something less hard-line contentious up-front, less in-your-face.'

'Oh.' Diane was crestfallen. 'I just had the idea, and . . .'

'And it's a really good idea, Diane, and it looks terrific, but for the dummy maybe we need to be a little pragmatic. Hey, is Pixhill married or anything? Girlfriend?'

'Oh, really.' Diane felt herself blush.

'Public schoolboys together.' Juanita raised an eyebrow. 'Both late thirties, unattached.'

'It's an appealing thought,' Diane concluded, 'but I don't think Archer is actually gay. Just doesn't have regular girlfriends.'

'Never mind, Tory Central Office'll find him a nice fiancée before the election. Then they'll part amicably when he wins. You watch.'

'I don't want to watch.'

'No.' Juanita lay back on the pillows. 'I can't help thinking we might have stopped it. And shafted the Glastonbury First movement along the way.'

Obviously meaning the Headlice thing. But as it had turned out, it was just as well they hadn't been to the police. Wearing her *Avalonian* hat, Diane had made a legitimate call to Street and learned from a detective sergeant that it was no longer a murder investigation. A post mortem had revealed that the young man, now formally identified as Alan Carl Gallagher, aged twenty, missing from his home since last summer, had had a weak heart and had taken a large quantity of drugs. It was very borderline now, the sergeant said, off the record.

'I still think somebody's been got at,' Juanita said. 'You can't just dismiss head injuries.'

'They virtually have.'

The sergeant had said the injuries were not sufficiently serious to have caused Alan's death. He might have been in a fight; he could just as easily have been stumbling around stoned out of his head and been superficially struck by a car. Or walked into a tree and then staggered back into his bus. Driven it into the woods because he couldn't see where the hell he was going. None of the travellers they'd spoken to had admitted knowing him, but then they wouldn't, would they? As for the false number plates on the bus, well, it was hard to find any of these hippy wrecks with genuine plates.

'Was it his own bus?'

'I don't know,' Diane said. 'I haven't seen it.'

It would be easy to tell. If, for instance, there were yellow stripes under some of the black. She'd been thinking a lot about the bizarre episode with the girl, Hecate, and the children with their spray cans. Somebody had told them to spray the bus black. To make it less conspicuous, less identifiable?

'I think the travellers killed him,' she said.

There'd been bad magic on the Tor that night. Colonel Pixhill would have understood, would have recognised what she'd seen in the sky. And again in the fire.

Powys was waiting for Diane in reception, a styrofoam cup in his hand. In a baggy sweater and jeans, he still looked a lot like his picture on the back of *The Old Golden Land*, although he must have been ever so young when that came out. At school, other girls had photos of Tom Cruise in their lockers; she dreamed about dishy J. M. Powys, earth-mysteries writer. How could she not trust him now?

'How is she?' Powys asked.

'A little overwrought, I think. I didn't tell her you were here. You don't mind, do you?'

He shook his head.

'There's a lot she isn't telling me,' Diane said. 'She keeps talking about coming home, but I think she needs to get as much as possible out of her system before she comes home.'

'You're a bit of a psychologist then, Diane?'

'I've been to enough,' she said.

He tossed his cup into a bin. 'I, um, meant in the Dion Fortune sense.'

'Oh,' she said. 'Yes. I know what you're asking. The answer's no. I've never had what you might call a practical involvement with the occult. Never even been to a seance. Tried to take up meditation once, but I was hopeless. I . . . things just sort of happen to me.'

When they were back in the car, because he was J. M. Powys, who dismissed nothing, she told him about the lightballs. About the Tor. And about the Third Nanny.

'You saw her?'

'I didn't exactly *see* her. I was . . . aware of her. Sitting on the edge of the bed.'

'And, um, what made you think this was Dion Fortune?'

'You're not going to put this in your book, are you?'

'Not if you don't want me to.'

And he wouldn't. Of course he wouldn't. He liked to think he'd gone way past the stage where books mattered more than people.

All the same, she proved difficult to pin down on this one. At first, she told him, she used to think she was a reincarnation of DF. But the basis for this seemed to be little more than a teenage crush on the novels and those initials.

(Powys didn't imagine Dan Frayne had any illusions about *his* initials.)

She wasn't quite sure when she'd first made a connection between DF and the Third Nanny, who, to Powys, sounded suspiciously like a fantasy figure to help her cope with life under the authority of the real ones.

'What happened to your mother?'

'She died when I was born. That is, I was born in rather a hurry after she fell down the stairs at Bowermead.'

'I'm sorry.'

'My father's rather held it against me ever since. I don't think he's ever been able to look at me without feeling a certain resentment.'

Powys thought this, and being brought up by starchy nannies, was enough to disarrange any kid's psychology.

Several miles further on, somewhere down the M5, she said, 'It isn't a coincidence.'

'No?'

'We were called back. You for John Cowper Powys, me for Dion Fortune.'

'Dion Fortune didn't have much time for JCP,' Powys pointed out. 'She even misspelt his name.'

'That was deliberate. A sort of smokescreen. If she didn't know him well enough to spell his name right, she could hardly be involved with him in a secret operation.'

'What secret operation was this exactly?'

'I don't know. But I think we have to find out. Why else have we been brought back?'

'I haven't exactly been brought back. I've never been here before. Also . . .'

'You're a Powys.'

'I've been commissioned to write a book, Diane. That's all.'

But it isn't all, is it? Is her Third Nanny on the edge of the bed any more crazy than having your living room repeatedly rearranged by a kinetic copy of A Glastonbury Romance?

Diane said, 'Do you believe in evil?'

'Probably. I mean, yes.'

'In Glastonbury?'

'Good as anywhere. Or as bad.'

'Colonel Pixhill believed in it very strongly at the end.'

'That's one very depressing book,' said Powys.

'People hate it in Glastonbury.'

'I can imagine they would. Doesn't fit the ethos.'

Diane said, 'There's an American called Dr Pelham Grainger, who lives locally and apparently maintains that we don't let enough darkness into our lives. I've taken over thirty orders for his book in the past fortnight.'

'I think somebody mentioned him a week or two ago. Sounds like a very sick man.'

She nodded and stroked Arnold and didn't say anything else until they were well past the Isle of Avalon sign.

'I've seen the Dark Chalice.'

Her voice seemed to reverberate, which didn't happen in Minis. Powys slowed down drastically, the lights of Glastonbury all around them now. There was a sort of shelter in the centre of the car park, under which Diane had left the van. Powys turned the Mini so that the headlights lit up the side of the van.

He was waiting. This could mean almost anything; the Dark Chalice seemed to be Pixhill's all-purpose metaphor for bad shit.

'Oh no,' said Diane.

Although it wasn't yet nine p.m., the car park seemed completely deserted. It was another bright, sharp night, the moon not long past full, the tower of St John's sticking up like a candlestick on the edge of a table.

Diane said, 'Oh, please . . .'

He followed her eyes.

'Oh.' He got out.

The back window of Diane's van had been smashed, so had the driver's side window; glass all over the seat. Across the side panels, where Diane had painted friendly pink spots, there was uneven, black, spray-paint lettering, six inches high.

Diane stared at the van in numbed silence. Powys squeezed her right hand with both of his. He saw the black paint was glistening, still damp.

'It was in the fire,' Diane said tonelessly. 'When Jim died. That was the second time. The first time was over the Tor. Like shadow hands holding up a shadow cup. That was when I felt the evil. I've never felt anything like it.'

'I'll call the police,' Powys said.

'No.'

'You can't just let them . . .'

'The police are never going to catch them. There's a garage I used to go to. I'll get them to take it away first thing tomorrow.'

'Bastards,' Powys said. 'Have you any idea who might . . .?'

'It doesn't matter,' Diane cried. She turned away from the van. 'It doesn't matter,' she whispered.

FOUR

HORRID BROWN FOUNTAIN

Woolly said, 'Mind if I move some of this stuff, Diane? I need to spread the maps out.'

She put on all the shop lights; it was a dark morning. 'Gosh, how many have you got?'

'Three. I need to put 'em all together. Think we're gonner have to use the floor. This is heavy shit, Diane, man. This is, like, end-of-the-world-scenario.'

Woolly squatted on the carpet and began to unfold an Ordnance Survey map, sliding one edge under two legs of the display table for current bestsellers. He'd phoned just after seven, to check if he could come round before the shop opened. He needed to lay something on her. Couldn't believe what he was seeing.

For once, Diane hadn't wanted to get up, not even for Woolly. She'd been out long after midnight. Yes, OK, she'd lied to J. M. Powys. It did matter about the van. It mattered terribly.

'I got the proof here, look, no hype,' Woolly said.

'Proof?'

'About the road. You all right, Diane?'

'Yes. Fine. Sorry. Go ahead.'

The maps were covered with little circles and ruler marks. All Woolly's Ordnance maps were customised into ley-line plans, with prehistoric sites – stones and burial mounds – and ancient churches, moats, beacon hills and things neatly encircled in red ink. People like Woolly could prove all kinds of wonderful things with maps and rulers and set-squares.

What you did was to find how many of the old sites fell into straight lines and then draw them in. It never failed; you'd finish up with a whole network of lines, some with four or five points, sometimes a whole star-formation of lines radiating out from a single point, indicating a very powerful ancient centre.

Glastonbury Tor, of course, was the classic example, perhaps the most important power centre in the whole of Western Europe. Sure enough, there it was on the second of Woolly's maps, with lines of force spraying out in all directions.

'Spent all night on this, Diane. Couldn't believe it myself at first, where the road goes. Bit of a mind-blower, girl. Don't know how we missed it, here of all places.'

Woolly was a very intelligent chap, but he'd done so many exotic drugs in his time that he tended to approach life obliquely, from strange directions. So that rather mundane things seemed, to him, quite astonishing.

Of course, there was the possibility that what Woolly saw was the truth and everyone else was blinded by the familiarity of things. Diane liked to think that, most of the time.

She made some tea. When she came back he had the three maps pushed together, taking up more than half the shop. He was thumbing through one of the paperback Dion Fortunes.

'Wish this lady was still around, Diane. She'd get us organised all right.'

Diane handed him his tea and said nothing.

'Ever heard of the Watchers of Avalon, Diane?'

'Sort of. The group she founded to defend Britain against Nazi black magic in World War Two?'

'I believe that,' Woolly said. 'Everybody goes on about the V-2 or whatever it was being the Nazis' secret weapon, but the *secret* secret weapon was heavy-duty magic. They were well into it. Now the Watchers, they were all over Britain, but they all concentrated on the Tor at certain prearranged times and like pooled their energy. Really heavy. A real reservoir of psychic power to keep the enemy out.'

'The Tor's a very powerful beacon,' Diane said. A few weeks ago, all this would have sent her into overdrive, but this morning, everything felt so dull and stagnant.

'Some people say the Watchers of Avalon are still around, you know. Not the original ones, like, but magical adepts who've picked up the banner. What I wanner know is, if they are around, what the hell they doing about this fuckin' road? Right.' Woolly rubbed his hands together. 'Got your notebook?'

'I've got a good memory. Oh gosh!'

'Huh?'

'Nothing. It's OK.'

What if Colonel Pixhill and John Cowper Powys were involved with DF in the Watchers of Avalon? Pixhill first came to Glastonbury in the War – while recovering from his wounds in fact. Was that how the three got together?

'OK,' Woolly said. 'Gimme a sec to get my head together. Everything'll be cool.'

'Everything will be cool,' repeated a voice as smooth as cashmere. 'Is this a cartographer's convention, Diane, or have I wandered into a timewarp?'

Woolly spun round in alarm.

Dark overcoat, briefcase, gloves. Diane's brother Archer in his city clothes.

'Leaving early to catch my train to London,' Archer said. 'Saw the lights. The sign said Closed but the door was slightly open. So I took the liberty of walking in.'

Woolly dived at his maps like a maniac, gathering them to his chest. The one held down by the table legs ripped in two places.

'Not inconvenient, I trust,' Archer said.

Young Paul, who thought even anoraks were a little avant garde, was wearing a sleeveless pullover in maroon. He was waving his arms about.

'Swear to God, Sam, I'm coming back from the Avalon Internet Group at Dean Wiggin's flat, I'm taking a short cut across the car park . . . and there she is. Got three, four spray cans and she's going at it like a loo . . . like mad.'

'Painting her van? At night?' Sam leaned back in his favourite director's chair, legs stretched out, hands behind his head. 'You don't by any chance take hallucinogenic drugs at meetings of the Avalon Internet Group?'

Paul looked insulted. The kid didn't even drink; his idea of hard drugs was extra-strong mints.

'Sam, I saw it.'

Sam needed to think about this. He'd been in the print-shop since seven, no need to be here, wasn't expecting Diane cracking the whip or anything. The *Avalonian* dummy was more or less in the can, just waiting for the interview the guy with the dog was doing with the bishop. So no sleep lost over *The Avalonian*.

Just Diane?

Daft eh? Found he couldn't sleep for ages last night, through . . . not exactly worrying about her. Trying to puzzle her out. Track down her motivations. Odd, that. Never lost a wink of sleep over Charlotte or the row with his dad. Or even getting arrested over the sabbing, come to that. Probably the last time was the fox cub. Six nights feeding the little guy with a dropper – seven, eight years ago, this must be, a hunt orphan from Pennard's land. Nearly got himself snatched by that bastard, Rankin – Hughie Painter shouting, *Leave it, Sam, they'll see your face.* He couldn't do that.

Rufus. Cute little guy. Still had that sweet, puppy smell. Used to fall asleep on Sam's knees. He'd cried like a baby into his pillow the night Rufus died.

'OK, Paul,' Sam said. 'You don't mention this to a soul.'

'No, Sam.'

'Good boy.' Sam sat up in his director's chair. Beyond puzzlement this time.

Verity arose at seven-thirty and made a point of not putting on any lights, doing her tenebral breathing as she found her way through the shadows to the kitchen.

Although it was the youngest and least museum-like part of the house, the Victorian kitchen was depressing in its own way. Those tall, dark-stained, fitted dressers leaving hardly any wall visible. Knotted, exposed wiring crawling along two beams like varicose veins. The water pipes coiling in the shadows, making intestinal noises.

In the drab stillness, the telephone rang just after eight a.m., rattling the plates on the dresser, the combined sound somehow reminding Verity of the shrill, protesting warble of the fire-engines trapped in Wellhouse Lane, less than half a mile away, while poor Mr Battle had burned to death.

She picked up the receiver sharply.

It was Dr Grainger; he came straight to the point.

'Verity, I've been thinking about this a good deal. Also discussing it, in confidence, with my partner, the psychotherapist Eloise Castell. Bottom line is, if you are going to gain any benefits from our work together, we need to get around to some corrective therapy for the house itself.'

'Yes, but Dr Grainger, I don't . . .' He was suddenly a runaway force in Glastonbury. The publication of his book, *Embracing the Dark*, had been brought forward to coincide with the Winter Solstice, the shortest, darkest day, and the *Sunday Times* had done an article on him for its colour magazine.

But she really couldn't have him tampering with the fabric of Meadwell.

'I would like to check this out soonest, Verity. Specifically the old well itself.'

'But you can't *get* to the well. It's sealed up, Dr Grainger. Concreted over. Because of contamination. There was a . . . a health risk.'

'Precisely. The sealing of the well put the house into a state of denial. What you have there is a vital subterranean artery you can no longer access. I say vital, because this was the reason for the house being built in this location. Could we say tomorrow? Eleven a.m.?'

'Oh, but I . . .' Verity frantically fingering her wooden beads. 'I would need to consult the Trust.'

And I'm afraid to. Because I don't know who controls the Trust any more or to what extent it still honours the Colonel's wishes.

'Verity,' he said with heavy patience. 'I ran into Oliver Pixhill last night. We discussed the problem at some length. Oliver is concerned about your situation. He wants to help you. He said to me, go ahead.'

'Go ahead?'

'And unblock the Meadwell.'

Afterwards, Verity, who had not been down to the old well in years, felt so jittery that she was obliged to take a measure of Dr Bach's Rescue Remedy before she was even able to leave the oppressive kitchen.

Archer stood in the doorway exuding Presence; Diane wondered if this was something they taught you at Conservative Central Office, how to walk into a room and dominate everybody. Or perhaps he'd just had lessons from Father.

'Councillor Woolaston.' Archer smiled, managing to make Diane feel as though he'd discovered her and Woolly dancing in the nude.

Woolly shoved roughly folded maps under his arm to shake hands. Archer said, 'I suspect we'll be seeing a good deal of each other in the years to come. Or perhaps not.'

'If you get elected,' Woolly said. Diane glanced at him; wasn't like Woolly to be so abrasive. He must have been very startled.

She saw Archer's full mouth develop a petulant twist, swiftly straightened. Too swiftly – as if he'd been studying his less appealing expressions on video, with a view to strangling them at birth.

'Quite,' Archer said pleasantly. 'Look, I don't want to intrude on you, Diane, if—'

''s OK,' Woolly said hurriedly. 'I was just off. Got this site-meeting out at Meare in half an hour. Catch you again, Diane.'

'Interesting to meet you, Councillor.' Archer watched him go, shaking his head almost kindly. 'Quaint little person. Surely the last of a dying breed.'

'He's a nice man, Archer.' Diane moved defensively behind the counter.

'I'm sure he is. Diane, reason I called, Father's been trying to reach you – with a conspicuous lack of success – to find out what you were doing for Christmas.'

'If you remember,' Diane said icily, 'the last time I saw Father was when he had me kidnapped.'

'Oh Diane . . .' Archer twitching off his gloves. 'What can one say? The old man was thinking of me. A trifle embarrassing if the news of one's election had appeared next to the arrest of one's sister, along with two dozen smelly hippies, for public order offences. But you're quite right, an over-reaction. Educated people make allowances for you now.'

Archer smiled his vulpine smile. She noticed he'd developed Lady Thatcher's mannerism of finishing a sentence by putting the head on one side and exposing the teeth.

'Archer . . .' Diane stopped suddenly, realising she was being given a chance to mention what the Rankins had done to Headlice.

Archer was watching her, unblinking, and Diane felt a stillness come upon the room. The colours of the books on the display stands seemed to be neutralising before her eyes.

She let her arms fall to her sides in defeat. 'It . . . it's just you can't do that, you know, that . . . that sort of thing.' The words mushy and inexact, not quite aware of what she was saying. 'I mean I'm twenty-seven, which . . . which makes me a . . . grown-up person, you know?' Blinking to clear her vision. 'I mean, what . . . what was he going to do, lock me in the attic?'

Archer retracted his smile. If he was relieved she hadn't mentioned the Headlice business he wasn't showing it.

'Diane, believe me, when Juanita Carey arrived to collect you, we couldn't have been more happy. A responsible woman, in spite of . . .'

Archer gesticulated at the books with a certain nose-wrinkling contempt.

'Really 'palling tragedy, though. Wondering if I ought to pop in and see her in hospital. Take a bunch of flaaahs.'

'Perhaps not,' Diane said carefully. She felt as if she were standing in a pool of grey water, its temperature just above her body heat.

'Whatever you think best. Anyway, we're all jolly happy to see you apparently settled and working on this little . . . ah . . . periodical . . . pamphlet thing.'

Diane let it go. They weren't making a great secret of *The Avalonian*, but the less Archer knew the better. She didn't want to talk about the new road either. And certainly not the Tor; Archer was its enemy. And hers.

'So.' He beamed. 'What *are* you doing for Christmas? Because, Father and I thought you might like to join us – family, friends, neighbours, Party people – at Bowermead. The usual Christmas Day gathering and then the hunt, of course, on Boxing Day. We couldn't possibly think of you being so close and not joining in the festive fun.'

Diane could almost feel the bloody dampness on her thighs as she remembered Archer's idea of festive fun. She could hardly see him now, the shop was so dark, its window and door clouded with fog. She heard her own voice say, 'Tell Father it's terribly kind of him, but I think Juanita's going to be out of hospital for Christmas. And she won't be able to use her hands much, you see. Not properly. Not for some time.'

'Ah, yes. How good you are, Diane. I shall try and explain it to Father.'

Diane felt a movement in the pool of mist at her side.

'Of course it was his original intention . . .' Archer's little smile was almost coy. '. . . to invite Patrick and his family.'

She clutched at the counter, feeling sick with hatred, the loathing solid and real inside her and also, somehow, existing separately, in the room

'If you'd then refused to come, he'd doubtless have sent Patrick to fetch you and it would all have been horribly embarrassing. Tact, diplomacy and forethought never being Father's middle names. Don't worry, my dear, I've talked him out of it.'

'Thank you,' Diane said on a long, volcanic breath. 'Thank you, Archer.'

'I'll be on my way then.' Archer slipped a glove over his hand, paused in the doorway. 'And when is this little paper of yours to be published?'

'Er . . . er, next year perhaps.'

'Oh, nothing imminent then?'

'We want to get it right.'

'Absolutely. I'm sure Father will be delighted to see you deploying your, ah, new-found journalistic skills.'

She saw how cold his eyes were.

'Even if it is in our backyard, as it were,' Archer said. 'Even if it scorns all our best endeavours.'

He raised a gloved hand. 'Look after yourself, Diane. Damned hippies and squatters are turning this town into a jungle. Drug-dealing. Burglaries. Muggings. Vandalism.' He caught her eyes. 'Graffiti.'

Diane's insides were already pumping like a sewage works as she slammed the door in his face and barely made it to the kitchen sink before her meagre carob-bar breakfast came up in a horrid brown fountain.

FIVE

ALL FOR REAL

Sam tried to gaze casually out of the print-shop window, his chair angled meaningfully away as Charlotte rushed out, slammed into her Golf – blatantly parked on the double-yellows, Daddy being in the same lodge as the chief superintendent – and wafted imperiously off down Magdalene Street.

'Bitch.' He saw two blokes unloading the lights for the Christmas tree in front of the bank. Some bloody Christmas this was going to be.

'What's that, Sam?'

'Didn't say a word, Paul.'

'Oh. Right. Thought you didn't.' Paul, young Mr Tact, went back to his work. He didn't like Charlotte, Sam could tell. He guessed the kid was still a bit scared of high-octane women, not realising they could be just as half-baked under the gloss.

Charlotte, eh? Like, what a snotty cow. All the advertising she could have pointed *The Avalonian*'s way . . . what with working for Stan Pike and Daddy being chairman of the Chamber of Trade and all this crap. She could even've put the arm on Pike to give *The Avalonian* the all-clear to his mates. 'It is not a hippy rag,' Sam had insisted. 'How many times I got to spell it out? It's a genuine, solid publication.'

'With Diane Ffitch?' Charlotte had replied just now. '*Diane Ffitch*? You call being edited by that fruitcake solid?'

'All right, stuff it, then,' Sam had snarled. 'We don't need Pike, bloody backstreet used-house dealer.'

Charlotte. Bloody Charlotte, eh? Things had been very much on the blink since he'd made that minor scene at the Glastonbury First gig over the old man and Archer Ffitch. Time to call it a day?

Three years, though. Three years of storms and upsets and sexy making-up sessions. Three years of political arguments and being produced as Charlotte's bit of rough at too many posh parties.

Naturally, she'd backed him all the way in starting up the print-shop, becoming a local businessman, like Daddy, like Stanlow Pike. When Sam became a businessman, Charlotte started circling dates on the calendar for the engagement party. Cracked it at last, brought the anarchist to heel.

Charlotte had got Sam the contract for printing all Pike and Corner's property brochures, which was a major deal.

The major deal . . . until Juanita Carey had come up with the idea for *The Avalonian*. Which little Charlotte, of course, didn't like the sound of at all, from the outset.

Sam lit a cigarette.

Another thing about Charlotte was the way she nagged him about his smoking. Like he was already her property and she was making sure he came with a full warranty. How could a woman of twenty-six come over so bloody middle-aged? Nil prospect of her moving into the flat without something official, on paper, signed in triplicate. Twice they'd almost wound it up. Trouble was, she looked so seriously edible, waiting for him by the market cross, parked on a double-yellow. Could he really stand to see her hanging out for some slimy accountant with a BMW?

Difficult one, that.

He brightened when he saw Diane crossing the road by the Christmas tree. She hadn't been in all morning, and after what Paul had said about her painting the van in the dark he'd kept thinking maybe he should take a walk up to the shop, check her out. Just that he didn't feel he knew her well enough to ask why she was behaving like a fruitcake.

She didn't come in. She didn't even glance at the shop, just walked past, like a bloody zombie, people getting out of her way. Sam watched her cross Magdalene Street and head straight for the Abbey gatehouse. She didn't go in there either, she turned her back on it, fell against the wall like a drunk trying to stay upright.

What the . . .?

Sam was up and out of the door, not giving himself time to think.

'Diane?'

When he ran across the road, a truck driver braking and blasting his horn, she looked, unseeing, in Sam's direction. He could see that she was shivering uncontrollably, like a long-term junkie run out of smack. Shit, the girl was ill.

'You all right? Something happened?'

'Oh.' Diane looked up, vaguely. 'Sam.'

'What's wrong?' A few people staring at them now, but not many because this was Glastonbury and there wasn't much they hadn't seen in these streets. 'Only Lady Loony,' he heard one woman with a kid and a shopping bag say knowingly to another and they both laughed and Sam wanted to kick their bloody arses halfway to Benedict Street.

Diane, face slightly blue, was staring vacantly across the road to where the two guys were untangling the Christmas tree lights. Sam took her arm.

'Come on. Come for a hot chocolate, Diane.' Easing her away from the wall. 'Catch your death.'

Darryl Davey came past with a couple of mates, nudging each other and smirking.

'Don't you say a fucking word, sunshine,' Sam snarled. Darryl narrowed his eyes and gave him the finger.

Tosser.

'You see . . . and this is strictly off the record . . .' The Bishop of Bath and Wells lit a thin roll-up. '. . . some of my predecessors have been frankly embarrassed at having Glastonbury in the diocese.'

The Bishop was a compact man in his early forties. He wore cord trousers and a purple denim shirt, his white clerical band under the button-down collar. Powys wondered if he always rolled his own cigarettes or just wanted to appear cool for the local radical rag.

'Point being, Joe, the Church of England might have owned the Abbey for most of the century, but the ambience remains RC, and I imagine many people still regard us being the landlords as the final insult. Even if we have tidied the place up, stopped it being treated as a convenient stone quarry for local builders.'

'But the Catholics aren't the problem right now, are they?' Powys said. 'You've got what we might call an older denomination to contend with.'

'Pagans.' The bishop laughed. 'Be so much easier if the buggers still wore horns and bones through their noses. But they're quite likely to be academics in suits.' He nodded towards the window. 'Could be a few hanging around the cathedral as we speak.' But he didn't seem to regard this as much of a threat.

They were in Wells, a very small city a short drive from Glastonbury. At a window table in a pub facing the cathedral. The bishop drank Perrier. His name was Liam Kelly; he didn't sound even vaguely Irish.

'But, you see, Joe ... are they really pagans? What you have today, as we approach the Millennium, is a great yearning for spirituality. We – the human race – have been everywhere and realised what a terribly small place the earth is, how finite are its resources.'

A micro-cassette machine lay on the table between them. The bishop pulled it a little closer.

'Even been to the moon, and what a dreadful anti-climax that was. So more people are realising there's only one real voyage of discovery left to them, and that is inwards. It's a very promising situation.'

'You think so?'

'You don't?'

The bishop seemed to see Powys for the first time, to wonder who he was. Powys hadn't mentioned his proposed book. Diane had arranged the interview – which, presumably, was why the bishop had agreed to do it; he hadn't been here long enough to risk offending the House of Pennard. How was he to know how things stood between Diane and her immediate family?

Powys said, 'You don't think inner trips can be a little risky for some people?'

'Are we on or off the record?'

'Whatever you like.' Powys stopped the tape.

'Look, I don't know precisely what kind of magazine this is, ah ... Joe. But if you can somehow get over the message that I don't regard my visit to Glastonbury next Thursday as any kind of crusade. Or the pagan element as the Enemy. I like to believe that we're all working towards the same goal. If, for instance, some women like to regard the Divinity as having a distinct feminine aspect, how can I legitimately argue against that? The battle for the ordination of women has been fought and won, and it's a victory I applaud.'

Not answering the question. Didn't seem to realise, either, that *The Avalonian* didn't yet exist and would hardly be on the streets in time to get over any message about Thursday.

'Goddess worshippers,' Powys said. 'You'll be meeting them?'

'On Thursday, as I say. Which is simply the shortest day as far as we're concerned. To them it's Christmas without the Christ – as yet. God, is that the time already? Sorry about this, but I do have to be in Bath for lunch.'

'Oh,' Powys realised. 'The Solstice. Thursday's the Winter Solstice. Won't the pagans be having their . . . whatever they do?'

The Bishop stood up. 'I don't know what they normally do, but on Thursday, before exchanging opinions about the future of Glastonbury, we shall go together at dawn to St Michael's Chapel, where I shall conduct a small service with carols which followers of the, ah, nature religion will find not incompatible – 'The Holly and the Ivy', this sort of thing.'

'St Michael's Chapel . . . Look, I'm sorry, I'm not too familiar with the geography, but that's part of the Abbey, is it?'

'No, no.' The Bishop finished his Perrier. 'It's the one on the Tor.'

Powys pocketed his tape machine. 'Let me get this right. You're going to the top of Glastonbury Tor with a bunch of pagans on the Winter Solstice. Doesn't it bother you, if you believe . . .'

Bishop Kelly laughed and shook his head. 'The Winter Solstice, as I say, is merely the shortest day. The "pagans", if we have to use that term, will be represented by Dame Wanda Carlisle, who I've already met socially and who is, in all other respects, a delightful person. And the Tor is, ah . . .'

'Just a hill?' Powys couldn't believe this.

'Indeed,' said the Bishop. 'Just a hill.'

'So what are your feelings about this plan to restrict public access?'

The Bishop smiled. 'Good talking to you, Joe. Hope to see you up there.'

*

Diane went over to sit in her usual red typist's chair. She looked pale as watered milk.

'Go on.' Sam turned on an extra bar of the electric fire and moved to the corner where Paul kept the tea and coffee and Diane's chocolate, everything washed and neatly arranged. 'What did the slimy bastard want?'

'Me for Christmas,' said Diane dolefully. 'At Bowermead. They have a gathering most years, and the awful Boxing Day hunt's been revived, so . . .'

'Has it now? Well, well. Going, are we?'

'Bowermead? For Christmas? Gosh, no. I might never get out again. They still have sort of dungeons underneath. Anyway, Juanita might be out of hospital by Christmas. She'll need a lot of help.'

'Right,' said Sam. 'Right. Soya cream in your chocolate?'

'Perhaps not. Sam . . .'

'Good job, we're clean out of soya cream. Sorry?'

'I . . . Does anything ever, you know, ever happen to you? The way it does to some people. Quite a . . . a bigger percentage of people than normal, I suppose. In Glastonbury.'

Boxing Day hunt, he was thinking. Got to have a go at this one. Especially after that 'MP-elect' bollocks. Make Christmas worth while, for once. Ring Hughie. Get some of the old crew in from Bristol.

'Sorry, Diane . . .?' God, but she looked tired. Wanted looking after, this kid.

Diane watched him, unblinking. 'I was saying, did you ever have . . . did anything ever happen to you that . . . that you couldn't explain? Like . . .'

'Oh, there's a whole lot of stuff I can't explain.' Sam dumped two spoonfuls of drinking chocolate into a mug. 'Why folks will cheat and lie for a few quid that isn't gonner make them happy. Why it's always the best people who wind up dead before their time. Why otherwise humane, civilised folks'll go out and make little animals run till they can't run no more and then watch 'em get ripped apart. I don't include your old man in this, mind. I can understand why he does it. It's because he's soulless and pig-thick.'

He pulled a cigarette out of the packet.

'Sorry. Shouldn't talk like that. He is your dad.'

Diane shrugged. She had her hands clasped between her knees. Every few moments her shoulders would shake like she was fighting off flu.

'I know what you're asking,' Sam wanted to put his arms around her. If he could get them all the way round. 'I'm just avoiding the question.'

Not the time to come on with the arms. Probably never would be, after he said what he had to say. Shit. Should have realised he'd have to deal with this at some point. Should've been prepared. Course, if he hadn't grown to like her so much, as a person, it wouldn't have been a problem. In fact he usually got quite a buzz out of laying it on people in this headcase town – the people who'd looked at him, with his tangled, shoulder-length hair and his bit of an earring, and made certain assumptions which were way, way out.

Both of them veggies, too. They agreed totally about animal rights – although Diane was a bit more discreet about it than Sam was; didn't seem to feel quite the same urge to go and beat the living shit out of a huntsman. And, OK, she had this incomprehensible appetite for these totally disgusting carob-covered cereal bars.

Beyond this, it got more difficult.

'Look at me,' Diane shook again. 'I've been like this all morning. Couldn't open the shop.'

'You seen a doctor?'

Diane smiled thinly. 'Not anything a doctor could deal with. I've spent most of the morning sitting in front of the fire trying to deal with it.'

'Archer.'

'Sam, a sort of . . . blind hatred comes over me.'

'Fair enough.'

'And when it does, things start to happen. Awfully strange things. In the room or wherever I am. Sometimes I can almost see it, see my own rage. I suppose it's always been there. He just touches something in me and sets it off.'

'Seems a perfectly normal reaction to me. We *are* talking about Archer Ffitch here.'

'When I was a child, I got a sort of perverse comfort from it. I would hug it to me. My hatred. Hug it to me like a dog. I think it's . . . it happened during the Glastonbury First meeting when he unveiled his plans for the Tor. It was as if the Tor knew what he was planning and hated him for it, and all that hatred is coming into me.'

'Ah,' said Sam, wishing he was out of here. 'Right.'

'And that's why the Tor's been coming through to me since I was a baby. The Tor knew what was going to happen as we approached the Millennium. It was all pre-ordained. Why Violet – Dion Fortune – was chosen to be my spirit guide. Because I have to stop them destroying the Tor.'

'Diane, they don't wanner destroy the Tor, they just wanner restrict—'

'It's the same thing.' Rage dancing in Diane's eyes. 'The Tor, the road scheme. It's all anti-spiritual. You ask Woolly. Woolly was in the shop this morning talking, you know, end-of-the-world scenario. 'What happens in Glastonbury affects the spiritual life of the entire nation. This is the cradle.'

'Diane, if Woolly runs out of dope it's an end-of-the-world scenario.' Sam handed her the mug. 'Drink your chocolate.'

Dammit, most situations you could work with people for years and they never needed to know where you stood on the big issues, which way you voted, etc.

Sam took a big breath, pulled on a handful of his long hair. Looked at Diane and kept seeing Rufus the fox cub.

'The thing is . . . I've got a big problem with all this, look. I'm like . . . coming from a different direction, right? Like, far as I can make out, you believe in just about the whole bit – UFOs, God, ghosts, the Holy Grail.'

'You have a way', Diane lowered her eyes, 'of making it all sound frightfully tawdry.'

'Whereas, I . . . I'm like . . . how can I put this . . . an atheist,' Sam said.

Diane looked up and sought his eyes. This time it was Sam who looked away.

From what seemed a long distance, he heard Diane whispering, 'You don't believe . . . in anything?'

'I believe in looking after the planet and, you know, each other, and not being cruel to animals. Or even people. Most of them.'

'You don't even believe in the possibility of anything?'

'I believe in cleaning up your own mess. I believe in being kind. But as for . . . you know . . .'

Diane said, very faintly, 'The otherworldly.'

'If you like. I think, quite honestly, I think it's all bollocks. The Grail, the Holy bloody Thorn. The Abbey – very pretty, look, but . . . it's all bollocks.'

In Glastonbury, he thought, you were allowed to be a Christian, a pagan, a Buddhist, a Hindu, a Muslim and maybe, at a pinch, a liberal kind of agnostic. Anything, but . . .

'Where I'm coming from,' Sam said, 'this is a town built on bollocks.'

Big, *big* patch of quiet.

Then Diane just said, 'Oh.'

And for that moment, and maybe the one after it, Sam Daniel wished he did believe in the resurrection of the body and the forgiveness of sins and the shroud of Turin and the holy virgin of Knock and the men in silver suits, the whole bloody shebang.

Diane was sitting there looking down at her clasped hands. She hadn't touched her chocolate.

It occurred to Sam, for the first time, seeing her half in shadow, eyes downcast, that she was actually kind of beautiful.

Diane stood up. 'I'd better go.'

No. Don't go. I could have second thoughts.

'Yeah,' he said. 'OK, then.'

At the door, he said, 'It's coming along really well, Diane. *The Avalonian.* If this was for real, I reckon we could have it on the streets before Christmas.'

Diane said very quietly, 'It's all for real. Everything's part of everything else, and it's all for real.'

SIX

SMALL THINGS

Juanita sat in the bedside chair and stared at her hands until her vision went blurred. 'There,' said Karen, the nurse. 'Isn't medical science wonderful?'

She was too upset to reply. Every time they unwrapped the dressings, the hands seemed to look more alien, the transplants in her palms the revolting pink of an old-fashioned condom. And shockingly clean, devoid of lines.

At first they'd looked like the hands of an excavated corpse which someone had joined to her wrists. Frankenstein hands. Now they were claws. She'd shrieked at the doctor, *I can't move them, oh Christ, I can't bend the fingers.* The doctor said they'd become more flexible. In time. And the pink would fade. In time. As would the pain.

Oh, sure, she knew she was lucky. Knew it could have been so much worse. If she hadn't covered her face, if she hadn't been wearing the Afghan.

And, just for a moment, she'd imagined how it would have been the other way round. If she'd died in flames and Jim had been left with hands which wouldn't hold a paintbrush, wouldn't paint with any delicacy perhaps ever again. Jim gazing into his beloved dusk and watching it recede.

About to cry, Juanita sat up in the chair. Think angry.

What beautiful hands you have, Juanita.

'Take it easy, now,' said Karen. She'd come on duty at four, as usual. Juanita's hands had been unwrapped since ten. She'd got dressed for the occasion, in the off-the-shoulder lemon top which Jim liked so much and a long, Aztec-patterned cotton skirt which lay easy on her flayed thighs.

Juanita looked up into the small face full of professional interest. A couple of times they'd sent a trauma counsellor to see her. At least, she'd claimed to be a trauma counsellor, her questions reflecting a certain concern for Juanita's mental-health. After all, what kind of normal person would hurl herself at the blazing, flaking corpse of even a close friend?

She said to Karen, 'Did you find out anything about Ruth Dunn?'

Karen looked even more anxious, then her face went blank. 'Talk about it later.'

'Come on, Karen, what did you find out?'

'Where's she now, Juanita? This woman.'

'Glastonbury.'

'Not in a hospital?'

'No.'

'Private clinic?'

'Nothing like that.'

'Thank Christ for that.'

'Jesus, Karen . . .'

'I'll see you later. Sister'll be on my back. We'll have a chat.'

Juanita glowered at the uniformed back. A hospital was like a police state. She thought about discharging herself, walking down to the motorway intersection. Holding up her weird hands to thumb a lift. Frighten the lorry drivers.

Then she sank back into the hard chair and wept.

Sam paced the office. He had to do something. Couldn't just sit around like a spare prick. Sod it. He snatched up the phone and rang Hughie Painter, Central Somerset's most experienced hunt-saboteur.

Mastersab, they called Hughie. Once jailed for three months after trying to ram a hunting horn down the throat of some pompous bloody Master of Foxhounds. A hero. A legend in sabbing circles. When you talked to Hughie on the phone you kept it short and careful.

'Half an hour, right? Under the Christmas tree? We'll be, like, anonymous figures in the crowd.' Sam laughed. 'OK. See you.'

About the only thing he could do for Diane was spoil Archer Ffitch's Boxing Day.

She couldn't bring herself to go back to the shop. She walked right past. Some people gave her sidelong glances. She knew she probably looked pretty awful.

She'd never felt so isolated. There wasn't anyone she could trust. How could . . . how could anyone live in Glastonbury and not believe in anything?

How could you be, like Sam, a good person who cared about people and animals and the welfare of the planet, and not believe that it all existed for some purpose? How could you live in Glastonbury and not feel *closer*?

Actually, she didn't feel close to anything. She felt used. The candyfloss sunbeams rolling down the Tor and the ice-cream lights at night giving way to fragmented images, sharp and threatening as slivers of glass, to the dark vaporous forms which passed as fast as birds. To the black, portentous symbols you could only wish you'd never seen.

All nonsense to Sam. All *bollocks*. She didn't know whether to pity him or envy him his freedom.

What he thought of her; this mattered more. Sam Daniel thought Diane Ffitch was a loony. It didn't matter that most people had thought this for years, were thinking it now as they watched her trooping up the street like a fat scarecrow. It suddenly mattered awfully that Sam now thought it too. It wounded her. It was terribly unfair.

There was a funny atmosphere in the town again, the shapes of the buildings sharp against a cold, grim sky, everything so vivid, a thunderstorm air of energy-in-waiting. She wished she could drive away for a while and think, but she hadn't even had the nerve to collect the van from the garage.

And of course that started her thinking about Archer again. That parting shot. He *knew* about the graffiti on the van. He might even have told them to do it.

He was taunting her. Why did he always have to do that?'

She wandered, inevitably, up Wellhouse Lane, past the trees which screened Chalice Orchard, where DF had lived. Probably fooling herself over that as well. What would the legendary high priestess of Isis want with someone like her?

There was an unhealthy engine noise behind her, then an ancient Land-Rover clattered alongside.

'Lookin' for me, Miss Diane?'

Oh gosh. Moulder. Forgotten all about the phone message. 'Hop in, my chicken.'

Another site-meeting, more disillusionment.

Under discussion this afternoon had been a Griff Daniel proposal for a new housing estate out on the Meare road. Green field site. Daniel's plan, an executive housing estate: four-bedroom luxury homes two bathrooms (with bidets) and . . . and this, as far as Woolly was concerned, was the worst of it . . . double garages. Double bloody garages!

A double garage said this: it said you were expected to have two cars and maybe a third and fourth in the driveway for your teenage kids.

Woolly had tried to explain to his colleagues on the planning sub-committee that the only way to avoid Gridlock Somerset by the year 2020 was to start building homes with single garages or even no bloody garages at all.

And did they listen, his council colleagues?

They looked at him in his red and yellow bobcap and his pink jeans and then they looked at each other and they smiled in that *He's from Glastonbury* kind of way. Except for Griff Daniel (at the meeting in his capacity as developer), who'd looked at Woolly like he hoped he'd die of something painful in the not too distant future.

Afterwards Woolly had gone to a pub out past Wells for a bite of lunch with Fred Harris, the elderly Wedmore councillor, Fred trying to talk a bit of sense into him. Be pragmatic, Fred said. Your time will come.

Ho ho. His time wouldn't come until they had a New Age party with about a dozen like-minded members (if you could find twelve like-minded New Agers) and a sympathetic central government. Which was about as likely as a Mothership from Alpha Centauri coming down to a civic reception on Glastonbury Tor.

On the way back to the poor, beleaguered Isle of Avalon, he shoved Julian Cope's *Autogeddon* into the cassette deck. *You and me, Jules, you and me.* Ah, but nobody took Julian Cope seriously either, possibly on account of him being the only rock star left who dressed like Woolly.

He'd go and see Diane again. Shook him up, that did, bloody Archer Ffitch strolling in just as he was about to lay it on Diane about what the new road would do to the St Michael Line. Coincidence, or what?

'OK,' Karen said. 'No names and you didn't get this from me, all right?'

Juanita nodded. Her mouth felt very dry. She needed to hear this but didn't want to. She composed herself, crossing her hands lightly – with these hands you had to do everything lightly – in her lap in the vinyl bedside armchair.

Karen sat down on the bed. 'Geriatric ward, all right? I'm not saying where. This is what I've been told. That situation, I've been there, I know how easy it is to become impatient when you're on your own at night and half of them are incontinent. A saint would blow, some nights.'

'She isn't', Juanita said, 'a saint.'

'I was just saying that. I just need to know before I go any further that she's not any kind of friend of yours.'

'I mistrust her. I think she's a dangerous megalomaniac, a bad person to be around. OK?'

'All right.' Karen lowered her voice. 'Well, this goes back twenty-odd years. It's small things. Hard to prove. Publicly fitting catheters to old men who don't need them. Putting bedpans just out of reach of the disabled ones and then not cleaning them up and leaving the bedding unchanged for hours. Telling them stuff their relatives have said about them never coming home again and renting out their rooms – when they haven't said anything of the sort. Stealing their sweets, taking away pictures of their grandchildren in the night. Telling them that there's, like, no God. That this is where it ends. Except for those who are . . . condemned to walk the ward. As – you know – as spirits. Take it from me, geriatrics are like little kids. They'll believe what you tell them.'

'Jesus. Those are small things?'

'Came to a head when Dunn left a dead woman on the ward all night, unscreened.'

Karen slid a robe around Juanita's bare shoulders. The warmth helped.

'Go on,' Juanita said.

'She took the Anglepoise lamp from the nurses' table and placed it on the dead woman's bedside table. So that it was lighting up the corpse's face – not a peaceful face, you know? Lit up for them all to see, all these old people, all night.'

'How do you know this?'

'Because a doctor came in unexpectedly, and she was reported.'

'She was sacked after that?'

'And blacklisted. The doctor did a good job, got a few signed statements, although the girls were pretty intimidated. God, I only had to mention the name Ruth Dunn to Jane, who came to us from Oxford . . . Anyway, Sister Dunn never worked in another general hospital . . . as far as they *know*. The next they heard of her she was a matron at a public school.'

'Where?'

'Dunno. But some of these fancy schools, they like a sadist, don't they? Just stay well away from that woman, my advice. I better go, Juanita, I'll be getting hauled over the coals.'

'Hang on. Could I talk to this Jane? What about the doctor who reported . . .'

'I shouldn't have told you her name. Leave her alone, Juanita, Jane's jittery enough at the best of times.'

'What about the doctor?'

Karen rose to her feet, expressionless. 'They say the doctor's died. That's all I know. You take care, Juanita.'

Puttering into Magdalene Street in his old but catalytically converted Renault Six, Woolly spotted the coloured lights of the Christmas tree. He liked coloured lights and he liked Christmas trees.

He wondered what it would be like if you could only see the tree lights instead of headlights. If the only sounds you could hear were, like, carol-singing and stuff, not the rumble of this twenty-ton truck coming up behind carrying God-knows-what to God-knows-where. All freight this size should be made to go by rail, was Woolly's view.

Fred Harris, the Wedmore councillor, who was a bit green around the edges, bless him, had patted him on the back as they straggled off Daniel's site. 'Never mind, old son. World'll catch up with you one day, look.' Fred always said that to Woolly.

Be dead by then, Woolly thought, as he drove down to where all the streets converged on the tree. He wondered why his cassette player had suddenly cut out.

'Forget it, my advice.' Hughie Painter pulled Sam out of the doorway of the Crown Hotel and up into High Street towards the NatWest bank and The George and Pilgrims. 'Jeez, was this your brilliant idea to come here? Can't hear yourself flaming talk.'

The kazoo band was doing a syncopated 'O Little Town of Bethlehem', kids singing along, a bunch of young drunks dancing in the street.

'Look, come on.' Sam hadn't been expecting this, not from Mastersab. 'They haven't done that hunt for three years at least, not on Boxing Day. Too expensive, look, too many people to entertain, too many hunt-followers. But now Pennard's pushing the boat out again for some reason, and you're saying . . .'

'I'm saying leave it. We got more important stuff to worry about.'

'No chance, Hughie. I'm gonner ruin that bastard's Christmas.'

Hughie pulled him up hard against the ancient walls of The George and Pilgrims and bawled into his ear, 'And how did you find out about it, eh, Sammy? Not been widely advertised, am I right?'

'Yeh, I know what you're thinking. She let it slip out by accident, OK?'

'Haw! You been set up, boy,' Hughie roared. He was about ten years older than Sam, grey in his beard. But Sam wasn't about to be humiliated.

'Hughie, this is straight up.' Sam was shouting too, now, and the words were coming very fast. 'She don't even speak to the old man. It's a dysfunctional family. Leastways, Diane's not functioning in it. I figured, what if we were to make a bit of a recce, maybe. Then we could have a meeting, draw up a ground plan, get it dead right, fuck these bastards good.'

He spotted his old man swaggering down the street with old Quentin Cotton, both of them wearing big shit-eating grins and enamel lapel badges with that picture of the Tor and a white no-entry sign slashed across it.

Sam wanted to leap out at the bastards, start a nice public barney, but Hughie held him back. 'What's got into you, boy?'

'What's got into me? Shit . . .'

'Listen!' Hughie yelled. 'The big issue right now has got to be the new road, right? The big wildlife issue. It's not just trees and fields, it's badger sets, the lot. Wholesale devastation. Word is we'll have bulldozers in by the end of January.'

'So?'

'So, naturally, we got to have the manpower ready. Like, not on bail.'

'Well, sure, I appreciate that, but this is . . .'

'They could start anytime, Sammy. Could be starting now, for all I know. Some civil servant, never been west of Basingstoke, gives the word, out go two dozen big, nasty blokes with chain-saws. Private contractors, that's the way they work it now. Time's money. Evil buggers. Whole armies of security guards.'

'Yeah, well, Pennard's in full support of the road. Archer certainly is. We could, like, work the wider message in somehow while disrupting their hunt.'

Hughie Painter shook his head in disgust. 'This is not so much the hunt you wanner target, this is Pennard himself, right? What's this sudden thing you got about that bugger? Something to prove, maybe?'

'Bollocks.' Sam felt himself going red.

'So what's the angle here?' Hughie grinned. 'Afraid we'll all think you sold out, going into this magazine thing with Big Di?'

'Piss off!' Sam wanted to hit him, half aware of how ridiculous this was because big Hughie was a really gentle guy, nobody ever got into a row with Hughie. He walked away into a soup of swirling street noise: carol-singing, laughter, whoops and cheers. He saw traders in the doorways of their shops, some of which seemed to have reopened, lots of children of all ages.

There was a roaring in his ears. He looked up at the tree, saw coloured lights floating down like snowflakes. What?

*

'Bloody thing,' Woolly shouted. 'Sheesh, nothing works for two weeks together these days.'

And it was because he was fiddling with his stereo, worrying about the tape snapping and getting all chewed up in the mechanism that he didn't notice it until it was almost on him.

'Oh shit!'

Sweat seemed to spring out of the wheel. It was like he'd suddenly woken up, lights all around him, the big truck behind, people waiting to cross, and this bus . . . rumbling in a leisurely, rickety way down the wrong side of the road, the driver grinning, or maybe the bus itself was grinning, its radiator grille hanging open between the bleary headlights.

Woolly hit the brakes. Hammered his foot into the pedal, wrenching at the wheel, lurching inside his seatbelt and feeling the Renault spinning side-on into the middle of the road and the bloody big lorry behind.

Gasp of airbrakes, screech and a ground-wobbling rumble, like an entire block of flats collapsing.

Blur of lights, a coloured blizzard.

Woolly sat for a long, isolated moment, noticing how bone-chilling cold it was in his car and that his throat was ash-dry. Only vaguely aware of the screaming all around him, whoops of terror and pain that didn't stop, not even when he was struggling to open his door through the Christmas branches.

SEVEN

LADY LOONY, COUNCILLOR CRACKPOT

Diane stared up at the cross.

'Did you make it yourself?'

What a blindingly stupid question. It was an abandoned telegraph pole with a fence post crudely nailed across it.

'Come away now,' Don Moulder said. 'I don't hang around here after dark no more.'

He led her out of the bottom field, up towards the farmhouse. It was nearly dark. The cold bit through her sweater. The Tor looked remote.

'Dogs won't go down there, n'more,' Don said. 'Night or day. What d'you say to that, Miss Diane?'

Nothing. She said nothing.

'Maybe you don't believe me.' Don pushed into the farmhouse kitchen, kicked off his wellies. Wife's WI night, he'd told Diane in the Land-Rover. They could talk freely. 'Thought if anyone'd believe me, it'd be you.'

'Because of my reputation as a loony.' The kitchen was unmodernised, pale green cupboards with ventilation holes in the doors and a big, bright fire in the range. Don Moulder waved her to a chair, sat down opposite.

'Did I say that?'

'Nobody ever has to.'

'I'm a frightened man, Miss Diane. Two years ago, I d'come to Jesus for protection, all the weirdies round here, the evil, heathen things I seen when I looks across at . . . that thing, that hill.'

'Can you tell me about it now? Exactly what you saw?'

He wouldn't talk much about it when they were down in the bottom field. He was genuinely afraid. She was remembering the night of the fire, the way he'd kept talking about the *black buzz*.

'I thought it was a one-off thing,' he said now. 'Somethin' they'd kind of left behind 'em, like most of 'em leaves ole rubbish, this lot leaves . . . well, all the drugs they takes, maybe something in the air, I don't know, I don't, 'twas just a small hope. But I makes the cross, I prays to the Lord to bless the field and I tries not to think about it. But then the dogs . . . the dogs won't go in there, look, not even in broad daylight. The dogs slinks off. They can sense evil, dogs can. Then – where are we now? – not last night, the night before, I'm doin' the rounds, padlockin' the sheds, when it comes again.'

He leaned close to her across the scuffed, Formica-top table.

'Engine noise. Lord above, it went through me like a bandsaw. I could smell it. The fumes of evil. I could no more've gone down that field than dug my own grave. So you tell me, Miss Diane. What was they at? What was those scruffy devils at on my land that night?'

What on earth could she tell him? What did she even know?

''Cause what I do know is, what I reckernise now is I seen it before. I made careful note of every one o' them hippy heaps as they come through the gate that day. Know what I remember? The ole radiator grille hangin' off like a scab. Stuck in my mind, that did. Lazy devils couldn't even be minded to screw the bloody radiator on. I remember thinkin' that. Aye, it stuck in my mind. And that's what I seen. What they done, Miss Diane, what they done in that buzz to taint my land?'

'Oh gosh.' The fire was so warm, she was so tired, all her caution dropped away. 'They . . . nothing happened in it while it was here. Not while I was here, anyway. But later I think it was found . . . Oh, look, it was the one they found at Stoke St Michael. The one with the body in it.'

Don Moulder sat up, stiff. 'By golly, I d'remember readin' 'bout that. I never thought. By the . . . How'd he die?'

'I don't know.'

He stood up, began rapidly to pace the kitchen. 'Why's he come here? Why's he come back here?' He went to the window, snatched the curtains across. He looked terrified.

326

'I don't know,' Diane said.

'I don't want 'im. I can't live with this. I don't want no dead hippy and his black buzz. Could you live with that – knowing it's out there? Black evil? I'm afeared to set foot outside that door when it's dark, case I hears it again, *chunner, chunner, chunner*. How'm I gonner do my lambin' now?'

'These things . . . it won't harm you, Mr Moulder.' But terror was contagious; Diane bit her lip.

'Won't it? Won't it, Miss? That cross don't keep it off. What kind of evil defies the Christ?'

'I don't know, I don't *know*.'

The cold blue flashing lights. The hysteria of ambulances. The stolid red hulk of a fire engine. Steam rising.

Figures were in motion in the half-light, fluorescent paramedics with stretchers and oxygen equipment. And out of the murky stew of noise – moans and yells, a baby crying and the escalating whirring, whining, keening of a saw attacking metal – there was a woman wailing.

'*Const . . . ance . . . !*'

The name caught in Sam's head. He heard it again in the squealing of the saw reaching a frenzy and the rending of metal before two firemen backed into view with most of a lorry door held between them, trampling sawn-off Christmas tree branches into the tarmac.

'*Naaaaaaaaaaaaaw!!!*'

Echoing across the market-place like some old street-trader's cry, a woman's shredded shriek. Close to Sam, a man was being eased out of a metal cave like a snail from its shell, squirming into vicious life when his boots touched the ground.

'. . . was that little tosser!' Jabbing a finger. 'Slams on and just fucking . . .'

A pool of newly spilled oil shimmering like smoked glass with beacon blue light. A police boot slapping into the pool.

'Get back. Get back, please.' A stretcher shape coming through: red blankets, paramedics.

As the policeman pushed him back, Sam saw the lorry skewed across the road, the new Christmas tree snapped like a matchstick, the lorry's crushed-in cab garlanded with branches and little coloured lights, red and yellow and green and white.

The cab was crushed because behind the tree had been the great rigid finger of the market cross. They'd had to cut away the side of the cab to get the driver out, and he was snarling in self-defence, '. . . didn't have no choice, mate, that fucking lunatic . . .'

'Come on, now, back,' a policeman snapped. 'It's not a flaming funfair. Everybody back!' The first ambulance squealing away, revealing a small, muddied, maroon car in the centre of the road. A sticker on its rear side window.

RESIST ROAD RAPE.

The car was a Renault Six. Sam stared at it in horror and disbelief.

'Ask him. Ask that little bastard!' the lorry driver yelled.

And there was Woolly standing in the middle of the road, blood on his fingers, one sleeve torn away and bloody skin peeling from his wrist like curled shavings from planed wood, and he was weeping. 'Oh, Jesus.' His face ragged. 'It . . . shit. It's . . . I'm going outer my fucking head, man.'

'You hear that, officer?' Ronnie Wilton, the butcher, normally a jovial bugger amid the blood and offal, his face bulging and twisting now. 'He's admitted it. You take that down. I'll be a witness, look.'

Another one who hadn't voted for Woolly.

'Yes, thank you, sir, now if you'd just . . .' One of the policemen wore glasses, twin ice-blue beacons strobing in the lenses, concealing expressions, feelings. 'Mr Woolaston, you better go in the ambulance.'

'No, I'm not taking up ambulance space.'

Woolly's agonised face was frozen by a flashgun, some Press photographer dodging in front. And then there was an awful sound – all the worse because in other circumstances you might have thought it was a howl of glee – as a ball of crushed and bloodied metal was handed through the despoiled jungle of the great, festive tree.

'Oh, *Chrrrrrist*.' Woolly's hands covered his face.

Sam saw that the metal ball handed from fireman to fireman was the crushed remains of a baby's pushchair.

*

Iridescent. Mesmeric.

With rage, it looked like.

Bad move, he thought. Wrong night. He would have turned round and left quietly, but she'd seen him.

Powys had started having second thoughts about this as soon as he was inside the hospital. If she wouldn't have visitors except for Diane, wouldn't even talk to Dan Frayne on the phone . . .

'If you're another one come to talk me out of it, you can sod off now,' said Mrs Juanita Carey, acid in her voice.

Powys said nothing. Just gave her a smile.

The session with the Rt Rev. Liam Kelly had left him disturbed. And dismayed that anyone who thought Glastonbury Tor was 'just a hill' could get to be Bishop of Bath and Wells. Wonderful material, obviously, for a book. He'd be there at dawn on Thursday, no question. Fascinating stuff.

Fascinating for an author. Fascinating if you were outside looking in. If you didn't let your viewpoint become cluttered by something plump and vulnerable.

All the stuff Diane had told him, about Dion Fortune, Pixhill and the Dark Chalice was still washing restlessly around his head. He'd wound up in Bristol because, to get a handle on whatever was happening, or whatever Diane imagined was happening, he needed to talk to someone who wasn't Diane. Someone who knew the score but was temporarily apart from the game.

Also – face it – he was very curious to meet Juanita Carey and, after what had happened to her van, there was a fairly good chance Diane would not be here tonight.

'You a friend of hers?' the nurse in the burns unit had asked him. Not waiting for an answer. 'Do you think it might be possible to talk a bit of sense into her?'

Oh.

Mrs Carey glared at him. She was fully dressed, which was a slight surprise. Long skirt full of exotic colours. Low-cut, sunny lemon top. Bright orange moccasins. Copious, dark hair down below her shoulders. Skin aglow.

Iridescent.

The bed between them, her eyes like distant warning lanterns.

He became aware of the way her arms were hanging unnaturally away from her like the arms of a dress shop mannequin plugged in at the shoulders the wrong way round. The hands frozen like a mannequin's but not with that fashioned abandon; they were both curled arthritically and as colourful in their way as the skirt.

'Um, Joe Powys,' he said. 'Dan Frayne sent me.'

The awful energy something like this generated. The town would be alive with it all night.

The sick mythology was already taking shape. Sam had heard one teenage girl telling another that the baby had been taken away in two shoeboxes.

'I can't believe it,' Hughie Painter said. Not the most original remark tonight. 'It's just . . . Could've been one of mine, you know?'

Not very original either. Sam watched two coppers taking measurements and photos. The container lorry – car parts for Swindon – had been pulled out of the market cross monument, council blokes checking out the stonework in case it was in danger of collapse.

'Think he'll be charged?'

'Woolly? I dunno.' Hughie was still looking quite white. 'Can you be done for slamming on your brakes without warning? Maybe.'

'If half these people had their way, the poor little bugger'd be hanged.'

'He didn't help himself,' Hughie said severely. 'You heard what he said when he got out of his car.'

'I didn't hear it. I was told. Every bugger's probably been told by now. So with Woolly's past, everybody naturally assumes he was doped up to the eyeballs. This'll finish him, Hughie. Who's gonner vote for him now?'

'Good news for your old man.'

'Yeah. Good news for Glastonbury First all round, once the weeping's over.'

'Aye. Well.' Hughie sniffed. 'I'm off home now, Sammy. Going to count my kids.'

Sam nodded and walked into the road, single-lane traffic going through sluggishly now. Counting his kids. A lot of mums and dads would be doing that tonight. Even Alternative mums and dads with a shelf full of meditation tapes and a cannabis plant in the greenhouse. Why did he think that even Hughie Painter, father of three, might well think twice about voting for Woolly again?

The fucking irony of it, though. The great anti-traffic evangelist. Slamming on in the middle of the rush hour for a bus that nobody else managed to see. Just swerving out into the centre of the road. The driver of the lorry behind him pulling the other way to avoid smashing into the back of Woolly, and the lorry going out of control and crunching through the Christmas tree, the people and the pram, smack into the side of the market cross.

Neither of them could've been going very fast. Not in the town centre, in the rush hour. But they didn't have to be.

Const . . . ance . . .

Ah, Jesus, was he going to hear that every time he walked past here, like the shriek was imprinted on the fabric of the street?

Constance Morgan. Four months old. Hardly aware she had a life before it was gone. Her mother, now in danger of losing a leg, was Kirsty Morgan.

Née Cotton.

Daughter of Quentin Cotton.

So the chairman of Glastonbury First loses his grandchild, gets his only daughter crippled in an accident caused by . . .

'I can't believe this,' Sam hissed.

''Scuse me, squire, would you mind?'

A bloke wanted to set up a black tripod. Sam moved back, thinking it was a police photographer, until the bloke slid a big video camera into the top of the tripod and a white light came on, revealing a woman in a sheepskin coat, very short blonde hair. Tammy White from BBC Bristol with a big boom microphone in a furry cover.

'What about we do it here, Rob?' Tammy White said. 'Can you get the lorry in?'

'Yeah, if the two of you come out a bit. That's fine. That'll do.'

Sam stepped into the doorway of the Crown Hotel as the camera light shone bright as day on the face of Archer Ffitch.

'Sorry to put you on the spot like this,' Tammy White said in a low, non-interviewing voice. 'They'll only use about half a minute, but I need to cover myself. Is that all right?'

'Anything you require, Tammy,' Archer said smoothly. 'It's a pretty difficult situation for me, but you've got your job to do.'

'I'm recording,' the cameraman said. 'In your own time, Tammy.'

Tammy White straightened up, held the microphone between her and Archer, just above waist level.

'Mr Ffitch, this is obviously a terrible thing to happen, particularly in the week before Christmas. What are your feelings?'

Archer said, 'It is *the* most appalling tragedy. People ... *children* ... gathering for this joyful occasion – the lighting of the Christmas tree ... My heart goes out to the family.'

'And you saw what happened?'

'I was returning from the station when we were held up. It had happened only minutes before and there was tremendous chaos. The driver was trapped in his cab, the poor mother was semi-conscious, and I don't think anyone realised at that stage that there was a pram underneath.'

Archer's voice faltered. Sam saw his jaw quiver. Sam's fists clenched.

Tammy White said, 'Now, you're one of the supporters of the plan for a Central Somerset relief road which many people are objecting to ...'

'Tammy,' Archer held up a restraining hand. 'This is not the time to make political capital. I realise that many *local* people will be saying that, if such a road existed, commercial traffic of this size would not be passing through Glastonbury. Personally, I would rather not comment at this stage especially as the leader of the campaign against this road is tonight being questioned by police in connection with the incident.'

'This is the second death in just over a month connected with traffic congestion in the town. The other involved a fire, which emergency services couldn't reach because of New Age travellers' vehicles on the approach road to Glastonbury Tor. You've initiated a campaign to limit access to the Tor. Do you think that's a related issue?'

Tammy made a face at the clumsiness of her question, but Archer was straight in there.

'I think what both these tragedies are telling us is that this is a town which has been getting seriously out of control. I think we have to calm down, consider whether we believe Glastonbury has been going in the right direction and then take steps to ensure the town is run for – and *by* – normal, decent, law-abiding people.'

Meaning, Avalon out, Woolaston out. Sam felt like rushing out there, making a scene, giving them some real footage for their programme.

'Thank you.' Tammy nodded to the cameraman to wind up.

'Got all you wanted?' Archer asked obligingly as the camera light went out.

'Fine. Unless you've got any views about the Bishop's meet-the-pagans mission on Thursday.'

'Silly man,' Archer said. 'Off the record, of course.'

'Also off the record,' murmured Tammy, 'the word is that not every member of your family is backing your Tor scheme.'

Archer smiled. 'Diane.'

'Just talk. As yet.'

'Look, strictly off the record,' Archer said awkwardly, 'we've all been terribly worried about Diane, who's in a . . . particularly delicate state . . . you remember she was at that awful fire? Plus, she's been working non-stop on this, ah, hippy magazine thing from early in the morning until late at night.'

'Must be a problem for you,' Tammy said ambiguously.

'Oh lord, yes.' Archer's expression was no longer visible. 'She's given us a few headaches in her time, you must have heard about all that, Tammy.'

'Well, you know . . .'

'God knows, we help her all we can. Try to help her. Ha ha.'

Sam was so blind furious he could have smashed his fist into the wall. The two-faced git. So smooth, so deft. Tossing his sister to the pack like a fox cub.

Mad, restless energy was pumping through Sam's body. No way he could go home, sit there with a can of lager and a sandwich and wait for the slimy turd to come up on the box. No way he could go to any pub in this town tonight and listen to the gloating gossip about how Councillor Crackpot had helped kill an innocent little baby.

Archer and Tammy and the cameraman were moving away. 'Really, very good of you to talk to us at a time like this, Mr Ffitch.'

'Archer, please. Probably be seeing a good deal more of each other in the months to come. Do you and your colleague have time for a drink?'

Sam watched them walk away from the mess of Magdalene Street. Wanted to scream at Archer's broad, dark back, like a hooligan.

No good.

He decided to go alone to Bowermead Hall, climb a few fences, jump a few streams, figure out how to sabotage the forthcoming Pennard Hunt.

EIGHT

SCORCHED EARTH

The case was very light, as though it contained nothing but discarded bandages and stale hospital air. Joe Powys carried it out to the car.

Outside, she seemed to wilt. Her blue three-quarter-length, belted coat looked too big for her; her gloves too small. She shouldn't be wearing gloves at all, according to the young doctor called George, who'd said to Powys, 'I hope you know what you're taking on, mate.'

Because she couldn't use either of her hands, Powys had signed her out. The little nurse called Karen had said, stone-faced, 'I hope you're proud of yourself,' and George, who had a half-grown beard, said, 'This is very silly, Mrs Carey.' Trying to sound grown-up. 'You're going to have a lot of pain, you know.'

Juanita had looked raw and frayed. 'For reasons I can't discuss, I'd be in a lot more mental anguish if I didn't get out. Can you get my case, Karen? Do I have a coat?'

'Juanita, does this have something to do with that woman? Sister Dunn?'

'Look, Karen, please, just leave it, all right? Think of the extra bed. Sorry. I really am grateful for everything you've done.'

No longer iridescent, Juanita Carey stood shivering in the hospital car park, looking at the filthy, dented white Mini. And at the black and white dog with enormous ears and only three legs.

'Um . . . Arnold,' Powys said.

Juanita instinctively put out a gloved hand to the dog, and then drew back.

'It's OK,' Powys said. 'He likes all women.' Before he realised that she was afraid of patting the dog because of her hands. That she was afraid to touch anything.

'Stupid,' she said. 'I had the physiotherapy, but told the shrink

335

to sod off. You've got to deal with things yourself, haven't you? Is there somewhere I can get some cigarettes?'

'We'll find somewhere.' He held open the passenger door for her, watched her get in without using her hands, holding them in front of her as if the gloves were borrowed and mustn't get dirty. She fell back into the little bucket seat, closed her eyes and breathed in.

They stopped at a newsagent's and he bought her forty Silk Cut. Unwrapped a packet, lit one for her.

'Sorry. This is pathetic. But I just feel so . . . frail. They tell you you're going to, but you don't really expect it. You're so looking forward to your first breath of real air. And real smoke.'

Waiting to get into the traffic, he was aware of her taking the cigarette from her lips, trapping it not very effectively between the very tips of her fingers. The next time he glanced at her she was shuddering, breathing very fast.

'Can we stop? I'm sorry.'

He pulled into the side of the road to a chorus of hooting, revved-up road rage from behind.

'Sorry.' She let him take the cigarette. 'Thanks. I nearly dropped it. This is ridiculous, I just . . . It's on fire, you know? It never occurred to me before that they were on fire. Christ.' She exhaled. 'I always thought if it ever came to this I'd get myself quietly put down.'

Powys said, 'Dan Frayne's been worried about you.'

'Good old Danny.' She leaned her head back over the seat, stared at the tear in the roof-fabric. 'Your publisher now?'

'Possibly.'

'You are the only one, aren't you? I mean he hasn't persuaded a whole bunch of esoteric authors to come to the aid of the disabled bookseller? I'm not going to find John Michell redecorating the flat, Colin Wilson hoovering the sitting room.'

Juanita sat up, laughed and coughed. 'God, what am I going to do if half of me's screaming for a cigarette and the other half's terrified to hold one? Don't forget to note this. For your report.'

'I'm doing a report?'

'For Danny. He's sent you to find out how crazy I've become, right? Why I tried to burn myself to death.'

'Well, no,' Powys said. 'The official brief is to find out how crazy Glastonbury's become.'

'Glastonbury's always been crazy. He knows that.'

He told her about the book Frayne wanted them to co-write. She spent some time examining her gloves.

'Forget it.' She didn't look up. 'He's just being kind. You don't need me. Were I to write about Glastonbury, the way I'm feeling now, it'd read like either *Paradise Lost* or Dante's *Inferno*. He doesn't want that. He sent you because he's feeling a bit of residual guilt from a long time ago, but he's afraid to come himself.'

'He's afraid to see you again. He thinks it might destroy his marriage.'

'Mr Smooth-mouth. If he saw me now, he'd be booking the hotel for his golden wedding.'

'I don't think so. Um . . . I've read your letters. Everything you ever wrote to Dan Frayne since about 1977.'

After a considered silence, she said, 'I may kill him for this.'

She held up a gloved hand. 'I'm not supposed to wear these. They're quite painful. 'I'm supposed to let the air get at my hands. How squeamish are you?'

'My dog has three legs,' Powys said.

Diane collapsed against the Abbey gates. Closed. As if God had shut His eyes.

She looked up at the charcoal sky through her tears.

How could you? Doesn't this town matter to you any more?

Across the street, men with chainsaws were cutting the remains of the Christmas tree into slices.

Don Moulder had driven her back into town until they came up against a traffic tailback and diversion signs. Diane had got out in the Safeway car park where Don could turn round. He'd been silent most of the way, then, as she was getting out, he'd said, 'Field I got next to the road, I agreed to let 'em have it for car parking. When the bishop comes to the Tor on Thursday. I been thinkin', maybe if I was to ask him – the bishop – to bless the bottom field. Sure to count for something, a bishop.'

Diane had nodded dubiously. 'Anything's worth a try.'

Minutes later, she was learning about the terrible accident from Matthew Banks, the tall, willowy herbalist, loading apples and grapes and Linda McCartney TV dinners into his 2CV.

'This is awful, Matthew. Why did he stop like that? Cat run across the road or something?'

'Oh, something bigger than that,' Matthew had said. 'So big that nobody else saw it.'

Diane turned her back on the Abbey, edged around the POLICE/ACCIDENT signs and the taped-off area and walked down Benedict Street, where Woolly had his shop.

She had to tell him. Not that it would help him much, credibility wise. The good news: somebody else believes you saw a black bus that wasn't there.

The bad news: it's Lady Loony.

You could see the big house now, the lights just coming on, winking through the stripped-off trees. Only, it wasn't a friendly wink; the lights were a baleful white. In Sam Daniel's view, Bowermead Hall made Dartmoor Prison look like the House at Pooh Corner.

The moon had risen over the woods, making it easier to see the footpath even when it got tangled. So far he was legal, not even trespassing, although you wouldn't know that from the signs.

New signs. Aggressive signs with red lettering.

PRIVATE LAND. KEEP OUT. SECURITY PATROLS. ALL TRESPASSERS WILL BE PROSECUTED.

Sam knew all these public paths. Two or three years ago, he and Hughie had joined a protest with the Ramblers' Association when Gerry Rankin had fenced off a right-of-way with barbed wire. They'd taken wire-cutters to the fence, and Rankin couldn't say anything apart from, *I'll remember your faces*. Which was when Hughie grew his beard.

There was plenty of new barbed wire now, dense and high. But there were ways. Rankin had to get in and out. Stay clear of the hall was the answer, go for Rankin's farmhouse, which was about five, six hundred yards from the Hall, tucked into the bottom of a wooded hill. The vineyards were the other side of it, facing the town and Glastonbury Tor. Between the farmhouse and the entrance to the vineyards Sam saw what looked like new hunt kennels: two long, low sheds in a cobbled yard.

He thought about the possibilities. Maybe he could pull a stroke the night before, like letting the hounds into the vineyards.

Or, presuming the meet was at the Old Bull like it used to be, with stirrup cups and all this shit . . . well, that was over three miles away, so they'd be using transport – horse transporters, dog wagons. Maybe he could find out tonight where they'd got the trucks. Then come up here very early Boxing Day morning and slash all the tyres.

Wilful damage, Sammy? Hughie's voice in his head. *They'll throw the book at you this time, son. You're known. You've been warned. Conditional discharge . . . conditional, yeh? Also, you just don't do this kind of stuff when you're angry. That's how you get nicked.*

'Oh. I see. You do it when you're feeling rather tolerant about bloodsports. My mistake.'

Sam stopped halfway over a rotting wooden stile. Bloody well talking to himself now. *You really are in a bad way now, Sammy. You know what this is? It's what love does to you.*

'Piss off. Don't be soft.'

A dog barked in the kennels, and then another.

Damn. Once they started, it would go on and on. That was why it was normally best to do a recce in the daytime. Come the innocent rambler bit if anyone saw you.

Except when they know your face . . .

Sam detoured off the path and into the woods behind the new kennels. He was on higher ground now and suddenly he could see the Tor, like an upturned paraffin funnel prodding the white moon.

The Tor would do that, suddenly come into view from nowhere. If poor bloody Woolly was here now, he'd be climbing to the top of the next hill to see if he could see the tower of Stoke St Michael church, which was the next point on his beloved St Michael Line.

Poor little sod. He'd probably be hounded out of town, out of Somerset in fact. And then the old man would swagger back with a bloody huge majority thanks to Glastonbury First, which stood for Traditional Standards and road safety and getting rid of nutters.

Sam kicked at a branch, which turned out to be dead and rotten. It shattered into a shower of sodden splinters and one lump flew into his face. *Bastards!*

Everything collapsing. Everything diseased. How could any silly bugger believe there was a God up there?

The full implications were only now becoming sickeningly clear. The way the scum was rising back to the top: the return of Councillor Griff, man of the people, and Archer Ffitch smarming his way into Parliament – the cool, blatant way Ffitch had planted the idea with the TV people that his little sister was a hopeless fruitcake and you mustn't hold her against him.

Sam peered down the slope towards the bulk of a barn. You'd get a couple of horse boxes in there, no problem. If he got here before daybreak, came round under cover of this wood, he could do all the tyres before breakfast. No way they'd get them all replaced in time. Not on Boxing Day. Hunt off. Piece of cake. Merry Christmas, Mr Fox.

So, need to check for padlocks on the doors. Might need some cutters.

Sammy, Going Equipped for Burglary is the charge, coppers find you with bolt cutters. You'll go down for three months and when you come out nobody respectable's going to give you any more work.

'Get off my back, Hughie!'

Sam was about to slide down the bank towards the big barn when he smelled something.

Smoke. Burning.

Well, he wasn't daft. If Pennard was hosting a top-people's barbecue over the next rise, he wanted to know about it.

He scrambled back up the slope, holding on to bushes, torch in his pocket. Slowing up the nearer he got to the top, trying not to breathe too loudly.

The hill was longer than it looked. Must have been two, three hundred yards. Scrambling to the top, he nearly toppled into empty air.

He dropped flat, didn't move, kept very quiet for two minutes, the acrid smell everywhere now. Peered over the unexpectedly abrupt edge – almost like a big slice had been taken out of the hill.

It had. That was precisely what had happened. You could make it out now: a big, wide trench. JCB job.

What we got here then, Sammy?

No sign of flames. No sounds, not even an owl. He was well out of sight of Bowermead Hall and, presumably, Rankin's farm. He pulled a torch from his jacket pocket, a Maglite, big beam. Snapped it on, stared in disbelief.

Shit on toast!

At first, Sam didn't understand. Used to be all woodland here. Lovely woods. Used to sneak in here as kids. It was legendary for conkers. Giant horse-chestnut trees. Also beech and sycamore and huge, thick oaks.

Now, for as far as the torch beam would stretch, it was a sea of stumps. And fallen tree trunks whose branches and winter foliage had been cut off, piled together and burned.

Burned. It was horrible. A massacre. When he switched off the torch he could detect glimmerings of red, the damped-down smouldering of bonfires.

I don't get it. I don't get it, Hughie.

Come on, Sammy, where's your brain gone? It's the road! The sensitive Glastonbury stretch of the Bath–Taunton fucking Relief Road! It's happening now. Here. In secret.

Sam felt like one of those poor bloody trees, all the sap in him drying up, everything crashing to earth around him. This was some of the finest broadleaf woodland in Somerset. A wildlife paradise, with badger sets and all kinds of birds and wild orchids.

Scorched earth, now. He scrambled down, stood in the deep, wide trench, flashed his torch from one side to the other. It was massive, surely twice as wide as a dual carriageway. But then, they had to allow for the banks, the verges and the hard shoulder.

It made some sense when you thought about it. If Pennard had sold a chunk of his precious land for the road, what he didn't want was a few hundred eco-guerrillas camping out on the site and living in the trees to prevent them being axed. This was a pre-emptive strike.

He shone his torch ahead of him. The beam faded out before the road did. When he looked up, he could see the Tor again, looking shadowy and majestic . . . and dead straight ahead.

The full horror of the plan, the awesome scale of it made him go cold. He'd never liked the idea, but he'd figured he could live with it. Not quite the stab to the heart it was to Woolly and those guys.

But suddenly he wanted to cry aloud. This was England. Ancient England. He could hear the traffic already, he could smell exhaust and diesel fumes. See the articulated lorries and holiday coaches and the flash gits in their Porsches, all the men like Archer Ffitch, all the women like Charlotte.

The hounds began to howl in their kennels. Heard him, maybe. So what? He was going to let this out, what they'd done – illegally, no doubt – and it would damage Pennard and Archer a whole lot more than just sabbing their hunt.

The howling went on. It dawned on Sam that this was no ordinary howling. He began to feel uncomfortable. Exposed. He moved away along the trench, walking quickly along the ruts, dodging the remains of bonfires, the hounds going at it all the time like the Wild Hunt of bloody Gwyn ap Nudd. It was creepy, like moving through an open wound, like he was stumbling into a bleak and ravaged future. Up on the banks, exposed, bare saplings were writhing and rattling.

Unexpectedly, he saw Glastonbury Tor again. It was a shock; it was so close, and sheer like a castle, the road aimed straight at it. It couldn't be, of course, because the published plan showed the route giving the Tor quite a wide berth; it just looked like it the way this section was aligned, like it would cut directly through the middle of the hill, under the tower.

The howling stopped. There was a great stillness. An icy stillness. Sam had that feeling of being watched. Of someone rearing up behind him.

He spun round irritably, and all the breath went out of him.

There was a man standing, staring silently up at Glastonbury Tor. An elderly, straight-backed man in an overcoat. He held a pipe in his mouth. Sam smelled the tobacco, just briefly. The old man's face was pale and hazy and fibrous, like soiled cotton-wool; there was a ridged scar under one eye.

Least it wasn't Pennard. Sam tried to laugh with relief, tried to speak to the old guy, but he couldn't find the breath.

The man turned very slowly to face him. Sam saw that he wore very long, dark trousers. So long that they covered up the shoes. In fact he couldn't see where the trousers ended.

This was because the old man was hovering about six inches above the rutted track. His rigid arm was pointing at the Tor. His jaw fell open, revealing no teeth, only a black void, and his eyes were like white gas.

The old man's scream was silent.

Unlike Sam's.

NINE

MEANINGLESS KIND OF
VIOLENCE

It must have been halfway down Benedict Street, where Woolly lived and worked, that Diane got a bad feeling. It said, *Go back*.

She stopped and frowned. She seemed to spend most of her life responding to feelings, waiting for signals and beacons on the horizon. Never seemed to think for herself. Never seemed to reason.

So she walked on. This had, after all, been one of her favourite places in all the world. Ever such a little shop, in a tiny square, at the end of a short alley off Benedict Street, and all it said over the door was: WOOLLY'S.

As a child of about eleven or twelve, she used to persuade Rankin to bring her into town to visit a friend. He didn't, of course, know who the friend was.

She'd spend hours watching Woolly in his workshop in the back. He was with a lady called Maria then. The business hadn't been going long, and they were mostly working on specialist jobs, recreating medieval string instruments for folk groups. Woolly was a fan of people like The Incredible String Band and Amazing Blondel who Diane was a bit too young to remember, but on their record sleeves they wore colourful, medieval patchwork clothes and Woolly said they came from a gentler time and she believed that. It always sounded like a different dimension. Like Middle Earth, everybody wearing floppy clothes and laughing a lot, light as butterflies.

Diane paused, sure she'd heard a footfall behind her. But there was nobody. It was unusually quiet, as though the tragedy had made people want to lock their front doors and cling to their families.

It must be wonderful to have a family you wanted to cling to.

She stopped.

A shadow had flitted around a corner about a hundred yards away and vanished into the alley leading to Woolly's square. And another one, another shadow. She saw them through a vague mist. So much mist on the street these nights.

Diane slipped into the doorway of a dry cleaner's about seventy yards away from Woolly's alley. Just as there came one of those sounds that instinctively made you cringe: the shattering of glass.

And then,

'Woolaston!' Echoing from the square. 'We've come for you, Woolaston! Get yourself out here, you murdering little fucker!'

A rolling, local accent. Young. Diane dragged in a long, trembling breath, held herself close to the shop door.

More breaking glass, but a blunter sound this time. She pictured a boot hacking out the shards left at the edges of the window.

Woolly's shop had just the one window, about the size of a living-room window in a small terraced house. It screened a little museum display of reproduction antique instruments, usually a narrow, eighteenth-century Spanish guitar and a tiny mandolin with lots of mother-of-pearl. And, unless he'd sold it at last, one of Woolly's own inventions with a long neck and a terracotta sound box the size of a football.

There was cackling male laughter, then a different voice, mock-official.

'Councillor Woolaston?'

Silence. Oh gosh, don't let him be in. But where would he be? Where could he go tonight and not have to endure the stares and the righteous abuse?

'Councillor Woolaston, sir!' Louder, rougher. A roar. 'You better get into your best suit and your dinky little bobcap. You just been invited to a special meeting of the beating-the-shit-out-of-mangy-little-hippies sub-committee.'

'And are you?' Juanita said.

'I doubt it. I doubt he was capable by then.'

The self-service restaurant had a Christmas tree and all the counter staff wore little Santa hats. It was quite crowded and

Juanita was feeling jittery, holding her hands in front of her like pieces of cracked porcelain.

She sat down at a window table, as far away from other people as possible. She needed to find out very quickly whether JM Powys was someone she could trust.

'So, if you aren't his son . . .?'

'Then it's probably in some way down to me. Some aspect of me comes down in the night, rearranges the shelves, untidies the room. Something in me that hates being a has-been recluse and would like to be a great and famous writer like his namesake. Something that wrecks the little refuge to force me to get my act together.'

'And dispatches you to Glastonbury?'

'That was Dan Frayne. And coincidence.'

'That's not very convincing, Mr Powys. I'm slightly horrified to hear myself say it, but this is one of those cases where the paranormal explanation seems the more logical.'

She watched him unwrap a straw and put it into her coffee.

'That's the slippery slope, Mrs Carey. Some things we are not meant to make sense of.'

'That's the coward's philosophy,' Juanita said. 'OK, it's been my philosophy too. Otherwise, Glastonbury buggers you up. Pixhill's parting message; ignore it at your peril. Glastonbury Buggers You Up.'

'And how did it bugger him up?' Powys asked. 'In the end.'

'He went out one cold morning in November and had a fatal coronary halfway up the Tor. They brought him back and laid him out on the dining table at Meadwell. Where he lay for three days, guarded by little Verity, his housekeeper. That, er . . . that room, according to legend, was where the last abbot of Glastonbury had his final meal. Before they strung him up. On the Tor. On November 15. Which was, of course . . .'

'The date Pixhill died?'

'Another coincidence for you.' Feeling slightly foolish, Juanita sipped her coffee through the straw, the first time she'd done this in public.

'Mrs Carey,' Powys said. 'I – I'm not sure how to put this – I seem to have walked into a . . . a situation.'

'Oh yes.'

'Diane says it's meant.'

'Diane thinks everything is meant,' Juanita said. 'Let me guess – you're John Cowper Powys, she's Dion Fortune and you've both been brought to Glastonbury to help deal with something of apocalyptic magnitude.'

Powys stirred his tea. 'So you think she's . . .?'

'Off her trolley?'

Juanita thought for a while, watching the young waiters looking overworked, underpaid and sullen in their Santa hats.

'No,' she said at last. 'There've been times when I've thought she was . . . shall we say psychologically stretched. A victim of her upbringing. Living a fantasy life of her own creation because real life at Cold Comfort Hall was so bloody dire and restrictive. I feel a bit ashamed of thinking that now.'

'Now?'

'Since the fire. Being in hospital you have a lot of time to think. That's not always good. I don't know. Maybe I'm just as screwed up as she is.'

'What do I do about these?' Powys pulled over a plate with two chocolate muffins on it.

'Embarrassing,' Juanita said. 'Can't pick it up, Powys. In hospital they fed me like an animal in the zoo. Little Karen was probably right, I could be in deep trouble out here.'

'How about this?' Powys presented a muffin in a napkin. 'I'll hold it while you take a bite. Or I could take a bite out of the other side at the same time and then everyone will think we're soppy lovers and they'll be embarrassed.'

Juanita smiled.

They'd smashed the window with a brick and pulled out about five instruments. The eighteenth-century-style guitar was clamped to the stomach of a stocky, wide-shouldered man who was standing in the middle of the street trying to prise heavy metal chords out of it.

Another, much younger person was banging on a shamanic drum with half a brick and bawling up at the window over the shop, 'Come on out, Woolly. Join the band. You little piece of dogshit.'

Diane had recognised him at once. It was Wayne Rankin. Eighteen years old, the farm manager's son who had kicked Headlice in the face while he lay on the ground.

She had crept to the corner of the cobbled alley. Could see them clearly under a tin-shaded exterior bulb. She might be called on to identify them if they got away before the police came.

If Woolly was inside he would surely have telephoned for help by now. If he wasn't, it was up to her; all the other premises in the little square were lock-up shops and there were no lights in the apartments or storerooms. No one had come out; either they hadn't heard the breaking glass and the shouting or they didn't want to get involved.

If there'd still been a policeman back in the town centre, she would have run to him. As it was, she would have to knock on someone's door.

The half-brick finally ruptured the parchment of the deep-bodied shamanic drum. Wayne Rankin let it fall, drew back his foot and sent the drum rolling down the cobbles like an empty barrel.

'Come on, Woolly!' the heavy man bellowed. 'We wants a private consultation with our councillor, look.' He gave up trying to find power chords on the little guitar, swung the instrument round by the neck and shattered it against the wall.

Diane cringed.

'That's what we're gonner do to you, Woolaston,' Wayne Rankin sang. 'You gonner come out, baby-killer?'

'We know you're in there.' The big man had put on an American cop voice. He pulled a beer can from his pocket and ripped at the ring-pull.

'Woolaston!' Wayne screeched. 'You don't come out, you piece of hippy shit, we're gonner have your door in.' He began to jump up and down on the soundbox of the little guitar.

It was too much. Diane's eyes flooded. They were making as much noise as they could, and where was everybody?

She couldn't stand it, turned away and walked blindly back up Benedict Street, determined to beat furiously on the first door with a light behind it.

It was no use pretending everything would return to shambolic normality because it wouldn't, Colonel Pixhill had been absolutely right, there was a growing darkness and an evil in this town which fed on division and extremism and prejudice. The road scheme, the Glastonbury First movement, issues which polarised people and led to tragedy and accusations and a really despicable, meaningless kind of violence, and . . .

And like a vision of the Grail, it came to Diane then what she must do. Here in Benedict Street, named after the little church, which may or may not be the resting place of the bones of St Benignus the hermit, she saw her direction.

She had to write about it. Like Pixhill had, but in a far more immediate way. She had to find the courage to throw journalistic balance to the winds and document it all and name names. Tell everyone about Headlice and Rankin's involvement, about the Glastonbury First movement and how it existed to split the town in two.

The Avalonian. They would bring out the first edition for Christmas. Late on Christmas Eve when there'd be no other papers until after the holiday.

Even if everyone rejected it and scorned it as Lady Loony's ravings. Even if Sam refused to get it printed because it wasn't up to his professional standards. Even if Juanita was frightfully angry and never spoke to her again because she'd gone down the same sad, dead-end road as Colonel Pixhill.

She had no choice.

Diane felt, for a moment, quite awesomely calm.

And then, in the shadows between streetlamps, she walked into a pair of open arms. 'Hey, now.' The long arms closed lovingly around her.

She thought, *Sam?*

She smelled beer. The arms manoeuvred her under a streetlamp.

'Who we got here then?'

The light splattered like egg yolk on a great shambling grin built around the kind of large, yellow teeth which, according to Sam, looked appealing on donkeys but rather less so on Darryl Davey.

Sam had had a lot to say, over the weeks, about Darryl: thick as shit but king of the third form on account of being overdeveloped for his age, like a shark in a goldfish tank.

'Lovely Lady Loony,' Darryl Davey said, holding her tightly to his body.

'Please excuse me.'

'I don't think so.'

She felt his hands through her sweater, clasped between her shoulder-blades.

'You're quite a handful, you are, my lover,' Darryl Davey said.

He began to move jerkily down the street, pushing her before him, his wiry red hair springing as he pressed himself against her.

'Stop it. How dare you?' He'd bulldozed her back to Woolly's alley.

'I do what I like, Lady Loony. Go on, struggle. Push them big titties out.'

'*Get off me! You disgusting . . .*'

'All right.' Darryl's hands parted and he stepped back. 'No problem.'

'Thank you.' Relief streamed through her.

Darryl grinned.

As arms in a thick check workshirt came around her from behind. Diane shrieked.

Darryl bellowed with laughter. Diane struggled and tried to turn her head to see the face, although she knew it must be the wide-shouldered man who'd smashed Woolly's guitar.

On the edge of her vision she saw Wayne Rankin slip back into the alley. He wouldn't want her to see him. She couldn't see the face of the man holding her; whenever she tried to twist away from him, he danced her around from behind. He was quite a bit shorter than Darryl. He pulled her to him and she felt something hard press into the base of her spine.

Darryl said conversationally, 'They d'say Sammy Daniel's been shaggin' you.'

'Leave me alone!'

'Ah, you can do better than him, my lover.'

Diane kicked back hard with her trainer. There was a grunt. 'Fuckin' fat slag.' A hand plunged into her coat and squeezed her left breast hard. She screamed out.

'Woolly! Call the p—'

Then she was choking on a mouthful of thick, leathery fingers and was hauled into the alley, the heels of her trainers bouncing on the cobbles.

In the little square, the tin-hatted bulb hung like a shower-spray over the smashed window and the broken string-instruments.

She was absolutely terrified now. It was already a sexual assault, and they knew she'd be able to identify them. This was more than drunken bravado, it was madness. *Division, extremism, prejudice . . . violence.*

'Take your dirty, common fingers out of her mouth, Leonard,' Darryl said. 'She's a lady. Deserves better than that.'

She was lowered to the cobbles, her head against the remains of the window.

'And she's gonner get better.' Darryl giggled. Fragments of broken glass fell into Diane's hair. 'And bigger.'

And then, fiddling with the zip of his jeans, Darryl Davey burned their boats.

'What you doin' hidin' in there, Wayne? She can't have you flogged now, boy.'

To her horror, Wayne Rankin emerged from Woolly's doorway and went to stand by Darryl so that she could clearly see his face. He stood like a man in an identification parade, expressionless, a wiry youth with close-cut hair like his father's.

Then the heavy man, Leonard, joined them, all three of them blocking the alley.

Wayne smiled slyly, 'All right there, Miss Diane?'

Lanky, shambling Darryl Davey started running his zip noisily up and down.

'If . . . if you go away now,' Diane said, her voice high and breathless, the taste of Leonard's fingers in her mouth, 'I won't say anything about this.'

There was dead silence. The three men looked at each other and then back at Diane.

'Ho fucking ho,' Darryl Davey said.

TEN

BLACK AS SIN

'Go on then!' Mrs Moulder yelled, back from the WI. 'Don't bugger about. Been a sight too many fires hereabouts.'

'You can't be sure,' Don protested feebly. 'Coulder been a glow from a torch, headlamps.'

'Well, seeing where it come from, that's not much better. You should never've let them hippies down there, I told you at the time.'

Halfway through the door, Don turned back. 'Let's call the police, then.'

'Don't be stupid. Farmer for near forty years and scared to go out on his own land. They've all heard about that cross, too. Lizzie Strode said is it true he's holding open-air services now?'

'They can mock! 'Tis a pit of sin, this place. A pit of sin!'

Don Moulder snatched his lamp from the big hook behind the door and walked into the dark. *Protect me, Lord, protect thy servant, yea though I walks into the valley of the shadow . . .*

Verity was in a stiff-backed kitchen chair, her back to the Aga, rereading John Cowper Powys's *Maiden Castle.*

The novel had been bought for her many, many years ago by her fiancé, Captain Hope, and she'd never been able to open it without picturing him: a strong, stocky man with a faintly piratical Errol Flynn air and a wide, white smile which would simply erupt across his face when she opened the door of her mother's house on a Sunday afternoon.

Captain Hope had been ten years older than Verity, who was twenty-five when they became engaged. He liked to call her 'the child bride', although this was more a reference to her stature than her years.

His sudden death from peritonitis, barely a month before the scheduled wedding day, had been followed a week later by her widowed mother's first stroke and then fifteen years of caring for her, increasingly querulous, before her death dispatched Verity, all alone into the world. Two unhappy housekeeping jobs had followed before she and Colonel Pixhill had found each other, recognising the qualities that each required for the quiet, untroubled life that never quite came about.

Colonel Pixhill was not at all like Bernard Hope, being more refined, less vigorous in his manner. But then, when they met, he was so much older. Verity had often wondered what might have developed had she met the Colonel twenty or thirty years earlier. Before the unfortunate Mrs Pixhill.

Before Oliver.

The mere thought of Oliver Pixhill spoiled her concentration and she found herself miserably counting the Christmas cards on the windowsill.

Seventeen. Fewer and fewer every year, as her friends died off and Verity was crossed from the lists of distant great-nieces and nephews who presumably thought she must be dead by now but did not think it worth a phone call to find out. She imagined that years after her departure, from the house or from life, whichever came first, there would still be a handful of small, cheap cards addressed to Miss V. Endicott, Meadwell, Glastonbury.

There was, quite simply, nobody left now to whom she might turn for help – having this afternoon telephoned the only contact number she now possessed for the Pixhill Trust. She'd at last reached a solicitor called Mr Kellogg and asked him if the Trust could prevent Dr Pelham Grainger from uncovering the Meadwell as, in her view, this would not be complying with the Colonel's wishes.

Mr Kellogg had laughed. Actually laughed.

'Miss Endicott, the Trust is entering a new era. Meadwell's a delightful and historic house and it's been hidden away for too long. While the Chalice Well gets tens of thousands of visitors, ours is ignored.'

'But that's because . . .'

'We want to see the Colonel take his place among the great pioneers of modern Glastonbury, along with . . . with all the others. And for Meadwell to become recognised as architecturally on a par with the Tribunal, The George and Pilgrims . . .'

'But the Colonel quite deliberately sealed up the well so that nobody . . .'

'Probably because he was unhappy about spending the money that would have been required to clean and repair it. But times change, Miss Endicott. There are now thousands of tourists with an unassuageable thirst for the Spiritual, and if this man Grainger can help put us on the map . . .'

Put us on the map!

Was Major Shepherd the last of them to realise that the Colonel's last wish had been for Meadwell to stay, for the foreseeable future, entirely *off* the map?

Any faint hopes that Mrs Rosemary Shepherd, the Major's widow, might have picked up his sword had been dispelled by a telephone call around teatime.

'Miss Endicott, I've been trying to clean out Tim's study, getting rid of all the silly books Pixhill made him read, and I keep falling over this blasted parcel – full of boring papers connected with the Pixhill diaries and addressed to a Mrs Carey. If I've phoned her once I've phoned her a dozen times. Keep getting the same tedious answering machine. Would you have any idea at all what on earth the problem is with this woman?'

Verity had explained that Mrs Carey was in hospital, having been injured in a serious fire.

'Oh. Well, how long's she going to be in hospital? Look, suppose I send this stuff to you, can you pass it on to her? Yes, that makes sense. I shall do that.'

Nothing makes sense any more, Verity thought.

Coming into Glastonbury, there were several police diversion signs. One said, AVOID TOWN CENTRE.

'Still got bloody roadworks, I see,' Juanita said. 'I'd ignore it. It's just to avoid congestion in the daytime.'

Seconds later they were stopped by a policeman.

'You're going to ask me if I can read, aren't you?' Powys said.

'I wouldn't insult you, sir. I was going to ask you which paper you worked for and then I saw the dog and Mrs Carey. Welcome home, Mrs Carey.'

'I'm sorry?' Juanita looked fogged.

'It's OK, you won't recognise me.' The policeman leaned on the wound-down window. 'I was at the fire.'

'Oh,' Juanita said.

'I'm glad to see you looking so much better. We were a bit worried about you. I put my jacket under your head. Tried to keep you calm until the ambulance got through. You kept saying, "Get the cat!" I thought, If there's a cat in there he can get himself out.'

Powys felt rather than saw Juanita go absolutely rigid.

The one time Don Moulder had felt safe going down to the bottom field was at dawn, when the cross would make a proud and rugged silhouette against the eastern sky and the Tor.

At night, no silhouette was a good silhouette.

Bloody woman. How could she have seen flames down here? And wouldn't it have been easy just to stop the car and have a quick glance over the hedge? She did it on purpose; sensed there was something he didn't like in the bottom field but wouldn't tell her.

Trouble with this field, you approached it from the farmhouse and you couldn't see what was inside it till you were practically through the gate.

Protect me, Lord.

Don slid the bar and walked in, praying under his breath.

No flames. No light at all, except from his lamp. Which he kept switched on and tightly in his right hand all the way to the cross.

Feeling safer when he reached the cross. He went to embrace it, that good and sturdy telegraph pole he'd bought for 50p when they moved the lines.

The cross felt oddly light when he threw his arms about it. And brittle, like a husk. He felt his fingers sinking in.

His arms dropped, nerveless, to his sides, the lamp still clutched in his right hand. He backed away and held up his left hand to the light. It was black.

He let out a cry as the wooden cross started to shiver.

Charcoal. It was burned to charcoal. Lord, how could it be?

How can it be, Lord? D'you hear me?

He shone the light on the cross. Black as soot. Black as sin. Burned to a black cinder and still standing, like the fire had come from inside.

This was what the missus seen? Not ten minutes ago, coming home from the WI, she'd seen the cross on fire?

Couldn't be.

Don flung himself at the cross and hugged it close, feeling it flaking in his arms, beginning to crumble.

He began to whimper. It was burned through, and worse than that, worse than that . . .

. . . Worse than that, it was cold.

In a corner of the field, an old engine cranked into unholy life.

Behind the barriers, the Christmas tree lay in slaughtered sections at the side of the road. Christmas had been cancelled and the market cross exposed again, a solitary finger accusing God.

Powys winced. 'I suppose you know this guy Woolaston.'

'Yes.' Her voice sounded slack. 'And Kirsty Cotton.'

He pulled sharply into the kerb just below Carey and Frayne. The pavements were deserted, most of the shop lights were out. Even The George and Pilgrims had looked quiet, a muted glow beyond the ancient windows.

'Woolly has a reputation', Juanita said, 'for being the slowest driver under seventy in the entire West Country. It doesn't bear thinking about.'

But she still sounded as if there was something else pressing on her mind, something the policeman had said before he told them about the horrific accident. Maybe it was just being reminded of the fire by someone else who'd been there. More likely, though, it was what the policeman had said about the cat. Had Jim Battle had a cat?

Powys climbed out of the Mini, took the suitcase from the boot, went round and opened Juanita's door wide.

It was a penetratingly cold night. She stood shivering in the road. Almost directly across the street, the goddess smouldered in purple, in one of the very few windows which remained lit.

'My God.' Juanita looked slowly around her as if she might be in the wrong town.

If it's all changed so much from this morning, Powys thought, what the hell must it seem like after more than a month?

She seemed unsteady. He put a hand under her arm, guided her to the pavement.

And stopped.

There was a new sign in the window of Carey and Frayne.

It had been pasted to the outside and was clearly legible under the streetlamp. He realised it was effectively covering a sign which the printer guy, Sam, had made and Diane had stuck up on the inside of the glass. The sign which said, COMING SOON – THE AVALONIAN.

This one was much bigger. It had foot-high black letters on luminous yellow paper, pasted the full width of the window right at the top, where you couldn't hope to reach it from outside. Whoever had done this must have had ladders. Or maybe parked a van on the pavement and stood on its roof.

The sign said, THE AVALOONIAN IS HERE.

ELEVEN

HOME TEMPLE

'It's all right.'

'Oh please . . . please, no . . . I won't tell any . . . Oh, no . . . no, please don't . . .'

'Shhhhhhh.'

'No! Get away from me! You dis—'

'Open your eyes, Diane. You're safe. Nobody's going to do anything to you.'

She opened her eyes. Into other eyes. Shut them in panic.

'Take it easy. You're all right.'

'Oh. Oh gosh.'

'You see?'

'Have they . . .?'

'Gone. Yes they have. They wouldn't tangle with me. Diane, my dear, you're trembling horribly.'

Light from the tin-shaded bulb sprayed down on her. Her relief turned it into golden tinsel.

'They were going to rape me.'

'I do believe they were,' said Ceridwen.

Juanita ran up the stairs with her coat flapping and her useless gloved hands held out in front of her like fins.

'Diane? Diane!'

Joe Powys followed, doing what Juanita couldn't, tossing doors open, smacking lights on.

He found her standing in the middle of the upstairs living room. She looked about to faint. He made her sit down.

'She's not here, Powys. Where is she? Why isn't she here?'

'Oh, hey, she could be anywhere. She's working flat out on *The Avalonian*. Goes to meetings and things. Teaches correspondents how to write shorter paragraphs.'

'Well, she can't have been here when whoever it was put that sign up.'

'They could have done it in the last few minutes. Anytime. These Glastonbury First guys move fast. What's more, nobody seems to stop them.'

'How do you know it's them?'

'I don't. But I can't think who else would want to discredit Diane. On the other hand, none of the Glastonbury First people I've met struck me as clever enough to think of that one.'

He helped her take off her coat and she sat there looking lost in the absurdly festive Aztec-pattern skirt and the lemon-coloured, off-the-shoulder top. Her face was white.

Powys had never been up here before. It was cosy: densepile carpet, many bookshelves; between them, paintings of luminous, twilight skies. Jim Battle.

'Let me moisten your lips. There. Better? Lie back on the sofa. That's it.'

'Where is this place?'

'A sanctuary.'

It was dark and warm. She could smell something musty but not unpleasant, not quite incense. Domini Dorrell-Adams and the angular woman, Jenna, had picked them up in a car. She vaguely remembered going through backstreets and across the car park.

Didn't remember arriving because she'd collapsed against Ceridwen, in shuddering tears, on the back seat of the car. Remembering Darryl Davey, his copper-wire hair, his buck teeth, his penis out. *Better than a tube of Smarties, my lover.*

'. . . terrible ordeal, Diane.'

'They . . . He put his . . .'

'But he's gone.'

'Yes.'

'Drink this.'

'What is it?'

'Only herbs.'

'It's sweet.'

'It's for shock. Drink it slowly. My, you've lost weight, Diane.'

'Don't seem to have had time for meals.'

'You need looking after. Shouldn't be on your own. Certainly not tonight.'

'No. I mean, I'll be OK.'

'Comfortable?'

'Mmmm. Thank you. Where's . . . where is this?'

'You've been here before, haven't you, Diane?'

'I don't think so.'

'It's Wanda's temple.'

'Oh.' She almost smiled. When she was up in Yorkshire, Juanita had sent her a two-page picture spread from *Hello!* magazine. It had said, *Dame Wanda Carlisle, newly adopted into the Pagan Faith, receives us in her Home Temple in Mystical Glastonbury.* The actress had been photographed in Egyptian costume. There'd been no mention of The Cauldron.

'Diane, listen to me.' Ceridwen's voice so close she could feel the warm breath on her cheek. 'I've dealt many times with this situation. If you're alone, you won't sleep. You won't feel secure. You know they know you can identify them. You'll feel so much safer here. There are plenty of rooms. And we shall watch over you.'

'Honestly, I . . .' She tried to lift her head from the soft cushion. It felt so incredibly heavy.

'Which brings us to the question of the police. Do you think we should call them? I think perhaps we should. Especially if one of the attackers works for your father . . .'

'Oh gosh, no. Please.'

'Unfortunately, I didn't see them do anything. They scattered when they saw me advancing. I could testify that they were there, of course. I know the rest would be your word against theirs, but . . .'

'No, really. My father mustn't know. That above all. Please don't tell the police. I don't think I could face it. I don't think I could summon the strength. I just feel, you know, so awfully tired.'

'Diane, I know you're there. Will you at least do me the common courtesy of returning my calls . . .?'

There were nine messages on the answering machine down in the shop. Most of them from Lord Pennard.

'Yes, well, not calling him back was the most sensible thing she could do under the circumstances,' Juanita said. 'His family have been pushing people around for centuries, and Diane's easy. If he gets to speak to her, he gets what he wants.'

'She does seem a bit malleable,' Powys said. 'For an upper-class rebel.'

'She's not a rebel, she . . . she's been pushed around all her life. Father, Archer, nannies . . . even the so-called Third bloody Nanny . . . That's your rebellion.'

'DF?'

'Right.' Juanita accepted a cigarette in her lips. 'Thanks.'

There was a different tone to Pennard's final message. *'Diane, this is difficult for me . . .'*

Juanita snorted smoke.

'. . . I should have talked to you properly that night . . .'

'Old bastard should have talked to her properly from when she was a kid,' Juanita said.

'. . . but we were both somewhat overwrought. I know what I did was high-handed. I'm sorry. I beg of you to telephone me at the earliest possible . . .'

'He can sound very plausible sometimes. If the chain-mail gauntlet doesn't work, slip on the white evening gloves.'

'Shush,' Powys said. 'This one sounds interesting.'

'. . . Mrs Shepherd in Coln St Mary, Gloucestershire. I understand you have had dealings with my late husband . . .'

Juanita went still. 'Late?'

'. . . who before he died was most perturbed that you had not contacted him after promising you would.'

'Oh my God,' said Juanita. 'He rang up the night before the fire. I'd forgotten all about it. I promised to go and see him, pick up some . . .'

'. . . papers, documents which, when I was sorting through his effects, I realised should have been collected by you. I have made several attempts to telephone you and I now merely wish to say that I am sending the package by courier to Miss Endicott at Meadwell. If you wish to collect them from her, that will be in order. Thank you.'

'Oh, shit.' Juanita extracted the cigarette, using the tips of her fingers. 'I should have gone over there the day I woke up in hospital. I don't think I've thought about it from that moment to this. Now the poor old boy's dead. He sounded awful, thinking about it, really ill. That's another one. Another one I've let down.'

'Oh, come on,' Powys said. 'Like you were supposed to ask the ambulance driver to take you to Bristol via Gloucester?'

'I wouldn't feel so bad if I'd even thought about him, just once.'

'*Diane . . . Diane, it's Woolly . . .*'

'Oh God, here we go.'

'*. . . got to talk. I'm at the end of . . . Oh fuck, we just got to talk . . . I'm at home. Please call me when you can. Please.*'

'There you are,' Powys said. 'That's where she's gone.'

'OK, if you hold the phone I'll call him.'

'Before you do, these papers. The ones that woman mentioned.'

'Oh. Well, it was strange. Normally I would've listened harder when he called, but that was a night we had other problems, with Ceridwen downstairs and hearing about this guy Headlice. Major Shepherd said . . . he said there was a missing chapter from Pixhill's diary that they couldn't publish for legal reasons. He said that it cast light on what was happening here. I don't know what he meant.'

'Why was he telling you, if it was unpublishable?'

'I don't know. He said Verity couldn't handle it on her own any more. God, how could I forget this?'

'I'd like to see this stuff,' Powys said.

Juanita said sharply, 'You're thinking about your book, aren't you? The Secret Pixhill Wasn't Allowed To Tell.'

She looked up in alarm as something fell against the shop door like a heavy refuse sack. Powys moved across and lifted up the blind.

'Diane, for Chrissake let me in. We've got to talk.'

'God,' Juanita said, 'it's . . .'

'Diane, listen . . .' the voice still slurred but low and urgent now. 'I know this isn't the best time. But I love you I love you Diane.'

'. . . Sam Daniel?'

TWELVE

FROM A HIGH SHELF

They took Sam upstairs. He was certainly pissed. But Juanita suspected there was more to it than that. Some imbalance, something which had toppled him from his comfortably cynical, nonchalant perch.

The sudden perception of a slow-burning desire for Diane?

Devastating, but not enough to do this to him. There was a kind of desperation here.

'Juanita? Is that Juanita?' Sam peered at her, eyes wide and blurred. A tremor went through him. 'I need to be sick.'

Powys showed him the lavatory and shut the door on him.

'I'm quite shocked,' Juanita said. 'I don't think I knew about this. I don't think that even in my wildest . . .'

'I may be wrong,' Powys said, 'but I don't think Diane knows about it either.'

'Christ,' said Juanita. 'The perfect suitor. A drunken, left-wing anti-bloodsports-campaigner. If only Pennard were here.' She collapsed into the sofa. 'OK, let's call Woolly. Ask him to keep her there for a while. Some things need to be put into perspective.'

Powys held the phone to her ear and called the number.

There was no answer.

Juanita swallowed. Her throat felt very dry. She found herself looking at one of Jim's pictures, was flung brutally back into the moments when she was ringing Jim and ringing and ringing, and he didn't answer, kept on not answering, that was when they went to the cottage.

'Juanita?'

Staring at the picture. Was it going dark? She must have told Karen, the nurse, about that when she was feverish. Karen had said next day, 'That happened to my gran the night before Grandad died.' It used to be well known. The pictures in the room go dark before a death.

'Come on . . .' Powys on his knees in front of her. 'Calm down, huh? Just tell me where he lives. I'll go and check this out. As soon as we make sure Sam's OK.'

'Powys, you think something's happened to her, don't you?'

'I'm more worried about you. You're not well. You're very pale.'

'I'm OK. Leave Sam to me. You go.'

'I'll leave Arnold. He's a dowser's dog.'

'What on earth does that mean?'

'Pray you never have to find out.' Powys produced his enigmatic earth-mystery-guru's smile, but she could tell it was a struggle.

There was the sound of the lavatory flushing.

'And then we need to talk,' he said. 'About what that policeman said. About Jim's cat.'

'Not his cat,' she said hoarsely. 'His hat.'

On his way out, Powys spotted on the table in the downstairs parlour, an ancient copy of *The Avalonian*. There was a drawing on the front of a woman looking up towards Glastonbury Tor.

He recognised her at once and felt an almost-aching sadness.

Despair made a cold compress on Verity's heart as she switched off the light and padded in her pom-pom slippers to the bed.

Dr Grainger had said, *Go to bed earlier in the winter, semi-hibernate like the animals. And, if sleep will not come, make use of the peaceful hours to commune with the dark, listen to the night sounds, the conversing of owls, the creaking and shifting of the house. Listen to the ancient, beating heart of Meadwell.*

Verity lay under the sheets with her eyes open, drawn to the windows, two chalky-grey rectangles like paving slabs. Like gravestones in the wall. There were no owls tonight. Occasionally she would hear traffic from the main road, half a mile away, but only the loudest lorries. She wished the road were close enough for headlights to flash on to the glass.

Dr Pel Grainger would wince at such defeatism.

What did Dr Grainger know?

Rolling over on her cold pillow, aware of that painful tug at her left hip.

Arthritis.

Although it would be more comfortable that way, she would not lie on her back, remembering how her mother had eventually died in the night and Verity had found her next morning, eyes wide open to the ceiling like a stone effigy upon a tomb.

Verity felt utterly lost. Almost wished that she could See.

Powys said, 'Woolly?'

The little guy dropped his shovel in alarm, spilling fragments and splinters of wood. Under the lamp projecting from the wall, his scalp gleamed through sparse hair. Behind him was a hole where a window had been.

'I'm sorry. We haven't met.' Powys felt foolish. There were shards of broken glass on the cobbles and remains of what might once have been a guitar.

He was getting a bad feeling. If Arnold had been here, Arnold would have growled that particular growl.

'Who are you?' Woolly retrieved the shovel, brandished it like a weapon. Powys swiftly identified himself.

'JM Powys.' Woolly smiled the smile of a man for whom everything comes too late. 'Heard you were in town. Tried to find you once. Ask your advice. Sheesh.'

He lowered the shovel. 'Been a bad night, JM. Bad as they get.'

'We picked up your message for Diane. On the answering machine.'

'Where is she?'

'We thought she might be here.'

'We?'

'Juanita Carey and me.'

'She's back?' Woolly ran a weary hand through his hair. 'Shit. She picks her nights, don't she? No, Diane's not here.'

'Has she been here?'

'I hope not. Spent the last hour walking. Got a taxi back from Street. Couldn't settle. That poor woman. Kirsty. I saw her face, you know, just before they sedated her. Gonner see that face for ever, man. Wiped out. How do you even start to live with that?'

Woolly patrolled the square in circles, not looking up.

'So I left the message for Diane then took off. Walked along Wearyall. One of my places. Fetched up at the Thorn. Prayed a bit, you know? Prayed to anything that would listen. Know who I felt like?' He looked at Powys at last. 'Judas fucking Iscariot. The chosen instrument of death. The Thorn . . . it felt hostile. Never felt like that before, man, never. Then I came back and found some upright citizen had decided to, like, express the feelings of the whole town.'

'You told the police about this?'

'You kidding? If they'd set light to the damn place I wouldn't feel I had the right to call the fire brigade. It's over, man. Not gonner walk away from this one. Don't deserve to.'

Woolly kicked away the neck of the broken guitar. Powys bent and picked it up. The strings were still attached to the bent machine heads.

'Who did this?'

'Does it matter? Town's crawling with vigilantes now. Glastonbury First; I thought it'd blow over. Keep quiet, don't make a big deal out of it, let it burn itself out. Sheesh, everything that happens deals 'em another ace. Jim Battle. And now—'

'You said "chosen".'

'Huh?'

'You said "chosen instrument of death". What did you mean?'

'Ah, you don't wanner hear this.' Woolly wiped his forehead. 'Seminal book for me, *The Old Golden Land*. Somebody said you'd changed. Thought it was all balls now. Didn't wanner have anything to do with leys and location-phenomena.'

Powys said nothing.

'That being the case, you'll be saying to yourself, What a shit-head – gets pissed, causes a truly horrible fatal accident and the best he can think of is to blame the paranormal. Get me outer here, you'll be thinking.'

Woolly was close to tears.

Powys thought about all the crazy stuff he'd heard tonight. He thought about Uncle Jack.

'Woolly,' he said, 'I think I'm changing back.'

Sam sat for a long time with his head in his hands.

'Take your time,' Juanita said.

Although she truly didn't think there was time. Too much happening too fast. It was like one of those Magic Eye pictures where there was a lot going on but it all looked like mush until your eye learned how to resolve the vibrating strands and then, in the centre of it all, was a shatteringly obvious symbol.

A very dark symbol.

'We had kind of a row,' Sam said. 'Diane said everything was real and everything was a part of everything else. Something like that.'

This was so close to Juanita's own thoughts that she had to drink some whisky very quickly, through her straw.

Sam had tried to clean himself up. He was wearing an old, torn army parka, camouflage trousers and walking boots.

'Where have you been, Sam?'

He sighed. 'Bowermead. Pennard's got a hunt coming off on Boxing Day. Thought I'd see how I could spoil the fun.'

'Rankin catch you?'

'No. Didn't see Rankin. I saw . . . I saw where hundreds of beautiful broadleaf trees had been destroyed. The ground all dug up and flattened. You know how poor old Woolly was saying they could start anywhere, at any time, clearing land for the new road?'

'This is for real, Sam?'

'Swear to God.' His hair was stuck to his forehead where he'd splashed cold water into his eyes. 'What I figured . . . Pennard's worried about hundreds of protesters descending on his woodland like at Newbury and Batheaston . . . so he's got in first. Destroyed his own trees. Remains of bonfires everywhere, where they burned the branches.'

'The mind boggles,' Juanita said. Dynamite stuff, certainly. But why would that send Sam off to get crawling drunk?

Take it slowly.

'Sam, does Diane know about this?'

He shook his head.

'Did she know you'd gone to Bowermead?'

'No. What happened, look, after the crash the telly were interviewing Archer Ffitch. He's coming out with all this pious, hypocritical shit, trying to lay it all on Woolly. And then, when the camera's off, he puts the knife in for Diane with the reporter. How they've tried to help her but she's a lost cause. Very sick girl, all this. Discreetly planting the information that Diane's batty and anything she says should be treated accordingly. Which would include anything printed in *The Avalonian*.'

Black lettering on yellow started to roll across Juanita's brain like one of those advertisements on a belt in the Post Office: OONIAN IS HERE . . . THE AVALOONIAN IS HERE . . . THE AVAL . . .'

'I just went insane. I wanted to go off, fuck up the Ffitches any way I could.'

'And now you can,' Juanita said. 'You can blow it to the papers about all the trees they've destroyed prematurely. Where did you get pissed, Sam?'

'Down the Rifleman's. Four double Scotches and a pint. On an empty stomach.'

'I'm missing something. How did you get from Bower-mead to the Rifleman's Arms?'

'Walked. Ran. Ran, mostly. Left the van back on the Pilton road. Wasn't going back that way. Oh Christ, Juanita, the reason we had the row, me and Diane, was over what you believed in and what you couldn't handle.'

'I'm surprised it took you so long. Working together so closely and her being of a mystical persuasion, while you . . .'

'Juanita . . .' Sam pushed the hair away from his eyes and his hands stayed clutched to either side of his head. 'So help me, I think I've seen a ghost.'

'Help yourself, JM.' Woolly pushed a bottle of Bell's across the workbench, untied his pathetic pony-tail. 'You won't mind if I don't.'

Powys poured less than half an inch of Scotch into a tumbler. He wasn't in a drinking mood either.

The little room was like the picture you had of the workshop of the man who made Pinocchio. Curved planes and fancy chisels and lots of tools you wouldn't know which end to pick them up with. And rich, woody smells.

'I'm out of here tomorrow,' Woolly said. 'Best thing. People don't want to see me around. Even my friends, they'll just be uncomfortable.'

'Where'll you go?'

'Dunno yet. Here I am one day, an old hippy in the place where all old hippies would want to come to die. Next day, boom. Outcast.'

Woolly lit a roll-up, like the Bishop of Bath and Wells.

'Sheesh,' he said vacantly.

'Look,' Powys said. 'I don't really know this place. I just came because somebody wanted me to write a book about the New Age culture.'

'Decline of,' Woolly said. ''Tis gonner be all washed up again. You know the last time this happened? 1539. The dissolution of the monasteries. When the State fitted up the Abbot here. Topped him.'

Woolly picked up a wooden guitar bridge with little holes for the strings to go through and began to sand it down with a small piece of glass-paper.

'I seen it coming a long way off, man. Just never thought it was gonner happen so fast. I knew there was gonner be a showdown and I knew I'd be at the centre of it. What I guessed was it'd be the road that brought it all to a climax. Big protest on the site, us occupying the trees they were gonner bring down, digging tunnels, forming human chains. Then this business with the Tor comes up. Need a human chain round that too. I had this feeling that was what I'd been born for. My destiny. To form human chains around a holy hill.'

Powys formed pictures of Woolly as this little Hereward the Wake figure rallying the New Age troops. Woolly on the TV news. Woolly in Sunday newspaper profiles.

'Stupid,' Woolly said. 'What I'd been born for was to help kill an innocent child at precisely the right time. Thereby making a key contribution to the Second Fall of Glastonbury. Apocalyptic, JM.'

He put down the wooden bridge.

Powys said, 'I don't understand.'

'OK.' Woolly started rolling the glass-paper between his hands. 'Let's start at the beginning. This is the most important spiritual power-centre in the country. Maybe in the Western World. This is where they brought the most powerful mystical artefact the world has ever known. Because it brings together Christianity and the old religions. The Chalice, right. Let's not call it the Holy Grail, let's just call it the Chalice. Whether it dispenses wine, water or just pure spirit, it's a symbol of harmony, right?'

'I'll go along with that.'

'Good. The Tor itself is like an upturned chalice, pouring spiritual energy into the earth and it flows out in all directions spreading harmony . . . at least, the possibility of harmony. And the strongest of those currents, cutting straight across Britain . . .'

'The St Michael Line. It doesn't stand up to too much scrutiny, Woolly. A lot of those St Michael churches miss the line by a mile.'

'Aw, shit, man, I walked that line. From St Michael's Mount to Bury Abbey. I *know* it exists.' Woolly touched the little scroll of glass-paper to his head. 'In here.'

Powys smiled. He had no quarrel with that. Not tonight.

'St Michael's the hard-man angel,' Woolly said. 'Defender of the spirit. Plays it straight. Literally. That line coming down across the countryside like a big sword. There's also the possibility of another current weaving in and out of the line. A feminine current this dowser guy found. The St Mary current. All very harmonious.'

'And then' – the thought came out of nowhere – 'somebody puts a new road through it.'

Woolly rose to his feet, picked up the wooden bridge, threw it into the air and caught it in triumph.

'It's about covert secularisation, JM. The State's always done it, because government – even the Vatican when they ran things – is anti-spirit. The State is about, like, rules and money. Spiritual values, they get in the way. But, shit, there ain't time to go into the politics of all that. You just got to look at the effects of this conflict on the ground – on the landscape.'

'When the Normans conquered England,' Powys said, 'and they wanted to establish a physical power base, they built their castles . . .'

'On ancient sacred burial mounds. You got it, JM. Course, when Christianity came they built their churches on mounds and inside stone circles, too, but that's OK, 'cause it's still spiritual.

But the number of Norman military strongholds built on pagan mounds is staggering. And it goes on. Where do the Army do their training – bloody Salisbury Plain. So all the countryside around Stonehenge is churned up by flaming tanks and splattered with Nissen huts and stuff. Then they ban free festivals at Stonehenge and that screws it for the genuine pagans and Druids who can't find sanctuary there any more.'

'Leaving Glastonbury Tor.'

'Leaving the Tor. Where Archer Ffitch and Griff Daniel and the G-1 crew propose to have "restricted access". They strangle the power-centre, pump the St Michael Line full of diesel fumes, negative emotions, road-rage, fatal crashes . . .'

The mention of fatal crashes seemed to drain the energy out of Woolly, as rapidly as if he'd been shot. He sat down.

'Is this paranoia, JM? I can show you the maps, how that road will be visible, to some extent, from every significant church, every ancient sacred site from Burrowbridge Mump to Solsbury Hill, where it meets up with that other evil little bypass. You won't be able to stand on any holy hill or in any St Michael churchyard without hearing the roar of transcontinental juggernauts. It's horrifying. Like I say, the worst thing to happen to this town since 1539.'

There was a thump inside Powys's head, as it all landed on him like a big, thick book from a very high shelf.

Sam brought the book up from the shop. 'This the one?'

Juanita nodded. 'Pop it down on the table. You'll have to flip through the pages for me.'

It was one of those Glastonbury-in-old-photos books. Not really Carey and Frayne subject-matter, with its sepia line-ups of long-dead councillors and women in big hats.

'Stop,' Juanita said. 'No, sorry, carry on. Skip this section. Hold it . . . there.'

Sam swallowed. Juanita extended, with some pain, a discoloured, lumpy forefinger.

Sam looked up from the book.

'Oh, Jesus God,' he said. 'He's younger, but—'

'But that's him?'

Sam nodded. His face looked as blurred and lost and scared and overwhelmed as one of the small boys in knee-length shorts on the very edge of the photograph.

The caption underneath said:

October 1954: Children from St Benedict's C of E Primary School receive their prizes from the vice-chairman of the school governors, Col. George Pixhill.

PART FIVE

. . . and though the well is dark with blood, the Tor is bright with fire.

Dion Fortune
Avalon of the Heart

ONE

CROWS' FEET DEEPENING

She awoke to the voice of Ceridwen.

The last transition for a woman can be a wonderful and fulfilling time . . . also a time of disillusion and decay, constantly chilled by the draught of death . . .

The moan of distress brought Powys rushing in. He saw her head twisting on the pillow in a dark swirl of hair, before she woke, big brown eyes full of dread and not recognising him at first.

Arnold whined, his outsize ears pricked up.

'Um, Joe Powys,' Powys reminded her. He'd spent the night under cushions and a rug on the living-room sofa.

Juanita blinked at him. 'Is she . . .?'

Powys shook his head. 'Sorry. No sign.'

The winter morning hung in the window like a damp rag. Juanita's head sank back. 'What are we going to do?'

On the wall opposite the bed was a Battle duskscape, the red light reduced to a thin line. Powys thought of the St Michael Line, a ghostly ribbon linking the high places.

And interlacing last night's feverish dreams.

While Arnold had stayed, watchful, in Juanita's bedroom.

'Maybe you could call her father,' Powys said.

'Like he'd tell me if she was there?'

'He might.'

'If she isn't there,' Juanita said, 'I don't think it would be good if he knew she was missing. I also suggested to Sam that we should keep quiet about what he saw – the road. Until we find Diane.' Gloomily, she contemplated her face in the dressing-table mirror. 'What's Woolly's state of mind?'

'Not good. Somebody smashed up his shop window last night, while he was out.'

'*No.*' Her face crumpling in pain. 'In Benedict Street? What's happening to people?'

'Glastonbury First vigilantes, Woolly reckons. Or maybe just ordinary citizens appalled that they voted for a man who caused the death of an innocent child after hallucinating a black bus in the rush hour.'

'What do *you* think he saw?'

'Well,' Powys said. 'If Sam Daniel, who you say is a confirmed unbeliever in *anything*, is categoric about seeing Pixhill's ghost then, um, anything's possible, isn't it?'

He held up the *Daily Press*.

Christmas Tree Horror

Most of the front page was filled by a panoramic picture of the fallen tree half-smothering the lorry. There was also a smiling mother-and-baby photo from the Cotton family album.

And one of a crazy man staring into the camera with eyes which were wide and glazed. He looked like a junkie or an absconder from some high-security psychiatric hospital. There was a grim-faced policeman on either side. The caption read: *'I'm shattered'* – *Councillor Edward Woolaston minutes after the horror.*

'He says he's leaving town. Doesn't want to make his friends uncomfortable.'

'He can't do that,' Juanita said firmly. 'I'll call him. We need Woolly.'

He sighed. 'There's something else.'

Along the bottom of the front page, it said:

MP moves on Tor Ban – page three.

'It seems', Powys said, his voice flat, 'that your ailing Member of Parliament, Sir Laurence Bowkett, is tabling a Private Member's Bill.'

He turned to page three and read:

' "The Glastonbury Tor (Limitation of Access) Bill is tabled with the full support of the local branches of the National Farmers' Union and the Country Landowners' Association. It is also understood to have considerable support inside the executive of the National Trust, which owns the Tor."'

'Oh my God.' Juanita slumped. 'This could be passed. It could be law. It could be law next year.'

She turned to Powys. 'I wasn't taking this in very well last night. Woolly sees it as some kind of Government conspiracy?'

'More of a cosmic conspiracy, I think. The Establishment becoming a tool for the forces of evil. Because of their economic tunnel-vision, governments are particularly susceptible.'

'To the forces of evil as symbolised by . . .'

'The Dark Chalice. If the Holy Grail is the symbol of harmony and light and the healing power of the spirit, the Dark Chalice – the anti-Grail – represents hatred and division, greed and corruption and . . . well, you get the idea.'

'And was there a Dark Chalice? Is there anything in British mythology corresponding with that?'

'Um . . . I reckon Pixhill invented it. He wanted a symbol. Something easily understood. Maybe it's taken on a life of its own. If Diane's seen it—'

Juanita sat up. '*Where?*'

'Sam, I think I got dis bug. Feel rotten, all bunged up, so it don't look like I'll be id for a couple of days. Sorry boss.'

Ah well. He was relieved, if anything. Couldn't sit here, after last night, and listen to Paul rabbiting on about megabytes and CD Rom.

The machine said, *Click, whirr.* That's the lot.

No word from Diane. His head throbbed. Where was she? Walked out of this door, very sad. *It's all real. Everything is part of everything else and it's all real.* An hour later it's all mayhem and chaos in Magdalene Street. Where was she?

It was nearly half-past nine. Outside, the town was wrapped in dour grey-brown fog. Sam stood at his window watching people moving about, not laughing, not wishing each other Merry Christmas.

A sombre stillness settled around him and the world seemed a denser place. He caught himself wondering if any of the muffled passers-by were ghosts, his mind still squirming away from the dismal image of an old man who could not speak, only scream in silence.

Shit, Sammy. Too heavy, son. What he should be doing was getting on to Hughie, hanging it on him about Pennard and the new road. Calling in the eco-troops. Mass protest, mass trespass.

Wait till we find Diane.

Would he ever find Diane?

Did anything ever happen to you that you couldn't explain?

'In the sky,' Powys said. 'Over the Tor. A cupped-hands effect. Something very dark between them. And also in the fire. At the heart of the flames.'

'When Jim . . .?'

He nodded. 'Or so she says.'

'Maybe she didn't tell me because she thought I'd dismiss it. She thinks I'm cynical.'

'Which you aren't, of course.'

'I've tried. God, I've tried.' She turned back to the mirror, shook her hair, winced. 'Look at that. Bloody hag. There was the residue of something before the fire. Funny, that very night I got all dressed up for Woolly's protest meeting, saw myself in a shop window and I was quite cheered. I thought, there's something left, you know? Now I'm a hag. The last transition. *Chilled by the draught of death.*'

Powys saw the reflection of her eyes widen in panic, the crows' feet deepening. 'That's absolutely not true, Juanita.' He stood up and came behind her, picking up a hairbrush from the dressing table. 'Tilt your head back.'

She closed her eyes. Brushing her hair, he felt the softness of the skin on her long neck. He thought of that yellowing cover of *The Avalonian*, the sylph in the nature-goddess headdress.

'There's something I haven't told you,' Juanita said.

Don Moulder waited until Mrs Moulder was out collecting the eggs and then he rang his neighbour, Melvyn Carter, and he said, 'That bit o' ground, Melvyn. I'm ready to talk, look. Now.'

Melvyn expressed surprise and deep suspicion on account of it was only two weeks since Don had refused to discuss even the possibility of selling Melvyn a certain four and a half acres of pasture at any price.

'I'll be reasonable, Melvyn, I promise you. In return I need a particular favour and nothin' else will do. Your son-in-law, look, still in the police is he? Oh. Inspector now, is it? Well, I d'need his help and I d'need it fast. With regards to . . .'

Don's hand sweating on the phone.

'. . . with regards to a certain buzz.'

Feeling better now it was out. The Lord had thrown him into the heart of the Great Conflict, and, Yea, though he walked through the valley of death, he would turn his face unto the light and not be afeared to put his arse on the line.

'His hat? They took his hat?'

'They seemed to find that funny,' Juanita said. 'I was bloody terrified. Totally convinced we were both going to die. How could they chop off his head and let me go? You think New Age travellers are either young idealists pioneering a new way of life or else sad, urban refugees who need to be perpetually stoned. But these were very sinister. The guy in the mask, I can still hear him whispering. Didn't speak. Just whispered. I swore to Jim I'd never tell a soul.'

'Can't harm him now.' Powys stood up. 'How about I run you a bath?'

'The story's not over. I saw his hat, I . . . I've been blocking this out, OK. You're the first person to hear this. I'd virtually talked myself into believing I'd imagined it. Until that copper . . .'

'Jim's cat.'

'When they hold the inquest on Jim, early in the new year, I'm going to have to give evidence. I'm going to have to explain why I ran at the house, why I . . .'

'I know.' Powys gently squeezed her shoulders.

'You *don't* know. That's the point. Nobody knows. They all think I threw myself on the bonfire all trussed up like some Indian wife. Even I . . .'

The phone rang. 'Ignore it,' Powys said. 'They'll leave a message. Go on.'

'What if it's Diane?'

'Diane wouldn't phone. She doesn't even know you're out of hospital.'

The ringing was cut off, snatched away by the answering machine.

'All right,' Juanita said. 'There's an ash tree overhanging the cottage, one of the branches almost touching the window. His hat was hanging from it. I was standing there with Diane and Don Moulder, hoping to God Jim wasn't within a mile of that fire, and I saw his hat. No mistake. Not a bunch of dead leaves, not a piece of cloth. It was the damned hat. I was furious. The travellers were blocking the road. I thought, they've set fire to his cottage and they've left his hat. A message. A taunt. So I – I mean, OK, irrationally, I can see that now – I just went after it. I tore my skirt and wrapped it round my face and I just . . .'

'OK,' he gripped her shoulders. 'Was he very attached to that hat?'

'Inseparable. Wore it riding his bike. Wore it painting in his garden.'

'In Celtic magic,' Powys said, 'a man's soul is in his head. The Celts kept heads in streams and wells. They made stone heads. Sorry, I'm thinking aloud, you don't want to hear this crap.'

'No, go on.'

'I was just thinking that if they went through all the ceremony of an execution, a beheading. And then they just took his hat . . .'

'He still died, didn't he?' Juanita said quietly. 'Within two days.'

'Possession of a man's hat, especially when that hat was such an essential part of what he was, would, they might think, give them access to his head. To his soul. To put thoughts there. To arouse certain feelings. Emotions. Sorry, I'm . . .'

Theorising. He felt very uncomfortable. This was the kind of theorising he'd sworn he was never going to do again.

'Emotions.' Juanita looked up at him. 'What did Diane tell you? About Jim and me?'

'That *you* just wanted to be friends.'

'OK. The situation was he'd left his wife. To come to the Vale of Avalon and paint. That was his dream. His Gauguin fantasy. Except the only vaguely dusky female he knew was me. And in all those years we just enjoyed each other's company. We had laughs.

And he looked at me and he patted my bum, and that was as far as it went and as far as he wanted it to go. Sure, he'd say, "If only I'd known you when I was younger," that sort of stuff. He enjoyed all that, the banter, the what if . . . But the truth was he didn't want to get involved with a woman again. Certainly wouldn't have one in his cottage. She might've fractured the idyll, messed up his routine.'

She was looking at the painting of the thin, red, glowing line.

'He was an obsessive painter. Increasingly. Obsessed with the mystery. That night, he was absolutely outraged at what the travellers were doing on the Tor. Spiritual vandalism. Maybe he sensed more than I did. He'd certainly become very attuned to the dusk. To the ending of a beautiful day.'

Nine o'clock passed and, with it, that last small hope – that Diane would arrive to open the shop.

Powys and Juanita sat in the shop and didn't open for business.

Juanita told herself the girl was scatty, easily deflected and sometimes she would let you down. Also that Diane was a grown woman and could look after herself, that to think otherwise was patronising and insulting.

So why did she feel desperate with anxiety?

The answering machine didn't do much to relieve it.

'Diane, it's Matthew Banks. That article of mine, for your dummy edition. We're going to have to scrap it. Something absolutely awful's happened. Please call me.'

TWO

OUR FIRST CHRISTMAS TREE

'Should they have let you come home?'

Matthew Banks was a very tall, spare, fastidious-looking man in his fifties. Waiting for him to arrive, Juanita had told Powys how Banks had sold the family garden centre to finance his self-published books on plant-lore. A fanatic, she said, but he knew his stuff.

'I can treat you,' Banks said. 'I can make you something up to put on those hands. You needn't have had grafts. Potato peelings. Forms a kind of skin.'

'Never mind, Matthew, too late.' Juanita was impatient. 'This is JM Powys, by the way, the author and, er, descendant of JC Powys.'

'Ah.' Banks inspected Powys down his half-glasses. '*The Old Golden Land*. You know, I . . .'

'And his dog, Arnold,' Juanita said. 'Let's not mess about. It opens at nine-thirty, doesn't it?'

Outside, the sleet was gathering force and every lamppost and signpost seemed to have one of those Glastonbury First stickers with the white slash across the Tor.

Banks tore one off as he passed. 'This should be stopped. You know we're going to turn tomorrow's Solstice Service into a sort of small-scale protest against this Tor lunacy. All the more urgent with Bowkett's blasted bill. If the Bishop's so keen on developing a sort of ecumenical attitude towards paganism, let him speak out against this.'

'You'd better make sure it is a small demo,' Juanita muttered through her scarf as they crossed into Magdalene Street. 'Or you'll be playing directly into their hands.'

She found herself glancing at every passing woman in the futile hope that one of them might turn out to be Diane.

'It will be discreet and dignified.' Banks strode through the Abbey gates, his jaw jutting.

*

It was Powys's first visit to the Abbey. Pity, he was thinking, that it should be at a time like this. For a reason like this.

They reached the modern visitor centre, where Banks was nodded through by the attendant but Powys paid for himself and Juanita. There were showcases inside the centre, and relics of stone and pottery, books and leaflets on sale, glossy pictures of sunset silhouettes. The centre-piece was a scale model of the original abbey in all its soaring, honeyed splendour. There were also several information boards, the first one telling the story of Joseph of Arimathea, said to have settled here with eleven disciples in AD 63.

And so – Juanita pale and muffled and following a three-legged dog – they entered the holyest erthe in all England: thirty-six acres of lawns and ruins. The reason for Glastonbury.

There was a tall wooden cross set in a vast lawn greying under a skim of sleet. The cross was modern but timelessly simple. Despite its size, it had humility; it said, *We're not even trying to compete.*

Powys saw the Abbey ruins stark beyond it. They'd always reached him, these ancient, spoiled places. More than palaces, more than cathedrals.

But there was no time to explore the ruins. Matthew Banks was striding, stork-like, towards a well-preserved grey chapel with a tiled roof and a tiny bell-tower.

On a small, walled lawn, with a path going by, stood a little tree. Arnold edged towards it.

'Perhaps not, Arnold,' Powys said.

Matthew Banks bit off a short, arid laugh. 'It really doesn't matter now.'

The Thorn. Another descendant of the staff of Joseph of Arimathea. This one was like the kind of tree a child draws, with its thin, grooved trunk and its clouded mesh of branches.

'I've seen the one on Wearyall Hill,' Powys said. 'Which is the actual?'

'They all are,' Banks said. 'Wearyall Hill was where the first one grew, but there's been a greater continuity of Holy Thorns here. This is the one most people see. For most visitors, this is *the* Holy Thorn. The one that flowers at Christmas. Should be flowering now.'

The Thorn wasn't in flower yet, although Powys could see what looked like buds.

Juanita said, 'Are you sure about this, Matthew? I mean, I don't know much about these things, but it looks as if it might flower.'

'Of course I'm sure,' Matthew Banks said harshly. 'It's dying.'

Juanita put out an inexperienced hand. The tree was like a curled-up hedgehog; you couldn't get inside it. She discovered, a little surprised, that she was crying quietly. It was only a tree, for God's sake. And whatever had happened here, it hardly compared with the arboreal massacre found by Sam Daniel.

'It was a bad summer,' Banks said. 'Phenomenally dry, into August. And then . . .'

'The Blight?'

'Which went on until the end of November. And then winter came in with a crunch. The strange part is, I examined the tree less than a week ago and it was thriving. I'd stand by that. It was ready to flower, as I say.'

'But if it wasn't lack of water?' Powys said.

'There *is* lack of water.' Banks bent, snapped off a twig easily between finger and thumb. 'Look. Feel it. Embrittled. Parched inside. This doesn't happen overnight.'

'No.' Cold on the outside, Juanita thought as Powys accepted the twig. Parched and arid inside. *Like me.*

Damn it, this wasn't the Holy Oak. It wasn't the Holy Giant Redwood. It wasn't even much of a myth: an old guy shoves his stick in the ground and it turns into the kind of arboreal runt that gardeners rip up and feed into the shredder. And yet that was why . . .

'There's a poetic truth about this little tree,' she said.

'Yes,' Powys said.

'You know what Pixhill said.'

'Oh please,' Banks snapped. 'Must we bring that man into this?'

'Pixhill had a dream, right?' Powys tossed the twig to the foot of the tree. 'Or claimed he had. Anyway, he goes all apocalyptic. *Dreamt I saw the Dark Chalice in the sky again, and the Meadwell was spewing black water from Hades and . . .'*

'Stop it!' Banks shouted. 'Merciful God, are things not bad enough? Must we talk like this?'

'Must we . . .?' Juanita stared at him in despair. 'Did it ever occur to you, Matthew, that not talking like this is what's allowed this situation to develop? You've all been so airy-fairy, peace and love, open up the healing forces of nature, that you haven't noticed it growing.'

Matthew Banks recoiled.

'Until it's everywhere.'

But he obviously didn't want to face anything apocalyptic. Not what Glastonbury mysticism was about.

'In *Avalon of the Heart*,' Powys said, 'Dion Fortune described the Thorn as our first Christmas tree. I like that.'

Juanita's eyes widened. 'I know what you're thinking. Do I?'

'I can't say that *I* do.' Banks was obviously feeling himself being pushed from centre-stage. 'What *are* you saying?'

'He's thinking about the other Christmas tree.'

'Oh, this is stupid.' Banks backed away from them.

'I don't think it is, Matthew. There's a malaise in this town.'

Powys said, 'I dreamt I saw the Dark Chalice in the sky again, and the Meadwell was spewing black water from Hades and . . .'

'*And I saw that Joseph's Holy Thorn*', Juanita said, '*had withered in the earth and . . .*'

'Stop it! Pixhill was a paranoid, sick old man.'

'*. . . and the Feet which walked in ancient times*,' Juanita was amazed she could remember this stuff, '*had walked again in the winter-hardened fields of Avalon. But this time . . .*'

Banks walked away in anguish, his head bowed like a monk's.

'*. . . This time*,' Powys said, '*they left cloven prints.* Jesus, Arnold . . .'

Juanita saw the dowser's dog whimpering and backing away from the murdered Thorn. Powys picked him up. Looking, Juanita thought, more concerned at the dog's reaction than anything.

'All I wanted', said Banks, when they caught him up, 'was for Diane to withdraw my article. Not to initiate a witchhunt. I wish I'd known this when I saw her last night.'

'Matthew, when did you see her?'

'Must have been before eight because Safeway was still open. Oh, and then I saw her again. With Jenna Gray.'

Juanita's hands began to throb; the gloves felt too tight.

Powys said, 'Where was this, Mr Banks?'

'From my . . . my friend's window.'

'You mean Mr Seward? What were they doing? Where did they go? This is very important, Matthew.'

'Well, I think they got out of a car. I wasn't paying much attention. Juanita, do you . . . do you think I should inform the Bishop?'

'What?' Juanita was making let's-get-out-of-here eye movements at Powys.

'About the Thorn. Should I tell him about the Thorn?'

'Well, his mob owns the Abbey. What do you think, Powys?'

'Whatever,' Powys said. 'Unless I've misunderstood the guy, he'll probably just send one of his minions to the nearest nursery for another one.'

'The bloody idiot,' Juanita said when they parted from Banks at the Gatehouse. 'How could she do this?'

The sleet was coming harder, looking thicker and whiter. A Christmassy crust was forming on the sawn-up sections of fir tree behind the barricades around the market cross.

'Banks has this intermittent thing going with an antiquarian bookseller called Godwin Seward. Seward's flat is more or less opposite Wanda Carlisle's house.'

'Where The Cauldron meets,' Powys said. 'But let's not jump to conclusions.'

'You sound like Banks. If I want to jump to conclusions . . .'

'How confident are you about facing this woman?' He looked at her hands.

'I'm not afraid.'

'I never thought you were. That's not what I meant. I just think a slanging match at this stage . . .'

'All I want is Diane out of there. At this stage.'

'Obviously,' Powys said. 'But what if she doesn't want to come?'

THREE

THE SOLSTICE TREE

Hello. Are you awake?

'I think so. A little.'

Comfortable?

'I think so.'

Let me moisten your lips.

It felt sweet on her lips. Her head felt very heavy. So did her eyelids, and yet they fell softly, like petals.

'It's very dark. I thought it was morning.'

Don't worry. Let me tell you a story. Yes? About a baby? Whose mother died when she was born?

'That's me. It's my story,' Diane whispered. She had to whisper. It was dark and she didn't want to waken the other patients.

That's right. Your mother died when you were born. She was actually dying when you were born.

'She fell downstairs.'

No, my dear, she was pushed downstairs. Everybody knows that.

'I don't understand.'

She did see you. She opened her eyes and saw you before she died. Did you know that?

'No.'

Lie back, now. Your lips are very dry. Drink some of this. Put your head back.

'Which hospital is this? Your uniform . . .'

Head back now . . . open your mouth . . . there. Relax. You're going to be fine.

'Did you know my mother?'

Like you, I didn't meet her until she was dying. I was your age then. Perhaps a little younger. I was an assistant midwife at the Belvedere. There were two of us. We put you in your mother's arms.

'Oh.'

She died holding you.

Diane knew she was crying.

Didn't you know that?

'No, I . . . it's so beautiful.'

She bleeds. We have put you in your mother's arms as she bleeds. Do you remember? Her arms around you. And she bleeds and bleeds. And her arms grow cold.

The petals of her eyelids floated like waterlilies on pools of tears.

You are lying in her dead arms. We leave you there in those dead arms. Until other arms encircle you.

Powys let the knocker fall twice, the sound tumbling away into the slender Georgian house.

The barbed tower of St John's soared above the surrounding roofs, almost shockingly close to this discreet but hardly modest pagan temple.

Nobody answered the knock. Powys glanced at Juanita for guidance.

'Try again.' She was tense. 'They've got to be here. Where else would they be?'

'You OK?'

Stupid question. She looked close to fainting, her face taut as parchment. It was a lovely face but not iridescent, not mesmeric. He wanted to take her home, come back alone. Smash a window with a brick, storm the place. Drag Diane out of there. Get them all the hell out of this increasingly *un*holy town before they, too, like Jim Battle, like Woolly, fell under the malaise.

Powys raised the knocker again. This time, when it fell back on the metal plate, the door glided eerily open. 'Of course,' Juanita said. 'Electronic.'

She followed him into the hallway. There was nobody waiting for them. He saw closed doors and . . .

'Bloody hell. What's that?'

In a corner, a tangle of dead branches rose sombrely from a black tub. The branches were wound with holly and mistletoe and there was a circle of small stones on the carpet around the tub.

'I suspect it's . . . what you might call a Solstice tree,' Juanita said.

On the topmost sprig, where the silver yuletide fairy might be expected to perch, a large, white mushroom sprouted flabbily.

'It's obscene.'

'. . .'s pretty, isn' it? 'S extremely . . . pretty.'

'God!' Powys found himself clutching Juanita's arm. One of the doors had opened; the shape which hung there was as white and moist as the mushroom.

She wore her druidic white robe with gold edging. It hung open, exposing a black satin shift. There was a huge gold torc around the neck, glittery slippers on the feet, a sheen of perspiration on the face.

'Who're you?' She was obviously pissed as a newt.

'Wanda,' Juanita thought rapidly. 'I'll come straight to the point. We're looking for Diane. You remember Diane?'

'Diane Fortune?' the Druid giggled. 'Oh gawd, Diane bloody Fortune.'

He should have recognised her; she was, after all, famous.

'That's right,' Juanita said tensely. 'Diane Fortune.'

The eyes unclouded for a moment. 'You're not Diane Fortune. I know who you are. You're that woman from the bookshop. Anita. Been away, haven't you? Something happened to you, what the hell was it? Come and tell me about it. Is this man with you?' She peered at Powys. 'Do I know you, darling? Think I'd've remembered. 'Stonishingly few shaggable men in this town. Place is full of *new* men, show 'em your tits and they offer to do the washing-up.'

Dame Wanda cackled.

Juanita adjusted a glove with her teeth. 'Wanda,' she said very deliberately, 'may I present JM Powys, the writer . . . and bastard son of John Cowper Powys. JM, this is Dame Wanda Carlisle.'

And whispered to Powys, 'Go with it. We have to make her talk. Put your hand up her robe if you have to.'

She was drowning.

In a red tide.

Thick, salty wetness in her mouth. She awoke in terror from a long, long, long sleep, with blood in her mouth.

Breath bubbling through blood.

Blood drying on cold arms.

She said, 'Please . . . Have I been in an accident?'

What makes you think that?

'I feel . . . I can't feel . . .'

No, lie down. You're all right. You're fine. No, you haven't been in an accident.'

'But I . . . No. I don't remember.'

But I'm sorry to tell you, my dear, I'm very sorry to tell you that you were attacked.

'I . . . I don't remember . . . I don't remember what . . .'

You were – be calm – you were raped, Diane.

'NoooOOOOO!'

Diane. Be calm, my dear. Give me your arm.

'D'you know what I thought?' Wanda Carlisle demanded. 'D'you know why I took a short while opening the door?' Thought it was little fucking Verity. My goddess, what a bore that woman is. Come in, come in. Solstice felishi . . . flicitations. Have some mulled Bowermead plonk. Dreadful piss.'

They followed her into the opulent room with the velvet drapes, the gold braiding and a superior coal-effect gas fire. Dame Wanda fumbled at the drinks cabinet and knocked over a brass lamp. 'Bloody thing.'

Powys righted the lamp. Wanda squinted at him. She wore lots of mascara which had blotched and run. She looked as though she'd been shot through both eyes.

When she flopped down on the sofa, Juanita sat next to her. 'Wanda, listen to me. Where's Diane? You remember Diane. Plump girl. Jenna brought her last night. And Ceridwen. Was Ceridwen here?'

'Nobody's here, darling, nobody 't all.'

'You're saying you're alone? All alone in this big house?'

Wanda poured wine, clumsily. 'We're all of us alone, Anita.'

'And chilled by the draught of death. Yeah. Wanda, where is Ceridwen?'

If she could use her hands, Powys thought, she'd be shaking the great actress until her torc rattled.

'C'ridwen's gawn. All gawn.'

'All? Who?'

'C'ridwen. Domini. Diane Fortune.'

'Diane. Diane is with them. Where? Where are they, Wanda?'

'Fuck should I know. I'm just an outer . . . outer circler. Don't tell *us* anything. I sit and I drink and I wait for Enlightenment.' She thrust a brimming wineglass at Juanita. 'Try this. Old Pennard makes it. Ghastly piss.'

Juanita didn't move. Powys swooped and plucked the glass from Wanda's hand, took a sip, grimaced. Wanda laughed.

'Treads the grapes himself, shouldn't wonder. They're on their uppers, you know, s'why he's so keen for the bloody road to go through. Done a dirty deal with Government for about fifty acres. Got a drink, have you, darling?'

'Yes,' said Juanita.

'But we're going . . .' Wanda stabbed her in the chest with a gold-encrusted forefinger, '. . . to stop them. Yes we are. C'ridwen will cast the most enormous sodding spell. Not that *I'll* be there. Bitches. I'm not toly . . . totally stupid. Know I'm just a figure-head. Also kept for menial chores like looking after little fucking Verity.'

'What's the problem with Verity? I thought you were friends.'

'Lord above,' said Wanda, 'I'm a fucking *actress*.' She leaned her head back into the sofa's gold-brocaded cushions. 'D'you know what I've to do today? Have to invite her for Solstice tomorrow. Gawds, up at dawn to join the fucking bishop on the Tor and then Verity for the duration. You imagine that? Verity for Solstice? Stringy old bird, no breast.'

Wanda cackled. She adjusted herself on the sofa, picked up an imaginary phone.

'Oh, but darling, you simply *must* come. No way can you spend Solstice alone in that dreary, dreary house. And the other point, you see, is Dilys – my housekeeper – has *gawn down* with this awful *bug*. Verity *would* you, *could* you . . . I've a lovely room, overlooking St John's . . .'

Wanda beamed. Lecturing Juanita now, pleased with herself. She seemed to have forgotten all about Powys.

'Double whammy, darling. You see, she'll be desperate to come, but she'll feel it her duty to stay in that hellhole – so the clincher will be the housekeeper line. Housemaid mentality, that woman.

Got to be *doing* for people or she doesn't feel jus . . . justified. In living.'

Powys nodded to Juanita and moved quietly to the door.

'Piece of cake,' Wanda was saying. 'Putty, that woman. Dear little parcel under the Solstice tree. Set of naff hankies with a mongrammed V. Basket of pot-pourri . . .'

Powys slipped out of the room and back down the thickly carpeted stairs.

He entered Cauldron country. There was a huge drawing room and library, perhaps two rooms knocked into one. A lecture room now, with about thirty chairs in rows. Shelves around the walls held about twice as many books as you could find in Carey and Frayne, but the same kind of stuff. Alphabetically arranged. Under Fortune, he found about forty volumes, some different editions of the same book. Under Powys, nothing.

Choosy. Or maybe no male authors.

On a plinth at the far end of the room sat an enormous, crude goddess-figure, not unlike the thing in the Goddess Shop window but carved out of oak with bangles and necklaces of mistletoe.

It was all very tidy. No smells of herbs or incense. But for the goddess, it might have been a conference suite in a hotel. There was another door, between bookshelves.

Powys found himself in Wanda's Home Temple.

'It didn't make sense,' he told Juanita outside. 'It was done up like Tutankhamun's tomb, only more comfortable. Sofas, drapes, nice coloured pillars. A stone altar, fat candles. It felt as phoney as that woman looks. Why did she come here?'

'Fell in love with the whole Avalon bit,' Juanita said. 'That's the official story. The truth is, she went to dry out at a discreet New-Agey sort of health hydro a couple of miles out of town. Ceridwen's friend Jenna worked there, realised that here was a woman with unlimited wealth in need of a Cause. The reason I know this, my reflexologist, Sarah, was doing sessions there two days a week. Jenna wasted no time introducing Wanda to Ceridwen. Who administered a little psychic psychotherapy. Next thing, Wanda's bought this house and is spending a bomb on it.'

'I don't claim to be heavily attuned to this kind of thing,' Powys said. 'But if there's ever been a heavy ritual in that house—'

'It's somewhere else, isn't it? This place is a front.'

Juanita shivered. She looked ill now; Powys was scared for her.

'When Wanda set up here, this was when The Cauldron really surfaced.' Over her scarf, Juanita's nose was blue. 'It became *the* goddess group virtually overnight. All kinds of women who'd never been seen at the Assembly Rooms attended Cauldron meetings and lectures because of Wanda. Including Verity.'

'The lady with the Pixhill papers. I think we need to collect them, don't you?'

'What about Diane?'

'She's not here, Juanita. She may have been brought here last night but they've taken her somewhere else. Where does Ceridwen live?'

'Tiny little flat near the Glastonbury Experience arcade. She won't be there. Too obvious.' Juanita walked to the end of the mews, where it led into High Street. 'Time is it?'

'Nearly ten-thirty.'

'She's been missing for over twelve hours.'

'We could tell the police.'

'She's twenty-seven. We can't say she's missing from home.'

Juanita's teeth were chattering. Her brown eyes were full of sickness.

'You're going home,' Powys said. 'Now.'

The sleet had eased, but it was very cold and the sky around the tower of St John's foamed with purplish cloud.

FOUR

PIXHILL'S GRAVE

For the first time, Pel Grainger had his partner with him, the psychotherapist and sociologist Eloise Castell, a slender blonde with a mid-European accent who never seemed to smile. Verity had seen her at gatherings of The Cauldron, but they had not spoken.

Shivering, despite her body-warmer, Verity followed the two of them up the garden under a hard sky which sporadically spat out sharp, grey fragments of itself. Verity felt an ominous tug on her hip with every step. It could not simply be arthritis; it had come too suddenly.

It felt like Colonel Pixhill's ghost. Urging her to stop them, bring these foolish people back.

But Dr Grainger was jovial and bulging with confidence. He hadn't even knocked at the door; she'd just seen them both walking briskly through the garden gate.

'See, just because people can't drink this water, Verity,' Dr Grainger called back cheerfully, 'that is no reason to seal the well.'

Against the weather, he wore a thick black cloak like the ones church ministers wore for winter funerals.

'But surely,' Verity ventured, hurrying to keep up, 'if anyone was ill, they could then sue us for some enormous amount.'

'Not if there's a sign specifically warning them not to drink. Hell, you seal off an old well, you're blocking an ancient energy flow. Water – and darkness – must not, not ever, be stifled.'

The garden, extending now to little more than three-quarters of an acre, was well tended by Verity close to the house, a small area of lawn which she kept mown and its edges neatly trimmed. Then it narrowed, a rockery began and so did the wilderness.

'Do be careful, Dr Grainger. Unfortunately, there are brambles and nettles. We did once have a part-time gardener. But when the well had to be sealed and people no longer came to it . . .'

'You know, Verity, the more I think about this, the more incredible ... See, it's clear from the name that this house was built in this location, all those centuries ago, precisely because of the well. No wonder it lost its identity, turned in on itself. You have a scythe or something?'

'I'm sorry, no.'

'That an old spade over there? Would you pass it to me? Thanks.'

He began to slash at the brambles, laying bare what used to be a narrow path. Verity, who hadn't been to this end of the garden in many years, seemed to remember there once being cobblestones.

Ms Castell made no attempt to assist – indeed seemed uninterested in what her partner was doing. She paid no heed to Verity either, but gazed beyond the boundary of Meadwell's land to where Glastonbury Tor hung above them, its base bristling with trees, its church tower black as a roosting crow.

Dr Grainger, his back to Verity, looked disturbingly Neanderthal as he swung the spade like an axe, smashing through a clump of tall thistles. Verity clutched her body-warmer to her throat. She saw that Ms Castell was watching her now, with a crooked little smile. *I don't like you*, Verity thought suddenly. She was not one to make snap decisions about people and wondered if this was another warning communicated to her by the Colonel.

Dr Grainger let out a small yip. 'Hey, I think we found it.' He stepped back. 'Goddam, is this a crime or is this a crime?'

They had emerged into a circle of concrete surrounded by a low wall, bramble-barbed and overhung with twisted, brittle bushes, most of them clearly dead or dying.

'Yeah,' said Dr Grainger. 'I feel it. All is cool.'

At the centre of the circle was a raised concrete plinth about four feet in diameter. He stabbed at it; the spade rang dully on the concrete.

Chalice Well, where the Holy Grail was said to have lain, was at the top of a lovely garden by the foot of Chalice Hill, which flanked the Tor. Below the well were circular pools of red-brown water. It was owned by the Chalice Well Trust, and on summer days people would pay an entrance fee and sit or lie on the grass, eyes closed, in meditation. Verity had always wanted to think the Meadwell had been like this once, a place of ancient peace.

It looked harsh and desolate now, and, in truth, she had never seen it otherwise. When she'd arrived to take up the post of housekeeper, the Meadwell had already been partially sealed and Colonel Pixhill never spoke of it.

'You have a pickaxe someplace?'

'Oh!' Verity stumbled, feeling a sudden, intense glow of pain at her hip. Almost immediately it began to fade. 'Dr Grainger, I really don't think . . .'

'Hmmm. There may be too much light. There a metal cover under here? Like with the Chalice Well?'

'I believe so, but . . .'

'Yeah,' he said thoughtfully. 'See, you hit it with harsh daylight after all these years, the shock could completely negate the effect. Am I right here, Eloise?'

Ms Castell stood back. 'I sink the well should certainly be in shadow when the cover is raised. The emanations will be powerful after all these years of confinement.'

'And the energy goes kind of . . . whoosh. Whereas we need a gentle, subtle . . . mingling.'

He made sinuous, snaking movements with his hands. Verity felt herself begin to tremble.

Ms Castell said, 'Maybe first we put over it a tent. To subdue the light, ya?'

Verity grasped the stump of a dead tree to steady herself.

'Dr Grainger, are you a Christian?'

'What?' The question seemed to throw him.

'I'm sorry, it's just that the type of clothing you habitually wear makes you seem rather like a priest, so I . . .'

'Well.' He gave it some thought, pursing his little round lips. 'I guess I think of myself as a scientist first. My life's a search for understanding. I don't like to be too much in awe. And also there's the tenebral conflict. "Out of the darkness and into the light." I can't buy that. Christianity makes too many naive assumptions, I guess. That answer your question?'

'Yes. I'm sorry.' Verity turned back to the old house crouching in the shadows of the grey morning. 'I don't think I can let you do this.'

Dr Grainger froze, the spade in mid-air. 'Whaaat?'

'I cannot let you expose the Meadwell.'

'Verity?' He peered at her as though he thought she might have been replaced by someone else and he hadn't noticed.

'I'm very sorry, Dr Grainger.' She rose up in her tiny shoes. 'The Colonel would not wish it.'

'The Colonel?' Dr Grainger was half-grinning in amazement. 'We are talking here about Pixhill? The *late* Pixhill?'

'I sink,' said Ms Castell in her somehow unconvincing mid-European murmur, 'zat Colonel Pixhill felt himself to be in a defensive position as regards the world in general. He wanted to close himself in, to seal up all points of access. The well permits water from the hill, maybe from under the Tor, to enter his domain, and so . . .' She shrugged.

All around lay rubble and uprooted dead bushes, their whitened branches like bones. Verity was beset by the disturbing sensation of Dr Grainger and Ms Castell hacking into Colonel Pixhill's grave. How dare this woman speculate about the Colonel's state of mind?

'Please leave.'

Dr Grainger kicked away a slab of concrete dislodged by his spade.

'I don't think so,' he said. 'This is important to me now.'

Juanita's head twisted on the pillow. Her hair felt damp on her neck. She could hardly focus on the thin red line slicing Jim's painting in half on the wall opposite the bed.

'I'm going to call a doctor,' Powys said. He sounded scared. That made it worse. She was frightened for Diane and he was scared for her.

'No. Have you got that? You know what a doctor would say. And I'm not. I'm not going back. Just been overdoing it. I need a rest. And the worry . . .'

A glass of still spring water stood on the bedside table, a red and white striped straw in it. She tried to sit up and take a sip. She fell back.

Powys held the glass for her. 'I'm not leaving you like this.'

'You've got to.' She tried to smile. 'Besides, you know how badly you want to know about the missing Pixhill stuff.'

'It'll wait.'

'It won't wait. None of this will wait.'

'OK, if you won't see a doctor, what about Banks?'

'I'd rather die, if you don't mind.'

'Christ, Juanita . . .'

'He's an old woman. He'll fuss around. OK, OK, call him. He's in the index.'

She closed her eyes. Patches of grey and black coalescing.

Last transition . . . disillusion and decay . . . draught of death.

'Hey . . . will you look at this?' Dr Grainger squatted down. 'It's iron and there's some kind of a symbol here, if I can just . . .'

'Get out,' Verity said icily.

'. . . get this slab of concrete out the way . . . Come check this out, Eloise. You know how the lid of the Chalice Well has these interlinked circles symbolising the conjoining of worlds? See, what we're looking at here . . .'

Verity flew at him.

The way Stella, the little cat, had flown at her from the cupboard on the night of the Abbot's Dinner. Unfortunately, she didn't have the claws for it; her housework-blunted nails raked ineffectually at his tight black shirt. She felt a wrench from her hip and stumbled.

'Verity, for Chrissakes, what the fuck is the matter with you?' The spade fell back into the beaten-down bushes behind Dr Grainger. Verity was aware of Eloise Castell drifting mildly away, watching the struggle with that same supercilious, unconcerned smile on her thin face.

'Please go!' Verity was on her knees in the dirt. 'Please leave at once.'

'Verity, c'mon, listen to me.' Grainger put his hands on her shoulders, holding her away from him, holding her down. 'Hear me out.'

'I don't want to know. I'm grateful for all your help. With the darkness. Please send me a bill.'

Her hip was aching abominably now but he wouldn't let her rise.

'Verity, listen up. My studies are entering a new phase, extending naturally into the psychic ecology of caves and tunnels, and ancient wells are an aspect of the subterranean tenebral network

I had neglected to consider. Until Eloise here made some connections for me. Now, if you think that the, ah, ambulant shade of Colonel Pixhill is gonna be offended, then we'll respect that. We'll replace the covering. Later. After we check it out.'

He was very strong. Verity couldn't move.

Ms Castell was kicking at the crumbled concrete with her cowboy boots. 'Pel, ve are vasting time. Maybe I fetch Oliver.'

'Verity,' Dr Grainger persisted with his well-honed soothing intensity, 'nobody appreciates more than I do the kinda stress you've been under. What the—?'

'Psychic ecology, eh?' The bushes parted. A man stood there. 'Subterranean tenebral network. Wow.'

The man wandered down from the bushes, a black and white dog at his heels.

'Sorry, I was just passing, couldn't help overhearing. Any chance you could decode this impenetrable jargon for me?'

Dr Grainger's grip on Verity's shoulders eased. She scrambled up.

'You see . . . I may be wrong here, but it sounded like . . . you know . . . complete bollocks.'

He stepped down to the Meadwell plinth. He was quite a young man, although his hair was grey. The dog did not follow him. It stopped at the edge of the bushes and growled. It had only three legs. The young man smiled.

'Bugger me, it's Pel Grainger, isn't it? Sorry, Doctor Grainger. That would be, I think, an honorary postal doctorate from somewhere like the University of Nerdsville, Indiana, right?'

'Who the fuck are you?' Dr Grainger picked up the spade.

'I'm the, um, earth-mysteries correspondent of *The Avalonian*. I'll be reviewing your book.' The young man shook his head. 'Serious bullshit, Pel, but you don't need me to tell you that.'

'You better watch your mouth . . .'

'Or you'll attack me with the spade?'

'Pel,' said Ms Castell. 'We go.'

Dr Grainger started forward.

'Pel,' snapped Ms Castell.

Dr Grainger snarled and hurled the spade to the ground.

*

Grainger and his partner walked back to the garden and down the path to the gate. Neither of them looked back.

Powys pushed some slabs of concrete back over the well cover with his shoe, waiting until they were off the premises before stepping down into a clump of dead thistles, stark as brown pylons.

He was glad to be away from Pixhill's well. As for Arnold – he wouldn't go near it.

'Thank you.' The little woman, Verity Endicott, smiled hesitantly. 'Thank you for your help.'

'It was a pleasure,' Powys said honestly.

'Would you like a cup of tea, perhaps?'

'I would love a cup of tea. I, um, I was coming to see you. I knocked on the front door, but everybody seemed to be up here, so . . .' He grinned apologetically. 'I slipped over into the field, came round the back way.'

He followed her back towards the house. 'You seem to be acquainted with Dr Grainger's work,' Miss Endicott said.

'A little.'

The doorway of Meadwell was like a fissure in an ancient tree. She vanished into it like an elf. He followed her.

Arnold didn't. Arnold shuffled around on the path, looking uncomfortable.

'OK,' Powys said. 'What's wrong?'

Arnold's first peculiar reaction had been when they turned into the Meadwell drive. Two yew trees meeting overhead, gnarled, full-bellied trees knotted with parasites. And Arnold had started to pant. When the house came into view, with its weathered stone, mullioned windows and leafless creepers like torn fishing nets on the rocks, the dog had begun to whine. He'd been OK once they got into the field, but he wouldn't go near the well.

Dowser's dog. Arnold used to go out with Henry. Dogs like to please. Sniff out drugs or dead bodies. Arnold was attuned to less physical items. Well, all dogs were psychic to an extent; just that Arnold had learned to tell you what most dogs would be surprised you didn't already know about.

'We'll discuss this later,' Powys told him, then picked him up, and carried him into the house. 'You don't mind dogs, Miss Endicott?'

'I love all animals.' A note of sadness there.

They entered the darkest room you could imagine in daylight. Stone walls like a castle. Corners which disappeared into black shadow. He made out a huge inglenook, like the maw of hell. A long, oak table. He stopped. This would just have to be the table where they'd laid out Colonel Pixhill.

'Please sit down,' Miss Endicott said. 'I'm sorry, I don't even know your name.'

'Powys.' He put Arnold down on the flagstones. 'Joe Powys.'

At that, Miss Endicott seemed to freeze. Her woodland mammal's eyes were startled and then confused. He saw that the skin around the eyes was doughy, suggesting exhaustion. Her dry, puckered lips formed the word –

Powys.

But only a thin ribbon of breath emerged. At that moment, Powys could almost swear the shadows in the room were moving. How could shadows move without light? He could never live here; he'd be constantly walking into the darkest corners just to reassure himself there was nothing there that really moved, always scared that there would be something – grisly shadow-teeth closing on his fingers.

'Powys?' said Miss Endicott. Her small eyes coming slowly to life, like the valves in an old radio.

As Arnold screamed.

It was a sound Powys had never heard from Arnold, nor from any dog. 'Hey.' He bent down and grabbed at him. Arnold's head came up, his ears flat, his eyes bulging with fear and a kind of fever; when Powys reached for him he lunged and snapped, his teeth clicking together in the air, once, like a mousetrap.

And then skittered away, his three sets of claws scraping frantically at the flags until he reached the oak door and began to hurl himself at it, as if he wanted to smash his own skull, break his own neck.

FIVE

PRE-ORDAINED

'Don't do this, Woolly,' Sam said. 'Whatever you got in mind, don't do it.'

At Woolly's shop, he'd found Hughie Painter and his brother Gav helping to board up the broken window. Woolly was loading stuff into his Renault. Looking uncharacteristically dowdy in dark jeans, a green waterproof jacket. He'd cut off his pony-tail, shaved his head at the front. He looked older and unhappy.

'Where you gonner go?' Sam planting himself between Woolly and the Renault's raised back door.

'Well, first off,' Woolly said, 'I'm going to the cops. To confess.'

'To what?'

'To whatever they wanner charge me with, man. Get it over, that's the main thing. Then I'm off to walk the Line. Park the car some place, take my bags and my tent. Walk the Line and think. Maybe when I get back, somebody'll've nicked the car, save me some hassle, 'cause I don't really wanner see that car again.'

Sam shook his head, mystified. 'Sorry, Woolly. Slight generation gap problem here. Walk the Line – is this some old Johnny Cash reference I wouldn't understand?'

Woolly smiled. 'Sam, man . . . the St Michael Line. I need to think. I need to walk until I'm shagged out, camp out by the Line and pray something sorts itself out. People don't wanner see me. I'm bad news, no getting round that.'

'No,' Sam said. 'You're wrong. Completely. You're the best councillor we ever had. 'Sides which, you'll die of exposure out there. Look . . . Here's Hughie – he's got masses of kids, Mr Fertile. Yet, here he is, nailing boards across your window. Hughie, come on, is Woolly gonner weather this one or isn't he?'

'Ain't that simple, Sammy,' said Big Hughie. 'My first reaction, I'm angry. I think why'd he do that? Is his brain even working? Then I think, well, he's a friend, he's a good guy. Best councillor, as you said, we ever had. Besides which, it could've been any one of us.'

Hughie brushed sawdust from his beard.

'What other people're gonner think, though, in the final analysis, I can't say. There's a lot of shit going round right now, Sammy, lot of extremism. So, well . . . maybe Woolly does need to get away for a while.'

Sam shoved his hands in his pockets. Not what he wanted to hear. He stared at his trainers for a couple of seconds.

'OK. Spare me two minutes, Woolly. Over there. Excuse us, lads.'

He led Woolly out of the square, away from Hughie and Gav, over towards St Benedict's, where it was quiet.

'I've been at a bit of a loose end this morning,' Sam said. 'I just walked round, looking for Diane, asking if anyone's seen her.'

'Diane's still missing?'

'Since last night.'

'Shit,' said Woolly. 'Like I know she's done this before, but . . .'

'I don't care if she's done it before or not. Things are different now.'

'Sheesh,' Woolly said, looking hard at Sam. 'I can see they are.'

'Yeah. Ain't life funny? Let me get this other thing out. I've been talking to people. In and out of the shops. People I haven't talked to in years. Both sides of the fence – what we thought was a fence. There's two topics on everybody's lips. The crash, obviously. But the other one's Bowkett and his Tor Bill. Most people, they just didn't realise. They just never thought it could happen.'

'Most people want it to happen,' Woolly said. 'They've had it with the New Age.'

'I reckon most people *don't* want it to happen. OK, maybe a lot do, but still less than half. Lot of folk out there got no big feelings about magic and earth-forces and all this crap, but they do care about freedom. And they don't want bloody Griff Daniel back.'

'So you stand against him. Take on your old man.'

'Aw, Woolly, some of these people like to go into the countryside and shoot rabbits, watch the hunt and that. They don't want me neither. But I reckon you'll see the size of the opposition, look, at dawn tomorrow, when the Bishop goes up the Tor. This

Christian-pagan common ground stuff, it might be crap, but if the Bishop comes out against Archer and Bowkett . . .'

'Better I'm not there, Sam. I got a bad feeling about that. Better I'm miles away.'

Sam had a major struggle with himself, at this point, not to tell Woolly about the evil road burrowing through Bowermead, leaving the ashes of slaughtered trees.

'Also,' Woolly said, 'on a personal level, this may be the last chance I get to walk the Line before it's sliced up.' He put out his hand. 'You're a good boy, Sam. I always said that. Diane could do worse.'

He shook Sam's hand solemnly and walked towards the church.

And Sam thought, with a horrible jolt, *He's not going to come back. Not ever. He's going to be found dead in his little tent near some forgotten standing stone.*

'Woolly!' His sense of loss compounded. 'Woolly, listen, you gotter help us. We're all shit scared here. About Diane. About the way this town's cracking up before our eyes. You can't just walk out on us. You can't!'

Verity unscrewed the top of the brown phial. 'Dr Bach's Rescue Remedy. If you can hold his mouth open, I shall put three drops on his tongue.'

'Does it work on dogs?' Powys held open the car door. It was snowing freely now.

'Why not?' said Verity simply. She leaned into the car from the other side. Arnold lay on the back seat, a tartan travelling rug half over him. Powys patted him and then, as if to give Arnold the chance to bite him, nuzzled his face into the furry neck.

Arnold licked him apologetically. It was different out here.

'Do you know what this is?' Powys asked her.

'I think I do.' Verity squeezed the rubber bulb on the end of the glass dropper, her wizened face tight with determination. They had bathed quite a deep cut beneath the dog's ear, where he'd caught it on a nail protruding from the door. They'd felt around his skull, finding no obvious damage. But his breathing was disturbingly erratic.

'It's simply the house,' Verity said, like she was shedding a great weight. 'All animals hate it here. A few weeks ago I had to take a very placid little cat to the Cats' Protection League to be re-homed. She went berserk. Attacked me.'

They sat in the front. The snow accumulated on the recumbent wipers. Powys was not anxious to go back in the house.

'How do you stand it?'

'I'm a very dense person. I do not See. And lately there's been Dr Grainger to . . . help me.'

'Help you to cope with the dark?'

'I thought he was harmless. I was very lonely, you see. And my friend Wanda Carlisle is very persuasive.'

'Between them they persuaded you that this tenebral therapy nonsense was going to help you cope with what the house was throwing at you?'

'That's exactly it. Foolish, wasn't I? And yet when Oliver Pixhill came and made it clear he wanted me out, Dr Grainger was very kind.'

'This is Colonel Pixhill's son?'

She nodded. 'I thought they didn't know each other. Dr Grainger appeared to be on my side. I thought he was harmless, you see.'

'He might be harmless. His theories might be complete bollocks. But bonding with the dark, while unlikely to cause problems in most places, could be . . . Well, in a place like this it could be close to suicidal.'

'I've been very stupid. Loneliness, I suppose.' Verity looked out at the snow. 'Do you know why *you're* here, Mr Powys?'

'Joe. I'm here to collect a parcel for Juanita Carey.'

She turned and examined his face.

'It's funny,' she said. 'You don't look at all like him.'

'Hawthorn. Hops. A little rosemary. Some other things,' Matthew Banks said.

'What's it for?' Juanita felt utterly limp. She'd drunk the herbal mixture and about three pints of water, most of which she'd surely sweated away.

It began in her feet, a prickly heat, like warm goose-pimples, crept up her legs like unwelcome, flaccid hands . . . and then her whole body, instant sauna, breasts and face burning up.

At least the duvet lay quite comfortably, for the first time, on her flayed thighs, to which Matthew had applied some ointment; it had stung like hell at first, but that was preferable to the other thing which came and came again, a hot tide, four or five times in an hour and left her flung against the headboard like a rag doll.

'What's happened to me? Did I just do too much too soon, or what?'

'Forgive me,' Matthew said. 'But when did you last have your period?'

No. No, no *no*.

'Missed one. Maybe two. Shock, they said. It's normal.'

The last transition for a woman . . .

'What are you suggesting?' She panicked, hitched herself up on her elbows. 'Listen, Christ, it doesn't happen like this, it can't be, I mean, it doesn't happen from *nothing* like *overnight*? It doesn't come at you time and time again. Not . . . nothing and then . . . Jesus Christ, Matthew . . .?'

'No.' He straightened the duvet. 'No. It shouldn't happen like that.'

They were all there. All the main ones, anyway: *Weymouth Sands, Maiden Castle, Wolf Solent, Porius, Morwyn, Owen Glendower, A Glastonbury Romance* – well, naturally. And the *Autobiography*.

Hardbacks, too, several in leather. She had them arranged in what might once have been a bread-oven in the jagged inglenook.

Powys shrank back. He'd never seen all the books together before. Like a reception committee.

Took you long enough, boy.

'What?' Almost a yelp. His senses swimming, or maybe drowning.

'I said I'd be most honoured', Verity repeated, 'if you would sign them for me. Later, perhaps?'

'I'm sorry?' He was imagining all the books spinning out of the black hole, whizzing around his head, blown by unearthly laughter.

'I doubted him. Poor Major Shepherd assured me that someone would come. He said I would know.'

'Um, look . . . Maybe we're both in danger of over-reacting. Do you think?'

The high melodrama of it might normally have made him smile. Anywhere but here, in a room like an ancient vault, haunted by the leather-bound spirit of Uncle Jack of blessed memory.

The collected works seemed to shimmer on the shelves in triumph. Pre-ordained. In this hard, cold, uncompromising house, it all seemed horribly pre-ordained.

He thought about what Diane had said. About the three of them. George Pixhill, John Cowper Powys and Dion Fortune. The Avalonians.

Grey-green light from mean, leaded windows tinctured the silver lettering on the spines of Uncle Jack's books. Verity and Powys sitting once more at the old, shadowed dining table, where the Colonel's body had lain in state. A brown teapot and cups on it now.

'He came here?' Powys said.

'Only once while I was here. A tall and immensely striking man with curly hair and a hooked nose. He sat . . . well, where you are sitting now. I was so much in awe, having read his work, that I could not speak to him, let alone ask for his signature on the books.'

A brown-paper parcel lay on the table between them.

'Are you going to open it?' Verity asked.

'It isn't addressed to me.'

Mrs J Carey. Very Private.

Very firmly written, fountain pen job.

'Do you know what's in here, Verity?'

'I'm perhaps as curious as you are, Mr . . . Joe.'

Powys felt on edge. The nervous part of him needed to be well out of Meadwell by nightfall. Something was building here, and it wasn't a new Jerusalem. Blake's *dark, Satanic mills*: in this house you could almost hear those mill wheels grinding.

The other side of Glastonbury. It had always been here.

As had Verity. And not being *sensitive* was not necessarily a defence. She'd survived, perhaps, because she hadn't yet been personally attacked. But now Grainger would go back and report to whoever had set him up – and Wanda – to come on to Verity, get inside Meadwell, and into the well itself, for whatever reason.

This puzzled him, too. If they wanted to penetrate that well, why not come at night – Grainger's chosen medium – go through the field, as Powys had done, hack it open at their leisure?

'Can I use your phone?'

The telephone was in the kitchen, a lighter room because of its white walls, one of which bulged out unpleasantly, like a corpse under a sheet.

Powys called Carey and Frayne. He didn't get the answering machine, he got Matthew Banks.

'She's sleeping at last,' Banks said. 'I've made her comfortable. She shouldn't be disturbed. I shall stay with her as long as I can.'

He left a severe pause.

'Glastonbury as we know it, Mr Powys, may be about to collapse into a chaos unseen since the Dark Ages, but, as Juanita appears to be my patient now, I must put her interests first. I hope you understand that.'

'Yes,' Powys said. 'I'm glad. If she wakes up before I'm back, tell her everything's . . . tell her I'm doing my best.'

Whatever that meant.

He went back to open the brown-paper parcel.

SIX

EXTREME AND EVERLASTING

THE OLD VICARAGE
COLN ST MARY
GLOUCESTERSHIRE

My dear Mrs Carey,

Your no doubt somewhat bewildered receipt of this parcel follows either my death or my discreet removal to some secluded nursing home where the wheelchairs are locked up at night to ensure the inmates do not escape!

No, do not mourn for me, my dear. Save all your grief. You may well need it.

Let me say, at the outset, that burdening you with this matter is something in the way of a last resort, the flailing gesture of an old, tired and sadly ineffectual man who has, for some years, been attempting to stay afloat in waters untold fathoms beyond his depth. I was hoping to, as they say, sort things out myself, with the help of others. This has clearly not been possible in the time left to me, especially as there now seem to be remarkably few 'others' I feel able to trust. Also the situation seems to have escalated at an alarming rate, as poor George implied it might as we approach the Millennium.

Be assured, however, that I would not expect you to do anything beyond coming to the rescue of my good and staunch friend, Verity Endicott, who is in grave and mortal danger, standing as she does directly in the path of (and, God help me, I do not exaggerate) an old and utterly merciless evil.

Oh, Mrs Carey, how it pains me to have to use language of such Biblical intensity. Yet I beg of you not to dismiss it as nonsense as I, to my shame, have done in the past.

As a highly intelligent and worldly woman, you must have wondered many times why, in seeking a strictly limited outlet for George Pixhill's Diary, we approached you. And, indeed, your shop was hardly picked at random from Yellow Pages. The truth is that, despite your merits as a bookseller (and, indeed, your not inconsiderable personal charms) you were chosen primarily because of your long association with Diane Ffitch, a young woman who, I am obliged to say, may now also be in danger of a most extreme and everlasting nature. I do not know the girl, but I rather suspect it would be unwise to show her this material directly. Perhaps the facts could be broken to her in stages. I leave this to your personal assessment of Miss Ffitch's state of mind.

As you can imagine, my association with Colonel George Pixhill (and how often I have cursed the poor man) has compelled me to delve, with a good deal of distaste, into arcane and occult matters better left, in my view, to moulder among the pages of ancient and disreputable books. Perhaps your professional knowledge of such volumes will render some of this more accessible to you than it has, over the years, been to me.

As I may have mentioned, the most important items here are the 'missing' sections of the Pixhill diaries which we were unable, for reasons which will become apparent, to publish.

You have probably asked yourself many times: what was the point in publishing the diaries at all and in such a restricted fashion? Well, firstly, as I have tried to explain, George was most insistent that his knowledge of the Dark Chalice should become not widely known but yet accessible to those who might find it meaningful, at a time when the two-thousand-year-old Glastonbury tradition would face a terrible challenge. (I believe that challenge is upon us – or, rather, upon YOU.)

Secondly, it is especially clear to me now that had we not published when we did the Pixhill diaries would NEVER have seen the light of day. I did not realise for a long time how close George was to the source of it and that some of the danger might emanate from within the Pixhill Trust itself. It can only have been a rare prescience on my part that persuaded me to publish the diaries when we did and to entrust them to an outside agency – that is, your good self.

How drastically things have changed in that short time. I had my health then and there was a sound nucleus of us old comrades at the heart of the Trust. As I write, I am the only founder member *left alive. When you read this, there will be none of us left unclaimed by disease, senility or accidents of the kind which tend to befall the elderly. Had I been a wiser man I might have sought protection.*

Ah, but we are old soldiers, used to an enemy we can perceive. How could we have had any idea of the possible implications of helping out a friend?

I have no more to say. Let George Pixhill speak for himself. Thank you, my dear. From wherever I am, I pray for you, for Verity and for Miss Ffitch.

God bless you all.

Timothy Shepherd.

Powys folded the letter.

In his head a big book fell from a shelf.

A tweed hat swung on a branch.

A steaming black bus roared through the night.

The irony of it did not escape Don Moulder.

He laid the ten-pound notes one by one in the scrap-dealer's outstretched hand.

'. . . three-thirty, three-forty, three-fifty.'

Fat grey snowflakes came down on the yard like sheep at feeding time.

'What you gonner do with it, then?' the scrap dealer asked.

'None o' your business.' Don Moulder wound the rubber band round the remains of his wad.

Three hundred and fifty. Exactly what he'd been paid for letting the parasites in. A terrible rip-off, but it could be bad luck to haggle.

'You wanner start 'im up, have a gander at the engine?' The dealer trying it on now.

'No, thank you.'

'Bloody morbid, you ask me,' said the dealer, bold bugger now he'd got his money.

'Well, no bugger is askin' you. So you keep your trap shut, mister.'

The scrap-dealer grinned, pocketed the money. The extra fifty for the time of delivery.

Don Moulder drew him a little map. 'After dark. Well after dark, all right? No need to knock on the door, I don't want the wife to know. You just leave it there, got that?'

Don walked out to his old Subaru. He didn't want anyone to see it till the Bishop arrived at dawn.

Verity put the letter down.

'Such a kind man,' she said.

'Is that all you can say?' Powys drank half his disgusting camomile tea without blinking. 'This guy thinks you're in mortal danger, standing – he picked up the letter – "in the path of – and, God help me, I do not exaggerate – an old and utterly merciless evil." What does he mean? Do you know? Do you have any idea?'

Verity went prim. 'I really don't consider myself qualified to attempt a definition.'

Powys tried another one. 'What does Grainger think is inside that well?'

'Energy. That is what he said. Energy which has been confined, stifled . . .'

'I heard that, Verity. I didn't believe it. I don't think you believed it.'

They had taken the parcel into the kitchen. Even with all its lights on, the dining room was not the most suitable place in which to read for long.

Verity poured him, to his dismay, more camomile tea.

'Joe, I'm sorry. You will have to excuse my apparent unwillingness to co-operate. I'm unsure. Unsure of what I know and what I only think I know. More than that, I'm unsure of how much the Colonel would wish me to say.'

'He's dead, Verity.'

'He remains, through his Trust, my employer.'

'Who runs the Trust now then?'

'Faceless people,' Verity said. 'Solicitors, accountants. And Oliver. I don't know how Oliver worked his way in. As a mere employee, I am not party to such administrative details.'

'But they didn't get on.'

'I fear that's something of an understatement. After Mrs Pixhill had her breakdown, she and the boy went to live in a rented flat in the town. Neither of them would have understood why the Colonel could not sell Meadwell.'

'Meadwell was the reason for her breakdown?'

'It couldn't have been easy,' Verity said, 'for any of them.'

'And Oliver was resentful?'

'Oliver hated his father, Joe. The thought that the work of the Trust might now be influenced by a man who would do anything to besmirch the Colonel's memory fills me with horror.'

'And what is the work of the Trust? What's its actual purpose?'

'Officially,' Verity said, 'to further the cause of peace and harmony in a troubled world. Rather inexact, I'm afraid.'

'But unofficially?'

'Unofficially . . .' Verity hesitated. 'Unofficially, to prevent Meadwell falling once more into the hands of the Ffitch family.'

'How did my mother die?'

I wondered when you would ask that.

'They told me what she died of. They never told me how she . . .'

Go on.

'I don't know what I'm asking.'

I think you do.

Sometimes she awoke thinking it was morning. Thinking she'd slept a very long time. Sometimes it was as if she'd only minutes before closed her eyes. Sometimes she felt relaxed, sometimes frightfully agitated. Always this question at the back of her mind.

'Someone . . . someone said she was pushed downstairs.'

Well, there you are. You do know, don't you? Do you need the bedpan again? Nurse, fetch a bedpan, please.

'Why won't you tell me? You were there. No one knows more than you.'

Because you must work it out for yourself. And decide what to do about it.

'Who pushed her?'

You know who pushed her. You were very small. Not yet born. But you know. Your mother told you. Through the blood.

SEVEN

LOURDES

And slowly it all began to make a kind of incredible sense.

As he read page after page of primitive typescript, Powys lost all contact with his surroundings. He was entering Pixhill's Avalon.

Here was the lost heart of the diaries. Insert the missing chapter, the missing parts of existing chapters and what you had was no longer the aimless ramblings of a man without a discernible purpose, but the record of a tense, thirty-year defence campaign by the stoical old soldier and – whether she was aware of it or not – a little spinster who could not See.

First, there was the section of the introduction bridging the void between Pixhill's vision of the Tor in a stifling tank and his arrival in Glastonbury. It opened with the Colonel back home, in a military hospital, where . . .

. . . trying to pin down the image, I produced drawing after drawing of the conical hill I had seen and showed it to everyone who came through the ward. They looked at my rough efforts, to humour me, I suppose, and shook their heads. Until, one day, a dapper man in a good-quality brown suit came to visit me. He pulled a chair close to the bed and took from an inside pocket one of my drawings which he said one of the doctors had passed on to him.

'Glastonbury Tor,' he said. 'In Somerset. There is no mistaking it. It is a place we ourselves have been made increasingly aware of lately.'

'We?' I said suspiciously. At which he took out his wallet and produced his papers. Quite an eye-opener. My visitor, one Stanley Willett, turned out to be a highly placed civil servant in the War Ministry. Intelligence, I guessed, for these fellows will never say as much.

He then began to question me closely about my apparent obsession with Glastonbury Tor. He started to throw names at me, one in particular. Had I had any contact, he demanded, with a certain Violet Mary Firth, known to her readers as Dion Fortune?

Well, of course, the name meant nothing at the time and it seemed to me that whatever line of research he was pursuing, I could be of no great assistance. But this was wartime. No time for secrets between fellows on the same side. I therefore, feeling somewhat embarrassed, related to Willett the circumstances of my vision in the desert.

To my surprise, he neither laughed at me nor attempted to belittle the experience. My life, I suppose, would have been happier if he had.

'Do you think the doctors would mind if I were to smoke?' he asked.

'Hardly,' I said. 'All the doctors smoke. Keeps this place going, tobacco.'

We both smoked in silence for some time and then he sat back and observed me shrewdly through his rimless spectacles.

'We've been studying your record, Pixhill. You're a man of intellect rather than action who nevertheless adapted to his circumstances with courage and resourcefulness. We could send you back to the front when you're fit to leave here.'

'As I fully expect you will,' I said.

'Or we could send you to Glastonbury.' He held up my drawing. 'To the Hill of Visions. A very significant spot. Did you know that? Think carefully before you answer.'

My immediate notion was that the Tor concealed some clandestine bomb-proof HQ. It would explain the Secret Service's concern, if some shell-shocked patient at a military hospital was turning out crude drawings of a secret subterranean refuge for Mr Churchill's War Cabinet.

But it was nothing so orthodox. For Mr Stanley Willett was to be my first introduction to Miss Dion Fortune and The Watchers of Avalon.

Powys sat up. So Fortune *had* been Pixhill's 'teacher'. How had Diane known? Pure guess? Wishful thinking?

He'd read about the Watchers of Avalon but, apart from DF, he didn't know who they were or precisely what they'd got up to.

He went outside to check on Arnold, let him out to relieve himself. Arnold did this on a rear wheel of the Mini and then immediately hopped back into the car.

It was nearly dark now and the snow was as fluffy as a sheepskin on the roof of the Mini. Against the snow, Meadwell looked even darker.

Violet Firth/Dion Fortune, said Willett, was an unqualified Freudian psychologist who had been drawn into the occult and had become a member of a rather fashionable magical society of the period known as The Hermetic Order of the Golden Dawn, among whose better-known adherents had been the poet WB Yeats and that sinister shyster Aleister Crowley. Miss Firth (or Mrs Evans, as she was then, though parted from her husband) went on to form her own occult fraternity called the Society of the Inner Light, which drew together her interest in both Christian and pagan mysticism. It was this loose organisation which interested Willett and his colleagues.

For Dion Fortune, it seemed, had joined the War.

We all knew of Hitler's obsession with the occult and Himmler's Aryan fantasies centred on his medieval Schloss. Dion Fortune, it seemed, was convinced the Nazis were using black magic against the Allies and that a suitable defence should be fashioned to harness the 'group mind' of the nation and shield our islands from this alleged psychic onslaught.

Members of the Society of the Inner Light throughout Britain were therefore recruited into the Watchers of Avalon and given their instructions in a series of monthly bulletins from DF herself, working both from London and from her home on the very flank of Glastonbury Tor. As Willett understood it, they were all to meditate at a prearranged time, simultaneously visualising the same powerful cabalistic symbols and forming a kind of psychic wall around these islands.

They were taught to visualise, as the mystical beating heart of the British psyche, a place referred to as the Cavern Under the Hill of Vision. Each week, the minds, the souls, the inner consciousness of the members of the Society of the Inner Light would 'gather' here. Glastonbury Tor, of course. I saw my own drawing with new eyes.

'Seemed harmless enough to us,' Willett said. 'Last thing we'd want to do is discourage this biddy. If all the harebrained mystics in the country are turning their minds against Hitler, it can't harm anyone's morale. But we would like to keep an eye on them. That's where you come in, Pixhill. You've had a rough time. Spot of convalescence in order, I think. Nice place, Somerset.'

'Oh dear,' I said. I felt an excitement tinged with a very definite trepidation. I remember wondering what the Cricketer had let me in for now.

'Perhaps, in a week or so, you could drift along to Glastonbury,' Willett suggested. 'Tell a few people about your, ah, vision. See who you encounter. If these people trust you, we'd like you to stay there. Keeping us informed from time to time about what exactly is going on.'

My eyes widened. 'You mean as a sort of secret agent? As a spy? Me? I was never a master of subterfuge. Not much of an actor, you know.'

Willett chuckled. 'Precisely. You have an honest ingenuous face, Pixhill. And I really don't think we should use words like spy, do you? Thing is – what we really want to know – is all this mumbo jumbo having any actual effect? The fact that you, yourself, stuck in a tank in Libya were getting pretty unmistakable pictures of their so-called Hill of Vision might well suggest that something is being . . . transmitted.'

I was staggered. Had I, in my weakened state, passed to a higher plane of consciousness and become the unwitting recipient of a psychic broadcast by the self-styled Watchers of Avalon?

'You see, if it turns out that this woman is having an impact,' said Willett, 'we want to know about it. Because if it actually works to some extent, I think you'll agree, it should hardly be left in the hands of a collection of eccentric women and fuddled old occultists, however well-intentioned they might be. Get my drift?'

Ah, the arrogance of the man to imagine that a bunch of War Office boffins could take over a mystical tradition over two thousand years old as a psychological weapon.

But, of course, I was intrigued. Whatever the source of that vision of the Tor, I was convinced it had saved my life. Perhaps this *was why. Perhaps this was the part I was destined to play in the liberation of the world from fascism.*

And so, ten days later, upon my discharge from hospital, I journeyed for the first time to Glastonbury.

At this point, the story was picked up by the text of the published diaries. Pixhill's arrival in Glastonbury, his impressions of the town and its people, their wartime spirit.

But in the published diaries, he was hazy about individuals. Especially one.

Powys felt a small thrill of unease. Pixhill's first description of her corresponded so closely to his own impression, formed out of *Avalon of the Heart*, that he couldn't believe he hadn't read it before.

She was waiting for me in the garden, a hefty, jovial woman, comfortably middle-aged. She wore a thick, blue woollen dress with several rows of beads on her mantelpiece bosom. A chairwoman-of-the-Women's-Institute sort of person. Certainly not my idea of a High Priestess of Isis.

'So,' she said. 'You are the young man who has come to our town in pursuit of a vision.'

I nodded, feeling duplicitous in the extreme.

I had been summoned – no better word for it – into the Presence. The previous evening I had spoken of my desert experience to the curious collection of misfits lodging at the house in which I had found accommodation, in the Bovetown area. Now I had been approached by a small boy in a schoolcap who informed me that Mrs Evans would be expecting me for tea at four-thirty.

Her bungalow, among the trees at Chalice Orchard, was a rather more primitive structure than it is today. Someone, it appeared, had donated to her an old army shed or Nissen hut. I had approached it as you would a shrine, with my head down. DF, of course, knew at once why I was almost afraid to raise my eyes.

'Wait,' she commanded. 'Don't look yet. Come this way.' She guided me through a well-tended garden fragrant with the perfume of herbs and on to a small paved area.

'Now,' she said. 'Look up.'

I could feel the blood literally draining from my face as I raised my eyes to the emerald majesty of that all-too-familiar sacred hill, its church tower rushing away from us into the clear spring sky. I do not know if I actually fell to my knees. I know I wanted to.

'Yes,' DF said, as I recovered my faculties. 'That is all I need to know. You are the one.'

I must have blinked. It was one of those moments when the world stands still and you know that your life is about to change for ever. How was I to know then that those moments are all too common-place in the rarefied air of Avalon? It doesn't matter, that was THE moment.

'Well, George,' said DF. 'Don't just stand there like a complete nincompoop. Follow me.'

I suppose that is what I did, from that day until she died a few all-too-short years later. She was the most remarkable person I have ever met. She taught me who I am. And that what we are is seldom what the world sees.

I cannot imagine how many hours I spent in the bungalow at Chalice Orchard, sitting on hand-made wooden chairs and sur-rounded by roughly thrown local pottery, homespun mats and linens, drinking tea from a pot which, as she told me proudly, it would have taken a sledge-hammer to crack. DF, born in North Wales of Yorkshire stock, liked things to be sturdy, honest and with-out compromise. It was hard to imagine her as a robe-and-pentacle person, although, when I saw her thus attired, I believed in her just as completely.

You are the one. As if she knew that I would come. But what would a woman like this want with an invalid soldier whose meta-physical experience was limited to the Cricketer and a fevered dream in a disabled tank? If the Watchers of Avalon needed advice on military tactics, there were surely better-informed sources than myself to tap.

'Ah, the Watchers,' she said when I let slip a reference. *As I had tried to explain to Willett, I have a limited capacity for subterfuge.* 'I won't embarrass you by asking how you knew about that. But yes, we use the idea of Gwyn's cavern as a focus, a gathering point. The energy here, as you obviously realise, is hugely powerful.'

Between DF and Willett, there was no contest as to who was the more formidable. 'I was approached by one of our Intelligence chaps', I confessed at our second meeting, 'to find out if you were having any effect on the Enemy.'

'Ha!' DF slapped her thigh. 'But how wonderful. They are taking us SERIOUSLY? A breakthrough indeed.'

'They do not like to dismiss the idea of a secret weapon,' I said.

At this she grew serious. 'George, you must not let them think of us as engaged in any kind of psychic warfare. Our role is one of protection. To ensure that no jackboot ever steps upon this sacred soil. We are all too aware of the laws of karma to attempt to invoke forces of an offensive nature. No matter how justified we may feel, to launch a psychic attack is to walk the Left Hand Path. The first step along this path is an easy one. To go back requires ten times the strength.'

At this point she produced a copy of a book she had published some years earlier entitled Psychic Self Defence.

'Let this be your bible, George. You are a trained soldier in a just cause. But to invoke negative forces even for a positive purpose can get you into a lot of trouble. As I know from personal experience. And incidentally this experience has a bearing on my reason for bringing you here.'

Bringing me here? But surely . . . I told her of my assumption that I had somehow 'tuned in' to a signal broadcast, as it were, by the Watchers.

'Oh no, George,' she said. 'The signal was for you. Or for someone who turned out to be you. For a vital and specific task, I have need of an individual who is clever but uncomplicated, strong but sensitive. I therefore placed what you might call an advertisement via the Inner Planes.'

Powys said, 'Colonel Pixhill came to Glastonbury after answering an advert DF placed on, um, the Inner Planes. Did you ever discuss this with him?'

'By the time I arrived,' Verity said, 'Mrs Evans was several years dead. No, he did not discuss her.'

The Inner Planes, Powys thought. The psychic Internet.

He sighed.

*

'The War will end,' DF said. 'It may take some time yet, but the Allies will win and Hitler will never land here. Our own small part in the defence of Britain will never be acknowledged, nor widely known, but that is as it should be.

'No, George, the reason I sent for you relates to a danger which far precedes the rise of Nazism and will be with us when Hitler is long gone. It may not become fully apparent again until the end of the century. And while I – and a certain gentleman – remain alive, it will certainly be contained. However, I suspect my own time here is limited . . .'

I protested; she was in formidable health. She held up a hand.

'Death is a mere station between trains, George. There's a spirit in Avalon which is far more important than the transition of individuals. I don't want that to die. Not again.'

'The Abbot. Abbot Whiting, Verity. This was the first death. The first death of the spirit of Avalon.'

'November 15th was a very solemn day for the Colonel. We have . . . a dinner. The Abbot's Dinner.'

Powys thought about what Woolly had said.

'Tis all gonner be washed up again . . . last time this happened . . . 1539, the dissolution of the monasteries, when the State fitted up the Abbot . . . Can you imagine what it was like here after that?

'When they hanged Whiting, stripped the Abbey, it took centuries to recover, and when the spirit came back it was in a different form. A recognition of the pagan element. But a kind of coming together.'

'This was the original message of The Cauldron,' Verity said. 'A convergence of goddess worship and the Marian tradition. I suppose this was what encouraged many of us to go to the lectures.'

'That and a chance to see inside Dame Wanda's house, perhaps.'

Verity smiled.

Right at the end of *Avalon of the Heart*, Powys thought, DF describes herself as an 'impenitent heathen' but she's got a soft spot for the Catholic Church, expresses the hope that Glastonbury will one day become the English Lourdes. This was over ten years before she summoned Pixhill.

So what did she discover that seemed to pose a threat to the Lourdes of the Grail?

DF asked me, 'What is it that nourishes the unique spirit of Avalon? What has made it the oldest place of pilgrimage in England?'

I could not think and she answered her own question.

'The Holy Grail, George, the cup of the Last Supper in which Joseph of Arimathea also caught the blood from the wound in Our Lord's side as he hung from the cross.'

She then related to me the story of the Grail. Of how an angel had told Joseph in a dream to carry the cup west across the sea until he saw a hill shaped like Mount Tabor and there to land and found a church. Of how Joseph knew he had come to the right place when he put his staff into the ground and it flowered.

The first church was where the Chapel of St Mary stands in the abbey grounds. The Grail was kept there for a while, possibly until the Dark Ages when that mysterious figure the Fisher King took it for safekeeping, first in a chamber under Chalice Hill and later in a spring of blood-red water, a spring already held sacred by the pagan priests and Druids. The Chalice Well.

'The Grail is seen by some as a Christianisation of the Celtic chalice, the Cauldron of Ceridwen,' said DF. 'At first, I, too, in my Freudian days, thought it was a symbol, a metaphor.'

'It exists?' I pursued, in some excitement. 'Have you seen it?'

DF shook her head sadly. 'I have not been permitted to see the Grail. Once, a man – I spoke of him earlier – said he would show it to me. He led me to an underground chamber, where he . . .'

Her face tautened and darkened visibly at this point. I sensed her power then, and it unnerved me rather. But gradually her features relaxed. She was silent for a moment.

'The vessel he showed me, by candlelight, was not the Grail. Quite the reverse. Quite the reverse.'

Powys put down the typescript.

This was it.

'OK, Verity,' he said. 'Tell me about the Dark Chalice.'

EIGHT

DEPTH OF EVIL

When the spotlight came on, it made the Mini look older and shabbier and the whole idea like a non-starter.

Too late to turn back now.

The man in the leather cap he presumed was Rankin looked deeply suspicious, especially when he saw the dog in the back of the car.

'It gets even worse, mate,' Powys said cheerfully. 'The only Department of Transport ID I've got is a driving licence.'

All you have to do is con them long enough to get into the Presence.

'Tell you what, let's forget it. I'll be back at the Ministry on Monday. I'll ring Lord Pennard from there. If you get any trouble before then you'll just have to ask the police to sort it out. We don't work weekends since the cutbacks. Oh, and if the Press ring just tell them no comment and hope for the best.'

Powys smiled blandly and got back in the Mini. 'Cheers, then.' He slammed the door.

Rankin opened it again. 'Look, hang on. You can understand . . . I mean, turning up in an old car with a dog in the back.'

'Sure, sure, I probably look like the local poacher.'

'I know all the local poachers,' Rankin said.

'Of course you do. Sorry. No, as you can imagine, after Newbury and Batheaston and Twyford Down, we've learned that going around in a Ministry Rover wearing a pinstripe suit and carrying a briefcase is rather asking for trouble.'

Rankin nodded tentatively. He was a hard-looking bastard in his fifties. A man with one boss.

'At Newbury,' Powys said, 'colleague of mine had all four tyres slashed and the words *Green Power* scratched across his bonnet in letters about a foot long. No bloody joke, especially as we're now obliged to keep a staff car for three years or eighty thousand miles, whichever . . .'

'All right,' Rankin said. 'I'll call the house, tell my wife you're on your way. Mr . . .'

'Powys.'

Had to give his real name in case they checked his ID. But he pronounced it *Poe-is*. No basic reason why the name should put Rankin or Pennard on their guard, but you could never be sure.

He drove up the straight drive, bare trees gathering snow either side, Rankin watching the gate. The road surface was pitted, an indication that Pennard had no money to throw away.

The house was as he'd imagined it, possibly even grimmer. Jacobean or earlier but shabbily Victorianised. No finesse. Didn't even look like local stone. Not many lights – economy again.

'Any thoughts, Arnold?'

Since his ordeal at Meadwell, Arnold had been a little diffident. Lying on his rug, slightly cool with Powys, not even glancing at Rankin.

Should have warned me, Powys.

'OK. I didn't know about that place. I really didn't know.'

Know now, though.

He parked the car directly in front of the house, at the foot of a flight of six steps, already slippery with trodden snow. There was an unattractive double-glazed porch. A light came on behind it; inside the porch, a door of heavy new oak was already open. A weathered-looking woman stood there. Tweed skirt and jacket, hair tightly braided.

'Mrs Rankin?'

Housekeeper. A tight ship. There was a son as well, training to be the Huntsman, in charge of the hounds, according to Verity who knew these things.

'Follow me, please.'

Inside, it looked and felt like an old-fashioned office complex. Heavy panelled doors in walls of butcher's shop white. All the interior lights had low-wattage bulbs on show through clear shades.

'Lord Pennard will see you in the gun-room.'

Not the old, mellow kind of gun-room with racks of Purdeys and the heads of victims on shields. There wasn't a single gun on show, only steel-fronted cabinets. There was a practical-looking

424

desk with a stack of copies of *Horse and Hound* and *Shooting Times* under a bright, white-shaded metal lamp. A leather chair and a straight-backed leather sofa of the kind you found in solicitors' waiting rooms. An electric fire was off.

If the only woman's touch at Bowermead was applied by Mrs Rankin, all of this figured. She didn't invite Powys to sit down and he didn't. He was in; that was what mattered.

Lord Pennard kept him waiting for ten minutes. Plenty of time for nervousness to develop. Well, nobody had said this was a good idea. There just wasn't another one. Juanita was ill, Diane was missing and Verity . . . little Verity was bearing up. Under the circumstances.

'Mr Powys.' He filled the doorway. He did not say Poeis.

Juanita awoke feeling sodden and soiled. The duvet limp on her like a tarpaulin. She couldn't bear it any longer, needed to get out of the bed into the shower, blast away the half-dried sweat which coated her like soured cream cheese.

Matthew turned on the shower for her.

'How long was I asleep?'

'No more than an hour, I'm afraid. You were rather distressed. Juanita, I shall have to go soon. I have to see Wanda Carlisle. I'm taking her to the Tor before dawn. To meet the Bishop. Need to get to bed early. Got an alarm call arranged for five. Sorry.'

'You've done too much for me already.' The water was hurting Juanita, coming down on her like hot nails; her flayed thighs were stinging like a very bad nettle rash. She held her arms out in front of her like a sleepwalker, to prevent contact with her precious hands. Only the pain kept her this side of hysteria.

When she could take no more she stepped out and into a towelling robe with wide, loose sleeves. She couldn't dry herself.

Matthew turned off the shower. She sat in front of the biggest radiator, drying inside the robe, afraid to ask him.

'Did I . . . while I was asleep?' She was just so exhausted.

'Juanita.' He pulled over a dining chair. 'A lot of women consult me now. They want a herbal alternative to HRT. Perhaps they find it easier to talk to me because I'm gay. But I do think I help them. It's just . . .'

'Matthew, I had none of these symptoms. Not even yesterday. Can shock bring it on? Is there – I mean it's not even overnight – but is there such a thing as an overnight menopause?'

His lips tightened like the thin red line in Jim's painting.

'I think you should see a doctor. I have to say I've never encountered anything like this before. I'm sorry, Juanita, I'm out of my depth.'

Powys had declined Pennard's offer of a whisky. Could have done with the courage, but a clear head made more sense.

'Our information is that it could happen anytime,' he said. 'We just thought you ought to be warned.'

'Why? They won't get in.' Lord Pennard snapped out a bunch of keys. He was dressed as though ready to stop them himself, khaki shirt, moleskin trousers. His eyes were piercingly blue, his hair a kind of gunmetal grey. 'Almost a pity. Haven't had a siege here in centuries.'

He crossed to the metal-doored cupboard, fitted a key into it, turned it anticlockwise twice. Both doors fell open.

A line of shotguns like black organ-pipes. Pennard took one down.

'You shoot, Powys?'

Powys shook his head. 'Not much need for it in the, um, DTIB. Not yet, anyway.'

'Wish there was then, do you?' Pennard took down a box of cartridges.

'My head of department has been known to express a desire to blow a few, um, protesters away.'

Pennard broke the gun, dropped in a cartridge, then another.

'So, let me get this absolutely straight. You've come here to inform me that a bunch of these eco-guerrilla chaps've caught a whisper that we've been pre-empting things on the new road. How d'you get that information?'

'We've, um, infiltrated the movement. Can't say more than that. Have to protect our informants, Lord Pennard.'

'Quite.' Pennard snapped the gun shut with a ferocious clack. Powys thought, If he's trying to intimidate me, he's . . . succeeding.

'Good of you to drop in and tell me, Powys. In your undercover attire, too. Suppose you need to mix with these scum, do you? Gather your intelligence?'

'Sometimes.'

The problem was he hadn't decided on an actual strategy, beyond getting in to see Pennard. Meeting the guy rather reduced the options. The handful of lords and dukes Powys had encountered while exploring their grounds for ancient sites had been generally affable, so confident of their status they could be almost humble.

'And you're prepared to protect us, are you?' Pennard said, gun in his arms. 'If things get rough?'

'Well, we, um, we value your co-operation in this rather delicate situation.'

'Delicate, Powys? What's delicate about it?'

'Well, some people seem to think the road will damage not so much the natural ecology as the, um, spiritual ecology.'

If he wasn't careful he'd be talking like Pel Grainger.

'In what way?' Pennard demanded.

'Well . . . these people consider this particular landscape to be sacred. More so than anywhere else in Britain.'

'Damned idiots, then, aren't they?'

'Depends on where you stand.'

'I stand on my own land, Powys. Where do you stand?'

'We civil servants,' Powys said, 'we generally stand where we're told to stand.'

Lord Pennard shouldered the twelve-bore. Sighted on the ceiling and then brought the barrel down until its two holes were aimed either side of the bridge of Powys's nose.

'Know what I think, Powys? I think you're a damned liar.'

Powys swallowed.

'To begin with,' Pennard said, 'I don't for one minute believe there's such an organisation as the Department of Transport Investigations Branch.'

He moved the gun barrel an inch or two to point at the leather bench sofa.

'Siddown.'

His eyes were diamond-hard. Powys sat.

'Let's have it, then.'

'All right.' Powys looked away from the gun. 'I said I was with the Department of Transport because you wouldn't have seen me if I'd told you who I really was.'

'Which is?'

'Oh, I'm just a bloke who writes daft books. And I've been helping out with the magazine Diane's going to be editing.'

'Where is my daughter?'

'I wondered if you might know.'

'I don't.'

'You ought to,' Powys said. 'Don't you think?'

Pennard was silent, the gun barrel steady.

'Um, do you really need that thing?'

Pennard lowered the twelve-bore, broke it. 'You're right.' He slipped out both cartridges. 'If the occasion arose, I could tear your head off with my bare hands.'

He hung the gun in the cupboard. Shut the doors and locked it.

Powys said, 'This thing you have about tearing people's heads off. Would that be hereditary by any chance?'

Lord Pennard went so stiff and so pale in the cold white lamplight that Powys thought for a moment that the occasion had arisen.

'You're either a brave man,' Pennard said, 'or an extremely desperate one.'

'And Verity, darling,' Wanda said on the telephone. 'You'll never guess what's happened.'

'No,' said Verity, 'I don't suppose I will.'

'Bloody woman always gets the flu at the wrong time. I mean, could you, would you . . .? For Solstice?'

Verity glanced at Councillor Woolaston who nodded.

'I suppose I am at rather a loose end.'

'Splendid. I'll have your room ready. Shall we say one hour?'

'I'm not happy about this,' Verity said, replacing the receiver. The kitchen pipes gurgled with an ominous glee.

'You're better out of this,' Councillor Woolaston said.

'It's not my place to be out of it.'

'You've done your time, Verity. You've served him well. Better than he had any right to demand.'

'It never was in his nature to demand. But I was thinking more of you. You should not be here alone.'

'I won't be alone,' he said, 'when they come to do the well.'

'Councillor Woolaston, I don't think you realise . . .'

The poor little man looked quite wretched, his eyes deep with sorrow, his beard almost white. She was sure his beard had not been white the last time she saw him.

'. . . the depth of . . . of evil . . . that is in this place. I know that sounds almost ridiculously melodramatic.'

The end wall of the kitchen seemed particularly swollen tonight, like an abscess about to burst.

'Oh,' said Councillor Woolaston with a nonchalance which only betrayed how little he now valued his own life and sanity, 'I think I do. I think I've known it for a long time. Go on, Verity, man. Wanda don't get her gin and Horlicks she'll never be up in time tomorrow.'

'I'll get my overnight case.'

'Don't forget to switch off all the lights,' said the little councillor.

Verity felt very afraid for him.

NINE

CONTAMINANT

Lord Pennard uncapped a new bottle of Famous Grouse. 'You'll have a drink.'

'No th—'

'Wasn't a question, Powys. You will have a drink.'

Powys shrugged. Pennard poured him an inch of Scotch in a thick tumbler and went to sit at his desk with the pile of hunting and shooting magazines.

'So that devious, milksop bastard Pixhill wrote it all down. If this is blackmail, Powys, have to tell you we're not a good prospect, the Ffitches. Haven't been for years.'

'Not since the great days of the Dark Chalice?'

'Bunkum.' Pennard gazed into his Scotch as if pictures might form there. 'Spent half a lifetime telling m'self that. Father was a great believer. Always react against our parents, isn't that the way of it?'

'Like Archer's reacted against you?'

Outside, the snow had turned back to rain and sprayed the window, which was protected by metal security blinds.

'Powys.' Pennard rolled the name around his mouth with a slosh of whisky. 'You a descendant of the old hack?'

'Maybe.'

'Met him a time or two. Thought a good deal of himself. Talked and bloody talked. But that's the Welsh for you.'

'He wasn't Welsh.'

'Bugger should have been then.'

'That's what he thought too,' Powys said. 'Did he talk much about the Chalice?'

'Not going to let that go, are you? No, he didn't. Learned his lesson by then. Some chap in town, forget his name, convinced he'd been portrayed in that damned great book as the villain of the piece. Sued the piss out of Powys. Made bugger-all from that book, in the end. Served him right.'

Powys smiled.

'Come along,' Pennard said. 'Get this over. Tell me what the bastard said.'

'You want the lot?'

'Got all night.'

I haven't, Powys thought, worrying about Juanita and Diane and Verity and everything that might need to be done before dawn.

'As far as I can gather,' he said, 'Your family seems to trace its roots in Somerset back to the mid-eighteenth century. At least the first Viscount Pennard . . .'

'1765. Roger Ffitch. Like my father.'

'But the Ffitches had held land in the area for a long time before that. Over two hundred years in fact. Basically, since 1539 and the dissolution of the monasteries. When a certain Ffitch was rewarded for services rendered to the king.'

'Pure legend.'

'It's all legend. But legends are often more persistent than facts.'

'Only if you permit it,' said Pennard. 'Get to the point.'

'OK. Fact: Glastonbury Abbey was very rich and powerful and built out of the very cradle of Christianity, and Henry VIII had to crush it. Fact: Abbot Whiting was a hard man to nail because he was an unassuming kind of guy who liked to help the poor and was consequently very well liked. So Henry's hit man, Cromwell, had to find a way of fitting Whiting up. Fact: in the end they found writings in Whiting's chambers criticising the king's latest divorce. Also a gold chalice. From the Abbey. Which he was accused of stealing.'

Lord Pennard appeared uninterested and drank some whisky.

'Pixhill seems to think this chalice was later awarded – along with a few hundred acres of land and a farmhouse later known as Meadwell – to the man who agreed to plant it. A Benedictine monk at the Abbey called Edmund Ffitch. Spelt F F Y C H E. Who happily dumped his calling, moved into Meadwell . . . and founded a famous dynasty. Fact?'

Pennard grunted. 'Inasmuch as Meadwell was our first home.'

'The legend, of course, is that when Whiting was hanged and then beheaded on the Tor, Ffitch collected his blood in that same chalice. In deliberate parody of Joseph of Arimathea catching Christ's blood, from that famous spear-wound on the cross, in what became the Holy Grail. Thereby founding another tradition.'

'As you say . . .' Pennard leaned back in his chair, stretched out his legs, chin on his chest. 'Legend. Little-known one, too. So little-known it was probably invented by Pixhill to bolster his own fantasy of himself as a crusader. Sad little man.'

'You did have a family chalice, though, didn't you?'

'I wouldn't know.' He sounded very bored. Or trying to sound bored. 'Certainly not in my time.'

'And in your time . . .' Powys was beginning to despair of denting the armour. '. . . That is, since the War, the family hasn't exactly prospered, has it? Investments collapsing. Bad seasons in the vineyards. Land having to be sold. Couldn't help noticing as I came in that you're down to using sixty-watt bulbs where you need hundreds.'

'You're an idiot, Powys.'

'Perhaps the family has always associated its good fortune with possession of the Chalice. Lose the Chalice, money starts to go down the toilet.'

'Powys, if your illustrious ancestor'd been able to make up stories as good as this he might even've profited from his scribblings. Drink up, man.'

He advanced on Powys with the bottle of Grouse.

'Of course there was a down side.' Powys looked up at him. 'Meadwell became somewhat . . . spiritually tainted? Hard to live in?'

'Always a miserable hole. Don't cover your glass, it's discourteous. Either drink with me or get out.'

Reluctantly, Powys accepted another inch of Scotch. 'So this place was built. Comparatively small at first but massively expanded after the industrial revolution. By the outbreak of the First World War, the family was very wealthy. Which brings us to the previous Viscount Pennard. Your father, Roger Ffitch. Bit of a lad, Roger. A bit cocky. Not being discourteous here, am I?'

'My father', Pennard said, no hint of a smile, 'would have pulled your head off quite a few minutes ago.'

'Did you admire him?'

'He was an obstinate man. Immensely brave. Would've received the VC after the Somme if he hadn't shafted the wrong General's daughter, but that's by the by. Since you ask, I did not admire him. He was a chancer. A gambler.'

'And not only with money?'

'No,' Pennard said soberly. 'Not only with money.'

'With his soul, in fact,' Powys said. 'Such as it was.'

Juanita dressed slowly, painfully and impractically. She still couldn't bear jeans, tight or otherwise, against her thighs. Her thickest skirt was black velvet, calf-length; she dragged it on, thumbs through the loops, then wriggled into a sloppy lemon sweater, the softest thing she had, and it still felt like stiff cardboard. Her skin was starting to feel moist again, her head an oven.

In the kitchen, she turned on the cold tap with her wrists, put her head under the jet. The water hurt, so cold it burned.

Matthew had left a glass of water with a straw. A note to say there was a light salad (which she could manage to eat) in the fridge (which she could manage to open).

Blinking, horrified, at the clock, she thought, Powys!

Nearly nine o'clock. Hours since he'd gone to Verity's. A long time since Matthew had delivered the message that Powys was 'doing his best'.

Whatever that meant.

And no word from Diane. Time to call the police? Time to call Pennard?

Christ's sake, stay cool.

Sick joke.

She went down to the shop. No messages on the answering machine. She rolled the phone from its rest, tapped out the Meadwell number with the tip of a thumb. Bent over the receiver, heard the number ring and ring and ring, no answer, no answer, oh no.

She staggered back upstairs to the living room. *He'll be back. He will be back.* A little surprised at how much she needed him to be back.

Him. Not just somebody to be with her, to open things and switch things on. Him. Joe Powys, burned-out earth-mysteries writer, another jaded Grail-seeker.

She eased herself into the sofa, her arms spread along its spine. Opposite her, Jim's depiction of the mystical roads converging on the Tor as beams of dying sun, which lit the fields but not the Tor – a black silhouette, a hill of shadow.

The picture's surface glistened and glowed tonight, as though the paint was wet again, as though the ghost of Jim Battle was breathing on it.

She didn't like that thought. Made her want to look away, but the colours burned out of the canvas, the sweat on her face felt as slick and rich as linseed oil. There was a sour tang of turps. She blinked; water filmed her eyes, colours smeared.

Then there was a small movement on the picture. Could be a fly from the attic. Could be a spider. Crawling along one of the red sunbeams. Following the line exactly, towards the Tor.

Nothing there. It was the fever.

The room tilted; she saw the fly on the move again.

Except it wasn't a fly any more. It was a small, black bus, swaying and rattling down the black road from the Tor, a noxious Dinky toy stinking of burning oil and diesel, smoke puffing around it, feeding the blossoming shadows in the room.

A thin scream ribboned between Juanita's lips as the carpet hardened under her feet like stone. Like tarmac.

She arose from the sofa, edged towards the door of the sitting room.

Keeping her mouth tight shut, refusing to let the scream out. Corrosive fumes stinging her nose and it wasn't just smoke and oil, there was a harsh, acrid animal stench, a tomcat smell a hundred times more pungent, and the bus was coming at her, spewing feral breath from the torn-scab radiator between its heartless yellow headlights.

Juanita burst out of the room, tugging the door shut behind her, shutting it all in there, and she carried on tugging and wrenching long after the catch had clicked into place.

Becoming gradually aware – almost with a sense of awe – that she was using her lurid, pink, patched-up Frankenstein hands. The right hand gripping the doorhandle, the left hand around the right hand, all melded together in a pulsing lump of crippled flesh.

Fused to the handle as Jim had been fused to his easels.

She felt no pain at all as she fell to her knees on the landing, unable to breathe, lungs full of black smoke, head full of burning and those other images she suppressed even in her dreams: the explosion of the sunset window, Jim's blackened, dead grin, his boiling eyes behind the twisted bars in her arms, her own hands torched in the night. Blue fire from sizzling fat.

The ash tree. The dangling hat.

And *then* the pain. As wild and brutal as crucifixion nails through both palms. And the breath pumped out of her in hiccuping yelps as one hand came free and prised the other from the handle, finger by finger.

Powys put it to Lord Pennard that when Roger Ffitch came back from the Trenches, he was in a very bad state, not so much physically as emotionally.

'Hell of a lot of chaps afflicted that way. Three weeks in some petty little skirmish these days and they're sent for counselling. Gulf War Syndrome. Falklands Fever. Any of them even imagine what it was like at the Somme?'

'But he did find counselling, didn't he?' Powys said.

'Did he?'

'He was directed to a psychoanalyst. New word in those days. Who he'd probably have rejected if she hadn't been blonde and twenty-nine years old. With a certain glint in her eye. I'd guess.'

For the first time, Pennard looked fleetingly nervous. 'You're not drinking,' he said. 'Not drinking with me.'

Watching him now, Powys could imagine the problems Violet Mary Firth must have had with his father.

'He would meet her at Meadwell – he didn't want his family to know, that would've been a sign of weakness. Not his style.'

'Not the family style.' Pennard almost smiled.

'Anyway, she does seem to have been able to help your old man with his nervous problems. Putting a stop to his recurring nightmares of the blood and the filth. Restoring his self-confidence. Getting rid of that embarrassing, nervous tic. Making it so he could function again. He must have been impressed. Although he wouldn't have shown it. Couldn't let women get above themselves, could you?'

Pennard didn't look at him.

'But he really wanted her,' Powys said. 'My guess is he sensed her power, something he'd never encountered before, and he wanted some of that, too.'

Pennard snorted.

'But because she was a woman, he had to subdue her. If she was into magic then he'd bloody well show her some magic. The Holy Grail? He'd show her a real grail.'

Pennard was looking at him now. This stuff was obviously new to him. 'Pixhill wrote about this?' He spoke almost mildly.

Powys nodded. 'Your father took Violet to see the Dark Chalice. And then, perhaps feeling that the power was at last his power, he tried to make love to her.'

Pennard scowled.

'Did he rape her, or did she manage to fight him off? I prefer to think she did. Big strong girl. Maybe he was still weakened by the War. Asthma, wasn't it? Still, she was furious – justifiably. This was the man she'd spent weeks helping out of his crisis. Maybe she'd even fancied him a little. Whatever, she didn't any more.'

He decided to pass over the next bit, how Violet's hurt and her craving for revenge had manifested into an elemental force in the form of a wolf. Stay close to established fact.

'Maybe a month later, Roger Ffitch comes crawling back to Violet. His nightmares have returned, worse than ever. What were those nightmares, do you know?'

Pennard grunted. 'Before my time, all this. If it ever happened. Which I doubt.'

'I don't think you do. I think it's making terrible sense to you now.'

'Don't you threaten me, you little shit . . .' Pennard half rose from his chair, fists clenched.

'Wasn't a threat. Jesus, you bastards are so . . .'

'Just finish your fucking story.' Pennard sat down again, and his hand shook as he poured himself more Scotch.

'All right. Your father sent a message to Violet. She refused, understandably enough, to go back to Meadwell. They met in The George and Pilgrims. She, um . . . well, she was shocked when she saw him. He'd lost over a stone in just a few weeks. He was getting no sleep, couldn't keep a meal down. His tic – that was back in a big way. And his asthma had worsened to the point of being life-threatening. He was a hollow-eyed mess, your dad, and he virtually threw himself at her feet, fighting for breath.'

'*Not* his style,' Pennard snapped, meaning not *our* style.

Powys shrugged.

'As it happened, Violet hadn't been too good herself since exposure to the Chalice. If you've ever read Pixhill's diary you'll know the kind of dreams she was getting. Glastonbury not as a peaceful haven but as a volatile, unstable place. And always potentially a battlefield. The Dark Chalice: could this be the anti-Grail? Was there a parallel tradition?'

'Absolute non . . . nonsense.' Pennard scowled at the break in his voice and cleared his throat. 'Fucking bunkum.'

'So Violet made a deal with your old man. She would treat him again, work with him. And he would let her dispose of the Chalice however she saw fit. Which wasn't going to be easy, she knew that. At that age she really didn't feel up to dealing with evil on this scale. My guess is she probably consulted her own teacher, Theodore Moriarty – he ran a clinic specialising in cases like Roger.'

'He went away,' Lord Pennard said suddenly. A look of astonishment crossed his face. 'My mother told me this, many years later. He went away for six months in 1920.'

'To a clinic?'

'This is ridiculous.' A wave of anger quite visibly went through him, shone in his eyes as his arm swept over the desk, sent the whisky bottle spinning across the room until it hit the gun cupboard.

'While he was away,' Powys said, 'being treated by . . . Dr Moriarty? . . . your mother co-operated fully with Violet. She gathered some people, leading magicians of the day, powerful pagans and, I suspect, Christian mystics. And they took the Dark Chalice and they hid it – just as Joseph of Arimathea or the Fisher King was said to have done with the Holy Grail – in a well.'

Pennard sighed. Powys heard the whisky gurgling out of the bottle into the industrial carpet below the gun cupboard.

'They did their best with the Meadwell. They blessed it in the name of God. They did a powerful binding ritual. But it's a bit like burying nuclear waste. It's not possible to destroy something like the Dark Chalice which exists on more than one level. You can only contain it and hope for the best. But it's a hell of a contaminant. I don't know where the well leads, but that's a black spring now. You can tell what it's done to the house.'

'I wouldn't know,' Pennard said. 'Not our house any more.'

'That was part of the deal. Roger Ffitch agreed that when he died, that house would be sold to Violet Firth. Who by this time had her own home and teaching base in Glastonbury. Documents were drawn up. Your mother, Lady Pennard, was party to it, of course. But Violet died first, in 1946, as I'd guess she knew she would, after her unique contribution to the Allied cause.'

'Met the woman once, you know. As a boy. Gave me a bag of sweets.' Lord Pennard actually smiled. 'Bullseyes. Never allowed bullseyes.'

'Did you like her?'

'Did, matter of fact. Jolly. Like a scoutmistress. Interfering bitch.'

'The Fall of the House of Pennard?'

'Bunkum. Useless businessman, my father. Incompetent. All there was to it. Never the same after the War. Cracked up. Spent most of his last years in bloody church.'

'Whatever, all the wealth the family acquired with the chalice began to drop away. So Pixhill says. He reckons you did everything in your power to get Meadwell back.'

'Bloody disgrace. Under the table deal while I was away on National Service. Bloody Pixhill. What damn right did he have to take away our property? Worth over a quarter of a million now, that house. Of course I tried to get it back. Who *was* the bloody man?'

'Just someone Violet could trust. She needed a custodian for Meadwell. She was only fifty-six when she died. Leukaemia. She'd known it was coming. Maybe years before, you know what these people are like. I doubt if it worried her. Death was just a station between trains. That was what she told Pixhill.'

Just saying it, hearing himself, Powys felt aglow with the certainty of it all. Confirmation now in every response from Pennard, every change in expression, every involuntary gesture.

'What changed?'

Pennard didn't reply. He reached for the whisky before remembering the bottle wasn't there any more.

'Why did you give up the fight to get Meadwell back?' Powys said.

'Legal costs.'

'No.'

'No. Of course not.' Pennard stood up. 'What's your angle on all this, Powys? What do you hope to get out of it? Book? Bloody bestseller?'

Powys shook his head. 'I'll be honest. I was going to tell you I'd publish the whole thing if you didn't play ball.'

'And now?'

'It's too heavy. Until just now I don't think I entirely believed it.' He leaned back at last on the stiff sofa. 'I don't want to threaten you. It would be the wrong thing to do. I won't write about it.'

Pennard looked at him for a long time. 'I'm inclined to believe you.'

'Then tell me what changed.'

'Why do you think I should?'

'Because I think it's something to do with Diane,' Powys said. 'Who, according to the late chairman of the Pixhill Trust, is in, and I quote, *danger of a most extreme and everlasting nature*. And she's disappeared.'

Lord Pennard collapsed into his chair. He suddenly looked much older.

TEN

SAVE THEM FROM THEMSELVES

'It was Archer, wasn't it?'

She kept opening her eyes but they wouldn't focus. She saw the blobs of faces around her in the gloom, but their features fled as she tried to identify them, flitting from one to another, very quickly. She thought she saw the Pilgrims: Rozzie and Mort and Viper and Gwyn. She must be hallucinating, dredging memories from the sludge of her subconscious. But in the end she could concentrate on only one thought.

'It was . . . Archer. Archer pushed her downstairs. Archer killed her.'

Capturing the certainty before sleep reached out for her.

'I've never met him,' Powys said reasonably. 'Never even seen him. Got no reason to think ill of him. Hell, I'm not even very political.'

Working on information now that he hadn't found in the Pixhill papers. Piecing together what he'd gleaned from Juanita and particularly from Verity. Verity who pattered about the streets and chatted innocuously, sometimes inanely. And heard things.

'Is this gossip?' Lord Pennard seemed stunned. 'Is this talked about?'

'I don't honestly think it is. It just . . . suggests itself. Maybe . . . maybe it suggested itself to you.'

'How can I discuss this with you? I've never even seen you before tonight. Certainly never heard of you. You lied to get in here; how do I know you're not lying now?'

Powys said nothing. Pennard had his head in his hands. He'd found another bottle of whisky.

'My wife died after falling downstairs. She'd been to the nursery. Liked to spend time there. Been redecorated, refurnished in pink. She had her bed moved into the next room. Said she knew it was going to be a girl because . . . a *wise woman* had told her. My wife believed in such nonsense. She'd sit in the nursery alone and read for hours, as though the fact of the pink paint could influence matters at that stage.'

He drank some whisky. His face no longer smooth and polished but blotched with tension.

'Closed that part of the house now. Don't heat it, don't light it. Let it damn well rot. If it falls down, it falls down.'

'Were you in the house at the time?'

'I was in here. Didn't like her in her maudlin, nursery-moping mood. One of the maids – still had maids then – came to tell me. They'd found my wife at the bottom of the stairs. Semi-conscious. Called the doctor. And the Belvedere, the private clinic. Sent a midwife with an assistant. Bugger-all use they were.'

'How near to time was she?'

'Seven months. Baby came out, but the damned placenta wouldn't. Because of the fall. Place was like the inside of an abattoir.'

He choked back something and became annoyed with himself and pushed all the bloodsports magazines to the floor.

Powys said, 'Someone told me Archer and his mother didn't get on.'

'Who told you?'

'Does it matter?'

'No. It's true. This . . . Dark Chalice business. This blasted woman . . . this Fortune . . . Firth biddy . . . spent a lot of time, apparently, with my mother while my father was away at his . . . clinic. Whatever she told her, my mother evidently passed on to Helen – my wife. One Christmas, few glasses of wine, told the boy about the legend of the Chalice. My wife was furious. Insisted it was up to the women of the family to exercise constant vigilance to counter any attempt arising from "male avarice or poverty", as she put it, to "unbind" the thing. Archer, of course, was immediately enchanted. *We'll get it back, Father, won't we?* Damn it, if he hadn't learned about it from me, someone would have told him. Sooner or later.'

'Was that why your wife was so determined to have a girl? Because the women . . .?'

'Doubtless. Archer was ten at the time. Don't think she was ever close to him again. Almost afraid of him. And, of course, he played up to that. I remember he once walked in while we were having dinner. Solemnly carrying a chalice with a candle burning in it. Said he'd found it buried in the grounds. Helen had hysterics. Turned out some boy had stolen the thing from St John's. I think Archer paid him. It was smoothed over.'

The sleet had stopped. It was very quiet in the gunroom.

After a while, Lord Pennard said, 'Had the sheets burned. And the mattress. And then the fucking bed. Chopped up and burned. Sat in the library window, all the lights out. Watching the bed blazing in the walled garden.'

Powys thought, nearly twenty-eight years ago, Pennard would have been around his own age. Never imagined he'd be feeling so sorry for the guy.

'Rankin did the burning. Been with us about a year. Soaked everything with paraffin. Lit up most of the lawn. When the fire burned low, Rankin went away. Then Archer came out.'

Pennard pushed his whisky away.

'Had enough. Can't get drunk any more. Can't get merry. Yes. Archer came out. Arms full of toys and baby bedding from the nursery. Pink teddy bear. I remember the pink teddy bear. With a bow. Archer burned them all. He was grinning. The baby was born. I couldn't look at her. She had blood on her. So I sat in the library in the dark and watched Archer burn all the toys. Saw his grinning face in the firelight.'

Lord Pennard began to weep.

After much frantic struggling, Juanita managed to get the shop door open and she threw herself out into the street, blue coat under her arm.

Into the empty town, moving in a staccato, sporadic fashion. Stubbornly doing 'normal' things. Taking in images of ordinariness. She walked across the zebra-crossing to the post office. Looked into the phone box, an old-fashioned red one but the coinbox and phone were modern. A stand-up sandwich board said:

LPs, TAPES,
CDs, BOOKS
BOUGHT, SOLD

On the other side, a sticker had been slapped across the board:

Put Glastonbury First
– TAME THE TOR.

It was cold, but the sleet had stopped, leaving a thin glaze of slush on the pavement; few feet tonight to trample it away. The sky was clear again, almost starlit. There could be a hard frost, icy roads.

Alone on High Street, Juanita felt utterly wretched, but she couldn't go back. Couldn't live with those pictures. Couldn't take them down or hide them away, that would be the final rejection for Jim.

She struggled into her coat and stood for a while outside the delicatessen near the crossing. She felt agitated. Her body twitching, itching. Her hands ached abominably. She felt used and betrayed. As if her body had been strengthened just sufficiently to support the mind-twisting terror which began with the painting altering, recreating itself in her head, an unseasonal fly from the attic mutating obscenely into a symbolic black bus.

There were no roads at all in that picture, no hazy ley-lines. Somehow her mind had created them as an opening for the horrid black bus which came out of the shadow-Tor and tunnelled into her brain.

A black bus was not a real hippy bus. Hippies had rainbow buses.

The Pilgrims, though, they were different. Gwyn ap Nudd, lord of darkness, his sickle raised. The Pilgrims laughing because they knew the Tor had betrayed Jim and Juanita. The hill of dreams where she'd sat all night and drunk cheap wine and watched for the good aliens, the mystic hill which Jim had painted reflecting the last light . . . had reversed dramatically into the negative image of itself, thus becoming a dark hill, and spewed out the black bus of death.

And the good, hopeful hippies who danced like butterflies and wished people love had given way to twisted, embittered hippies, children of the Dark Chalice.

She felt the whole town twisting and turning and tightening around her like the grey snake-hair of the black priestess, Ceridwen.

Who had Diane.

'Diane!' Juanita screamed. 'Where are you? Answer me!'

Nobody answered her. Alone on the cold wet street, she sobbed and scuttled away, a Verity in the making.

There were questions he didn't have to ask any more.

Like why Lord Pennard had abandoned attempts to get Meadwell back.

Why he'd placed his daughter in the care of strict, old-fashioned nannies who would take no nonsense. Who could be relied upon to keep her away from Archer.

Why he'd sent her away to school after school. Why he wanted her to marry a man in distant Yorkshire.

'You could never be sure, could you? Whether it was real or the whole thing was fantasy. Whether Archer had actually pushed his mother downstairs and might one day do something similar to Diane. You were just trying to keep them apart as long as it was in your power to do so.'

'He's my only son.' When Pennard looked up, his face had hardened again. 'My heir. The next Viscount Pennard. And before that he'll be the MP for Mendip South. It's coming right again, Powys. We're selling the land for the road. The future's sound. We never needed the bloody chalice.'

'That's what Archer thinks too, is it?'

'Get out. Go on.' Pennard turned away. 'We never had this conversation. I've never seen you in my life. Just get out of my house.'

'Do you know where your daughter is now? Have you any idea?'

'Get out!'

'Don't you think it might be a good idea to report her missing? To the police? They'd listen to you. They'd pull out the stops.'

Pennard didn't reply. He didn't move. He was like marble.

Powys found his own way out down a shabby, leather-smelling passageway, frugally lit.

Rankin was waiting for him at the front door.

'Get what you wanted?'

'More or less, thanks.'

'I was listening,' Rankin said. 'Other side of the door.'

'What?'

'The aristocracy.' Rankin shook his head. 'Sometimes they can be very naive. Quite often we have to save them from themselves.'

He was half a head taller than Powys, held himself very straight. His face was without expression.

'Because we need them, you see. They're our backbone. You might not think much of him and his kind, Mr Poe-is, but they've made this country what it is. They deserve our protection.'

'Most people have to protect themselves,' Powys said nervously.

'I can't let you spread this around,' Rankin said, very matter-of-fact. 'You know that. I had my son break into your car, take it round the back of the house for tonight. We've killed your dog, sorry about that. Sorry about all of this, but I take my job seriously and that man in there and what he stands for is worth ten of you and all the pathetic sods down in that town, with their medallions and their dowsing sticks. You understand that, don't you, sir? All I'm saying, this is nothing personal.'

Rankin held open the door.

'After you,' he said.

ELEVEN

BLOOD OF THE GODDESS

Powys went quietly.

Rankin held open the double-glazed door of the porch for him. Not good form to soil your master's premises. Powys noticed that it was cheap, aluminium double-glazing. The economic way to cut heating bills.

He felt almost light-headed as he turned to Rankin and said, 'You don't really have to do this, do you? You don't have to kill me?'

Wanting to sound at least frightened but aware that it only came out puzzled. Faintly incredulous that there could still be men like Rankin who would murder without compunction if it was a matter of supporting the system which supported them.

Wondering distantly, as if he was watching from above or on a closed-circuit TV, how exactly it would be done. One of those SAS blows that drove your nose bones into your brain, perhaps. Or a slim knife to the heart. He wondered if his body would end up drawn and quartered like Abbot Whiting's and buried under what would become the Central Somerset (Bath-Taunton) Relief Road.

'It's the way things are,' Rankin said apologetically. Immediately outside the door he put on his leather cap. 'Preserving what has to be preserved. So much of it's gone, you see.'

'Yes.' Arnold was gone. *We've killed your dog, sorry about that.*

Well, that wouldn't be hard, a three-legged dog, recovering from shock. While Rankin was neatly closing the porch door, he thought about Arnold, the night the vet had taken his leg off, everything they'd been through since, the long walks along Offa's Dyke after which he'd sometimes have to carry Arnold home.

'Please,' he said, knowing this time that there were real tears in his eyes. 'Can't you . . .?'

And seeing a definite naked contempt in Rankin's eyes in the half second before he felt his face contort in blind fury as he sank his left fist into the man's gut.

Distantly aware, as Rankin doubled up, of all his rediscovered New Age credentials floating away into the ether. Surprised at the surge of maddened strength, which hurled Rankin back into the porch, snarling,

'. . . fucking scumbag cunt . . .' A face smashing again and again into the double-glazed door, which did not break.

Aware with a sense of dismay that it was his voice and Rankin's face. Fully aware that all this would have been entirely beyond him if Rankin had not blithely mentioned having killed his dog.

'Hey, shit, come on . . .' Pulling on Powys's shoulder. 'Stop it. You don't wanner go to gaol for shit like this.'

Powys's hands were covered in blood. He got back to his feet.

Rankin sat up on the top step and spat out blood. His eyes were moving, coldly weighing up the situation, working out his best move.

Powys kicked him in the throat.

'Bugger me,' Sam Daniel said, as Rankin went down gagging. 'I thought this was the Age of Aquarius. Just let's get the hell out, eh?'

Powys remembered now. How he'd called up Woolly on the offchance he was still around, needing someone to be at Meadwell if Verity got the call from Wanda. And Woolly had turned up with Sam who'd offered to go with Powys to Bowermead Hall. Slipped out of the car at the bottom of the drive to find his own discreet way in, keep an eye out.

'He killed Arnold,' Powys said. Rankin didn't move, lay wheezing quietly to himself.

'He what?'

'Where's the car?'

'It's down there, by those bushes,' Sam said. 'You left it unlocked, remember? I let the handbrake off and rolled it a few yards to the bushes, out of the light. To give me some cover, as we eco-guerrillas say.'

'Arnold?'

'He's lying on his rug. What did you think?'

447

'Why would this guy say he'd killed him?'

'It's the kind of guy he is, Powys. Or maybe he was going to. Or maybe somebody else . . . Shit.'

Powys turned and saw a mirror image of Rankin at the foot of the steps.

'Dad?'

'This is Wayne Rankin,' Sam said. 'He's training to be as big a psycho as his old man.'

Wayne Rankin was looking at Powys's hands. 'What you done to my dad?'

'Your dad,' Sam said, 'made a slight miscalculation about the aggression quotient of New Age Man. Now just back off, son, it's two against one and neither of us is in the best of moods.'

Rankin moaned.

'You can get him to hospital when we've gone, look.' Sam walked slowly down the steps. Wayne Rankin moved away, but he didn't take his eyes from Sam.

'You're a friend of Lady Loony, yeah?'

Sam stopped.

'We banged her last night,' Wayne said.

Sam froze.

Wayne kept on backing off. 'Gave her a good seeing-to.'

'Don't react,' Powys said in a low voice. 'If his dad lied about the dog . . .'

'Come here, Wayne,' Sam said. 'Tell me all about it.'

'Three of us.' Wayne had vanished beyond the feeble house lights. 'One after the other.'

Sam charged out. Powys grabbed his arm. 'Don't go out there. He'll be waiting.'

Wayne Rankin's voice came out of the darkness.

'Squealed like a stuck pig, she did.'

Woolly told himself he and Meadwell deserved each other. Sitting in the dark here was probably as close as you could get on this earth to authentic purgatory.

Sitting waiting for Pel Grainger.

He'd actually been at that lecture of Grainger's at the Assembly Rooms. Been unimpressed. Superficial bullshit. Even if you could welcome the night like you did daylight, how was that really going to expand your life?'

The exercise, when Grainger had all the lights put out, that felt good. On the surface, it was the harmless kind of meditation exercise Woolly'd done a thousand times. But that night it produced a serious buzz.

But that was a weird night anyway. Woolly had had to leave before the end after getting a message that somebody was smashing windows out on the street. Whatever you were doing that night, it was going to be intense, off the wall. Something had been happening. Somebody doing something. He should have seen it then.

Dark Chalice rising.

He wondered what he'd really do when they came for the well.

Simple, JM Powys had said. You just call the police. Report intruders. Let them handle it. Nobody knows you're there; don't enlighten them. Don't even think of going out there after them.

But he might. The fuzz might not make it in time. And he didn't have a lot to lose. He might well go out there. Needing to do something.

Dark Chalice rising. Corrupting everyone in its path.

Like Grainger. Grainger had been corrupted.

He could stop Grainger, if he was on his own. Pompous, fat git. Woolly felt he really needed to stop somebody. He was feeling totally useless. A whole pile of bad shit coming down and nothing that soon-to-be-former Councillor Woolaston could do about it.

Right now, he didn't want to leave this kitchen. Wasn't that wimpy? He didn't want to go anywhere in this spooky old house. Just to sit tight by the Aga, listen for a car, the sound of the gate opening, and then maybe . . .

Face it, any kind of action outside was better than being in here. Little Verity had to be a really strong person to have survived this. A really *good* person, Mother Teresa class.

Even on top of the Aga, he was still cold. Moonlight fluttered in through the high window like the ribbons on a shroud.

This was an evil house. As black as the black bus.

He kept thinking about that bus. Was it his own private demon? Was it a representation of everything he most feared: the fast-breeding traffic monster which fed on the English countryside? Had that bus come out of his own head, bred from his own paranoia?

Woolly projected himself back ... back into the car, coming down along Magdalene Street, seeing the tree lights. He remembered thinking how nice that was, what a really good vibe Christmas put into the town. Trying to see those lights in his mind before they all went up in the air and he saw the other lights, the wishy-washy yellow either side of a peeling grille.

Was there a driver? He peered harder down his dope-scarred memory.

Focusing on the headlights, on that grille that was like a lopsided, evil grin full of rusty teeth. Into the window. This really old-fashioned window, with a divider strip of rusting chrome.

His hands groping up the side of the Aga in the dark, the warm shiny metal, like he was climbing up on to the bonnet of the bus, peering in through that window. If he could only see the driver's face, he'd know.

He could feel the engine throbbing now under his feet. Could see the street. Hang on, this was wrong, had to get down High Street from the top. Coming down from Chilkwell Street, left into High Street, down towards the Post Office and the zebra crossing, under the wash of amber streetlight, the big steering wheel vibrating under his hands, that loose spring irritating his bum, gotta patch that seat, glaring through the muck on the windscreen.

Driving the bus. Driving the black bus.

'I never wanted children,' Juanita said hoarsely.

She found she was talking to the purple-spotlit pot goddesses in the window of the shop belonging to Domini Dorrell-Adams.

'It was always going to be, you know, a wonderful place to bring kids into. Not just Glastonbury – the new world we were going to make. Everybody loving one another. We didn't, of course. We still had our petty jealousies, prejudices, infidelities. But the fact that we felt it was *possible* for everyone to love each other. That we could aspire to it.'

The pot goddesses leered.

'And when it all started to go down the drain I didn't want to bring kids into it any more. That was why Danny left really. He wanted offspring. He wanted his own little Glastonbury family. But you can't be an ordinary guy in Glastonbury, it's not allowed.'

One of the purple spot-bulbs in the Goddess Shop window went out, with a little *phut* she could hear even through the glass.

Phut. Gone.

Like golden-haired Domini's marriage. Like Jim Battle and his cottage and his paintings. Like Headlice.

How swiftly lights were snuffed in this small town. How quickly they were forgotten. All that energy going bad. No place to raise a child. And too late now, anyway.

She heard laughter behind her. Laughter as light as a ball of windblown paper.

She turned slowly.

In the middle of the road stood Ceridwen in darkest robes.

Juanita went very still.

There was a hazy light around Ceridwen. Her hair, like grey snakes, sprayed out into this light, which was purple like the spotlit goddess.

Well, she'd dreamed of this moment, the big confrontation.

But on *her* terms. By daylight. In Ceridwen's tacky fortune teller's booth. Or Wanda's house, where there were things to smash, candles to knock over. When she wasn't feeling sick and feverish and broken and . . .

Ceridwen laughed.

. . . and disillusioned and decaying, constantly chilled by the draught of death.

She began to pant, looking down at the hands she hadn't been able to straighten out since they'd gripped the door handle. An old woman's curling claws . . .

'The goddess comes in three aspects,' Ceridwen said, her voice echoing, as if the whole street, the town, the world was empty, apart from the two of them. She was looking past Juanita at the Goddess Shop.

'Virgin,' she said.

Juanita turned in time to see another purple bulb going pop, putting the smaller goddesses into darkness.

Now there was only one bulb remaining. It lit the largest of Domini's pot goddesses, purpling her pendulous breasts. The obese idol squatted smugly on her swag of white satin and simpered.

While, from the large black hole at the top of her rough-glazed thighs, a dark fluid was dripping, making viscous rivulets on the white satin.

Juanita backed away. She could almost smell it. She tasted bile.

She looked up at the tower of St John's, but it looked coldly down, spurning her. And the dark, taunting, menstrual blood of the goddess soaked into the satin.

'Mother,' Ceridwen hissed.

As the last bulb went out.

Phut.

Just like the baby Juanita had had aborted. Secretly. Danny's baby. Danny becoming terrifyingly un-Danny when he heard. Danny throwing every book in the shop to the floor. Pushing over the shelf-units, smashing up the window display and walking out and never returning, never setting foot on the holy Isle of Avalon again.

Juanita turned to face the road and Ceridwen's white, hazy pointing finger.

There was a moment of stillness. A moment of knowing it was not as it seemed. A smell of fumes, souring the apple-scented woodsmoke from the chimneys, bad energy forming a grounded cloud.

And then, with a sensation of pins and needles in both feet, the flush began.

The big one. The flush of flushes. She felt fire in her limbs, a fire that dried her blood and her juices. She felt her skin slacken, her breasts shrivelling into pockets of old leather, her mouth stretching into a scream which she knew would crack her face into a spiderweb of deep, blackening fissures.

'Hag,' Ceridwen said.

Juanita raised her hands like the claws they so much resembled and rushed out at her, shrieking hatred and despair.

But Ceridwen's image went out like another lightbulb and there was nothing in the middle of the road but Juanita.

And the big black bus. Bellowing and farting smoke. With its radiator hanging off.

She felt the buildings tremble and wrapped her arms around her sagging body. As if that would hold her together.

TWELVE

MY GODDESS

Sam threw open the Bowermead gates, ran back and jumped back in the Mini.

'Wayne hangs out with Darryl Davey,' he said. 'Of the Provisional Glastonbury First Brigade. If that yellow-toothed twat . . .'

'Sam, he was lying. He was winding you up. I'm not even going to mention it to Juanita, the state she's in already. It could, however, be a police matter. Whatever they did.'

'You think the police got a better chance of finding her than we do?'

'They could pull this Davey in.'

'I could pull him in. Go round the pubs till I find him.'

'And get filled in by his mates.' Powys drove out of the Bowermead turning towards the lights of Glastonbury. 'Time is it?'

'Gone ten. What did you get out of Pennard?'

'Too much whisky.'

'Didn't do you much harm when it came to dealing with Rankin. If we *both* went round the pubs . . .'

'I'd rather you went to Meadwell, keep Woolly company. Because that's where they'll show up. Sooner rather than later.'

'You think?'

'I know. Sam, who else is in The Cauldron apart from Ceridwen?'

'Depends what you mean by "in".' Sam had Arnold on his knee, clutching the dog to his chest. 'A whole lot of women go to the meetings.'

'I mean the so-called Inner Circle.'

'There's a woman called Jenna thinks she's well-in. I dunno.'

'You see, we need to find out where the Inner Circle meets. That's where she'll be. I mean Diane.'

'Wanda Carlisle's, surely?'

'It's a front. Just like her. Nothing happens there. It's somewhere else.'

'I don't get this, Powys. Surely they're all going up the Tor with the Bishop for this Solstice dawn crap. They'll be at Wanda's.'

'I think you'll find they aren't all going up. Wanda's going alone with the Bishop. That's a measure of how important they think it is. She's about as half-arsed as he is. Two lightweights representing the great traditions of paganism and Christianity on the most powerful, hallowed site in Britain. It doesn't make sense. And yet it's got to. It's bloody got to.'

Sam said, 'Woolly's coming out with all this stuff about the biggest blow against spirituality since 1539. I mean, what kind of blow was that really? The Roman Church was pretty bloody corrupt by the Reformation. The Popes were just more bent politicians in tall hats. Something had to give.'

'It was a blow to Glastonbury. If you try not to get spirituality confused with organised religion, you find you can keep a better perspective. What about Archer Ffitch? Where might he be? He got any kind of apartment in Glastonbury? A girlfriend?'

'You're joking. Archer Ffitch . . . No, he's got a place in London. Or maybe he shares somewhere with Oliver Pixhill. But nowhere in Glastonbury. Anyway, Diane wouldn't be with Archer. Diane's not been having good feelings about Archer.'

Powys glanced sharply at him. 'What's that mean?'

'She said – and I was a bit cynical about this at the time – that she sometimes feels her hate for Archer has a life of its own.'

'Say that again. Try and remember exactly what she said.'

Sam tried. Powys listened, transfixed, gripping the steering wheel hard, and tried not to crash the car.

He drove into Chilkwell Street, indicated left for the town centre. He needed to talk to Juanita. And he needed a copy of Dion Fortune's *Psychic Self-Defence*. Fast.

'I just want Diane,' Sam said. 'That's all. If those scumbags . . .'

Halfway down High Street, Powys braked hard behind a stationary bus. A big, obviously decrepit black bus, stopped in the middle of the road.

'It's another accident,' Sam said. 'I don't believe this.'

Powys pulled out alongside the bus, switched on his headlights. A woman in a blue coat was lying in the road.

He came out of the car so fast he lost his balance – effects of the whisky, shouldn't even be driving – and pitched over in the road, hitting his head on the kerb and rolling over, buildings of brick and stone spinning overhead, lights coming on in windows over upside-down shop signs, pale amber streetlamps, a church tower with a dusting of weak stars around its crown of stone thorns.

The bus had huge, balding tyres. Bloody thing shouldn't even be on the road. A few people were gathering. He kept hearing the words 'not again' again and again and again.

He crawled towards the wheels, pulling himself up. Saw a guy bending over the body. The body wrapped in the blue coat. She said she always wore something blue. Lucky colour. Nothing would happen to you if you wore blue.

'. . . can't credit it.' The driver of the bus, presumably, fat guy in an anorak with a Castrol sticker. 'I mean, I *know* this town. I know where Wellhouse Lane is. But I didn't turn into Wellhouse Lane, did I? I come down here. If I'd got it right, she wouldn't . . . But, like, anyway she just comes leaping out like . . . Christ, I never slammed on like that before, thought I was gonner have a heart attack.'

Powys stumbled to where she lay. She was very still. The coat had come loose. Her long neck shone light brown under the head-lights, faintly freckled. Her eyes were fully open. Big brown eyes. One arm flung out.

The hand ungloved, a livid pink.

'Powys.' Nothing moving but her lips. 'You're crying.'

Woolly's guts turned over and he threw up in the sink. He could smell smoke and diesel and burnt rubber.

He turned on the taps. Let the water, hot and cold, splatter down on his face and neck for over a minute, until the old pipes were snorting and gurgling like a bad case of dysentery.

Woolly washed his hands, wiped them on his jeans. That was it. He went and put on all the lights in the kitchen.

Just for a minute. Just to get rid of the image of Juanita's face in the headlights before he trod the brakes, screaming out loud, praying to God, forcing his whole being into his feet and those brakes.

A lesson.

Never close your eyes at Meadwell.

She sat on the bed in the lamplight.

The lamp in the stone and timber-framed bedroom had a Tiffany shade almost matching the stained glass in the apex of the Gothic windows. The bulb in the lamp flickered, perhaps it would go out soon.

'I don't like bulbs that do that.' Her arms were by her sides, held away from her body.

'I'll get them to change it,' Powys said.

They were in his ancient, mellow, timbered room at The George and Pilgrims. Juanita wouldn't go home, wouldn't go back to the shop. *It's infected*, she'd kept saying. She'd stood up shakily in the road. Unhurt. *How can you be hurt by a phantom bus?* Giggling hysterically. At least the driver was happy. Powys had handed his car keys to Sam: 'Mead-well, quickly.'

Her blue coat lay on the floor by the bed. Arnold had curled up on it.

'I couldn't move.' Her loose sweater had slipped down over one shoulder. 'I didn't want to move. It was very peaceful in the road. Can't remember ever feeling as peaceful. I lay and I stared up at that torn radiator grille and I waited to die.'

He sat down next to her on the bed, looked hard into her dulled eyes. 'How do you feel now?'

'Not here. I feel like I'm not here.'

'Listen. Juanita.' He wanted to touch her. Didn't know where it was safe to. 'It was a real bus, OK? Sam talked to the driver. He's a scrap-dealer from Taunton. He was delivering the bus to a Mr Moulder, who has a farm up Wellhouse Lane.'

The eyes wavered.

'But he took the wrong turning. He doesn't know why he did that because he knows Glastonbury very well, but he took a wrong turning. He came down High Street and there you were in the middle of the road. He said he braked so hard he nearly had a heart attack and still he thought he'd killed you. And I . . . me too, you know?'

Joe Powys's head fell into Juanita's lap. He felt brittle and exhausted like the Holy Thorn. No sap left. He knew more than his mind could handle about Pixhill and Dion Fortune and the dark heritage of the Ffitches. And yet he knew nothing. He'd very nearly murdered a man in a rush of mindless violence. He'd thought his dog had been killed. Also the woman he really . . .

He felt Juanita's lips on his hair.

'You were crying,' she said. 'You thought I was dead and you were crying.'

'I shouldn't have cried.' He sat up. 'It's only a station between trains.'

'What?'

He kissed her. Her cheeks were wet and hot, her lips dry and cracked. He moistened them with his tongue, felt her shiver. Her face at last moved under his and her arms went around him. Just her arms.

Powys hugged Juanita and they stayed like that, dazed and weeping, for several minutes. Only in Glastonbury. Who said that?

'I'm a mess,' she said. 'It isn't possible to be a bigger mess than me. I don't even know what's real. I don't trust my eyes, I don't trust my body . . .'

'I'm real. I think.'

She pulled away from him.

'Listen, I'm serious. Of all the things that've happened to me tonight, I don't know which ones are real. You tell me that bus was real . . . an hour or two ago I saw that bus in a painting – that actual bus, with its radiator . . . and then I saw one of the Goddess Shop pots bloody well menstruating. And there was Ceridwen in her robes in the middle of the road. Talking to me. Instructing me that I was now officially a hag, which . . . which makes a lot of sense when you've had about two hundred hot flushes . . . I do mean two hundred very real hot flushes, which Matthew Banks will confirm. I'm a hag. A crone. Look at me.'

She wore no make-up. She was very beautiful. She was to die for.

'Look at me.' She began to cry.

He kissed her. His hands slid under her sloppy sweater. There was nothing there but warm skin.

'Um, would you mind if . . .?'

'You don't want this kind of hassle, Powys.'

He could hardly breathe. He fumbled the sweater over her speckled shoulders, draping it over Arnold, who murmured but didn't move.

'OK.' Juanita was looking down at herself. 'It's a relief. I thought they were going to be around my navel.'

Powys touched a brown nipple with his tongue. It had an aureole of freckles.

'Dion Fortune would have understood.' He tossed his sweater on Arnold and wriggled out of his jeans. 'What you've been through.'

'Mmm?'

'Psychic attack, Juanita. Nobody but nobody has two hundred hot flushes out of the blue in a few hours.' He unzipped her velvet skirt. 'That woman really hates you. We're going to have to break the spell.'

Guiding her back on to the bed, this creaky Victorian four-poster. The mattress was rather too high just to fall back on. He lifted her in his arms; she felt unnervingly light, a bit cold.

'Say, *I am very beautiful.* Say, *I am a goddess.*'

Sliding her into bed.

She said, 'I know what this is. You've seen that bloody picture of me, haven't you?'

'*The Avalonian,*' Powys said. 'Issue Six. And nothing's changed.'

'No?' She lifted the sheet with an elbow. 'This is where they took away the skin. To repair the hands. It means – this is the principal sick joke – it means I can't take any pressure on my thighs.'

Juanita closed her eyes, laughing. Her arms wide open, a hand on each pillow. It was the first time he'd ever seen her relaxed.

'Not a problem.' His lips moving down to the scars where the strips of skin had been scraped away. 'Too rough?'

'Nnnnnn.'

And slowly up to the bush. Juanita moaned, her legs opening. 'Turn on your side maybe?'

She said softly, 'This is ridiculous. This . . . Oh . . . my . . . God.'

'My *goddess*,' Powys breathed.

Around midnight, he returned from Carey and Frayne with a suitcase. He also had a tray of tea from the George and Pilgrims kitchens.

Juanita was sitting up in bed. She had the sweater on. He poured tea. 'I forgot the straw.'

'Typical,' Juanita said. 'And so little to think about.'

'Um, I'm going to say this now. Ever since I saw that photograph of you in Dan's office . . .'

She put a discoloured finger to his lips.

'Don't say any more. It's bad luck.'

'That's an old Avalonian superstition, is it?'

'It's how I feel, OK?'

'OK.' He put the book on the bed, turned it towards her. It was a hardback copy of *Psychic Self-Defence* by Dion Fortune. 'Have you read this?'

'Bits of it.'

'You read the werewolf story?'

'Where she conjures the elemental beast?'

'Let's read it again.'

He opened the book under the Tiffany lamp, whose bulb no longer flickered.

'Listen to this,' Powys said.

'CHAPTER ONE
SIGNS OF PSYCHIC ATTACK

We live in the midst of invisible forces whose effects alone we perceive . . . Normally . . . we are protected by our very incapacity to perceive.'

'Verity,' Juanita said.

'Just a passing thought. OK. It's about page fifty. Ah. "I had received serious injury from someone who, at considerable cost to myself, I had disinterestedly helped, and I was sorely tempted to retaliate. Lying on my bed resting one afternoon . . ." '

'Her resentment materialises at the bedside.' Juanita shuddered. 'As a kind of grey wolf.'

Powys sat on the bed. Held a cup of tea to her lips.

'Before we read the rest, I have to tell you where I went this evening.'

'It's like a truly horrible Grimm's fairytale,' Juanita said.

After he'd told her about Violet and Roger Ffitch and Pixhill, he told her about Archer. The blood and the fire and the pink teddy.

'No wonder the nannies were horrible,' Juanita said. 'Those weren't nannies, they were bodyguards.'

'He never knew for sure,' Powys said. 'And he still doesn't know. That's what he's had to live with. Makes you feel sorry for the old bastard, doesn't it?'

'It makes a lot of things clear. Poor kid. The retained placenta – I vaguely knew about that. Not being well up in midwifery, I didn't know about the amount of blood-letting it caused. Did I tell you that when she was little – and not so little – she used to go missing? And quite often she'd be found asleep in the Chalice Well garden.'

'The Blood Well.'

'A well's a kind of symbolic womb, isn't it? She was going back to what she couldn't remember. Oh, Powys . . .'

'I know. We've got to find her. All this gets worse.'

He picked up the book.

'Now Violet – no-nonsense type, even then – is more than a bit alarmed at what she's conjured. She tries the stern approach: *down boy*. And to her faint surprise the wolf turns into a dog and trots off and fades away. But Violet's not daft, and she's not terribly surprised when another woman in the house gets into a flap, claiming her dreams have been disrupted by images of wolves and when she woke up there were eyes shining at her from a corner of the room. Violet's seriously disturbed by now. She goes off to see Doc Moriarty, her teacher, and he confirms her worst fears.'

'That the beast is part of her. And that if she doesn't get it back she'll be, er . . .'

'No longer a nice person,' Powys said. 'It's a Left-Hand Path situation. If she doesn't get it back, she'll be on the Satanic slippery slope.'

'But she does get it back, doesn't she?'

'Not easily. But, yeh, in the end it all worked out because she helped Roger with his problem and she put the Dark Chalice on hold. With a little help from George Pixhill and the man I hesitate to call Uncle Jack.'

'This is leading somewhere, isn't it?'

Powys poured the rest of the tea. 'According to Sam, on at least two occasions recently, Diane's felt her rage at Archer – which probably goes back even farther than she knows – becoming almost . . . detached from her. Fermenting into patches of mist. Feral smells in the room.'

'Oh my God.'

'How much has she studied Dion Fortune? Would she know that story?'

'Oh dear. What you have to understand about Diane is that she doesn't have the magician mentality. Even if you believe in reincarnation the idea of her being the next life of Dion Fortune is slightly preposterous. Diane's a romantic, a mystic, very probably more than a bit psychic . . .'

'Someone who, if DF is still around in some form, she might want to protect?'

'The Third Nanny,' Juanita said. 'Sits on the bed and doesn't leave a dent in the mattress. Or something. The more you think about it, the more you realise that if anyone needs a third nanny, it's Diane.'

'But, look – this is important – you don't think Diane's capable of conjuring an elemental force?'

'Are you kidding?'

'In that case, someone's sending it to her. Someone who's been working over a long period to corrupt her.'

Juanita closed her eyes.

'Someone,' Powys said, 'who wanted her back in Glastonbury at this particular time. Who was disturbing her dreams, making her restless, sending her images of the Tor. A very practised magician – or group of magicians – who can conjure elementals. Like the wolf-thing. Like a black bus, in fact.'

'Why would Moulder have a bus delivered? Jesus, Powys, none of this is making sense. I'm not up to making sense of it. Let's just call the police.'

'The police wouldn't be able to find her. And even if they did, they wouldn't know how to handle any of this. It's down to us. Or you.'

Juanita shrank back against the oak headboard. She looked very small and frail in the four-poster.

'You've got to rediscover the Goddess,' Powys said. 'In yourself. You've got to go back to the heart.'

THIRTEEN

EVE OF MIDWINTER

In the Meadwell kitchen, Woolly and Sam were playing three-card brag by torchlight.

'Where'd you learn to play like this?' Sam said. 'Old hippies, taking people's money is not what they're about.'

Every time he lost, it was down to Sam to go and check they were alone, which meant an ominous trek through that bloody eerie dining room.

'You're just not concentrating,' Woolly said. 'I can understand that. But you got to keep playing, man. You let go of your mind in this house, it . . . You just don't, OK.'

'Something happen to you?'

'I don't know,' Woolly growled. 'That's the other thing, you never quite know.'

'Some things you know,' Sam said, not thinking of the house.

Woolly picked up on it. He grinned. 'She's a wonderful girl, Sammy. Surprised me, though, I got to say. You coming round to it. After that Charlotte.'

'Mmm, well,' Sam said. 'Something happened.'

'Like?'

'Like why a confirmed atheist and non-believer in anything you can't either spend or save from predatory upper-class gits with hunting horns is suddenly scared to go in that room next door.'

'Oh,' said Woolly. 'Like that.'

'I've seen . . . bloody Pixhill,' Sam said. 'I've seen Pixhill, OK? Old bloke in a deerstalker hat. Though I like to think he wouldn't ever have stalked a deer. And don't ask me – don't anybody *ever* ask me – about his eyes.'

'Sheesh,' Woolly said. 'When was this?'

And so Sam told him. And because it was cards-on-the-table night, he told Woolly about the devastation of the trees. The road.

Woolly threw his newly dealt hand on the table.

'You're not winding me up?'

'Tonight I'm not winding anybody up, Woolly. Tonight, winding up is on hold.'

'I don't know what to do,' Woolly said.

'Don't do anything. Juanita said to hang on.'

'Until when?'

'I don't know. Until we got Diane back.'

'You know what I think?' Woolly said.

'I don't even like to ask.'

'I think we got a battle on two levels here. On the material level, the Glastonbury First bit, the road, Bowkett's Bill. And all the side effects that lot's having on the invisible layers. Or maybe it's the other way around, and G-1 and the bypass, the whole thing's a manifestation of something going down on the Inner Planes.'

'Oh shit,' said Sam. 'I'm not *that* much of a sodding convert.'

'So what I think . . . I just think it's time we threw everything we got at this situation.'

'You're just saying that 'cause you reckon you got nothing to lose.'

'Maybe,' Woolly said. 'Does it matter? Where's Verity keep the phone?'

'Never was any good at keeping my trap shut.' Sam stared at his cards. 'Aw, for fuck's sake, Woolly, you dealt me a bloody king-flush and threw your cards in.'

'Yeah, well,' Woolly said, 'it was about time I took a stroll. After I use the phone.'

They entered the cradle.

Henry VIII could steal the gold, pull down the walls, Powys thought, but the fat bastard couldn't take away the atmosphere.

Sometimes, when I am alone in the Abbey grounds, Colonel Pixhill had written, *I become afraid of my own reverie, afraid that my soul will rise before its time.*

Even at night it was not eerie. Merely awesome.

Juanita knew how to get in. She said most locals did. You just had to be quiet as you climbed over a certain garden wall in a backstreet. In the old days, Juanita said, many a bottle of Mateus

Rosé had been consumed under a full moon on the holyest erthe in all England.

They'd gone back to the main entrance. Near the dying Thorn. This was the way to approach it, Juanita said.

Beyond the wooden cross, uneven stone walls had evolved into a kind of organic life, could almost have been close-cut, layered hedges. Other walls, other buildings, heaps of hallowed rubble, were all features in what, even without the lawns and the manicuring, was a garden.

Powys laid down the suitcase on the dark grass. It was cold and wet, but the snow had gone.

This, in the beginning and at the end, was the heart. This was where it all came together. Thirty-six secret, walled acres in what was still the centre of the town. Glastonbury's streets guarding their Abbey like . . .

Like the Holy Grail.

His gaze was raised to the focal point, the summit of the ruins. He'd seen pictures of it many times: the light flowing like a river between twin towers.

Except they weren't towers. And your second concept – an arch with the top part missing – they weren't that either. They were the ends of two high, buttressed walls, a flawed mirror image of each other, but they rose like forearms from elbows resting on the green turf. Ending in compliant, cupped hands . . . hands which could almost be supporting an invisible bowl.

Powys felt Juanita's tentative arm against his and realised he'd been standing here staring, for several minutes, at the moon through the space between the stone hands.

'It's like they're holding a chalice,' he said. 'Or waiting for one.'

'They say – some people say – this is the heart chakra in the body of the earth. The higher emotional centre.'

'I know.' You could almost swear it was warmer in here than the other side of the walls. 'You warm enough?'

Juanita nodded. She was wearing the long woollen cloak he'd brought from her wardrobe.

'Somehow,' Powys said, 'I can't quite believe that when we talk of the Dark Chalice we mean the gold cup planted on Abbot

Whiting by Edmund Ffitch. I still think it's a metaphor. An ancient symbol of division, intolerance.'

'If the Holy Grail is a symbol of conciliation, both a pagan and a Christian symbol . . .'

'The anti-Grail. It's logical to believe there's always been an anti-Grail. These things have their time. It's as if, when Henry destroyed all this, he was caught up in something that was *trying* to happen. They all were. Abbot Whiting – nice guy, kind to the poor. They put his head on the Abbey gates, isn't that right? The whole town must have been absolutely flattened, people terrified.'

'Not least', Juanita said, 'because this was the place where Jesus himself walked.'

'You believe that?'

Juanita looked up at the hands of stone accepting the invisible chalice. 'Sure. Why not? If his rich Uncle Joe wanted to broaden his horizons.'

'So when the Abbot was killed and the building violated and vandalised . . . by the King of England, they must have . . .' Powys hesitated.

'They must have questioned the very existence of God.' Juanita stood in front of him. 'It would have taken a long time to get back to that level of spirituality. We thought that maybe we were close to it once. Now it's gone the other way.'

Standing here, in the silence of the ruins, on the eve of midwinter, Powys could almost feel the Veil shredding like a cobweb.

'OK?'

Juanita nodded. He pulled at the ties which fastened the cloak at her neck.

She raised her arms, her crippled hands in the cup formation, like the great stone buttresses, and the cloak fell away from her shoulders and dropped to the grass.

Powys caught his breath.

Juanita shone in the moonlight.

She was wearing the dress last featured on the front of *The Avalonian*. Issue Six.

*

467

'Sammy,' Woolly hissed. 'They're here.'

Heart in his mouth, he'd been upstairs to the lavatory. The torch lighting up the dirty black beams and all those doorways, some of them ajar, shadows oozing out. And on his way back, glancing out the window at the top of the stairs, he'd seen the sidelights moving very slowly up the drive.

'What do we do?' Sam whispered. 'We call the cops?'

'I reckon we see who it is first. If it's Grainger I don't reckon we need bother the fuzz.'

'Christ,' said Sam. 'You still call them the fuzz after all these years?'

But Woolly had crept out into the dining room, a sliver of moonlight thin as fuse-wire on the table where Pixhill had lain.

Sam shivered. Funny, it really did go up your spine. Any normal, earthly fear, like having the crap beaten out of you by a master of foxhounds, it never happened like that.

Woolly was standing on a chair to see out of the high window.

'Two of them. Men.'

'Grainger?'

'Don't look like it. Both tallish guys.'

'Shit,' said Sam.

'One's got a pickaxe.'

'Double shit.'

Woolly dropped to the floor. 'You wanner go for this or what?'

'Maybe not. Maybe we should play safe. You want me to ring the cops, being as how I'm slightly less well known to them at this moment in time?'

'Only, one of 'em's your mate, Mr Davey,' said Woolly.

'Ah.' Sam rubbed his jaw. 'Well. This changes things just slightly.'

Powys wondered afterwards if perhaps he'd fallen asleep. Which seemed, in the normal way of things, unlikely, on the eve of mid-winter, sitting on a low stone wall under an icy moon.

If he hadn't fallen asleep, then it wasn't a dream.

In this dream, the one that wasn't, Juanita stood on one side of what tourists sometimes saw as a broken archway, where the stone arms reached for the chalice.

On the other side of the archway that wasn't, stood another woman.

Both white, incandescent in the moonlight.

When Powys either awoke or didn't, Juanita was alone.

Woolly came out of the garden shed. 'Ain't much useful in there, man, to be honest.'

He handed Sam a garden fork.

'It's got a wonky handle.'

'The alternative's a bent lawn-rake.'

'What's yours, then?'

'I'm a man of peace, remember?' Woolly whispered. 'Come on, move it.'

They climbed over into the field. Under the moon, the Tor looked surprisingly sinister. Sam figured he was seeing it from the same angle as when . . .

Don't think about it.

'You know your way round here? Shit, this field's waterlogged.'

'Couple of hours it'll be ice-logged,' Woolly muttered. 'Sure, I used to do a bit of gardening for the Colonel. He had a greenhouse then. I figured maybe I could grow certain exotic plants on the side, like. Never thought he'd know what one looked like. Still, he was very nice about it. Died the following year, poor old soul.'

Sam looked up at the Tor. Something was bothering him.

'Woolly, where I saw this road, look. There's no way they could run it through there. I was so blown away by . . . you know, *him* . . . that I just didn't figure it out proper. I remember thinking it looked like it was aimed straight at the centre of the Tor, under the tower. And, like, you see it from here, that's where it would have to go, else Meadwell'd be right in the middle of the central reservation, and it's a double-listed building, so that's out, right?'

'What you saying? And keep your bloody voice down.'

'I don't think that excavation's anything to do with the road. Not directly.'

'So what was it?'

'Fuck knows. You're the earth-mysteries expert.'

'Think about it later,' Woolly said. 'We got to scare these bastards away before they have the top of that well off.'

By moonlight, they skirted the edge of the field, keeping to the hedge. They heard the clunk of a pickaxe on concrete, saw the muffled glow of a lamp on the ground. Sam moved quietly through the shallow drainage ditch, his shoes and the bottoms of his jeans soaked through. There was an old stile he vaguely remembered from his days with the Ramblers' Association. From way back, when there was like a little pilgrims' way to the Meadwell.

Amazingly, he found the stile, tested it with one foot. Seemed solid enough to stand on, so he stood on it. He signalled to Woolly. Then, just as the pickaxe struck metal, he bawled out,

'Avon and Somerset Police. Don't no bugger move!'

And then he was over the stile and going hard for Darryl Davey, swinging the garden fork like an axe at a tree.

Darryl had started to run, and the shaft of the fork caught him under both knees and he came down on the concrete with a smack. Sam was aware of the other guy legging it, but that didn't matter because the lamp on the ground showed him where to put the fork.

Like hard under Darryl's chin.

Woolly was with him now. 'You see who the other bloke was?'

'Don't give a shit. This is my man. Darryl, as I recall, it was in 1972 when you persuaded me to part with my dinner money or face a difficult nosebleed situation. I got to tell you, you got precisely five seconds to say what you done with Diane, else it's a prong up each nostril and then I start beating your lovely big teeth out with the handle, look. And after that . . .'

Darryl twisted his neck round and a rusting prong nudged his Adam's apple. He screamed. 'Where's them cops?'

'Four,' Sam said. 'Three. Two . . .'

'I don't fucking know, do I?' Darryl began to cough.

Sam raised a foot.

'Leave it out,' Woolly said. 'He can't say much with your shoe on his gob.'

'One,' Sam said.

'No, listen . . . All we done was scare her. Then Ceridwen comes in and tells us to piss off. I don't know what they done with her after that, honest to . . .'

'Where was this, Darryl?'

'Outside Woolaston's shop. Len and Wayne done his window, right. I'm following Lady L . . . Diane.'

'Following her, why?'

''Cause they told me to.'

'Who?'

'Like . . . your old man, yeah?'

'Shit,' Sam said in disgust. 'You get your orders from the old man?'

'Sometimes.'

Woolly said, 'Who was with you, then?'

Darryl went silent.

'We missed that, Darryl,' Sam said.

'You can kill me,' Darryl Davey shouted. 'But I ain't sayin' no more.'

So they let him go. They let the bastard go.

They went back to the house and they put on every light in the place.

It was gone three a.m.

'Would you trust Darryl Davey with anything worth knowing?' Woolly said.

'Would you trust my old man?'

'Not unless I had no choice,' Woolly said. 'Go on. Go get him, boy.'

'I'm not leaving you here, Woolly. What if the other bugger comes back?'

'Then I'll handle it. Go, Sammy.'

'Can't we both go? This well thing, is that really so . . .?'

'Yeh. It is. It is, Sammy. Go.'

Sam drove away from Meadwell in Joe Powys's Mini. Glad, on one level, to be leaving Meadwell. Not glad to be leaving Woolly.

Premonition?

Not that much of a convert.

FOURTEEN

PALE LIGHTBALL

She felt her anger like a bed of white-hot coals in her solar plexus. Her eyes, wide open, watched the mist rising, weaving between the great pillars.

Diane watched the tendrils of cold steam interlacing in the air above her, hearing Archer's politician's voice, dark as old oak seasoned by his heritage.

All I need to know is, do you, the people of Glastonbury, want it to happen?

. . . damned hippies and squatters . . . turning this town into a jungle . . .

Archer. Who, all through their childhood, had watched her from a distance. Which was frightfully easy to do at Bowermead. Archer's face, still as an owl's, amid the branches of a tree as she pushed her doll's pram through the wood, an enormous pine cone suddenly landing like a grenade on its blankets. Archer's petulant expression seen from a high chair across the table, a spoon at his big, moist lips.

Diane bit the bedclothes.

Archer's finger at his lips. *Shhhhh.* Almost a man now, very strong as he lifted her out of bed and carried her in his arms down the stairs, Diane drowsy, half-hypnotised, aged seven?

Down through the grounds, sweet-scented in the summer night, and Oliver Pixhill waiting in the shrubbery. Almost dawn as they carried her, half-fascinated, mostly terrified, to the place where the Tor was a huge fairy castle.

Bring out the lights, Diane . . .

Diane felt starved and ill. She was drenched in the sort of spasmodic sweat which keeps congealing on your face, thick and sour as days-old milk. She was here because she was ill.

It was a hospital, wasn't it?

*

472

The old man had a big house now, self-built to a much higher standard than his usual crap, in an acre of ill-gotten ground set back from decently surburban Leg of Mutton Road. Far enough off the road to make it what Griff Daniel would call 'exclusive'.

But near enough to cause him serious aggro with his nice neighbours if there should be a high-decibel altercation resulting from the distinguished builder refusing to admit his prodigal son at half-past three in the morning.

Sam started politely. He rang the bell.

There was no response.

This time Sam kept his finger on the bell and at the same time battered his knuckles on the panel below the tasteless slab of bullseye glass.

Above the front porch, a bedroom window opened and a security spotbulb threw a circle of light around Sam.

'What the bloody hell you think you're doing?'

Sam stood openly in the middle of the circle of light. 'Well, I could do a tap-dance, Dad. Sing a couple of songs. Bit of a cabaret for the neighbours. Or you could just let me in and we'll have a little chat. And, yeah, I do know it's half-past three.'

'Bugger off,' said Griff Daniel.

'On the other hand, to save a bit of time I could just put that sundial through your lounge window.'

'And set the burglar alarm off, and I could have you banged up for the night. Now, for the last time . . .'

'I'd like that,' Sam said. 'I could sit in the station down at Street and keep the night shift entertained with your life history, culminating in your arrangement with Darryl Davey, Len Whatsisname and Wayne Rankin. It's cold, Dad, I'm not gonner piss about . . .'

Three minutes later, Griff let him in. Paisley dressing-gown and a face like a gargoyle with stone-fatigue.

'You got a bloody nerve, boy.'

'Yeah, well, we'll skip over the pleasantries, if you don't mind.' Sam pushed past him, through the hall and into a split-level lounge with a floor-to-ceiling rainbow stone fireplace and a cocktail bar with mirrors. He didn't have time to laugh. 'Things I need to know now, or, swear to God, I'll put you under so much shit it'll take more than a JCB . . .'

'You got nothin' on me, boy.' Griff glanced back at the stairs. 'No!' Waving a dismissive hand.

'Bring her down,' Sam said. 'Let's have a party.' He didn't want the old man's latest scrubber cluttering the place up, but anything to cause more disruption . . .

However, when the woman appeared in the doorway, clutching a white robe to her scrawny throat, she wasn't what he was expecting.

It was Jenna. From The Cauldron. Ceridwen's pipe-cleaner.

It didn't make sense. What was she doing here with the old man? Why wasn't she with Ceridwen and the rest of the so-called Inner Circle?

And Diane.

'Where's Diane?' Sam said weakly. 'That's all I wanner know.'

Griff Daniel sneered and dropped into a kingsize easy chair. 'You stupid little sod. Never did know when you were playin' outer your league.'

'And what about you?'

'I know my level.'

'And her?'

Jenna stared at him, her lips like a thin zip.

'Why aren't you with Ceridwen?'

'She knows her level, too,' Griff said.

'I thought you were a lesbian,' Sam said. 'I thought that was what the Inner Circle was about.'

'The Inner Circle isn't what you think,' Jenna said. 'And I'm not in it. And not all feminists are lesbians – that's something he would say.'

This was weird. Sam shook his head in non-comprehension. It was kind of sick.

'Don't think this is no more than a loose sexual arrangement,' Jenna said haughtily. 'He isn't going to be wearing an earring.'

'Go away, boy,' Griff Daniel said. 'We don't know nothin'. Somethin' I've learned these past few weeks. Local politics is my pond, look. Local politics is knowing which people to help when they d' want you, and when to keep out of it. Some things, 'tis better to know nothin'.'

Sam clenched his fists.

474

'Shut the door on your way out,' Griff said.

But when Sam was on his way out he thought of something the old man *did* know.

Mist, still rising around the bed like smoke. In a perverse way, Diane found this comforting. It suited her mood, enclosed her dark thoughts.

In the midst of it, she thought for a moment that she could see a very pale lightball.

When she was very young she used to go all trembly and run downstairs, and Father snorted impatiently and the nannies said, Nonsense, child, and felt for a temperature.

Nannies.

There was a certain sort of nanny – later known as a governess – which Father expressly sought out. Nannies one and two, both the same, the sort which was supposed to have yellowed and faded from the scene along with crinolines and parasols. The sort which, in the 1960s, still addressed their charges as 'child'. The sort which, as you grew older, you realised should never be consulted about occurrences such as lights around the Tor.

And then there was the Third Nanny.

Her memories of the Third Nanny remained vague and elusive. She remembered laughter; the Third Nanny was the only one of them that ever laughed. And one other thing: she would sit on the edge of the bed, but never left a dent in the mattress when she arose.

The pale lightball hovered. Part of her wanted to clutch at it and part of her wanted to push it away.

In the end that was what she did, for lightballs belonged to childhood, and she was grown up now.

She wondered what day it was. Was it Christmas yet? Always hated Christmas. All those fruity-voiced oafs smelling of drink and cigars, and then going stiffly to church. *'Merry Christmas, m'Lord, Merry Christmas. Thank you, m'Lord, very kind, very kind of you . . .'* And Boxing Days echoing to the horrid peremptory, blood-lusting blast of the hunting horn. *'Time we had you riding, Diane.' 'Doubt if we've got a horse fat enough and stupid enough, Father, ha ha . . .'*

'Time to wake up, Diane.' Ceridwen was at her bedside.

'It's still dark.'

'It will soon be dawn.'

Ceridwen no longer wore the starched uniform of the nurse or the nanny, but a long purple robe.

'This is not a hospital, is it?'

'It has made you well, however,' Ceridwen said. 'You've learned what you needed to learn. Without this knowledge you could never be free.'

'I . . . I suppose that's true.'

She had dreamed of blood. The blood around her birth. She had remembered her mother's cooling arms. She knew who had murdered her mother. She was, at last, approaching an understanding of who she was.

'You once came to me to ask if you were an incarnation of Dion Fortune. You always knew that, didn't you?'

'I . . .'

Ceridwen went down on her knees at the bottom of the bed. 'I honour you, Diane Fortune.'

And then there was a rustling all around her, and other people in robes emerged from behind the pillars, bearing candles. Among them, faces she knew.

Rozzie and Mort and Viper and Hecate, the girl who had been so rude to her and had made the children paint the bus black.

They all dropped to their knees.

And then Gwyn appeared, tall and bearded in a shroud of mist, and he held up his sickle before throwing it to the ground at the bottom of the bed. And all the people in the room said in unison, 'We honour you, Diane Fortune.'

Verity awoke into shrilling darkness and clicked off her travel alarm.

She had slept for four hours, after making Wanda's supper and mugs of calming cocoa. Wanda, who had drunk too much, had been in one of her unpleasant, resentful moods at being obliged to rise before dawn to put on a public relations sideshow with a bloody Christian.

The luminous hands of the travel alarm told Verity it was five-thirty. She arose at once, against the tug from her hip, into the tainted luxury of her suite at Wanda's.

Tainted by guilt. She arose into guilt. She had deserted her post. She had allowed Mr Powys to guide her away from the 'grave and mortal danger' foretold by Major Shepherd.

And left little Councillor Woolaston in its path.

Perhaps that part was over. Perhaps the intruders had been caught and detained by the police.

And perhaps something horrible had occurred.

Verity washed in cold water, for the heating had not yet come on. She heard the first spatter of sleet against the window.

She felt sick to her soul.

FIFTEEN

LIGHTS GO OUT

Woolly played patience at the kitchen table and didn't once win.

Life was like this. All you could do was keep turning over the cards, never knowing how they were stacked.

Of course, this wasn't the case with everybody. Some people cheated, and some people actually knew how to shuffle the pack. Glastonbury had far more than the average number of people who thought they knew how to stack the deck, but Woolly had no illusions.

He dealt himself three more and turned over the stack, but nothing would fit.

He knew he'd done one good thing this past night. Couldn't figure how he'd done it. Maybe, just that once, he'd turned the right card. Maybe he'd found an opening in the house's black atmosphere. Whatever, something had let him take the wheel of the black bus, and he'd saved a life.

Woolly hoped it was a good life.

He was hoping this when the lights began to go out.

Powys put his hands on her shoulders and was horrified. There was a layer of frost on the muslin.

'I'm all right,' she said. 'Leave me.'

'You're not.' He thought, what are we doing? What have I done? She's had pneumonia, she's been through hell.

Just for odd moments he'd thought, *this is it*. Without quite knowing what he meant, or even what he hoped for.

It had been a really crazy thing to do. Madness. He opened the suitcase and took out her cloak and put it around her shoulders. Very gently, he brought her to her feet. Her face was very close, but he couldn't see it very well. The moon had gone, the mist had arisen, there was a thin and icy wind.

478

'I c-could see her.' A tremor in Juanita's voice. 'She was in a grey place and she was lying down. I g-got a feeling of terrible confusion. I tried to tell her I was there. Sure she knew at one point. But then she turned away.'

She buried her head in his chest and he held her under the arms of the Abbey as the sleet came, deceptively gentle at first.

'I felt a light go out,' Juanita said.

As they came back over the wall, Juanita shivering inside the cloak, Powys heard the rumble of traffic, the criss-cross of headlights on the stone.

Two vans came out of High Street; he turned and saw them enter Wellhouse Lane. An ancient, clattering Land-Rover followed. And then – oh God – a bus.

A couple of dozen people were walking up High Street. They wore big boots and carried backpacks and rucksacks.

'What's happening?'

'You don't know?' a young woman said. 'Demo, mate.'

'Where are you from?'

A bloke said, 'Bristol Eco-guerrillas. BEG. Except we don't. Be people here from all over the country by morning. You know they started the road?'

A woman spotted Juanita in her cloak. 'You one of the pagans? It's getting, like, a bit confused. Groups everywhere been waiting for the call on the road, you know?'

Someone leaned out of the back of a truck. 'Happy Solstice, sister!'

'Let's get out of here,' Juanita whispered. Powys wasn't aware until they were heading through the already crowded central car park to the back entrance of The George and Pilgrims, that she'd taken his hand.

In hers.

Shortly before seven, Matthew Banks and his friend, the secondhand bookseller, called for Wanda in Matthew's Discovery. Wanda was petulant and bothered about her clothes, settling at last for the capacious black and white cape and a black, wide-brimmed hat which Verity knew would be blown away by the wind on top of the Tor.

'You'll have to carry my bag, darling,' she snapped at Verity. 'I can't manage *everything*. The bloody, bloody Bishop. Why couldn't he have simply waited until the Summer Solstice?'

'I'm not coming.' Verity handed Matthew the flask of coffee she'd made for Wanda and a half bottle of Glenmorangie.

'Don't be ridiculous, get in the car.'

'I'm needed at Meadwell.'

'That damned house needs nobody. Except possibly a demolition crew. Now get in, Verity.'

'I'm sorry, Wanda. I should never have come here. I know you couldn't refuse. I know how much you owe Ceridwen.'

'What on earth are you talking about?'

'They made you invite me to stay, didn't they?'

'What utter non—'

'To get me out of the way. Well, you can tell them I'm going back.'

She turned her back on the Discovery and walked off down the mews. Someone would give her a lift, perhaps.

'Verity!' Wanda screeched. 'I've done everything for you, you sad little woman!'

Don Moulder was manning his field gate, keping the riffraff out, shouting at them that it was private property.

Who were all these buggers? They never said this. There'd been talk of a small demonstration against Bowkett's Restriction of Access Bill (of which Don Moulder was fully in favour).

'No, you can't!' he roared at some cretin in a cagoule leaning out of his car and waving a twenty-pound note. 'This is the official car park.'

At last, two new-looking cars prodded through the cold mist which was alternating with freezing clear spells and sudden wintry mist, the Tor appearing and disappearing against a filthy night sky.

'Mr Moulder? Peter Wakely, Archdeacon.'

'Thank Christ.'

'Indeed,' shouted the Archdeacon. 'The Bishop's behind me in the BMW. Just tell us where to go.'

'Over there. Under the tree. By the buzz.'

Don Moulder didn't look at the bus. He hadn't been close to it. Hadn't even liked putting the keys in his pocket. Maybe the Bishop could bless them too. And then he'd sell the bus back to the scrapyard for half of what he'd paid. Give the proceeds to charity. Thus cleansing himself and his land.

The Bishop was wearing a tweed overcoat, buttoned around a purple neckpiece. He stepped out under an umbrella.

'Morning, your grace. Donald Moulder. This is my field.'

'Good morning, Mr Moulder. And a very fine field. Wonderful view of the Tor.'

'About the buzz, Bishop . . .'

'The buzz?'

'I spoke to a feller in your office. Reverend Williams, could've been. Arranging for you to help me with this buzz. This one behind you.'

'My God,' said the Bishop, 'I don't think we can tow it away.'

'To cleanse it, Bishop. To free this buzz and my field from unwanted presences. This Reverend Williams said you could, like, exorcise it . . .'

'I'm sure he said no such thing, Mr Moulder.' The Archdeacon, a powerfully built man in a Goretex jacket, thrust himself behind them like a bodyguard. 'I think you must have misunderstood.'

'You sayin' this man lied to me?'

'He was in no position to make any such promise and on a day like this, with a schedule like ours . . . I suggest you write to the diocese. I'm sorry, Mr Moulder, we do have to get on.'

'Drop us a line,' said the Bishop, as he was hustled towards the field gate.

Don Moulder looked back towards the bus. All he could see in the darkness was a great black bulge in the field and the glimmer of the scablike radiator grille, rust on it like dried blood on grinning teeth. Grinning at Don Moulder's stupidity.

As the Bishop's party left the field, another BMW pulled halfway through the gate, a head leaned out of the driver's window.

'Mr Moulder!'

Archer Ffitch's voice.

'Hell's going on?'

Don wandered over. 'Somebody told 'em the new road's under way.'

'But that's nonsense.'

'You tell them that. Looks like hundreds of the bolshie devils, comin' from all over, look. Won't do your campaign no harm, though, will it, Mr Archer? You wanner get up there, argue with 'em. Be telly crews in a bit. Make the most of it, I would.'

He knew he sounded like a ranting lunatic.

'I'll come later,' Archer said. 'I have to see my father.'

He reversed out of the field. Don Moulder followed him, not looking back. People with torches and backpacks were swarming all over the lane. It was like Armageddon.

They went into The George and Pilgrims through the back door and quietly up the narrow stairs to Powys's room.

When Arnold leapt up at her, Juanita pushed both hands into his fur. Powys looking on, not sure if the dream was over.

Juanita held both hands under the Tiffany lamp. They were still luridly discoloured, but she could flex the fingers without pain. She reached up, very hesitantly, and untied her cloak.

Juanita and Powys looked at each other. Neither said a word. Powys pushed his hands through his hair, sat down on the bed.

'I suppose', Juanita said after a minute, 'that most people would say it was a nervous thing. That I . . . you know . . . I could probably have used them any time. But I was scared to.'

'Is that what you think?'

She thought about it. 'If that was the case I think I'd have been able to use them when I wasn't thinking about it. Like when we were making love.'

'How long have you known?'

'I suspected from the moment I put my hands up before the stone arms. To receive the Chalice. I didn't think about it again.'

'Juanita . . .'

'Mmm?'

'Who was the other woman?'

'Did you see another woman?'

'I think I did.'

'There was power there, wasn't there?'

482

'A lot.' He couldn't stop looking at her hands; they were loosely clasped in front of her against the muslin dress. 'A whole reservoir.'

He felt her stare.

'What?' he said.

'Nothing. I don't know. Listen, maybe . . . Maybe it wasn't the right time.'

'What does that mean?'

'I need to wash. I'll think about it.' She seemed unhurried suddenly.

'I'll take Arnold round the block,' he said.

In the middle of the car park, Arnold taking a leak against the church wall, Powys encountered Sam Daniel.

'Powys, where the hell you been?'

'Around.' What was he supposed to say? He couldn't explain any of it.

'It's chaos up there. Gonner be a lot of trouble, count on it. Woolly. He wouldn't listen. Half the bloody Green Party's moved in over the last couple of hours.'

'He told them about the road, didn't he?'

'And he was wrong. It's not a road. I seen my dad. He did the work, his lads, his JCB.'

'What do you mean it's not a road?'

'You got a map?'

'I can find a map. Come up to the room, Sam.'

'You think this is important?'

'Could be,' Powys said. 'I mean anything could be important, couldn't it, at this stage. What time's dawn? Eight?'

'I never notice.'

They heard the angry warble of a police car.

'Bloody hell,' Sam said, 'word's finally got through to Street.'

Verity had walked all the way back to Meadwell, as quickly as she could manage with her dragging hip.

She pushed open the garden gate. Over her head, the yew trees clasped each other against the ice-barbed, predawn wind. Councillor Woolaston's Renault car was parked under the wall.

483

No other car, thank God, was there. All the lights in the house were out. Verity dug into the pocket of her winter coat for her keys.

She didn't need them. The door swung lazily open at a touch, as though the house was yawning with boredom.

Verity entered silently. And then, lest he thought she was the expected intruder, she called out,

'Mr Woolaston. Don't be alarmed. It's Verity Endicott!'

He didn't reply. It had been a long vigil; perhaps he had fallen asleep.

In the hall, all was normal: the dark tobacco pillars lounged like greasy old men and the water pipes bulged and croaked. *Welcome home. Heh heh heh*, the pipes seemed to belch. There was a sour and salty smell in the air. As if the house had broken wind in her face.

And she knew then, before she even noticed that the dining room door was ajar.

'Archer's orders, this was,' Sam said. 'Not the old man.'

Powys had found the Mendip Hill (West) Ordnance Survey map downstairs among a rack of tourist guides. They had it spread over the bed.

'Here's the Tor, right? Here's Meadwell. And here's Bowermead Hall.'

'I should have noticed that.' Powys pencilled it in. 'They're in a straight line. You'd probably miss it because it runs so close to the St Michael Line. But it *is* a ley . . . see, it goes on . . . a mound here and through this farm called Southbarrow farm.'

'So they built Bowermead Hall on an old ley-line.' Juanita had changed back into her sweater and skirt, combed her hair. 'Why would they do that?'

'OK,' Powys said. 'If, say, they thought Meadwell was too small and dismal to live in, maybe a little too close to the Tor for comfort, but they wanted to retain the link. Maybe even strengthen it, by adding another point to the line. And this is where they chopped down the trees. Dug it out. They dug out the ley?'

'You get an immaculate view of the Tor,' Sam said. 'Side of it I've never seen before. Like at Meadwell, but even more dramatic.'

'And that was where you saw . . .'

'Him. Pixhill. I think it upset him.'

Juanita was tracing the line with a forefinger. Possibly, Powys thought, for the sheer novelty of being able to do that. He noticed she was breathing faster.

'Sam, what's here?'

The tip of her finger quivering.

Sam peered at the map. 'Resr, what's that mean?'

'Reservoir,' Powys said.

'Oh my God.' Juanita closed and opened her eyes three times. She was looking at the bed next to where Powys sat. 'That's it.'

'What?'

'It's where she is. This reservoir.'

Sam stiffened. 'Drowned.'

'It's disused,' Juanita said. 'It's a big grey place with . . .' She closed her eyes again, '. . . three grey, concrete pillars.'

'What's up with her?' Sam was spooked. 'Where's she getting this from?'

Arnold stood up on all three legs and Powys, seeing his big ears go back and his hairy snout rise, dived to the floor and clapped a hand around it.

'He was gonner howl, wasn't he?'

Juanita smoothed the quilt next to where Powys had sat.

'Never a dent,' she said.

Upon the long oak table, on which the Colonel's coffin had lain for three days and nights, little Councillor Woolaston now lay dead.

Verity wept over his horribly disfigured corpse.

Be assured that I would not expect you to do anything beyond coming to the rescue of my good and staunch friend, Verity Endicott, who is in grave and mortal danger, standing as she does directly in the path of (and, God help me, I do not exaggerate) an old and utterly merciless evil.

She backed away from the body, not through fear or revulsion at the way the head had been smashed – nose and teeth broken, the blood pooled in sunken cheeks – but to give vent to her feelings.

'How I *hate* you,' she told Meadwell.

And then thought of the well itself. It would be opened now.

SIXTEEN

YES, NANNY

She lay back and let her eyelids fall. The pillows were soft and cool. The back of her head felt heavy, like a bag of potatoes. She let her arms flop by her sides. The anger, still burning somewhere below her abdomen was at odds, though not uncomfortably so, with the supine state of her body. She was, surprisingly, reaching a state of relaxation. But then, she was getting rather good at that.

Diane smiled.

The earliest light had hardened the tower on Glastonbury Tor into a rigid finger which poked and gouged blood from the raw flesh of the winter sky.

It was not yet seven-thirty. A false dawn, Don Moulder thought, watching from his top field through binoculars.

Lights showed where the protesters were scattered like maggots all around the Tor, but Don reckoned the police wouldn't let them go up. For their own safety no doubt. He'd half expected there to be a counter-demonstration by the Glastonbury First people, but they were lying low. Sensibly. Let the New Age hooligans dig their own grave would be their line.

He could see the handful of folk starting to wind their way up the Tor under a big lamp. Dame Wanda the beacon, in her black and white cape and her big hat. Pretty tame pagan, all the same. Too cold, no doubt, for the old Egyptian priestess get-up from *Hello!* magazine. Poor bloody Christian, too, that bishop, with his smarmy ways and his entourage and his minders.

Don focused the glasses on a very bright spotlight, setting up a small figure in a sheepskin coat, the collar up around short blonde hair. Tammy White, BBC Bristol. Don had relented and allowed Tammy and her cameraman to park in the bottom field. Tammy had parked her white Peugeot right side on to that bloody bus, God save her news-hungry little soul.

The sky was on the move again, darkening up again. Knew it was a false dawn.

Not seen weather like this in a good long while. First one thing then another. Like the heavens couldn't make up their minds which way to turn.

'OK.' Powys was driving. 'How we going to do this? Do we go in through the Bowermead entrance or what? How d'you get in that night, Sam?'

'Parked on the road, scraped through a couple of hedges. But it took me bloody ages, Powys. We don't have that kind of time. I say we go in. State you left him last night, I don't reckon Rankin's gonner do much. Juanita?'

'Do it.'

Powys cut the headlights at the entrance to the drive. Sam did the gates. Nobody came out to stop him, but when they reached the house there was a grey BMW parked on the forecourt.

'Archer's home,' Juanita said.

'Head down there.' Sam pointed to an avenue of trees. 'Takes you past the barn, past the hunt kennels. We wake the dogs, nothing we can do about that. Only problem is, it's a dead end. They come down here in a couple of Range Rovers, we're screwed.'

Powys paused, holding the Mini on the clutch.

Juanita sighed. 'You want to know how certain I am about this, don't you?'

Neither of them answered.

'It was like a Ouija board is all I can say. Something was moving my finger on the map. Just like something gave me a jolt when you came out with the word "reservoir" earlier.'

'Oh, shit,' Sam said. 'I don't like this.'

'I wouldn't like it either, Sam, except whatever we picked up, we picked it up in the Abbey. I wouldn't like to believe you can pick up anything bad there.'

Powys let out the clutch. 'You saw her sitting on the bed, didn't you?'

'Just like you in the Abbey, I don't know what I saw.'

Arnold sat on his rug on the back seat, next to Juanita. Powys watched him for a moment in the mirror. 'He knows what he saw.'

In the mirror Powys saw a figure emerge on to the steps, watching them, as they passed under the avenue of trees.

She was starting to enjoy her anger and felt no guilt about this. Light dripped on to her eyelids like syrup. And in the cushiony hinterland of sleep, in those moments when the senses mingle and then dissolve, when fragments of whispered words are sometimes heard and strange responses sought, Diane's rage fermented pleasurably into the darkest of wines . . .

The barns bulked to the right. 'Kennels beyond that,' Sam said. 'Then you got no road left.'

The Mini went into a dip. Powys knew he wasn't going to make it up the other side.

'OK, leave it here. You're out of sight.'

They all got out. Sam took the torch, led them up the side of the hill, Powys concerned when Juanita slipped and went down on her hands.

'OK?'

'Seem to be. It makes no sense but I do seem to be.'

'Not a hag then. Not tainted by the whatsit of death.'

'I feel like I may live for ever. That probably means I'm going to die. Jesus God, will you look at that.'

It looked like what Sam had thought it was. The devastation before a motorway goes through. The outraged stubble of a speedily shaven forest. You could almost hear the screams of the trees. If trees had ghosts, this place would be haunted for centuries.

'I've seen this before,' Powys said. 'They're reawakening the ley. They're going to either bring something down from the Tor or . . .'

'Or send something up,' Juanita said.

'Is that you talking or . . .?'

'I don't know. Do we have to walk through this?'

'Yeah.' Sam stepped over a watery rut. 'Sorry about this.'

Somewhere behind them, a hound began to howl. Powys looked sternly at Arnold, hopping between their legs, before he remembered that Arnold rarely responded to other dogs.

'Where'd you see Pixhill?'

'Shut up,' Sam said

'Don't worry. They rarely appear to more than one person. I think they're scared.'

'Ha ha.' Then Sam gasped.

Powys stopped. The Tor had arisen before them, a huge black wedding cake surrounded by candles.

'Lamps?'

'The protesters,' Sam said. 'Woolly's eco-army on the march. Swelling the ranks of the locals opposing the Tame the Tor Bill. Got here in no time, didn't they? All those little idealists phoning each other, spreading the word. Taking a day off work, those who've still got jobs. Piling into their cars and vans and trucks. Makes you proud to be British, don't it?'

'They'll go to the Tor first, and then they'll start looking for the road.'

'Do you think we oughter make sure they find it?'

'That's not a bad idea, Sam.'

'Give me something to think about. Like the night I first came this way, I was figuring out how best to sab the hunt. Trying to work off my temper at Archer.'

Juanita said, 'You know what will happen if Diane does that. If she lets go of the elemental.'

'What d'you mean?'

'She won't be the Diane you know and . . . and love.'

'She'll always be the Diane I know and love,' Sam said. 'That girl don't change.'

'Yes, she would, Sam.'

'You can't go bad, Juanita, not like that.'

'Absolutely like that. That's the only sure way to go completely bad. I'm not trying to scare you. I'm just trying to explain what this is about.'

Sam didn't like this. 'Where's the old cynicism, Juanita?'

'Cynicism is no defence. We're close to the reservoir. I feel close.'

'How can you know that? You're just . . . Jesus . . .'

Powys handed Sam his car keys and held out his hand for the torch. 'Do something practical, Sam. You'll feel better. There's a can of petrol in the boot, Juanita's matches in the glove compartment.'

He watched Sam moving away, hunched up against the unknown. Looked around for his dog. 'Arnold?'

Silence.

And then a sharp cry that he wasn't sure he'd heard at all. Wasn't sure if it was in his head. He looked at Juanita, wondering if she'd heard it.

'It said "fetch",' Juanita said.

There was a distant, muffled yip, an Arnold noise.

Then more silence.

It was coming light. Don Moulder, against all his best intentions, had moved closer, right to the edge of his top field, from where he could see the figures moving up the Tor quite clearly now.

He wondered what the Bishop was saying to Dame Wanda Carlisle. Discussing the terrible weather or Wanda's famous roles.

It was a joke. Even Don could see that. Where was that bloody Ceridwen? Why wasn't she up there?

Bloody joke. A stunt for Miss Tammy White.

Its fur was as harsh as a new hairbrush. It brushed her left arm, raising goosebumps.

It lay there quite still, but with a kind of coiled and eager tension about it. She could feel its back alongside her, its spine pressed against her. It was lean but it was heavy. It was beginning to breathe.

She put out her arm. Felt an almost liquid frigidity around her hand, over the wrist, almost to the elbow, like frogspawn in a half-frozen pond.

It turned its grey head, and the only white light in the room was in its long, predator's teeth and the only colour in the room was the still, cold yellow of its eyes.

I am yours.

'I can't,' Diane said.

'He killed your mother.' Ceridwen spoke softly. 'She stood at the top of the stairs. She was always very careful coming down them, afraid that the size of her belly would make her overbalance. She came down one stair at a time. One hand on the banister, the other holding the pink teddy she'd bought for her baby daughter. The teddy had a bow around its neck. Do you remember that teddy?'

'No.'

'Of course you don't. Because Archer burned it on the bonfire your father had Rankin build to destroy the blood-caked sheets. All the toys your mother had bought for you, Archer threw them on the bonfire, horrid yellow flames leaping into the night. He killed your mother and then he burned her dreams . . .'

Diane's head turned in anguish on the pillow. She saw the flames in the eyes of the beast.

'Let it go,' Ceridwen said, ever so softly.

'Yes.' Diane closed her eyes. 'Yes Nanny.'

SEVENTEEN

OURS

The sky over the Tor was, for a moment, as bright and shiny as the membrane over a cow's eye. And then it blistered, lost its focus. A fan of flickering colours sprayed up behind the tower before the ragged-edged clouds closed in, like the night coming back, and there was a low roaring like thunder deep underground, and Don Moulder got scared.

He was a superstitious man. Weren't all good farmers superstitious? Wasn't this what it was all about? Understanding nature. Getting a *feeling* for nature. 'Cause nature, whatever they said, nature wasn't scientific. And a dawn that couldn't decide whether to break was not in Don Moulder's previous experience, not even living where he did.

So Don, as a superstitious man, thought straight off, *They done wrong. The whole thing. Wrong. Christians and pagans. Conciliation, you can't have it. Isn't meant. There is but one God and He is sore offended.* And not only at the trendy bishop and the crazy pagan actress, neither of whom was up to the job. Not only at them, but at the bloody ole mad farmer who'd brought back Satan's buzz. Why the hell had he ever done that?

Miss Diane. She'd brought that thing in. Miss bloody Lady Loony. What she'd got, it was catching.

The heavens over the Tor, still locked in debate, had gone into black and white. Like Dame Wanda's cloak. Another Lady Loony. All drawn to that abnormal hill. Maybe Griff Daniel was right when he said they oughter run a JCB through Glastonbury Tor. No more Tor, no more loonies, no more bad dreams for honest God-fearing farmers.

All of a sudden, the sky above the tower went as black as Old Nick's arsehole and there was a great loud crack that had Don Moulder backing off in something like cold terror.

*

She saw the pale lightball again. It shimmered like a second chance, but she made the black mist cloud over it. Out of the foetid, feral-scented air, Ceridwen spoke and the voice came gutturally, like a burp, from out of Diane's own solar plexus.

There. That's better.

Ceridwen smiled and stood before her. Diane felt very weak, enormously relieved. But the relief enclosed an equally enormous sense of loss which she couldn't comprehend. It was like a nightmare where you'd done something frightfully wrong but awoke before you could put it right, and so the relief was relief only at having awakened.

There were more smiles. She saw little Rozzie, her monkey face split in two with glee; Mort, with his braided hair and his warrior's face and, inside his robe, the biggest dick you ever saw. She squirmed in the hospital bed. Visiting time? But it wasn't right. Was it?

'Welcome, sister.' Ceridwen stood in the misty candle-light between the great, grey concrete pillars, her serpentine hair alive with electricity. 'Welcome to the Inner Circle.'

'Where's it gone?'

'It? Why, it's gone about its business,' Ceridwen said. Ceridwen had been with her for ever. She must accept this.

Diane giggled. She did. She felt better. The truth was she'd never been so relieved. That was the truth, wasn't it?

She clutched the darkness to her body, wallowed in the dank, cloudy vapour, got high on the stench.

A man she didn't know said, 'I think there's someone outside.'

'So let them in. It's probably Gwyn. You remember Gwyn, don't you Diane?'

When the wooden doors opened, Diane expected a great and hurtful surge of daylight, but thankfully there was only more darkness. And people.

'Well, my goodness,' said Ceridwen, and she no longer looked quite so happy. 'If it isn't sister Carey.'

It was like entering an elf's house in a children's storybook, but vaster inside: the hall of the Mountain King, the subterranean lair of Gwyn ap Nudd.

In fact, it was a small storage reservoir, half underground, with a mound over it like a tumulus. It must have been out of commission for over twenty years judging by the size of some of the trees which overgrew it. But it was the dream temple. A hollow shell inside organic matter. Directly on the ley. Virtually under the Tor itself. Any time other than this, Powys would have been fascinated.

Inside, there were no trappings of a temple, white or black. No pentagrams, no inverted crosses. Only a few dark couches and rugs between the utility concrete pillars, brown-stained like nicotine fingers. Bizarrely, in the very centre of the former reservoir, there was a utility hospital bed, metal framed, white sheeted.

Diane lay on it.

She'd lost a lot of weight. She had an unhealthy pallor, obvious even down here. She inspected them curiously, her mouth tilted into a smile you could only call complacent. She showed no relief at their arrival.

For the first time, Powys saw Ceridwen, a heavy, wild-haired woman, an old hippy gone to hard. She was studying Juanita in the light of candles held by others, men and women in ratty-looking robes.

'You look well,' she said to Juanita, possibly surprised.

'That's because I'm one of your failures, Ceridwen,' Juanita smiled pleasantly, the goddess shining in her – Ceridwen would see that.

'I don't have failures,' Ceridwen said coldly. 'Some things merely take longer than others.'

'Well,' Juanita was brisk. 'We won't waste your time. We've come to collect Diane.'

Smiles vanished, but Ceridwen seemed unfazed. 'So take her. Why not? Diane, look who's here.'

Juanita said, 'Diane?'

Diane wore a black nightdress. It didn't look right on her. Or maybe – Powys acknowledged a cold feeling in his gut – maybe it did.

'Diane?' Juanita said again, approaching tentatively. Powys just hoping it wasn't too late, praying the girl would see the light around her and rush to her.

Diane gave Juanita an uncharacteristically coquettish smile.

494

'Fuck off,' she said sweetly. Behind her, the big wooden doors closed and a shutter clanged in Powys's head.

'OK.' Juanita turned abruptly away from the bed. Powys thought she must be a good deal less cool than she looked. Forehead furrowed, she faced Ceridwen close up. 'What exactly have you done?'

'I've set her free,' Ceridwen said simply. 'Haven't I, Diane?'

'Yes, Nanny,' Diane said and giggled.

Powys said, 'She's told her about Archer.'

'Of course,' Ceridwen said to Juanita, goddess to goddess, dark to light.

'And she's conjured DF's pet elemental?' Powys said. 'The wolf from the North?'

'And sent it on its way!' Ceridwen's voice ringing. 'If you only knew the beauty of it, Mr JM Powys.' But still looking at Juanita.

'You want to explain it to me?'

Ceridwen smiled at Juanita.

'I'll tell *you*, then,' Powys said, realising, with a feeling of deep sickness, that he could. 'Goes back to 1919. When Roger Ffitch had the opportunity to lure DF – even then potentially the strongest magician in the whole of the Western Tradition – on to the dark path. By exposing her to the Chalice.'

Ceridwen didn't react.

'And possibly his cock,' Powys said. 'Because Roger wasn't subtle.'

If they were going to get Diane out of here, they'd have to play for time. Sam's fires would bring people – any people would do.

'All she had to do,' Powys said, 'was release that black elemental force against him. The Dark Chalice – him being a Ffitch – would have shielded him. And both of them would have lived happily and Satanically ever after. They might even have married. Right?'

Ceridwen turned at last to look at him.

'Unfortunately,' Powys said, 'it rebounded. As these things often do.'

'Seldom do,' Ceridwen said.

'But then you would say that, wouldn't you?'

Making himself meet her brooding, dark brown gaze.

'Being a crazy old ratbag.' He smiled at her, his insides freezing up at her expression. This woman was steeped in it.

'Anyway,' he said. 'She did produce it. But she immediately saw what she'd done and eventually she got it back. Which was tough, a lot tougher than letting it go. But it made her a better person and stronger. Better equipped, anyway, to deal with what she'd stumbled on.'

Ceridwen's steady gaze was a long tunnel, no light at the end. No end, in fact.

'The Chalice,' Powys said. 'A receptacle for evil. Naturally, she wanted to destroy it. The way she'd wanted to destroy Roger Ffitch. But the very act of destruction was negative and it rebounded. Violet was very confused.'

'She could have had it all,' Ceridwen said.

'If that's your idea of having it all,' Powys said mildly. 'It just shows how bloody shallow you bastards are. Anyway, she went back to Dr Moriarty for advice and maybe he put her on to a third party – not an occultist, but certainly a visionary. Someone already obsessed with the concept of the Holy Grail.'

He held on to Ceridwen's gaze, talking slowly, holding the floor. Aware of Juanita moving closer to Diane.

'John Cowper Powys. A man with a lot of personal hang-ups. A seriously flawed character. But a bit older than Violet. And smart. I can hear DF and JCP talking long into the night, working out the implications of Grail versus anti-Grail.'

'And realising,' Ceridwen said, 'as you obviously cannot grasp, that they were dealing with a very ancient duality.'

'That everything has its negative? That without evil, how could we comprehend good?'

'That without the sterility of what you naively call good,' said Ceridwen, 'we cannot appreciate the beauty of what you call evil.'

'Bloody hell, Ruth,' Powys said admiringly, 'you'll be converting me.'

'I wouldn't want you as a convert,' Ceridwen said. 'You're no more use than your grandfather or whatever he was.'

'Probably not,' Powys conceded. 'But they did manage it, didn't they? DF would have decided they needed to conduct a binding ritual. To put the Chalice itself – if not the force behind it – into cold storage. And give the Ffitches at least a chance of salvation. It would've been JCP who worked out how to do it, how to put the arm on Roger – who, by now, was back into his nightmares and vulnerable. So they bound the Chalice. To the general benefit of mankind. But no help to the Ffitches. Their fortunes hit the skids. Since when . . .' He shrugged, '. . . the Dark Chalice has become a legendary prize for, um, certain species of spiritual pond-life.'

The tall guy with the pigtail stepped forward, holding his metal candlestick like a sword. 'You don't have to take this.'

'Let him finish.'

'I'm nearly there anyway.' Thinking of Diane in the hospital bed, Ceridwen, the nurse, an idea was forming. 'To liberate the Dark Chalice and whatever it represents, you had to actually corrupt the spirit of DF. Which is no small undertaking. It involved creating and developing a whole person. You were there when Diane was born, weren't you?'

'Yes.' Ceridwen looked uncertain and then her face broke into a beam, like the sun actually shining out of an arse, he thought. 'Yes. She knows that. I was her midwife.'

He imagined Juanita's eyes opening wider at that. She must be no more than a couple of yards away from where Diane lay seemingly unaware of any of them through the residual haze of whatever she'd been given to sedate her.

'I don't know what you planted in that baby,' he said. 'But you obviously thought you had to kill her mother to keep it alive.'

'Archer killed their mother,' Ceridwen said sharply. 'It was quite simple. He was a child, with a child's simplistic views. She was coming between him and his dreams of restoring the family's wealth and influence.'

'I bet he didn't do it on his own, though.'

'You're fantasising, Mr JM Powys. But that's your profession, isn't it?'

'I bet you had a little tug on the old umbilical, didn't you, Ruth?'

Her face told him it was inspired. *Thank you, God. Thank you, DF. Thank you, Uncle Jack.*

Ceridwen recovered rapidly, Powys thinking how two-dimensional these people were. 'It doesn't matter now,' she said. 'Diane's beast is loose. The bind is broken. The Chalice is back in the world.'

The reservoir doors opened. Archer Ffitch stood there. He showed no surprise. He'd been here before, of course he had. He must have seen the Mini vanish in the direction of the barns and known where they were going.

'Sorry to intrude.' Archer wore a dark suit, but he'd taken off his tie. He was sweating. 'But all of a sudden, one begins to feel safer down here. Tricky phase. Transition. All that. Difficult to settle. Until Oliver gets the family trophy out of the well.'

Right, Powys thought. They would have to cancel out DF before they dare uncover that well. The unbinding of the Chalice was a number of strands entwining simultaneously, something finally pulling them tight, just as Ceridwen must have sealed the fate of Lady Pennard by one wrench on the umbilicus.

He looked at Diane's face, the eyes flickering vaguely behind the twisted, narcotic glaze. It was unreal. It was insane. Diane had been brought up from birth to develop a hatred for her brother, to have that hatred fine-tuned to a pitch where it could be released as an entity in itself, dragging down the entity's original, unwitting creator.

Juanita was standing only a yard away from Diane, but it was a very long yard.

'Come down, Archer!' Ceridwen called out, almost gaily. 'We'll look after you.' She turned to Powys. 'As we always have. Ever since his schooldays. I was their matron, did you know that, at school? Archer and Oliver Pixhill. Always inseparable.'

'Let me get this right,' Juanita said. 'This would be after you were fired from the hospital in Oxfordshire for persecuting geriatrics?'

Ceridwen turned slowly and jabbed a blunt forefinger at her. 'I know what you've been doing. I know you've been leeching on DF's residue.'

'Or perhaps she's been feeding me,' Juanita said softly.

'I don't care if she's been feeding you,' Ceridwen snarled. 'She's over now, Juanita. Or she's ours – she has that choice. Oblivion. Or the shadier path.'

All this time Diane had been quite silent. Sitting up in her bed like some soiled fairytale princess.

'Come on, Diane,' Juanita said.

'Yes. Go on. Do,' Ceridwen shrieked. 'Go with her, Diane. Take it out into the world.' And to Juanita, 'She'll destroy you.

She was always going to destroy you. And then she'll come back. She has to.'

Powys was aware of a deepening of the atmosphere in the concrete chamber, as though it had become a hall of mirrors and went on and on until the Tor rose above it, a nightmare corruption of the Cavern Under the Hill of Dreams. A picture began to form in his head of Diane in five or ten years' time: no more the scatty but tolerable Lady Loony; instead, a fat and blackened sly-eyed whore, a parasite in high society, vampish fallen sister of the Conservative MP for Mendip South.

Fetch!

He heard it with bell-like clarity in his head. No one reacted. The silence was dull, yet charged.

And then, limping down the middle of this endless chamber, he saw – *Oh, no* – the familiar black and white, amiably lopsided dowser's dog.

Arnold pattered to the bed where Diane sat up. There was a ball in Arnold's mouth. A ball of pure, white light. Powys saw it and then he didn't.

Diane shrank back into the metal bars of the headboard. Powys watched, as though from far away, as though it was happening in a movie. Becoming only gradually aware that no one else was looking at the dog or the bed or Diane or him, but at the open doorway behind Archer.

Where Lord Pennard stood in heavy tweed shooting jacket and plus fours, the dawn welling wildly up behind him.

'Archer?' Pennard's voice rang like steel around the concrete chamber. 'Where are you, boy?'

'Father.' Archer didn't move. 'Go away. This is nothing to do with you. Go back to the house.'

'Who are these people, Archer?'

'Not your problem, OK? We'll talk later.'

'Is that Diane down there? I can't see.'

'Will you leave this to me?'

'I wanted very much to believe in you, Archer,' Pennard said. 'Damn it, I *had* to believe. To support the future. For the simple sake of our continuity, I had to believe that you didn't . . .'

'I . . . didn't . . . kill her.' Archer ground it out through his teeth. 'What can I do to convince you? *I . . . didn't fucking . . . kill my fucking mother!*'

'You sicken me,' Pennard said sorrowfully. 'Perhaps you always did. But now you frighten me too. And that . . . that is something I really can't live with.'

'Wait!' Archer moved into the pink light at the entrance. 'Listen to me! You want to know who killed her?' He turned to point into the darkness. The very heart of the darkness. '*She* did. You see her? You recognise her? That's your midwife, Father. From the Belvedere clinic. Ask her. *Ask* her!'

The moment seemed to last for ever. Archer's finger frozen in the dawn.

The finger still hanging there as Powys saw Archer's head burst like a bud into flower. A free-form flower of red and pink and grey.

And by the time his brain had registered the explosion, seen the smoke from the twelve-bore, heard the shouting and the screams, Pennard was raising the gun again and the shot from the second barrel took Ceridwen in the throat and she seemed to float to her knees, astonishment in the deep brown eyes and blood pumping down the robe, splashing on the concrete as her head fell off into her lap.

There was an instant of hollow nothingness.

At first, Powys thought he was trembling. But it was the ground. The ground was trembling.

Still it didn't occur to him what was happening.

At least, not until he saw the cracks appear in the grey concrete pillars of the old storage reservoir and he thought idly what a hell of a flood there would be if it was still in use.

Then, amid the incomprehension which preceded the stampede, he saw Juanita dragging Diane from the hospital bed, and when his legs would move again he ran to help her and they pulled her, kicking and squealing out of the reservoir and into the bleak beginnings of the shortest day and the stubbly wasteland from where Sam Daniel's trio of petrol-fired beacons sent signals, too late, to Glastonbury Tor.

EIGHTEEN

DF

At first, Powys thought it must be a frenzied, knee-jerk reaction to Sam's beacon fires and then he saw that the three of them were running against a tide of panic. Breaking on the Tor, flowing across the fields. So many frightened people, so much smoke, so many abandoned protest-placards. He couldn't see Sam anywhere.

He thought he heard another shot. Or maybe he knew that, for what remained of the honour of that family, there was, sooner or later, going to be another shot.

A big-eyed girl in an orange waterproof collided with him. He helped her up. 'What's happening? What's exploded?'

'Earthquake. Tremor. The tower's collapsing. Jesus. Stones and stuff crashing down. Like the Middle Ages all over again.'

'What?' Powys looked up at the Tor. The shell of the St Michael tower looked full and firm as ever against the pink-streaked Solstice dawn.

'The rest of the church came down in the Middle Ages.' A guy with a beard dragging the girl away. 'Leaving just the tower. Doomsday, man. Doomsday.'

Juanita heard none of this. She was listening to only one voice and that voice came from far inside her and it was saying, *Just get her out of here. Get her away.*

Diane was wrapped in Juanita's coat – so much weight gone now that it almost fitted. Her feet sliding about in the clumping shoes Juanita had snatched from Ceridwen's corpse. Diane seemed completely fogged, walking, head bowed, between Juanita and Powys, Arnold hopping ahead of them. Juanita wondering if anyone else had seen the ball of light in the dog's mouth or heard that headmistressy voice: *Fetch!*

Occasionally, without looking up, Diane giggled. Sister Dunn and her drugs. Drugs that might keep you permanently at that stage between waking and sleeping when, as DF put it, the etheric so easily extrudes. Drugs which might make it difficult to absorb the full emotional impact of your father discharging his shotgun into the admittedly unloved face of your only brother.

Juanita had seen this happen from behind, feeling a light splash of something like lukewarm soup on her forehead, refusing to give in to the nausea, concentrating on Diane.

Who, as they were approaching Wellhouse Lane across the field, stopped at a stile.

Juanita followed her eyes. They were just a hedge and a gate away from Don Moulder's infamous bottom field. Juanita caught her breath. In one corner was parked a black bus. She turned away at once and, for the first time, Diane's eyes met hers and an odd, mute plea passed between them, the struggle of something attempting to surface.

Juanita glanced quickly at Powys.

The glance said, *Leave us*.

'Be careful,' Powys said.

There was a wintry silence around Meadwell.

The gate seemed to click against it when Powys lifted the latch. He saw the house door hanging open, but he didn't go in.

Verity was standing on the path, a rigid porcelain doll in a body-warmer.

She saw him, bit her lip. And then beckoned, turning away to walk across the lawn to the wilderness part, and Arnold set off after her, which was curious.

The air was icy-still and the tower on the Tor seemed suspended in milky light. Verity led Powys to the concrete plinth, a perfectly circular black hole in it now. A rusting cast-iron lid lay amid the rubble.

So Oliver Pixhill had done it. Feeling so tired he could hardly stand, Powys contemplated the final irony of a Dark Chalice liberated into a world where the only remaining Ffitch had tripped over from airy-fairy to obscenely possessed.

Verity said nothing. From the wet grass to one side, she produced a big, red, rubber-covered flashlight and handed it to Powys.

He knelt above the hole and shone it down, recoiling at once, looking up at Verity.

'Oliver Pixhill,' she said.

'Dead?'

'He . . . he was down there when the tremor came. That is, I suppose . . . Perhaps he lost his balance.'

He glanced back down the well, without the light. All you could see was a white hand, fingers bent.

What did it mean?

'Most likely he was waiting for the dawn, Verity. He had to bring out the Chalice at dawn. At that moment. It was as if they knew about the earth-tremor. Or that something would happen.'

He was thinking of the alignment of the Tor, Meadwell, Bowermead. The reservoir precisely on it. The way the road had been dug out. The way the trees had been taken out. A build-up of violence.

'Maybe they needed to unblock the well in advance, like you let old wine breathe for a while.'

But what they really needed was for Verity to lay down her defences and invite Grainger in to do it. The little woman was as much a part of the defence system as the binding ritual itself. She had to be gently defused, like a bomb.

'Getting you out of the house was a last resort,' he said. 'But if you hadn't responded to Wanda's invitation, they'd have had to use a blunter instrument.'

Verity winced. But he knew that Oliver Pixhill could never have killed Verity. Such a forcefield surrounding her, the little woman who could not See.

'Have you called the police?'

'Oh. No. I've been praying. With Mr Woolaston.'

'Woolly . . .?'

She let him in through the back door so he wouldn't have to see Woolly, whose battered body she'd sat beside for perhaps two hours. Unconcerned about the smells, the atmosphere of brutal violence. She'd lived in the ever-darkening Meadwell; she did not See. Powys couldn't believe how strong she was.

Surprisingly, Arnold followed him in.

A plastic bag stood upside down, covering something on the table. On the bag, it said, SAFEWAY.

He swallowed. He was very scared. Rose light dribbled in from the high window, tinting the bulging white walls with the effect of watered blood.

'Don't you go near it, Mr Powys,' Verity said.

He stared at it, bitter and sickened. Whatever it was, Woolly had died for it. Beaten to death with a brick. The bag went in and out of focus. He wanted to find that same brick and hammer the Chalice flat.

'We should never have left him,' he said. 'We should've called the police.'

'No. It was my fault, if anyone's. I should have stayed. It was my duty.'

'And then you'd have been . . .' He shook his head. 'We were expecting Grainger. We didn't know what we were dealing with.'

'I must have arrived quite soon after . . . That is, I didn't know he was still here. There was just the hole. I thought he'd gone. I thought it was too late. I went back to the house and sat with Mr Woolaston. Praying.'

How could she explain any of this to the police? Still, someone would have to try.

'Do you wish to see it, Mr Powys?'

'Why not?' he said wearily.

Verity grasped the ears of the plastic bag and tugged.

Arnold sat at the foot of the table and growled, but didn't move, as Powys looked, with revulsion, at the Dark Chalice.

Don Moulder unlocked the bus, pulled back the rusted sliding door.

When Juanita tried to follow Diane, she shook her head. She took off Juanita's coat, handed it to her.

Moulder's eyes widened at the long, black nightdress. 'What's she gonner do?' He watched Diane as she stepped from the platform into the body of the bus. 'Because that buzz, look, that buzz is full of evil, Mrs Carey, I don't care what anybody says.'

'In that case come away, Don. We'll wait over by the gate. Whatever happens you don't want to see it, do you?'

'I don't understand none o' this no more.' He was wheezing a bit, looking starved. "Tis a black day, Mrs Carey. You coulder sworn that ole tower, he were gonner go, look. Swayed, like in a gale. Some masonry come down, they d' say. The Bishop, his face was as white as his collar, look. You had the feeling we was barely ... barely a breath away from ... I dunno ... the end of it. The ole sky changin' colour, night a-changin' back to day and day to night. I never, all my years at this farm, never seen nothin' like it.'

Diane appeared at the bus door. She sat on the platform and took off Ceridwen's shoes, tossed them on to the grass.

Then she went back.

It happened very quickly. Almost as soon as she entered the bus, she knew it was waiting for her.

It was just as she'd last seen it. The seat and the couch bolted to the floor, the cast-iron stove, the filthy windows you could hardly see out of. This was where something began.

'Oh!' A sudden stomach cramp made her double up and then fall to her knees. The pain was briefly horrible and when it ebbed she found she had both arms curled around the bus pole. She felt like Ulysses, when he lashed himself to the ship's mast to prevent him responding to the call of the Sirens.

When the sob came, it seemed to have travelled a long way. All the way from North Yorkshire. In a white delivery van with pink spots.

Diane hugged herself to the pole. The sob seemed to make the pole quiver and the whole bus tremble. At some point, it had begun to creak, its chassis groaning as if in some frightful arthritic pain. Diane clung to the pole, she and the bus bound together in the longing for release. The dark air seemed to be rushing past as she and the old bus strained to shed their burdensome bulk, to soar serenely towards ...

The light?

But just as she was beginning to feel ever so shimmery, as if those excess pounds had begun to float away and she could be as slim as a faun, gossamer-light, as beautiful as a May queen, as pure as a vestal virgin ... just as the warmth spread over her tummy and down between her legs and she yearned to touch it . . . and just as she began to uncurl her arms from the pole . . .

'*Stop!*'

A bell rang, quite sharply.

Diane's neck arched, her arms still enfolded around the metal pole, her head thrown back, and, oh lord, the bus began to move. It had been the bell which told the driver to start and stop. It had rung only once, but it kept on in Diane's head, a tiny, shiny *ting*.

And then her face was slapped.

Quite lightly, but it was done. A voice, crisp as the snapping of a wafer.

Don't you dare!

The other cheek was slapped, and this time it was not done lightly, but briskly and efficiently and it stung, spinning Diane around to look up, eyes wide and straining with shock, beyond the platform, along the deck of the bus.

'Who . . . who are you . . .?' Her voice faltered and she hugged the pole. It had not been an ordinary slap, and she went clammy with fright at what was beginning to happen.

For, along the deck, all the interior lightbulbs were coming on: small yellow ones in circular holders set into the curved metal ceiling just above the windows. The bulbs were feeble, nicotine-grimed, dust-filmed and fly-spattered. And they didn't work. They didn't work any more, those lights.

The lights that didn't work shone bleakly down on two rows of seats. They put a worn sheen on dark red vinyl. They reflected dully from chromed metal corners.

Diane began to blink in terror, wet with live sweat. Lights where the lights were broken. Seats, where there weren't any seats. This was a Bolton Corporation bus again, which rattled and hissed down grim, twilit streets.

About halfway down the bus, there was a blur of presence, a haze of movement.

The bell rang again, *ting*. The scene froze. Clinging to the pole, Diane saw a grey finger curled in the air. There was a red push-button in the curved part of the roof, and a grey finger crooked over it.

The grind and hiss of faraway brakes, a smell of old polish, damp raincoats and perspiration.

The pole was cold in Diane's arms, cold against her cheek.

Come on now . . . pull . . .'self . . .'gether . . . not a baby.

The words happened in the air, like the brake-hiss. Diane saw a grey lady. Severe hair enclosing a face without features, only sternness. A hat. Large beads. The face was a swirling of grey, black and white particles, like blown cigarette ash.

Diane tried to pull herself to her feet, using the pole, but she couldn't feel her feet at all.

And the woman glided towards her along the bus's dusty aisle. Diane began to gasp convulsively with fear; the shiny pole misted from her breath.

None of . . .'onsense now . . .

The voice was thin and fractured like a car-radio on FM during a storm in the hills. Diane sagged against the pole. Sorrow settled in her chest. Sorrow received from the grey woman, sorrow shimmering in the vagueness of her, in the half-formed face like a scratched old photograph.

The scent of old dust and lavender.

'Nanny . . .'

Essence of long-ago nights, pillows damp with tears, lonely little motherless girl in a house of cold leather, guns and uncompromising maleness.

Diane's arms pulled away from the pole at last and she came to her feet and reached out for the crumbling bundle of dusty, moth-ravaged fragments, as the lights in the bus died, one by one.

'Oh, Nanny . . .'

And she saw, in a corner, the yellow eyes in the mist. The eyes of her own hatred, the evil in her.

Diane felt her stomach shrivel in disgust. She just wasn't that kind of person. She had no natural aggression. She was the sort who ran away and hid and never wanted to harm anyone or anything.

. . . allow it, then . . .

'What?'

. . . take your . . .'edicine, girl . . . swallow it!

Diane closed her eyes.

Do it now! Now!

Diane opened her mouth.

She breathed it in.

And it filled her.

Inflating her cheeks, swelling her throat and then her breast, bloating her abdomen and finally throwing her to her knees, her arms outstretched like a legless, rocking doll.

So cold . . . so cold inside her that it froze her eyes wide and stiffened her tongue. She saw her arms and hands and then her lower body become luminously blue, radiating icy light, and she had no control over any of it, was aware of being squeezed out, reduced to a small, helpless fragment of consciousness, a particle of floating fear, only a moment away from ceasing to exist.

She watched her radiant body tossed on to its back on the filthy floor of the bus like an old mattress, was aware of the air coming out like vomit, in a long *swoooooosh*, as if someone was sitting on her stomach.

Diane rolled over. It seemed as if she'd been separated from her body for a long time, but it must have been no more than a couple of seconds. It felt strange to want to move an arm and for that arm to move. She began to crawl, and as the energy returned so did the panic, in a rush.

The Dark Chalice glistened palely on the kitchen table.

'That's disgusting,' Powys said. The words sounding so trite and ludicrous he almost broke out laughing.

Its base was of old, blackened oak, like the beams of Meadwell.

The wrists emerged from the oak like the stems of yellowing fungi. Whatever kept the bones of the hands and fingers together, it still held strong and the skeletal hands still gripped the bowl of bone, the upturned cranium.

'Who is it, Verity?'

Verity said nothing.

'Is this . . . I mean, is this the Abbot?'

Verity pulled the Safeway bag back over the horror.

She'd said vaguely that she must have found it by the side of the well. Where he'd placed it so that he would have both hands free to pull himself out.

Powys banished for ever an image that came to him of Verity, fresh from her discovery of murdered Woolly, kicking Oliver

Pixhill's groping fingers from the rim of the well, shutting out his scream.

She came down from the bus in floods of tears. She didn't know if it was over. How was she ever going to know?

She saw Juanita and Don Moulder over by the gate. On the other side of it, Joe Powys stood with little Verity and Arnold the dog, who had brought the lightball into the cold heart of it all.

And then came a strange jolt in her breast.

He was shambling slowly across the field towards the bus, his head down as if he was scared to look at her. His buccaneer's hair was matted, he'd lost his famous earring.

Diane, full of tearful longing but still uncertain, looked back along the deck of the bus.

Go, said the Third Nanny.

She had a nice smile.

EPILOGUE

Prophecy is a dangerous trade, but we may hazard the guess that history will look back to our English Jerusalem as the cradle of many things that have gone to enrich the spiritual heritage of our race.

Dion Fortune
Avalon of the Heart

FOR MYSTICISM . . . PSYCHIC STUDIES
. . . EARTH MYSTERIES . . . ESOTERICA

CAREY AND FRAYNE
Booksellers
High Street
Glastonbury

Prop. Juanita Carey

24 December

Danny,

OH GOD, Danny where do I start?

Where's it going to END?

You'll have read the papers, seen the TV reports (all concentrating on the Pennard madness, nobody making the right connections) and I know Powys phoned you.

Maybe this is entirely superfluous. As usual, I don't know whether I'm writing to you or to myself.

Today, I'm going to try to have a long talk with Diane. I've seen a lot of her, of course, but there's always been someone else there. Policemen. Her solicitor, Quentin Cotton. And Sam, of course – she's moved into his flat, doesn't like to let him out of her sight. She hasn't really taken it all in, of course. Still talks about her father as if he were still alive and still the owner of Bowermead Hall.

Which SHE is now, of course. I don't think any of us have quite taken that in.

'Two hundred acres,' Powys keeps saying. 'Three vineyards. And a pack of hunting hounds.' At which he grins delightedly at Sam, and Sam looks terribly embarrassed.

We're still staying, Powys and me, at The George and Pilgrims. He brought the old Amstrad across and I sit at the window and tap out this nonsense, looking down on High Street, very un-Christmas Eve, but still there, you know? Still there. Still with the candle lit in the window of the Wicked Wax Co. Even the quake didn't put that candle out.

And I think I'm happy. Happier than I've been since I don't know when. There's no calm before a storm, only tension. After the storm, that's where you find calm.

I feel guilty about this. Guilty because I'm glad – have to be frank and honest here – that old Pennard killed Archer and, especially, the hateful psychopath Ceridwen. I can still see Pennard framed in the entrance of the reservoir. Where he was always grey and heavy to me, there seemed to be a pure, fresh light in him as he raised that gun. Which just has to be very wrong, doesn't it? God knows, I hate and fear guns as much as Sam Daniel. I'm sorry – ignore this bit, I'm mixed up, there's too much I don't understand.

And yet aspects of it are coming clearer all the time. It was only yesterday that it occurred to me that out of all those appalling people in the reservoir – and I recognised many of them from that night on the Tor – there was one missing.

It was the man who called himself Gwyn ap Nudd. The man in the hairy mask.

I'm almost certain now that behind that mask was Oliver Pixhill. Diane told me how the whole attitude of the travellers' convoy began to change as they approached the start of the St Michael Line at Bury St Edmunds. What I suppose you would have to call a dark element entered. The less serious ones – the colourful, circusy types – had dropped away so that the only remaining members of the original group Diane had joined up with in Yorkshire were this boy Headlice and his so-called girlfriend.

Headlice – no home, estranged from his family, very much a lost boy.

They needed a sacrifice, you see. To activate the dark side of the Tor on the anniversary of the execution of Abbot Whiting. Powys, who (when pushed) will admit to knowing a little about these things, says the rootless, anonymous travelling population is regarded by working black magicians as a very accessible source of human sacrifices. Even babies, whose births are unregistered. Doesn't bear thinking about.

We know from Diane that Headlice had been 'prepared'. Made to walk backwards into every church along the St Michael Line – how more obviously satanic can you get? But this kid, from what Diane says about him, would have done it without a qualm, equating anti-Christian with anti-Establishment. (Which is utterly wrong; when the Arimathean planted his staff on Wearyall Hill, the pagans were The Establishment and Christianity was seriously radical, man . . .)

Who actually killed Headlice is no more clear than it ever was. Was it Gwyn or Mort? Or Rankin and his son. Or all of them, as, with hindsight, they seem to have been basically on the same side.

A sacrifice? Do I believe that, really? Well, people have died on the Tor in strange circumstances. And Jim . . .

Jim. Yes. Why did Jim die? Was it a case of Gwyn/Oliver spotting an opportunity for another Abbot's Night sacrifice, feeling that this bolshy little guy had been delivered into his hands? It will remain a mystery. He always treasured Mystery.

Oliver. How can we ever know what drove that bastard? Apart, that is, from years of resentment at his father and exposure, through Archer, to the allure of the Dark Chalice.

They were very close friends from an early age, Archer and Oliver. Doubtless, Archer initially cultivated Oliver to get close to Meadwell and the family chalice he probably believed was calling out to him. Perhaps this is why Colonel Pixhill encouraged his poor wife to leave with his son, sensing the evil growing in the kid.

By this time, Archer and Oliver were at boarding school together – in Wiltshire or somewhere, I forget. Who should be the matron there but one Ruth Dunn? Was this coincidence? I don't think it was. Dunn would already have been a serious, practising occultist by then. Who knows what she did with those two boys, what perversity they conjured between them.

It's my feeling that, while Archer initially dominated Oliver Pixhill, it was soon Oliver who was controlling Archer. I suspect he became genuinely powerful, in a Charles Manson-like way. I can imagine him getting a great buzz out of dumping his city suit every so often, stopping shaving and joining up with the travellers as their revered shaman, collecting around him a group of the kind of insane *occultists this society attracts and acquiring the kind of reputation that scares off the routine travellers.*

And always, in the background, there was Ceridwen. I have no explanation for her. A psychopath is a psychopath, and there are more around than we think. Even in Glastonbury. Thank God her husband got the kids is all I can say.

Ceridwen, Oliver, Archer – THIS was the Inner Circle. These were the people playing with the volatile Glastonbury atmosphere. I don't like to even imagine what went on down in that disused reservoir, the 'perfect temple', as Powys called it because of its alignment – an alignment they strengthened in the hope of somehow taking control of the Tor. They nearly did it too. With the proposed Restriction of Access, the Tor would very soon cease to be everyman's temple. Much of poor Woolly's paranoia seems to have been well founded and it makes you fear for Stonehenge.

Without Archer's influence, I suspect the Tame the Tor Bill will fade ignominiously away. As for the road – well, for a start, Diane's instructed Quentin Cotton to tear up any agreement for the sale of land to the Department of Transport. She insists she'll actually invite the eco-guerrillas on to her property if it comes to it. I suspect, in the end, we might at least force a change of route.

We'll fight, anyway. We have a lot of battles ahead. Not least to clear Woolly's name. I want to have some kind of Woolaston memorial – this is very important to me. And I want to publish The Avalonian *before March. One of the issues I want to raise with Diane.*

The earth tremor? I don't know what caused it. Was it a timely geological anomaly? Or was it the conflict of good and evil forces in a psychic hothouse climate? Some are saying it was the Tor announcing its refusal to be tamed. Others maintain it was a manifestation of God's outrage at a bishop attempting conciliation with the pagans. It's interesting to me that it happened when the two great spiritual forces were represented on the top of the Tor by two distinctly weak links – Wanda and the bishop, not enough power between them to keep a cigarette alight. If you imagine a fuse box: when the power overloads, it's the slenderest thread that breaks. I think if you'd had Ceridwen up there facing . . . well, maybe even me, the way I was feeling that day and maybe still am . . . then perhaps the tower would have come down. I'm not kidding.

You may have detected that I'm feeling so much better, more energised, much more positive about the town, about its future. Yes, I believe we CAN all live together. I believe we must invoke the Grail, which stands for tolerance and acceptance.

(I won't say peace and love.)

And the Dark Chalice, the anti-Grail?

I never saw it. Thank God.

With Don Moulder's permission, Verity (she wouldn't let anyone else touch it) placed the grisly item in the black bus, exactly where the radiator grille was coming off.

And then we set fire to the bus.

Well, we didn't know what else to do. We burned that damned bus to an absolute shell, and then we paid to have it taken away. We figured maybe the link was broken with the end of the last male Pennard. The speculation in the papers is that Pennard killed his son by accident while attempting to drive out New Age travellers setting up some kind of squat in the disused reservoir on his land. The fact that one of these people seemed to be a well-established Glastonbury citizen was one of the puzzles requiring further investigation. Another was the apparent murder of Councillor Edward Woolaston by Archer Ffitch's agent, Oliver Pixhill, at his father's former house.

Verity is still staying with a somewhat chastened Wanda. I am expecting the Home Temple to be dismantled. Diane says she hopes to persuade Verity to run Bowermead until she decides what to do with it. The Rankins have gone, of course. Just disappeared. Hardly a surprise. Sam's been going to Bowermead to feed the hounds, convinced he can 'reform' them. When I start to get depressed about Woolly and Jim, the thought of Sam as some kind of Pennard consort – and particularly what that will do to his revered father – always brings me round. I mean, can you IMAGINE Sam with the hunting and shooting mob at meetings of the Country Landowners' Association? I just love it.

As for your Glastonbury book, co-authored by JM Powys and myself – we may well get around to it, although it's unlikely to contain much of the above.

We're taking things day by day. And night by night.

Love,

J

CLOSING CREDITS

As with all stories set in Glastonbury, this was a *mélange* of myth, legend, fiction and even fact. I can't even remember the crossover points, but that's the Isle of Avalon for you.

The layout and history of the town are more or less as described, although small reinventions were necessary.

Dion Fortune and John Cowper Powys were both profoundly affected by Glastonbury, but whether or not they ever met remains a mystery. I like to think they did, and that DF's misspelling of the great man's name was an example of her irrepressible humour. As you may have deduced, I'm an admirer of DF, whose novels – particularly *The Sea Priestess*, for which Mrs Carey has good reason to be grateful – deserve to be far better known. The story of the wolf-like elemental can be found in her essential handbook, *Psychic Self-Defence*. I soul-searched before linking it with the Ffitch family, especially when my word-processor mysteriously refused to print the first four versions. But she did seem to accept the one you read earlier. Thanks, DF. *Phew . . .*

Thanks also to Peter James for planting the word 'Glastonbury'. Everyone I went to for information was amazingly helpful. Here they are, in alphabetical order: Penny Arnold, Pam Baker, Jim Barrington, Patrick Benham (author of *The Avalonians*), Paul Broadhurst, Simon Buxton, Carol Clewlow, Paul Devereux, Michael Dobbs, Anne Dowling, Bob Fells, Ron Fouracres, Jamie George, Tony Heath, Peter Heaton, Wendy Holborrow, Rachel Humphries, Tina Lukins, Cameron McConnell, Jeanine McMullen, Hamish Miller, Graham Nown, Ruth Prince, Serena and Colva Roney-Dougall, Fred Slater, Cynthia Straddling, Taunton General Hospital Accident Unit and Herbert Williams.

And ultimate thanks to my brilliant wife and live-in editor, Carol, who helped shape the plot, curbed a few excesses and then

516

spent many long days and nights transforming, page by page, what might have been a Ratners' chalice into the nearest we could get to an authentic Grail.